CONT

GW01457846

*I raise a glass
to you all, lovely people.
Thank you for being here with me.*

**Not that glass!**

# A NOTE BEFORE WE BEGIN

Lovely people, thank you for joining me once again as we explore a slightly darker side to Yorkshire than the Beaufort Scales books might have us expect. I hope you've enjoyed *All Out of Leeds* and *What Happened in London*, and are now firmly acquainted with the need to carry chocolate, ducks, and a very large stick at all times. (One just never knows when they'll be needed.)

I just wanted to add a quick note here about reading order, in case you're a little puzzled by what a certain annoying journalist might or might not know.

*What Happened in London* took place before Adams ventured north, then we had a little jump to *All Out of Leeds*, which occurred after the events of Beaufort Scales' third book, *A Manor of Life & Death*. This book slots in after *Game of Scones* in that series (and you can find the reading order at kmwatt.com/di-adams, should you fancy it).

So the question is, will you be lost if you haven't read the Beaufort books? No, not at all. What about the previous Adams books? Maybe a little, mostly as regards the importance of ducks and chocolate, but not really.

Although I would recommend checking who brewed your beer. You know, just to be safe.

Now grab your very big stick and let's get started …

# SO MUCH BULL

DI Adams sprinted across the field, head down, arms pumping, the long grass snatching at her ankles, and hoped in some distracted part of her mind that she didn't stick her foot in a rabbit hole.

"Adams!" Collins yelled behind her. "*Stop!*"

She ignored him entirely. Stopping was not an option. There was a gate in the drystone wall ahead of her, looking desperately distant, but it was the only option she could see.

"*Adams!*" Collins shouted again. "Don't run from it! Run *at* it and *dodge!*"

It was entirely possible that DI Colin Collins knew what he was talking about, given that this was far more his area of expertise than it was hers, but she wasn't about to test that out. Hooves pounded the sun-warmed ground behind her, and a snort came from close enough that she could've sworn she felt the wind of it on the back of her neck. She swerved hard, sliding in the grass and almost falling, but caught herself on one hand, recovered, and pelted off at right angles to her previous track.

"That's it!" Collins shouted. "Keep going!"

"*Do something!*" she yelled back at him, then concentrated on running again as the hooves bore down on her once more. She swerved a second time, back onto her original path, as 800-odd furiously grunting kilos of tawny copper hair and muscle surged past. And horns. Such excessive horns.

"*Hey!*" Collins was shouting. "Hey, over here! Coo! *Coo!*"

It was not a *coo*, it wasn't even a cow, it was a bull, and a very angry one at that, looking *nothing* like the cute postcards of Highland coos that packed the souvenir shops. Not that Adams was looking too closely at it right now. She made one more sliding turn, the bull tearing past her under its own thundering momentum, then corrected course and sprinted hard for the gate while it was still trying to turn back. She could hear Collins shouting behind her, but if he was attempting to create a distraction it wasn't working, and if he was giving directions she wasn't listening.

She hit the gate so hard she almost bounced off it, but instead used the momentum to launch herself up and over the top, tumbling ungracefully onto the faint, overgrown track beyond and rolling once before she managed to catch herself and scramble into a crouch. The wooden gate looked hideously flimsy, and the bull was bearing down on it in a snorting, thundering fury. Adams had a vision of the beast plunging straight through the fragile barrier, smashing it apart and squishing her like roadkill. She flung herself off the rutted track and into the dubious shelter of the wall, out of its line of sight, and braced herself for the sound of shattering timber, wondering if she'd end up playing some sort of high-stakes leapfrog over the wall to stay ahead of the damn thing. But the bull came to a skidding, snorting halt. She could hear it huffing and stomping on the far side of the wall, but when she leaned forward to peer at the gate, it was just surveying the track with an air of satisfaction, apparently happy to have banished the interloper. She sank back on her haunches, head down and elbows on her knees, hands dangling between them as she panted.

"Adams?" Collins called. "You alright?"

She looked down at herself. At some point in the preceding fifteen minutes she'd stepped in at least one cow pat, put her knee in another, and managed to cover her trousers in dandelion fluff. But, on the upside, she was neither gored nor crushed. She looked up as something huffed at her in a rather gentler register to the bull, and discovered a Labrador-sized, dreadlocked grey dog watching her, eyes hidden behind his hair and his tail waving gently.

"Some help you were," she said. He tipped his head. She could hardly blame him. If she'd been able to prance along the top of walls she'd probably have gone for that option too, rather than the run-for-your-life one. On the other hand, she also knew that animals were somewhat unnerved by Dandy, so she couldn't help feeling he might also be at least slightly responsible for the enraged attack launched on her by what Collins had insisted was one of the most docile cattle breeds.

"Adams?" Collins shouted again.

She stood up, dusting her trousers off ineffectually. "Yeah, fine."

Collins' voice went up an octave. "*Adams!*"

She looked up. The bull was gone, an outraged, oversized missile pounding back toward Collins, who had made it almost into the middle of the field in his pursuit of Adams. He was already running, a big man hardly built for speed, but currently demonstrating a pace that could've put Usain Bolt to shame. It was no match for the bull, though, and Adams ran to the gate, clambering up a couple of rungs to perch there, waving and shouting. The bull paid no more attention to her than it had to Collins earlier, single-minded in its pursuit.

"Just run *at* it!" she shouted, and was pretty sure he said something which wasn't aimed at the bull. He zigzagged across the field, short-cropped hair gleaming in the sun and his shirt straining at the seams with the unaccustomed exertion. The bull tried to follow him, but it couldn't make the turns as quickly as he could, and Collins didn't bother with gates or stiles. He made it to one of the drystone walls that enclosed the field and flung himself up and over, taking half a dozen old grey rocks from the top with him and yelping as he fell.

The bull slowed to a trot then an amble, lifting its horned head and rolling its shoulders. The sunlight gave its hair burnished ends, and turned the horns into gleaming weapons. It looked at Adams, then back at the wall, and snorted.

Adams scowled at it, then yelled, "Collins?"

The bull gave her a final, disinterested look, then dropped its head to munch on a little grass. She supposed chasing police officers built up quite an appetite.

Collins' red face appeared over the wall. "You were only meant to distract the bloody thing so I could get a look at its ear tag."

"I distracted it," she called back. "I distracted it so much, it just about flattened me."

"That's not a distraction. A distraction's waving a bit and getting its attention, not playing chase with it."

She turned her scowl on him, feeling the effect was diminished somewhat by the expanse of the field between them. "I used to work proper cases, you know. Murders. Drug gangs. *Actual crime.*"

"You chose to come to the country. This *is* a proper case up here." He examined his palms, grimacing. "I landed in a cow pat."

"A proper case? It's a missing bull, not the sodding crown jewels."

"A *stolen* bull with a pedigree longer than the damn king. A bull whose semen's probably worth more than the crown jewels, and has likely been used to knock up a bunch of cows without authorisation."

Adams crossed her arms over her chest, still perched on the gate, and stared at him.

His voice had broken slightly on the last line, and he threw his hands up. "I know, I know. But a prize-winning bull like this has seriously expensive semen."

Adams snorted. She couldn't help it. It was ridiculous, but what could she do? This was her life now. As if moving up to Leeds from London hadn't been enough. Moving *north*, when as far as her mum was concerned, anything beyond Watford Gap was a lawless wilderness populated by feral, blue-painted men wearing kilts. At least in Leeds she'd been in a city, with city problems and city crime, which helped ease the worst sting of her homesickness. She still missed the jagged, vibrant edges of the city that had birthed her, even the muscular, hungry turn of the Thames and its brutal secrets, although one of those secrets had been what sent her fleeing. Even so, Leeds had been alright. Leeds had been *comprehensible*.

But now, after finding herself constantly tangled up in the surprisingly criminal doings of the small, bucolic village of Toot Hansell, deep in the Yorkshire Dales, she'd ended up transferring out of West Yorkshire Police and into not just the larger area of *North* Yorkshire Police, but specifically the painfully rural and city-free Craven district. Which enabled her to keep a closer eye on Toot Hansell than she really wanted to (although she had to admit she needed to, because Toot Hansell involved a lot of what she termed *other* cases, which were categorically not covered by police training and which most people didn't even know existed), and also involved far too much livestock for her liking.

Those *other* cases she'd dealt with since moving north had involved, among others, dragons (friendly, for the most part); goblins (very much not friendly, and in fact rather bite-y); strange creatures living in the walls of stately homes; talking cats; enchanted necklaces; duck ponds that were only bottomless sometimes; and far too much crime for any tranquil Yorkshire village to justify. She'd also somehow acquired an invisible dog, or rather a dandy, although she still wasn't sure what that was, who was currently standing next to her with his paws on the gate and his tongue lolling happily. None of it made sense, and she still wondered sometimes if her official reason for transferring out of London, which was recorded as being due to a mental health break brought on by a traumatic case (monsters living under bridges and stealing children *are* fairly traumatic when one, as a sensible person, doesn't believe monsters exist. Or non-human monsters, anyway), had maybe been more accurate than she'd thought and she was imagining everything.

She certainly hadn't imagined the bull, though. "Collins?"

"Yeah?"

"Is it too late to reverse my transfer?"

"Absolutely. You'll never get out. It's going to be escaped sheep and stolen bulls until retirement, when you'll get a smallholding and take up goat-farming."

She scowled at him. "If I get a smallholding, you can send in the professionals. Yorkshire will have finally broken me."

He grinned. "You love it, really. Come on. We've found the right bull, anyway. Need to talk to old Daniel up at the farm and find out just how he acquired An Gaidheal Boidheach of Craven Highland Reds."

"Are you sure it's the right one?" she asked. "Did you ask it? Take its hoof-prints?"

"No. I did manage to get a look at its tag while it was chasing you, though."

"Glad I could help." She jumped down from the gate and surveyed the field she was currently in. It looked a bit boggy to the right, so she headed along the wall to the left. She'd have to follow it around and find another gate or stile to skirt the bull's field.

Bogs and bulls. These were the sort of things she worried about now. She squinted at the rolling land, the grass a long and vibrant green, the grey stone of the walls enduring like the bones of the country below the deeply blue and cloud-scraped sky. The sun was still high, even as summer loosed its grip on the high fells and deep valleys, the tarns and rivers and forests, and the smell of crushed grass and sleeping earth rose around her as she walked. A skylark dropped burbling notes from high above, and a couple of small, drably plumaged birds spun and darted ahead, hunting for sustenance in the long grass.

She supposed she didn't *hate* it. But the smallholding would definitely be a step too far.

BACK AT THE CAR, Adams scrubbed at the knee of her trousers with a rag, trying to get the worst of the cowpat off. She'd evidently slid through it, as the muck was deeply ingrained.

"You might want to start carrying some bin bags in the back," Collins said, dousing his hands in antibacterial spray. "They come in really handy for things like this."

"I have bin bags," she said, and pointed into the boot, where an assortment of black bags were bundled around something. "My wellies and coveralls are still in there after the pig farm incident. I'm too scared to open them."

"You're going to have to get used to a bit of muck."

She shook her head. "I don't mind muck. But this is *pig* muck. And now bulls. I did not sign up for bulls."

"What, the bulls are worse than goblins?"

Adams glanced around to make sure they weren't going to be overheard, but the farmyard where they'd parked was empty. "Goblins can't squash me."

"You can't tell me bulls are worse than the Toot Hansell Women's Institute, though."

He was grinning broadly now, and Adams sighed. For all the strange and – she hated the word, but – *magical* cases she'd been dealing with, it was true that the largest complicating factor were the ten ladies of a certain age who made up the Toot Hansell Women's Institute and had somehow made themselves ground zero for all peculiar happenings in the Dales.

"I really think I've made a mistake," she said aloud. "I'm pretty certain I can transfer back."

"Maud won't let you. She'll probably send me off instead, and then you'll have to deal with livestock cases all on your lonesome."

She gave him a horrified look, and her phone jangled in her pocket. She dug it out, frowning at the display. It read *DC James Hamilton*. She'd worked with him in Leeds, but since transferring, there was no reason for them to still be in contact. They'd been colleagues, not friends. She hit *answer* anyway.

"Hamilton?" she said.

"James," he replied.

She swallowed a sigh. "Sorry, James. What's up?"

"Can't I just call for a catch up?"

"You can. But I doubt you did."

He gave a little snort that was half-amused, and said, "Can you talk?"

She glanced at Collins, who was leaning against the car and looking across at the farmhouse. They'd already been in to visit the farmer, who had made a lot of protestations about how he'd found the bull wandering about loose and had taken it in out of the kindness of his heart. He'd even suggested that they should be investigating the bull's owner for animal neglect and maltreatment. None of which had convinced even Adams with her minimal knowledge of the intricacy of cattle pedigrees and breeding practices.

"Yeah, I can talk. What's happening? Is everything alright?"

"Not entirely. Do you remember when you were still here?" He stopped, as if unsure how to continue.

"Wasn't that long ago," Adams said. "I haven't completely wiped it from my memory."

"Right, yeah. Um – there were a couple of weird things, weren't there?"

Adams winced. There had been a couple of weird things. There had been a stolen necklace, which had turned out to be not just a necklace, but the repository of a dead sorcerer's power. It, along with the dead sorcerer's book, had almost been responsible for a large proportion of Leeds's more enterprising magic workers being burned to death by a corrupt police officer. James had got himself kidnapped in the middle of that mess, but due to some rather special tea didn't remember the stranger aspects of the case (there had been tentacles involved at one point).

There had also been a previous, smaller incident, which James did remember fully. He'd been mugged by what he insisted – without an awful lot of conviction – was a pack of children. Although there weren't many children who squatted in broken-down pubs, singing the Doctor Who theme and mugging large, fit runners. Adams had sorted that out too, and had done her best to keep James out of the rather more esoteric elements that kept sneaking into her job uninvited. She would have liked to have kept herself out of them as well, but unfortunately it was becoming clearer and clearer that she had no more choice in that than she had about dealing with bulls.

"Yeah, there were some weird things," she said to James. "And?"

"I mean, I don't know *exactly*. It's more an impression, you know? Like a hunch, maybe?"

Adams looked at the sky. There was no use being impatient with him. Just because she dealt with the weird on a regular basis didn't mean anyone else did. "Not super helpful, James. Can you be a bit more specific?"

He sighed on the other end of the line. "Right, okay. Someone gifted us a few crates of artisan beer the other day. You know the beer festival's coming up in Harrogate?"

"Yes, I had heard about it." Harrogate wasn't part of Craven, but it was within the North Yorkshire Police area, and everyone was aware of the festival. Nothing like an end-of-summer celebration of beer to legitimise some serious day drinking, followed by some afternoon brawling and evening driving under the influence.

James took a breath. "I suppose it was a bit of a promo for one of the festival breweries. Even though it's not our patch, you know how these things go. A little incentive to not keep too close an eye on stuff."

"Sure." Adams looked at Collins, who raised his eyebrows at her. She shrugged.

Sounding as if he were choosing his words carefully, James said, "And since that happened, things have got a little weird."

"Define weird."

"Well. When it came in, I was on shift, so I didn't have any. Plus beer makes me bloated."

"Good to know."

"Sorry. Anyhow, Temper had some, and Isha, plus a few other people who were knocking off."

"And?" Adams asked, trying not to feel a little stab of guilt at Isha's name. Isha had been … well, she'd been Isha, and Adams had walked out of Leeds without much of a glance back. She hadn't spoken to Leeds's computer tech since.

"And people have been acting really strange since."

"Strange in what way?" she asked, trying to hold onto her patience.

"Temper's really angry all the time."

Adams rubbed her forehead with her free hand. "Temper's always angry. Hence the name." It was actually DCI *Temple*, but Temper suited him much better.

"Not like this. He threw a journalist in a cell for three hours just because he asked a question about car thefts."

"*Huh*. Okay. That's a lot even for him."

"Yeah. And Isha's been poking around in the station computer system and doing things like releasing wage details to show gender gaps, and compiling promotion records to prove, ah, certain people are being held back. Which I totally support," he added hurriedly. "Only it means everyone's getting their backs up, and refusing to work with each other, and it's just a whole thing."

Adams looked at Dandy, who was sitting by the back of the car, watching her intently. She couldn't fault Isha's motivations, but creating chaos for the sake of it was out of character. She was hardly some power-drunk hacker. If Isha was going to do something like this, she'd have had a 96-point action plan, three backup options, six virtual escape routes, and would have pulled off a bloodless coup before lunch with no way to trace it back to her. "Okay, that does sound odd."

"I didn't know who else to talk to about it," James said.

"I'm not going *near* Temper. There's some other strange stuff going on too, and I can't even say why I think it's *off*, you know? It's only a hunch. I suppose I could report it to HR, but ..."

"Don't do that," Adams replied. "I'll head over this afternoon and you can update me fully."

"Really?" James sounded so relieved, she had a momentary flash of guilt over her impatience.

"Sure. I'll see you soon." She hung up and looked at Collins, who gave her a questioning look.

"Your expertise being called in?"

"Seems so. DC in Leeds is a bit worried about some artisan beer, apparently."

Collins nodded. "I see the appeal. But it lacks a certain excitement when compared to bulls, wouldn't you say?"

"I think I'll manage." Adams shut the boot and swung into the car, hoping Collins was right. Hoping there really was no excitement involved, and that James's sense for weird cases was rather less attuned than her own.

She wasn't sure she could be that lucky, though.

# 2

# TOTALLY NIDDERED

Adams left Collins at the Skipton station to write up the bull case, pointing out that it only made sense for him to do it, being the rural expert and all. He seemed unimpressed by that, but also relieved that her Leeds trip didn't involve him, as if the very idea of subjecting himself to the city when he didn't need to was horrifying. So she went home to change into clean trousers and top up her coffee mug, then headed out of Skipton with her windows down and Dandy sitting on the passenger seat next to her, his snout pointed into the wind and his dreadlocks blown back to reveal those unsettling, LED-red eyes.

The road wasn't too busy, clear of commuters in the middle of the day, and the ever-present summer caravans fading with the season. The banks were covered in trees, still summer-lush, and sandwich vans with hand-painted signs were pulled into lay-bys, while the long green skirts of the hills pooled around houses and hamlets as they traipsed off to the horizon. The villages she passed through slowed the route more than the traffic did, Ilkley a tangle of houses that trapped her for a moment before releasing her into a wilderness of moors. Then Guiseley swelled up along the road, linking to Yeadon, then past Kirkstall Abbey and on, the villages' borders blending irrevocably into one another, breeding industrial parks and shopping centres, the houses becoming more and more crammed in. Adams had a moment of claustrophobia which astonished her. This should feel normal to her, even *under*developed compared to London, but somehow, after the rambling, wild expanses of the Dales and even Skipton, with the hard shoulder of the grey fell rising above it and the wide high skies and resolute trees and stone-stitched fields and endless wind, the thought of all this condensed humanity was setting discomfort creeping up on her.

She wasn't sure she liked the development.

THANKFULLY, she didn't panic and flee at the sight of the city centre, or have a moment of overwhelm at the press of traffic and noise, so she wasn't too far gone yet. She pulled into a car park attached to the market, not far from the station, then texted James. She got out of the car while she waited for him, stretching, and watched Dandy following his nose to the bus station, investigating the comings and goings of the arrivals. Or looking to see if he could nab himself a Gregg's pasty, more like. She let him go. She'd discovered that Dandy had his own way of navigating places and distances, and he always turned up again. Plus, she had yet to figure out how one trained an invisible dog, so the odds of him returning when she called were entirely dependent on how he was feeling at the time.

She didn't have to wait long before she spotted James hurrying toward her, a tall, lanky lad who looked as if he hadn't quite grown into all his limbs yet. His hair was cropped shorter than the last time she'd seen him, but otherwise he looked no different.

Adams had been leaning against the car, and now she pushed herself upright. "Coffee," she said, by way of greeting.

James grinned at her. "There's a surprise. No decent coffee out in the Dales, is there?"

"It's not bad. Not what you'd call world class though, either."

"Best get you dosed up, then." He looked around, nose wrinkling. "Can you smell manure?"

"Almost constantly," Adams said.

They walked to the nearest coffee shop, exchanging the sort of desultory conversation of colleagues who had never quite made it to the friends stage. She thought he looked tired, shadows under his eyes and unfamiliar lines around the corners of his mouth.

Once they'd ordered and sat at an outside table, far enough from the next occupied one not to be overhead, she said, "Has everything been alright down here?"

"Mostly. It's just this whole beer thing," he said.

"Are you sure it's the beer? End of summer, everyone gets a bit scratchy." Nothing like a long hot summer to bring out the anti in the social experiment. Police ended up stretched pretty thin, and that helped no one.

"Some stuff, sure. But it's not about a few people getting roughed up, or someone putting the boot in when they can get away with it."

Adams grimaced. There were still plenty of the old guard around who felt like that was all part of being a copper, and not a small portion of the new guard wanted things to continue that way, too. Trickier these days, with cameras everywhere and all the phones, but there was always going to be that faction who thought they *should* be able to get away with it, and would when they could. "Been a bit of that going on, has there?"

James shrugged. "Always is." There was something distasteful yet resigned in how he said it, and Adams pushed down a little surge of annoyance. It wasn't something anyone should be *resigned* about.

"So what's the deal with the beer, then?" she asked, her tone shorter than she'd intended.

"It came in on Friday," he said. "Fair few crates, all spread about through the station, and we got one. Temper handed it out for a post-summer toast."

So four days ago. Adams frowned. "Everyone drank it at work?"

James shrugged. "It was for whoever was off-shift."

She supposed that was fair enough, but wondered how many people who'd had it had really been off-shift. Temper was hardly at the forefront of modern thinking. Not being able to drink at work probably felt a bit nanny-state to him.

"And then what?" she asked.

James grimaced. "Like I say, it's more a sense that something's *off* than anything that concrete."

"It's evidently concrete enough that you called me."

He looked at his coffee cup. "I know. I thought you'd maybe understand, or have some insights. What Isha's doing with the wages and stuff is right but also not, you know? And Temper's stalking about the place muttering that we're being hamstrung by political limitations—"

"He what?" That was far too close to what she'd just been thinking.

"You know how old school he is. He abides by the rules, but you always get the feeling he hates it. Now it's as if it's just all become too much and he's building up to *doing* something. Like locking up that journalist just for asking questions. As if he's finally decided to just run things as he wants."

Adams knew at least one journalist who could do with being locked up occasionally, but had to agree that actually doing it was both excessive and likely to be counterproductive. She was surprised there hadn't been a storm on social media about it already. Or maybe there had been – she never went on any of the platforms unless she had to. "Anything else?"

"Penny—"

"Penny?"

"Penny. Older woman, blonde bob, likes parakeets?"

Adams looked at him blankly.

James sighed. "DI Mitchell. Desk-based, absolutely gifted with anything to do with numbers."

"Oh. Right. Sure."

"She came in with a fancy new sports car this morning. Said it was a lease, but it'd be a *really* expensive one."

Adams frowned, something in the pit of her stomach tightening. That sounded far too much like the case involving the sorcerer's necklace. That was gone, though, gone and hidden, so this had to be something else entirely. She rubbed her fingertips together, feeling that little frisson, warning and delight, that meant she was onto something. Someone shouted inside, and she looked around, wincing as she saw Dandy winding his way through the tables.

"I had a coffee *right there*," an aggrieved-looking man was saying. "Right there!"

"Did you drop it?" his companion asked.

"Don't you think I'd be able to see it if I had?"

She tried to frown a warning at Dandy without anyone noticing.

"Are you alright?" James asked.

"Sorry, yes. Just thinking. Anyone else?"

"Well, Ste— DS Morton keeps appearing places and laughing about it."

Adams turned her frown on him. "Appearing and laughing about it?"

"Yeah, like there's no one there then he just *appears*, and it's enough to make you drop your cuppa. He thinks it's hilarious."

"You mean he's hiding or something?"

"No, I mean like this morning there was no one in front of my desk, then the next instant he was sitting on the edge of it. I just about had a heart attack."

"So he crawled up to your desk along the floor, maybe?"

"Maybe? But he didn't jump into sight or anything like that. He was just *there*. And DC Robbins climbed in the window yesterday."

"What window?"

"A window on our floor. Turns out some of them open."

Adams tried to ignore Dandy cleaning out the empty mugs on the next table. "But that's the fifth floor."

"I know. He climbed up the side of the building. No harness, nothing like that."

Adams considered it. Robbins was older, but very fit, and she knew he was into rock climbing and so on, mostly because he made sure that *everyone* knew he was into rock climbing and so on. It was at least 80 per cent of his personality, from memory. But no one gets to work by climbing in a fifth-floor window, no matter how into rock climbing and so on they are.

"And this all happened after they had the beer?"

"Yes."

"And other people who had it?"

"Nothing big that I've noticed," James said. "It feels like the whole place is on edge, though. Just waiting for something to happen. Isha's thing with the wages could really set something off."

Adams rubbed the nape of her neck. "What was the beer called?"

James pulled an envelope from the back pocket of his trousers and handed it to her. "I couldn't get any of the bottles. The ones that are left are still in Temper's office, and I'm not messing with that."

"Fair enough," she said, opening the envelope. There was a label in it, but it had stuck to the envelope, so she couldn't get it out. She peered at it in place, a well-printed sepia-toned graphic giving it the artisan-standard rustic look. It bore the portrait of an otter with surprisingly muscular crossed arms, wearing a flat cap and winking, and was called Niddered Ale.

"The back label's in there too," James said. "The address is in Knaresborough."

Knaresborough was a small town adjoining Harrogate, divided from it by a railway crossing and home to a tall, spindly bridge that spanned the River Nidd and raised the hair on the back of Adams' neck, even if the worst she'd seen underneath it were swans and pedalos. She checked the address but it didn't mean anything to her, just gave the name of the brewery itself as Dixon's Draughts.

"Any chance of getting hold of a bottle at some point?" she asked him. "We should get it tested, at least."

"I nabbed a couple of empties out of the bin on Monday when I realised what was happening, and took them to the lab."

"Nice work. Did they come back with anything yet?"

"No," he said with a sigh. "Just beer, no contaminants or anything weird. And I suppose it could've been a new batch, since I didn't get the original bottles that were drunk on Friday, but it seems unlikely they'd be any different."

"Does seem unlikely," Adams agreed.

"And I didn't know how to explain to anyone else that things are just *off*, but I figured you'd get it."

Adams grimaced. Mitchell had her numbers, Robbins had his rock climbing, and she apparently had being the resident expert in things that are just *off*. Or weird. She fended Dandy away with her knee as he tried to reach her coffee. "Alright. I'll take a look into it."

James let out a sigh in a great gust, as if he'd been clinging to it since she'd arrived. "Thank you. Really. That's amazing."

"I have no idea if I can find anything out," she warned him, pocketing the label. "It might not even *be* anything."

"Sure, sure. Do you need help? I can come with you to the brewery."

"No, you're alright." The last thing she wanted to do was pull him into this, assuming it *was* a this. Because if there was something weird about the beer, something more than just hot days and stressful nights and the built-up tension of the endless, grinding job, of dealing with humans being their worst selves over and over, then she was the one who had to handle it. If he could stay out of it, he should. Once one was in, there was no coming out. She was sure of that. And being *in*, seeing the hidden angles of the world, meant that one was seen as well. She could feel the scrutiny of hidden things all the time now, and found the gazes of non-human Folk on her more often than she liked to think about. Which was *fine*, in a strange way, but also wasn't. Because their scrutiny reminded her that she was no longer entirely part of the human world. She'd slipped through its gaps, straddling the Folk and more familiar world with one precarious foothold in each, and she didn't know how long she could hold on, or what would happen if she slipped.

She didn't wish that on anyone else.

"No," she said aloud. "It's not Craven, but it's North Yorkshire. I can argue I've got a bit of a right to be poking about there. You not so much."

"Fair enough. If you need backup, just tell me, though."

"Sure. First thing, though, is see if you can get hold of one of those bottles from Temper's office."

James winced, but said, "Will do."

She drained the last of her coffee, ignoring Dandy's disappointed huff, and got up. "Cheers, James. If anything else happens, let me know, alright? Keep me updated, especially if it gets any more weird."

"Got it. I hope nothing else happens, though. I feel like I'm the only sane one in the building at the moment."

"That's probably the case most of the time," she said, and he looked inordinately flattered. "If any more beer arrives, grab one of those too, so we can compare. And try not to let anyone drink any more of it."

He snorted at that. "It's a police station. Do you really think anyone's *not* going to drink it?"

"Well, there's that," she said. She raised her hand in farewell and headed back to the car, Dandy loping ahead of her down the pavement and winding through the oblivious pedestrians. The city smelled of exhaust and spent adrenaline and hot tarmac, and over it all she caught a whiff of manure, oddly reassuring.

Which seemed like a bad sign. She couldn't be getting attached to the stink of the countryside. She was pretty sure she had moral objections to that.

She swung into the car, settling herself into the seat and tapping the address from the beer label into the GPS. Traffic would be beginning to snarl up, and the road to Harrogate might be a straight shot, but there was no motorway or dual carriageway. She glanced at her watch. By the time she made it through Harrogate to Knaresborough the odds were good the brewery would be shut. Although, given the fact they were gearing up for the beer festival, maybe not.

She tapped her fingers on the steering wheel, considering it. It wasn't *on* the route back to Skipton, but it wasn't a huge amount out of the way. And the usual roads back to Skipton would be just as tangled with traffic as the Harrogate one, so it wasn't like she was going to be losing much time. Besides, her fingers still had that nervy, insistent tingle to them, begging for a puzzle to solve.

She looked at Dandy, who panted coffee-flavoured breath at her. "I'm sure it's not good for you, you know," she said, and he shut his mouth with a snap. She scratched him behind the ears then pulled out of the car park and back onto the roads, winding out of Leeds as the evening traffic swelled around her, riding the start of rush hour into the unspooling suburbs and forging on toward wider spaces, feeling an unexpected surge of relief as the city fell away.

Unexpected, but not entirely unwelcome.

# 3

# CLOSE ENCOUNTERS OF A
# POSH KIND

THE ROAD TO KNARESBOROUGH TOOK ADAMS NORTH OUT OF Leeds, creeping through the familiar clutter of houses and shops and cafes in Chapel Allerton and Moortown before the traffic slowly began to free up a bit, the sky growing bigger as fields started to interrupt the houses, then eventually replace them. The thin grey line of the road ran between drystone walls and tree-cluttered fields, encroached on here and there by flower-studded hamlets, then finally slipped down toward the roundabouts that circled Harrogate. The GPS indicated right, taking a route that skirted the town and would carry on directly to Knaresborough, but on impulse Adams kept on straight, thinking she could pass by where the beer festival was setting up first.

Within about ten minutes she was cursing her lack of local knowledge, the lack of driving skills in the general population, and the absolute refusal of the apparently offended GPS to offer her any other options. The traffic crawled, narrowing into the bottleneck of the main road through Harrogate, and by the time the tree-lined fields gave way to large gates enclosing generous houses, Adams was in no mood to appreciate any of it. Besides, she had doubts about anyone who'd choose to live in the middle of this morass of traffic.

Although, she had to admit as the long green swath of the Stray heaved into view, paths lined with graceful trees and the bright, neat grass pocked with walkers and runners and people throwing balls for dogs, that it had its good points. Harrogate was an old spa town, with the green spaces of the Stray and the Valley Gardens at its heart, full of tall, deeply fancy houses that attempted to hold themselves somewhat apart from the town centre and its bustle of chain stores and supermarkets. But, as with everywhere, the borders were smudged. The Victorian Turkish Baths were still in use, lush with rich colours, old tiles, and genteelly faded glamour, but the same building encompassed a personality-free, fruit-machine-adorned chain pub. Surrounding it were art galleries and bespoke tailors, kebab joints and dubious late-night venues, designer boutiques and antique dealers and phone shops of questionable provenance. And everywhere were green spaces and sun-drenched benches and flower baskets hanging from lamp-posts, a steady thread of nature stitching the town together.

Adams crept slowly through the crammed streets, trying to appreciate the vivid green of the Stray but mostly cursing herself for thinking this was a good idea. She'd probably have been at the brewery by now if she'd gone the way the GPS had suggested. And she'd likely be home if she hadn't decided to visit a brewery that was likely closed. She was here now, though, so she just took advantage of the slow traffic to pull onto the edge of the Stray, sticking her permit in the wind-screen and jogging across the lush grass toward a circle of white canvas marquees. There were a couple of workers still dealing with a stack of interlocking floorboards, and she slowed as she reached them, Dandy running past her to dive into the nearest tent, where the floor had yet to be installed. He rolled wildly in the grass then cavorted about the empty space, dreadlocks flying. The marquee had clear plastic panels in the sides, and she could see him bouncing up and down inside, which was at least mildly distracting.

"Afternoon," she called to the two men, who looked at her without much interest.

"Hiya," the youngest one said.

"DI Adams, North Yorkshire Police," she said, showing her ID. "When does the festival kick off?"

"Thursday," the younger man said. He had dark, flawless skin and high cheekbones, and his bare arms were finely muscled.

"Is it all taking place in here?" Adams asked, waving at the marquees. There were a dozen of them, all still empty shells at the moment, and they formed a circle around an empty centre where she imagined picnic tables might be set up later.

"Mostly," the older man replied. He was the polar opposite of the young man, pale and bulky and dusted with sunburn. "The bars and pubs'll all have the local beers on, and there's going to be food trucks and that lot coming too. But this is the centre of it all, as it were."

"By Thursday?" Adams asked. It was Tuesday night already.

The older man winked. "Just you wait and see," he said. "We're right quick once we're going."

"If you say so. Do you have a list of who's in what tent?"

"Marquee," the young man said, then looked embarrassed. "Sorry."

"Each marquee, then."

"Nah, not our job," the older man said. "We just put them together. About to knock off and grab a pint, though. Want to join us?"

"No," Adams said. "Police officer, remember?"

"Still drink beer, don't you?"

"Not when I'm working."

"Right you are," the man said, unbothered, and he and the young man returned to slotting the last few floorboards in place. Adams headed back to the car, clicking her fingers at Dandy, who was still cavorting about the empty marquee happily. Something about the hollow, expectant structures made her uneasy, deposited here in the centre of town like eggs at its heart, waiting to hatch.

Although that was likely her head getting away on her. They were *tents*, not bloody alien cocoons.

Sorry, *marquees*.

THE ROUTE to Knaresborough saw the outskirts of Harrogate merge into Starbeck, which seemed to have neither beck nor stars that she could see. It did have a higher proportion of takeaways and tanning shops, and distinctly fewer designer boutiques than Harrogate, though. Then she was out into a swathe of farmland, trees crowding the road to both sides and the ubiquitous golf course laying claim to half of it.

Knaresborough was across a stretch of the River Nidd, little red rowing boats tied docilely to the bank below and walkers strolling on the paths, but Adams' GPS told her to turn left before she reached it. She slowed, spotting signs pointing right to Mother Shipton's Cave, breathlessly proclaiming her as the most famous fortune-teller to ever have existed in England. There was also meant to be a well that turned things to stone, which Adams found at least as interesting as the idea of the fortune-teller. She knew a few people she'd like to drop in there.

Knowing what she now did about the less usual Folk of

the world, Adams suspected that Mother Shipton had been no more a fortune-teller or witch than she was. Folk tended to keep themselves rather more hidden, and Adams couldn't blame them. Humans weren't great with anything *different*, particularly if those with the differences happened to be female, as the witch trials rather aptly illustrated. Although Mother Shipton was long past worrying about such things, so who knew?

She turned left, obeying the nagging GPS and leaving the petrifying well behind her, the scent of the river and damp earth drifting in the open windows. The road was narrow but well kept, and when she emerged from the trees she found a bank of wooden signs, all for different businesses, crowned with one that neatly identified the area as *Feather-stone Manor*. She frowned at it. That had been the name on the beer label, but she'd expected an industrial estate, not a farm. As she followed the gravel lane, though, it soon became clear that the landowner had been diversifying. The signs pointed her on past a couple of junctions, and led into a cluster of buildings, some old, remodelled stone structures, others newer, wooden, custom-built ones. She stopped, looking around curiously. The first few places offered a CrossFit, an accountant, a printer, and a place that made organic skincare. There was no office or security, no one to check in with or ask questions of, so she drove slowly on, fields washing away to her right and trees forming a pretty backdrop to the buildings on her left.

It didn't take long to find the brewery. It was the last building in the little collection, and the biggest there, still mostly built out of original, heavy grey stone and looking like it must've been a barn once. It was two storeys, but with only narrow windows in the top floor, and had big double doors to the front as well as a smaller one to the left of them. A large sign matching the sepia tones of the beer label hung over the double doors, reading *Dixon's Draughts*, and Adams could smell the heavy scent of yeast and hops as she pulled up in front of it. No one was about that she could see, but she got out and went to bang on the door anyway.

There was no response from inside, and she stepped back, tucking her hands into her pockets and looking around at Dandy, who was still standing by the car, his snout lifted to the air. She wondered if the yeasty smell was getting to him. It was strong enough.

The crunch of gravel caught her attention, and she turned to see a tall, lean man with vaguely unkempt brown hair ambling toward her, two border collies flanking him with their ears back and their sharp eyes on Dandy.

"Can I help you?" the man called. He was wearing Hunter wellies and a Barbour gilet over a checked shirt, and she half expected him to have some sort of Landed Gentry™ label floating over his head. Maybe this place was less farmland than country estate land.

"DI Adams, North Yorkshire Police," she said. "I was hoping to have a word with someone from the brewery."

"North Yorkshire Police? I hope there's not a problem." His voice didn't hold the almost incomprehensibly posh tones she'd expected, but was lazy and softened at the edges to something warmer and more accessible.

"No, not at all," she said. "Just a couple of routine inquiries. You are?"

"Oh, sorry," he said, stopping in front of her and extending his hand. "Rory Acklesfield."

"Are you the landowner, Mr Acklesfield?"

"Rory," he said, smiling at her. He had a good smile, broad and friendly, and his hand felt calloused as they shook. "And yes."

She returned his smile with a nod and said, "How long has the brewery been here?"

"Oh, a couple of years now," he said. "One of the first tenants when I started renting the buildings out."

"Recent, is this?" She nodded at the collection of buildings.

"Fairly. These old places are a bloody fortune to keep up. So either you open them to tourists, or you find another way to make some money. The house isn't fancy enough for showing, plus it's in such a state someone'd be sure to fall through the floor, and I can't afford to get sued." He grinned at her, and she couldn't help smiling back. "Plus I can't stand the idea of people traipsing around the house anyway. I'd have to pick up my dirty laundry, for a start."

"That does sound like a nightmare." Adams was trying to ignore Dandy, who was standing on the roof of her car, staring at the brewery while the border collies circled below like a couple of furry, cruising orcas.

"Yeah, really not worth it. So I put the money into doing up the outbuildings and renting them out instead. Got a handful on the other side of the property too, plus a couple of holiday lets. Doesn't make a fortune, but it's enough to keep me going."

"How many businesses do you have here altogether?"

"Half a dozen here and the same over the other side. I rent fields as well, for grazing."

"Can't be doing too badly on that." She was only half listening, as Dandy had just sailed over the dogs' heads and loped off toward the trees that edged the buildings, ignoring his pursuers.

"House eats it all," Rory said. "But it's something. So is there anything I can help you with? I can't let you into the brewery, unfortunately. Not without a warrant, at least."

"That won't be necessary." Dandy vanished, and she hoped he didn't do anything nasty to the dogs. They didn't seem like they wanted to bite him, exactly. Maybe with all those dreadlocks they thought he was a stray sheep. "What are their normal hours here?"

"I think they're usually in by nine, out by five. Something like that, anyway. Do you want me to get them to call you?"

"No, that's fine. I'll come by again. Do you know what their participation in the beer festival is going to be like, by any chance?"

"I know they were gearing up for it," he said, rubbing a hand through his hair. "They've been pretty busy. Alistair – he's the owner – was trying out some new recipe, apparently."

"Oh? Have you tried it?"

"No, not much of a beer man. I prefer to stick to whisky, myself."

"Right." Adams examined the bland stone front of the brewery again. It hardly looked like a den of iniquity, and nothing about it was setting off any particular instincts, general cop ones or other. There was nothing to say the beer hadn't been tampered with after leaving the brewery, after all. If it even had been, and it wasn't just the stress of the long, un-Yorkshire-like hot summer.

"Alistair what?" she asked.

"Oh – Alistair Dixon." Rory looked around. "Where did the dogs go?"

Adams waved vaguely. "Into the trees, I think."

"Probably after a rabbit," he said, and whistled sharply, a loud, piercing sound that made Adams wince. He looked back at her and said, "Do you have a card?"

"Sure." Adams found one in her pocket and handed it to him. "I'm not based in Harrogate, though, so you might be better contacting the station here if you need something."

He gave her that grin again, the corners of his eyes crinkling. "You never know when you might need a police officer. Always good to be able to put a face to the force and all that."

She raised her eyebrows. "I suppose. But this isn't really my patch. I'm based out of Skipton."

"That's a nice town. I get to Skipton sometimes. Great pork pies."

"I'm vegetarian," she said, and he laughed.

"In that case I recommend the cheese scones at The Three Sheep. Truly excellent. And you can get them with extra cheese and chutney."

"Good to know."

"Of course, Detective Inspector," he said. "Do you have a first name by any chance?"

"DI Adams is fine."

"Fair enough." The corner of his mouth twitched up, though, and he stepped back, hands in his pockets as he looked around for the dogs again. "*Oi!*" he shouted. "Midge! Pinto! *Heel!*"

Adams nodded at him and headed back to the car. He was whistling again as she pulled away, and she glanced in the rearview mirror in time to spot the two border collies darting out of the trees, lean and lithe as they ran to him. She looked away just as Dandy stuck his face into hers, lapping her cheek with a hot tongue.

She almost swerved, swearing as she recovered. "Stop *doing* that," she said to him. "I'm going to have to get you a damn bell."

He whined, trying to rest his chin on her forearm as she drove.

"What? Were the nice dogs mean to you?"

Dandy straightened up, then put his chin on her arm again.

"They seemed alright. You were the one winding them up, running off into the trees like that."

He huffed and turned to look out the side window, evidently disagreeing with her diagnosis of the situation. She scratched the back of his neck as they rumbled down the lane, back toward the road. She hadn't been able to see anything weird about the brewery, and Rory – Acklesfield – had seemed alright, as far as that went. Dandy certainly hadn't been bothered by him.

She'd still follow it up, come and talk to Alistair Dixon tomorrow. But she did wonder if James was maybe jumping to conclusions, if the events of the summer so far, the necklace and the kidnapping and the mugging by diminutive Doctor Who fanatics, was taking a toll. It would make sense. Maybe she should be worrying about James rather than about the brewery. She sighed, rolling her shoulders against the sudden weight of the thought. She'd thought she'd got this sorted out. If she couldn't arrest someone, she could hit them with a very big stick, or possibly with her metal, rubber-duck-shaped keychain, which was surprisingly effective. But neither approach was going to work with an anxious DC who'd had one too many brushes with the unknown.

She pulled back onto the road and turned right to begin the trek home to Skipton, the long, late summer evening lying low across the fields around her, golden and mellow and full of magic.

# 4

# EXCESSIVE EVEN FOR A JOURNALIST

ENOUGH OF THAT RICH EVENING LIGHT WAS HANGING ON WHEN Adams got home that she went straight out again, running in the deep shadows of the town while the sun still burnished the tops of the buildings and reached for the still waters of the canal. Dandy ranged easily alongside her, and when they passed through a break in the buildings and were caught by the sun, his shadow muddled up with hers, indistinguishable. She wondered if other people could see it, or if it was as invisible as he was. It'd be a bit weird if they could, a shadow without a dog, but humans had a remarkable talent for explaining away anything they were uncomfortable with. Adams stumbled on the thought. *We*, she amended, with a touch of horror. *We* have a remarkable talent for explaining things away.

Dandy was easy company, keeping close to her as they ran through town then up to the woods that enveloped the castle, looping through the worn dirt tracks before skirting the moat and heading down to the canal, racing the lengthening shadows of the evening along the towpath. Town was crowded, long queues waiting at the fish and chip shop, and the roads and pavements outside the pubs crammed with both tourists and locals.

Adams' gaze drifted over them as she ran, observing without seeming to. Part of it was simple cop awareness, looking for the groups that were a little too drunk, the ones whose voices were a little too loud, the ones who were staggering a little too much. Looking, too, for those who moved among the drinkers with sharp eyes and quick, deliberate movements, their heads down and their faces shadowed as they looked for a bag left unattended, a phone on a table while someone's back was turned, a wallet not pocketed deep enough.

There wasn't much to be seen, though, and there was a certain mellowness to the whole scene. It was Tuesday evening in a Yorkshire market town, after all, not London on a Friday night. Skipton still had its moments, of course, once the pubs were letting out and the booze had been flowing for a while. The combination of the heat of the day and the aggression brought on by the drink was the same everywhere. It didn't matter if it was London or North Yorkshire or the far reaches of some Scottish highland, it was just all human nature.

But brewing trouble wasn't the only thing she was looking for as she ran, and the second thing wasn't quite as simple to define. It was simply an *otherness*. People who were somehow a little more clear-cut, who seemed to exist a touch more fully in the world than others. And, more often than not, those people weren't quite as human as those around them. Maybe they had hooves instead of feet, or wings tucked tight against their backs, or horns, or maybe their eyes just weren't quite *right*. For the most part, they went unremarked, just as Dandy's shadow would if anyone had seen it. Such *otherness* couldn't exist, so it didn't, and the Folk passed quietly beneath the attention of most humans, which was the safest option for everyone involved. Certainly for the Folk, as if humans had burned their own for being witches, what would they do to a faun? A faery? A *goblin?*

Actually, in Adams' experience, goblins would deserve the horror the average human might feel on seeing them, but she still couldn't condone *burning* them. That was unnecessary. It seemed that most Folk, like most humans, had their own lives to live, and they went about them as well as they could. So as she ran, she looked for Folk not because she thought they were intrinsically a problem – certainly no more so than the average boozed-up human – but because she wanted to know what was there. What she'd spent her whole life resolutely not seeing.

Although she had a feeling she'd been seeing it for a lot longer than she realised, even if she'd only had to face it in London, with the creatures under the bridge. That had been almost insurmountably difficult, her whole understanding of the world upended, and she'd had migraines at first, just as she'd had when she first got to Toot Hansell and stumbled across dragons. She didn't get migraines anymore, and she saw Folk everywhere, which she blamed firmly on the dragons and the Toot Hansell Women's Institute. She'd walked away from this other facet of the world after London, after all, and they'd just bloody well dragged her back into it, armed with tea and baked goods and an insufferable *enthusiasm*. She knew that wasn't entirely fair, that she'd have been stuck in this strange between-worlds state regardless, but dragons had broad shoulders and ladies of a certain age even more so. And sometimes she still needed someone to blame at least a little.

But now she watched the Folk, and she knew they watched her back. She had an idea they worried *she* might be a problem. She wasn't, of course, no more than she was for any humans simply out for a good time. She'd only be a problem if *they* were a problem, and she had no idea how she communicated that, except by doing what she'd always done. Watch, wait, and step in when she needed to.

AT HOME she heated up some leftover takeaway curry from the night before, sending a mental message to her mum that at least it wasn't instant noodles, *and* it was a vegetable curry, so absolutely one of her five a day. She gave Dandy some rotisserie chicken she'd shredded off the carcass, although she still wasn't entirely sure why she kept feeding him. He seemed to fend perfectly well for himself, and constantly turned up with stolen bones from who knew where. But she felt guilty if she ate and he didn't, and as she had discovered very quickly that he was no more inclined to eat dog food than she was, she bought him whatever meat was on special at the supermarket. Which was slightly awkward considering she'd been a vegetarian for years, and every time she ran into someone from the station they'd look at the packs of short-dated meats in her trolley and raise their eyebrows at her. She'd then explain that she was feeding the neighbourhood cats, to which they would always suggest that cat food was probably a better choice, and she'd have to come up with some excuse about why the strays were apparently not content with Whiskas.

In short, having an invisible dog was difficult and small towns were complicated, and she did miss the anonymity of living in a city. She settled on the sofa with her bowl of curry in one hand and her laptop in the other, Dandy flopping at her feet. She rubbed his belly with one bare foot while she ate the curry absently, searching for the brewery online. It didn't tell her a lot. It was indeed owned by one Alastair Dixon, who had a history of working for other artisan breweries in Yorkshire, including some prize-winning ones. Dixon's Draughts had come into being two years ago, and had been a mild success so far. Nothing exceptional, but towns like Harrogate were always happy to welcome anything artisan and local. Add in organic and he was onto a winner.

She couldn't find anything else out about either the breweries or Alistair himself. He had a good social media presence, as far as she understood it, with a decent following, and she couldn't dig up any unpleasant stories about the beer having peculiar side effects or anything like that. She supposed it could be a bad batch that had got contaminated, which should be easy enough to check. As long as they still had the rest in the back of the brewery and hadn't distributed it yet. But there was nothing more she could do tonight.

She closed the laptop and set it aside, stretching out on the sofa and enjoying the unaccustomed freedom of the evening. That was one thing about small towns she felt she could get used to. There was still plenty of work, of course, but there were also nights like this. Just her and Dandy ensconced in the snug downstairs of her rented house, listening to the last of the birdsong coming in through the windows and watching the night creep in, carrying with it the scent of dew in new grass and the old damp of distant trees.

It wasn't *awful*.

SHE DIDN'T GO STRAIGHT to the brewery the next morning, but instead drove to the station first, jealously guarding her travel mug of coffee from Dandy. Invisible dogs apparently had an insatiable appetite for coffee, and he'd already stolen one mug in the moment it took her to get her jacket on. She had a feeling she'd brought this on herself, by allowing him to have all her coffee grounds, and rather than making him happy it seemed to have convinced him that all coffee in a ten-k radius was actually intended for him.

He trotted after her as she ambled into the station, nodding to PC McCleod at the front desk. He managed something like a smile back, and a garbled sentence that might have been a greeting. Adams still wasn't quite sure what she'd done to inspire such fear in him, but she'd definitely done it well. She wished she knew, so she could at least take credit for it.

Collins was already at his desk in the little office they shared, the small window cracked open to allow the crisp morning air in, a mug of tea and a bacon butty sitting in front of him.

"Morning," she said. "Low cholesterol bacon, is it?"

He scowled at her. "I'm allowed a bacon butty. Wednesday's my midweek treat day."

"You're allowed to do whatever you want," she said. "Just don't tell your aunt." Collins' aunt Miriam was one of the less terrifying members of the Toot Hansell Women's Institute, and while she was not usually particularly intimidating, she had very clear views about what her nephew's diet should look like since he got diagnosed with high cholesterol.

"What came of your trip to Leeds yesterday, then?" Collins asked, then looked around warily, one hand protectively over his sandwich. "Is Dandy in here?"

"Yes. Guard that bacon butty with your life."

"You need to train him better. How am I meant to guard my sandwich when I can't even see what I'm guarding it from?"

She sat down, clicking her fingers at Dandy. He seemed torn between stalking the sandwich and her coffee, so just flopped to the ground and rolled onto his back instead, apparently overcome. "You're safe for now. James seems to feel they've been given some contaminated beer that's having really strange side effects."

"Strange how?"

"Eh." Adams wrinkled her nose. She really hated the word *magic*. Magic was rabbits out of hats and pigeons up your sleeve, not things with teeth and claws and different relationships to the physics of the universe.

"Toot Hansell strange?" Collins suggested around a mouthful of bacon butty.

"Yeah. That's a good way to put it."

"Okay, so where are you with it?"

"No full bottles to run tests on, but James got the lab to test some dregs and they came up with nothing. The brewery's in Knaresborough and I checked it out on the way home, but I was too late to talk to anyone. I'm going to head back there shortly."

"You want company?"

"I don't think so at this stage," she said. "I'll let you get on with the handling of the livestock and I'll see what I can come up with on a slightly more civilised case."

"You love it, really," Collins said.

"I really don't," she replied. She logged into her computer, taking a quick look at her list of reports waiting to be filed. She was behind, which wasn't unusual, but she didn't feel she was so far behind that she had to finish anything now. She'd get to it later. She gave Collins a wary look. "Anything we need to do for yesterday?"

He made her wait until he'd finished chewing and washed down his bite of sandwich with a mouthful of tea before he said, "No, I'm mostly finished with the report. Got a couple of follow-up calls to make, but I can deal with that."

She grinned at him. "I'll buy you another bacon butty for that."

He started to answer and was interrupted by a knock on the door. "Come in," he called.

The dark-haired head of one of Adams' least favourite people appeared around the door. "Morning, inspectors."

"What do you want, Mr Giles?" Adams asked.

"Ervin." He had the sort of dimples that probably made some people a little bit soft at the knees. "And is that any sort of greeting? I've brought you coffee."

"I've got coffee," she replied, holding her mug up.

"You can never have too much coffee," he said.

Collins laughed. "He's a man after your own heart, Adams."

"I doubt that," she replied, and said to Ervin, "You're bringing us coffee and sneaking in here first thing in the morning. What do you want?"

Ervin emerged into the room properly, and both inspectors stared at him.

"Bloody hell," Collins said. "Who gave you the shiner?"

The journalist crossed to the desk to set the coffee down, the shadow of a bruise spreading across his left cheek and his eye swollen partly shut. He still grinned as he looked at Adams, though. "Your old boss." He set a takeaway cup in front of her. "Triple shot Americano." He turned to Collins and offloaded a second one. "Chai latte on almond milk."

"Excellent," Collins said. "Be nice to him, Adams. He comes bearing gifts."

She ignored that and said, "My old boss? Were you the journalist DCI Temple locked up?"

Ervin settled himself in one of the wobbly chairs facing their desks, crossing one ankle over his opposite knee and picking up his own coffee. "That was indeed me. And I wanted to have a word with you about it."

"*DCI Temple* gave you a shiner?" Collins asked. "I mean … What did you do?"

"Victim blaming," Ervin said, pointing at him.

Adams sniffed her new cup of coffee, then tipped most of it into her travel mug and gave the rest to Dandy. "I don't know. I've wanted to hit you at least a few times."

"You've only met me a few times," Ervin pointed out.

Collins snorted laughter. "I think that was her point, lad."

Ervin scowled at both of them, pulling his cup close to his chest as Dandy snuffled at it. "Sit," he said, and Dandy sat. Adams sighed. One of the things that annoyed her the most about Ervin was the fact he could see Dandy. He didn't actually realise the dog was anything other than an ordinary dog, and was the only other person she'd come across who could see him besides the cat and the dragons, and she wasn't sure that was entirely relevant. Cats saw the world differently, and dragons had been around long enough to be able to see anything. Another human being able to see Dandy felt *significant,* and she didn't like it.

"What happened?" she asked.

"Well, I had a couple of questions about a spate of luxury car thefts," he said. "For an article, you know."

"And what, he just walloped you out of nowhere for asking about the thefts?"

Ervin grimaced. "It was a Friday afternoon, and there were some beers out on one of the desks. And I *might* have made a small joke about drinking on the job."

Collins looked at Adams. "Drinking on the job? Is that a city thing?"

She gave him a scowl then looked back at Ervin. "And?"

"And he dragged me off to a cell, and when I pointed out that I could write up this sort of threat to journalistic integrity, he clocked me."

"So you *were* annoying," Adams said.

"It's been said that I can be. But that should *not* have got me a punch."

Adams sighed. She wanted to disagree with him just on principle, but she couldn't. "No, fair. That shouldn't have got you a punch, and I don't see why he chucked you in the lockup for asking about a story. But why are you here? I'm not even West Yorkshire Police anymore, let alone Leeds. I can't do anything."

"No, maybe not." He hesitated, looking from Collins back to her. "But it was the beer."

"The beer," Adams said.

"Yeah. This is going to sound a bit mad, but I recognised the beer on the deck. It's from Dixon's Draughts, and they've been giving out samples around the place."

"Niddered Ale?" Adams asked.

"That's it. You know it?"

"Heard of it. And?"

"This is the bit that's going to sound mad. This isn't the only weird thing I've come across in relation to that beer. We had a load dropped off at the newspaper." He twisted in the chair, pulling the side of his T-shirt up to reveal a large purple bruise blossoming on his ribs.

"Bloody *hell*," Collins said. "You're not in Fight Club, are you?"

"First rule of Fight Club—"

"Who did it?" Adams interrupted.

Ervin pulled his shirt back down. "My editor-in-chief threw a journalism award at me. And before you say it, yes, I'm annoying. But no, I'm not that annoying."

"You kind of are," Adams said, but with no heat. "And your editor had had the beer?"

"Almost everyone did except me. I had a stinking hangover and couldn't have had a drink to save my life. Next thing I know, I've been half impaled with a journalism award and everyone else is just acting *weird*. I head off to do some work, thinking it'll all blow over, and next thing I'm being attacked by a DCI." He shrugged, leaning back in his chair and watching Adams with sharp dark eyes.

"And," she said, because though he was annoying, he wasn't slow.

He grinned at her, giving it the dimples again. "*And*, I found at least four other places where similar things have happened. Beer comes in, everything gets a bit out of hand. It's not people getting drunk because we're talking one beer. And it's not just violence. There's other stuff."

"Such as?" Adams asked, thinking of Robbins climbing in the fifth-floor windows.

"Such as our quickest reporter, the one who always has to write all the articles that fall behind. She's producing stuff so fast I swear it's hitting the website *before* I've seen the news come in. Like she's predicting it. And I watched this ..." He hesitated. "I don't know how to say it."

"I thought you worked with words," Collins said, and Ervin made a face.

"This really ... well-endowed woman—" He broke off as Adams growled. "Generous? Buxom?"

"Worse," Adams said. "We get the picture. Hurry up."

"Right. Yes. Um, she was jumping over cars in the parking lot."

"Sorry, what?" Collins said.

"*Exactly.* I don't know what's going on. But I felt I should tell you." He nodded at Adams.

"Why me?" she asked.

Ervin hesitated. "I'm not sure, exactly. But weird stuff does seem to happen around you." He patted Dandy on the head, and Adams and Collins exchanged glances. The reason Ervin didn't realise Dandy was invisible was that a certain cat had wiped his memory of his previous encounters of a somewhat magical nature. But the cat had warned them that it got more and more difficult to do with every encounter, more and more *damaging*, and that for some people it simply never takes properly. Adams had a feeling Ervin was one of those people.

"What do you think?" he asked her now. "You think it's a story?"

"I think you should give me all the details, and I'll look into it."

"I'll email you what I've got, but it's no more than what I've told you. I can look into it with you, though."

"I think you should probably just lie low and try not to get punched again," Adams said.

Ervin frowned. "A little bit of gratitude wouldn't go amiss. Where would you be without me?"

"See," Collins said, "that's why you end up with shiners. Just don't know when to stop, do you?"

"I do."

"You really don't," Adams said. "Send me that email." She ushered him out of the office. The last thing she needed was the cat having to wipe the journalist's memory again. He was annoying enough with his brain not too messed with.

# 5

## THE THREAT OF A CUPPA

With Ervin packed off, Collins and Adams looked at each other in the quiet of the office.

"What're you thinking?" Collins asked.

"That James might be onto something," Adams said. She wasn't sure if she was relieved or not – it meant she wasn't going to have to do some sort of mental wellness check on the DC, but it also meant someone was dosing up half the county with mysterious brews.

"Certainly seems like something's going on there," Collins said, sipping his almond-spice whatever and making an appreciative noise. "Doesn't mean it's something Toot Hansell, though."

"No," Adams admitted. "But have you heard of any sort of food poisoning that'd have people jumping over cars?"

"That's a fair point. Just saying that simply because we're used to things being a bit weird, doesn't mean they're anything other than human weird."

"I'd rather we weren't used to things being a bit weird. I would like a plain, human explanation."

"Let's see what we can find out at the brewery, then,"

Collins said, getting up. "I think I should come, off the back of that."

Adams stretched. "Sure. I'll meet you there. I might go on to Leeds after, see if James was able to nab one of the bottles from the station."

"You could just call him."

"Maybe." She didn't elaborate, and Collins just shrugged as she led the way out the door. Yes, she could just call him. But she also wanted to see him face to face, to make sure he was alright. He had been too hesitant, too uneasy the day before, with his bewildered references to weird cases. And just as she got the feeling that Ervin was a little too perceptive for the cat's brainwashing or whatever it was to entirely work, so she felt that James put too much faith in the world being as he believed it to be. If he was struggling, things maybe coming unravelled at the edges as he noticed truths that didn't fit his reality, then she might need to have a word with him. Him, or the cat. The cat might be an easier option, actually. If James got upset and needed some hand-holding, she was *definitely* calling the cat.

THE ROAD to Knaresborough was quiet, Collins' Audi trailing her at a steady distance but otherwise traffic was sparse and sedate. The route rolled through the variegated greens of farms and open spaces, framed with drystone walls and lines of trees marking out the paths of streams. The sky was cluttered with grey clouds that let shafts of sunlight through, spotlighting distant buildings or copses of trees, and Adams had the feeling she was driving through some half-forgotten pastoral painting, bucolic and unreal. Other than Dandy panting on her shoulder, having decided her window was better than his. That was very real and not at all bucolic.

She pulled off the main road toward Featherstone Manor and rumbled up the long gravel lane to the collection of outbuildings, creeping through them to park near the trees at a decent distance from the brewery itself. She got out, stretching, and examined the old barn. Neither door was open, but a selection of vehicles were parked out front, including a van with the brewery's logo on its side, a flashy red BMW, and a few cars that looked as though they'd got in some arguments with the drystone walls and come off worst.

Collins pulled in next to her and got out, looking around appraisingly. Even without the sunlight from yesterday the whole place had a mellow, warm feel to it, the gravel unmarred by potholes and the buildings well-kept. A few of them, the brewery included, had barrels turned into planters outside them, jumbles of flowers lending a rather more civilised air to things than the average industrial estate aspired to.

"Flash place," Collins said. "Part of the old grounds, is it?"

"Half a dozen companies here, and about the same on the other side," Adams said. "Holiday lets too. And fields for sheep."

Collins raised his eyebrows. "Done your research, have you?"

"Ran into the landowner last night. Rory Acklesfield. Said that Alistair Dixon is the owner here, but he hasn't noticed anything odd going on."

"Would depend how much time he spends down here," Collins pointed out. "Unless he's personally involved, he's unlikely to know if they're fiddling with their beer."

"True."

Collins fell into step with her as they headed for the brewery. "Cameras," he said, lifting his chin at one of the trees, and she followed his gaze. Sure enough, there was a security camera squirrelled away on one of the branches, aiming down the lane. It'd show anyone arriving and leaving.

"That might be handy."

No one had emerged from the brewery since they'd arrived, and Adams knocked on the office door. There was no response, so she headed to the big double doors instead, giving Dandy a puzzled look as she did so. He'd stayed by the car, watching her with an anxious tilt to his head, his floppy ears back as far as they'd go. He hadn't seemed too keen last night, either, but now he seemed determined to keep an overly safe distance. She knocked on the barn doors, wondering if there were charms on the place. He hadn't liked the sorcerer's house in Leeds, either, but that had been drenched in deep-seated magic. Perhaps it was just the hoppy stink he objected to.

There was no response, so she knocked again, using the side of her fist this time, a *come on then let's be having you* knock, and the door popped open almost immediately, a young man with long blond hair tied back from his face scowling at her.

"Easy," he said. "We're not deaf."

"Didn't answer though, did you?"

He waved behind him, his bare arms lean and muscled under a tank top. "We're working."

"Us too," she said, showing him her ID. "DIs Adams and Collins, North Yorkshire Police. We're looking for Alistair Dixon."

"Parking ticket?" He grinned as he said it, revealing canines that were just slightly too long.

"Something like that." She returned the grin with a half smile, and the young man turned into the bright-lit interior of the brewery, leaving the door open as he ambled away, shouting, "Someone for Al!" as he went. Adams watched him, her smile fading. She wasn't certain – it was so bloody *hard* to be certain about any of these things – but she thought he maybe had those slightly crisper edges to him, that sense of being more deeply *here* than most people.

Then again, maybe it was just the light. The whole place was flooded with white, sharp illumination from banks of bulbs set into the high ceiling. Despite the two-storey build there was no top floor, and the interior was both cavernous and crowded, the walls lined with the hulking forms of gleaming copper vats, held off the ground by disturbingly spindly legs. Pipes spiralled off in every direction, stainless steel reflecting the light where there wasn't more copper, and wheeled ladders leaned against a couple of the vats, allowing access to the double-stacked ones. Little round portholes offered glimpses inside them, and a cluster of industrial-style tables and stools were lined up in the stretch of open floor in the centre of the building. Crates of beer bottles were stacked on them, and the air was thick with the scent of fermentation. Half a dozen workers in T-shirts and jeans moved about, peering into the vats and writing things on clipboards and lugging crates, none of them paying any but the most cursory attention to the inspectors.

"Pretty nice set-up," Collins observed.

"Looks like a mad scientist's lab," Adams said. "Or an alchemist's."

"You would think that. Do you even drink beer?"

"Sure. More a whisky person, though."

"That's even more like alchemy."

"But it's tastier alchemy."

"Still. I'd prefer Harrogate springs to peat bogs," Collins said. "They still bottle water here, you know."

"I do now."

A tall man with broad shoulders wound his way past the vats and ambled over to them, his teeth very white as he smiled. Adams had that same sense of his canines being too long and his edges being too sharp, but she was starting to feel like she was seeing ghosts in shadows now. Not *everyone* could be Folk.

"Morning," he said. "How can I help?"

"DIs Adams and Collins," Adams said, pointing at each of them in turn.

He raised his eyebrows slightly, still smiling. "Two detective inspectors. Bloody hell, what did we do?"

Adams gave him a tight, polite smile. "Can we talk to you for a moment?"

"Of course." He pointed at the doors, and as they stepped back outside he walked past them, heading to the office door with the sun turning his brown hair glossy and shot with gold. "It'll be a bit quieter than in here."

"Nice set-up," Collins said, still peering into the barn. "Love the copper."

The brewer stopped, looking back at him. "Nice, isn't it? Proper classic look."

"It is that," Collins said thoughtfully, and Adams raised her eyebrows at him. He didn't say anything else, and they followed the brewer into the office. It was small and cluttered, mostly taken up by a desk filled with order books and flyers for the upcoming beer festival, but there were two folding chairs leaning against one wall and he shook them out to set them in front of the desk, then took the office chair on the other side.

Adams nodded at the flyers. "You must be busy with this."

"Very much so. We're launching a new brew, and it could be a real turning point for us."

"Seems risky, launching something untested at a festival."

"Well, it's not entirely untested. We've been giving out samples, doing taster nights, that sort of thing. Feedback's been really good so far."

"Where do you give out samples?" Collins asked.

The brewer grinned. "What station are you two from?"

"Skipton," Collins admitted.

"So you've heard it's gone out to Harrogate, then." He stood and picked up a crate from the floor behind the chair, setting it on top of the desk. He winked at them. "There you go. Can't have you missing out."

"That's not why we're here," Adams said.

"Oh?"

"You sent some to the Leeds city centre station as well."

He frowned, tapping his fingers on the side of the crate. They were long and slim, the nails hard and slightly dirty. "Huh. Well, one of the delivery drivers lives in Leeds, so maybe they had some left and dropped it there. Wasn't on the list."

Adams examined him. She couldn't get a read on him, couldn't tell if he was telling the truth or not, and she had a sudden, irrational rush of irritation at Dandy for not being here, as if his presence would be enough to make things clearer. Or at least he might give her some sort of signal about the brewer, something to indicate if he smelled shifty or duplicitous. Not that Dandy tended to be that helpful. She still hadn't worked out how much use her invisible sidekick was, and the only thing she was sure of was that it was all on his own terms. "We've had reports of some interesting side effects."

"Side effects? I mean, it's beer. We're fully organic, made with Harrogate spring water, pretty much as clean as you can get, but it's still beer. A bit of excess'll get you some side effects, for sure."

"I'm not talking about people being drunk, or hungover. More like odd behaviour."

"Define odd."

Adams sighed. "Look, is there any way it could've been

contaminated? Over-fermented, or under-fermented or something like that?"

"Absolutely not. We have very strict quality control," the brewer said. "We've got a clean hygiene licence, and we adhere strictly to brewing standards. I can show you the recipe, give you some extra bottles to take away and test." He spread his fingers on the desk. "Whatever you want."

"We'll take some of those bottles," she said. "And do you have a list of everywhere you've sent samples?"

"Of course," he replied, opening a laptop that was half-submerged in a drift of order forms. "I'll print it for you." He clicked through a few things and added, "You can take that crate, and I'll give you another, too. You pick the bottles, so you know I'm not fobbing you off." He looked up at her with a sudden grin. "Then when you've seen they're clean you can have a wee drink to celebrate."

"That won't be necessary," Adams said.

"Go on. Can't hurt, can it?"

"Might as well," Collins said, and Adams gave him a disbelieving look. He'd been quiet for a while, looking around the office thoughtfully. "Fully copper?" he said now.

"Eh?" The brewer looked up, frowning, as the printer clunked into life under the desk.

"The vats. All copper?"

"All the way through."

Collins nodded. "Harder to clean, isn't it?"

"It's traditional. We wanted to really go back to basics. Keep it authentic."

"Higher risk of contamination, though."

The brewer shrugged, poking his computer. "Colour cartridge empty? It's *black and white*, you piece— Anyway. Yes. But you can test the beer and see that there *is* no contamination." He clicked something, and gave a grunt of triumph as the printer whirred, then sighed. "Paper jam.

Hang on, won't be a moment." He vanished under the desk, and Adams raised her eyebrows at Collins. He shrugged.

Ten minutes later they were walking back to their cars, Collins clutching a crate of twelve assorted bottles. Not all of them were Niddered Ale, the others bearing names such as Twisted Knickers and Quacking Good, but Adams had also taken half a dozen bottles of the Niddered Ale from different crates. If James had managed to get one from the station, they could at least compare them.

"What was the copper thing?" she asked Collins as he put the crate in the back of her car.

"I've done a bit of home brewing. Got interested in the theory behind it, but of course couldn't really do a full set-up. I did some brewery tours, though, and usually even if the tanks *look* copper, they're only copper on the outside. The inside's stainless, because it's easier to sterilise."

"Isn't copper poisoning a thing, too?"

"No proven risk of that, even with fully copper tanks. But a fungal contamination or something along those lines could be a possibility."

They both looked at the bottles.

"You're not giving it all to Leeds to test, are you?" Collins asked.

"Why?"

"Well. Seems a shame, is all."

She stared at him. "It's causing erratic behaviour. You can't seriously want to drink it."

He shrugged. "If it comes back clear …"

Adams shook her head, closing the boot, and looked around for Dandy. He wasn't in sight, and she was about to tell Collins they might as well head off when someone shouted, "Midge! *Midge!* Get back here! Pinto!"

She grimaced and turned toward the shout, seeing Rory

striding up the lane, his hair dishevelled in the wind, pointing at the ground by his side enthusiastically.

"*Heel!*" he yelled, and the two border collies, who were scrabbling at the trunk of a tree, ignored him entirely. "You'd think you'd never seen a bloody squirrel— Oh, hello, DI Adams." A smile blossomed across his face.

"Mr Acklesfield."

"Rory." He ambled over to join them, offering a hand to Collins. They were almost the same height, even if Rory was leaner and rangier, and Adams had a sudden desire to find something to stand on.

"DI Collins," Collins said.

"Pleasure. Would you *heel!*" he yelled again, and Adams squinted at the tree. Dandy was perched on a branch, looking down at the dogs with his tongue lolling gently. She had an idea he was laughing.

Rory waved vaguely at the brewery. "So you managed to speak to Alistair, then."

"We did," Adams replied.

"Get everything you need?"

"For now."

"Good, good. Anything I can help you with?"

"No, we're fine," Adams replied, ignoring Collins looking from Rory to her with a broad grin spreading across his face, making it rounder and more boyish than ever.

"Great." Rory clapped his hands at the dogs, then shrugged. "Daft mutts. I was just about to go back up to the house for a cuppa. Can I offer you something?"

"Wouldn't say no," Collins said, still grinning, and Adams shot him a sharp look.

"No, we're working," she said, opening the car door and climbing in. "Thanks anyway."

"Right you are," Rory said. "Stop by next time. I'll give you a tour of the house."

"Sounds good," Collins said, and Rory gave him a friendly clap on the shoulder, then bent down so he could wave through the car window at Adams. She nodded stiffly and started the engine, watching him march off toward his dogs, whistling to them as he went.

Collins leaned down to look at her. "I think you're in there, Adams. Fancy a bit of landed gentry, do you?"

"I do not."

"Aw, go on. I can just see you as lady of the manor."

"Don't we have a case to look into?"

Collins nodded at Rory, who was pulling the dogs away from the tree by their collars. "I think he wants to look into your case."

"That's not even— That doesn't even make *sense.*"

"When you're that rich you don't have to make sense."

"You go have a bloody cuppa with him, then," she said, and put the car in gear. She pulled onto the lane and headed away a little too quickly, raising puffs of dust from the unsealed surface, and glimpsed Collins still grinning to himself in her rearview mirror.

"Bloody children," she muttered, and nodded at Rory as she drove around him. He waved cheerily, and Dandy bounded into view, chasing the car down the lane with his dreadlocks flying majestically. The border collies just about pulled Rory over as they bounced and barked, and Adams wrinkled her nose. Served him right for being so … something.

# 6

## A MUSICAL INTERLUDE

THE FIRST PLACE ON THE BREWERY'S LIST OF SAMPLE DELIVERIES was a gym where Starbeck blurred into Harrogate, a big building sitting alone in a concrete car park, the front perked up with some slightly windburned potted trees. A couple of big canvas signs promised the first month free and a person-alised programme, and at one side of the car park a big, bearded man wearing a black T-shirt that couldn't contain his biceps was bellowing at four sweating women and two nauseous-looking men as they flipped tyres, whipped ropes, and flung themselves through various bodyweight exercises. The only one who looked to be enjoying herself was a large woman in a bright pink singlet, who shrieked, *"Wheee!"* when she star-jumped at the top of each burpee.

Adams watched them for a moment, as she waited for Collins to park next to her and get out. One of the men abandoned his tyre and bolted for the closest potted tree, one hand over his mouth.

*"Not there!"* the bearded man bellowed, but he was too late.

Adams grimaced and looked at Collins instead.

"Ah, fitness," he said. "Look how healthy it is."

"There are other forms of fitness," she pointed out, as the man wiped his mouth and staggered back to his tyre. Dandy had joined the two women currently using the ropes, jumping them like he was playing skip rope.

"I prefer the ones that don't involve vomiting," Collins said, and they headed for the building, skirting the violated tree carefully.

The reception area was compact and immaculately clean, all in tones of black and grey, with occasional splashes of burnt orange to liven things up. There were a couple of doors to one side, labelled *toilet* and *private*, and the entrance to a corridor, with signs saying *gym* and *spin* and *classes,* and arrows pointing in various directions. Some instrumental music drifted about the place, and a little circle of soft chairs surrounded a coffee table in front of a high counter. The top of someone's head was just visible over it, and its owner peered over the edge at them, then stood up, revealing themselves to be not much taller standing than they had been sitting.

"Hello," the young woman said brightly. She had very precise eyebrows and a wide, warm smile. "Can I help you?"

Adams introduced herself and Collins, and before she could say anything else the young woman clapped her hands and said, "Wonderful! We have a discount for police officers. We'd be very happy to get you set up with a new routine. I can see if someone's free now?"

"No, that's fine," Adams said, looking at the young woman's name tag. "Frankie?"

"Frankie Holland," she said. "I mean, Frances." She looked from one of them to the other, her smile trembling at the edges and her eyes too big. "What can I help you with?"

Adams watched her for a moment before answering. Dandy had come in with them, and he was sitting on one of the chairs, not offering much in the way of insight, so she just said, "We understand some beers were delivered here from Dixon's Draughts the other day. Samples."

"Yes?" Frankie said.

"Yes they were?"

She'd been looking a bit pale, but now she went pink, her cheeks hectic with colour. "Oh. Sorry. Yes, they were. Sorry."

"And has anyone tried them yet?"

She looked down at her hands and mumbled something.

"Sorry?" Adams asked.

Frankie took a deep breath, her skinny shoulders heaving. "Yes. We had them that same night. After we knocked off, you know?"

Adams looked at Collins, who shrugged. She turned back to Frankie. "Did anyone mention noticing any strange side effects?"

"What do you mean? Like food poisoning or something?" Her voice was squeaky, and she was deeply interested in the pen she was holding, her gaze fixed on it.

"Maybe," Adams said. "Or maybe people seemed to get drunk really quickly? Possibly started behaving erratically?"

Frankie hesitated, then shook her head carefully. "Not really. It was all fine. Everything was fine. Really fine."

"Are you sure? No one's going to be in any trouble."

Frankie shot her a timid look. "Why are you asking, then?"

"There's a possibility the batch was contaminated. We're just trying to find out if anyone was affected."

There was silence again, Frankie twisting the pen back and forth in her fingers, her cheeks so red she looked as if she were about to combust. Adams looked at Collins, raising her eyebrows, and he cleared his throat, tucking his hands into his pockets and rocking on his heels as he looked at the ceiling.

"You know, *I* thought I drank something dodgy once," he said, his voice thoughtful, and Frankie stole a glance at him. He didn't look at her, just continued, "I was probably about your age, and I went to Majorca on a lads' holiday. Bloody wild, it was. I mean, not a lot of sex on the beach in Skipton, is there?"

Adams made a startled noise, and Frankie gave something like a giggle.

"The cocktail, not the act," Collins added. "Anyway, I woke up the second morning on a beach on the wrong side of the island, wearing the top half of a donkey costume and a neon green tutu, with no idea how I got there."

Adams looked at him blankly. She was all for being relatable, at least in other people, but she wasn't sure Collins was doing much for the credentials of the police right at this moment.

Frankie was smiling, though. "Did you *really?*"

"Absolutely," he replied, smiling back. "I tried to tell everyone my drink was spiked, but I'm pretty sure it was entirely self-inflicted." He rubbed the back of his head. "I was hungover for the entire rest of the week, and I've never been that drunk again. I don't recommend it to anyone."

Frankie gave a very small nod, her eyes still wide.

Collins winked at her. "These things happen, don't they? To most of us, anyway." He jerked a thumb at Adams. "My colleague here, on the other hand, runs every morning, *and* she's a vegetarian. I've never even seen her drink a beer."

"I drink beer," Adams protested.

"Light, or alcohol-free?"

"Well ... look, I told you I prefer whisky."

Collins dropped his voice conspiratorially and leaned toward Frankie. "I don't reckon she *ever* had a misspent youth."

Frankie laughed then, and it was almost entirely natural.

"Okay, something kind of weird did happen," she said to Collins.

"Do tell," he said, grinning back and, Adams was sure, radiating smugness in her general direction.

Frankie shot a look at Adams, who spread her hands. "Like I said, no one's in trouble here. We're just trying to find out if something's up with these beers."

Frankie hesitated a moment longer, then said, "I'll show you." She picked up a phone and shoved it into the pocket of her gym hoody, then emerged from behind the desk and led the way toward the corridor. Collins and Adams exchanged glances (his was definitely at least a little smug), then followed. Frankie was even smaller than she'd looked behind the desk, barely coming up to Adams' shoulder, and proportionately petite. It looked like it would have taken about four of her to make up one of Collins.

The main room of the gym was mostly empty, the morning exercisers already done and gone and the lunchtime ones still to arrive. There was a man walking on a treadmill with a movie playing on his tablet, and a young woman running backward on another. Someone was rowing frantically to nowhere, and an older man in a skimpy singlet was doing bicep curls in the mirror. None of them looked around as Frankie led them to the lat pulldown machine. She adjusted the weight to its maximum, checked the room cautiously, then said, "This is what happened."

She took hold of the bar in one hand and, as casually as if she were putting down her toothbrush, pulled the cable to its full extension. The weights flew up so fast they almost slammed into the top of the machine, and Collins said something unrepeatable. Adams just stared, first at the weights then at Frankie, who eased the weights back down carefully.

"That happened after the *beer*?" Adams managed finally. "To everyone?"

"No," Frankie said. "I've always been pretty strong for my size. I work out a lot. I know I don't look like it, but I do. This is impossible, though."

"Yes," Adams and Collins said together, then Adams added, "When did you realise?"

Frankie grimaced. "One of the trainers … Ugh. Look, he's never done anything *wrong*, exactly, but he's just *there*, you know? Always stands a bit too close, or comes and adjusts me when I'm working out without asking. *Touches* me."

Adams found her expression matching the young woman's. "I know the type," she said, and wished that wasn't the thing that could instantly connect them.

Frankie gave her a grateful look, though. "He was there, when we were having the beers, and he adjusted my hair. I told him not to, but he did it again, and I … I pushed him."

Neither Adams nor Collins answered at first, then Adams said, "And?"

"And that's when I found out about the whole superstrength thing." Frankie pointed across the gym, to where cracks spider-webbed across the plaster wall to one side of a stretching area full of mats and Swiss balls.

"Wow," Adams said, once she'd managed to find the word.

"Yeah. And we were standing like halfway across the room. Nobody saw what happened, they just saw him crash into the wall, so they thought he was messing around." She hesitated. "He didn't come in today, and I thought maybe he'd reported me and that's why you were here."

"As far as I know, no," Adams said. "And I doubt he will."

"No," Collins agreed. "A bit embarrassing, I'd imagine. For someone like that."

"I hope I didn't hurt him," Frankie said. "I really didn't mean to. I just wanted him to stop *touching* me."

"A few bruises will be good for him," Adams said, and Collins gave her an amused look. "I mean, that's not my official stance, obviously." Collins and his bloody *relatability* were catching, evidently. "Did anyone else mention anything weird happening?"

"As far as I know, everyone else was fine. Do you think it's going to last long?"

"Not sure, I'm afraid."

"I mean, it was right satisfying yesterday, but this morning I was running late and ripped the door off my car. And I broke my mug mashing the tea. I'd quite like it to stop now."

"Well, we're looking into it," Adams said, and gave Frankie her card. "We'll let you know if we find out how to stop it. Get in touch if you hear about anyone else having any effects, okay?"

"Okay," Frankie said, and gave Collins a shy look. "I liked your story. It's really cool hearing about old people doing stuff like that."

She headed back toward the reception as Collins stared after her, his face blank. Adams bit her lip as she followed, ignoring Dandy trying to get a grip on a Swiss ball. She was pretty sure he couldn't steal it.

In the car park, the boot-campers were alternating between bear-crawling and frog-hopping across the tarmac, and Adams cleared her throat a couple of times before she trusted herself enough to say, "Where d'you want to try next?"

"A plastic surgeon's, I think," Collins said, and she burst out laughing, trying to smother it with one hand. He scowled at her. "Oh, *that* you laugh at. Can barely get a smile out of you normally."

"That's not true. And, to be fair, it *was* hilarious."

"I thought I was bonding with her, and she thought I was her grandad telling stories from the war," he complained.

"Oh, she didn't. Her dad, perhaps."

"You are *not* funny."

"She was, though."

"No, she bloody well wasn't."

"She was *devastatingly* funny."

"I think you should go back to Leeds," he told her, beeping his car open. "Or London. I've gone right off you."

"But who would make sure you got home safe?" she asked, leaning down to look at him as he got in. "And took your meds on time?"

"I liked you better without a sense of humour."

Adams straightened up, still laughing, then stopped abruptly as Dandy bounced across the car park, chasing a bright blue Swiss ball, Frankie running after him. "Oh, *bollocks.*"

"Serves you right," Collins said. "Sort your invisible dog out, then let's go interview someone who's actually out of high school."

THEY CHOSE the radio station next because it was the closest to them, and even in the middle of the day the traffic around Harrogate was enough to make Adams daydream about those big American pickups with oversized wheels that could roll over anything. She'd managed to get to the Swiss ball before it rolled into the road, and handed it back to Frankie while explaining that it must've rolled through a puddle, and that was the cause of its sliminess. The young woman had seemed a little dubious, then spotted the vomit in the tree pot, dropped the ball in horror, and marched off to thoroughly berate the trainer. Adams left her to it, hoping the trainer didn't make the mistake of calling her *love* or trying to pat her on the shoulder.

Welly Wave FM was based out of a four-storey office

building that huddled with two other matching buildings amid a near-empty car park. There seemed to be at least as many empty floors as occupied ones, and the outsides of the buildings were a little stained and neglected. A large canvas sign with a logo featuring a black and white cow gripping a red welly in its teeth was hanging under the windows on the top floor of one of the buildings, with chunky text reading *Welly Wave FM! Your Local Stomping Station!*

Adams and Collins found the door to the building's lobby open, a wedge of wood stopping it shutting properly, and they let themselves in then traipsed up the stairs, Dandy trotting ahead of them. In the hall upstairs they found a sticker of the station's logo plastered to a door, the edges curling slightly, and beyond that a reception desk and a few plastic chairs. Music was playing a little too loudly, some sort of remix of half a dozen songs, and there didn't seem to be anyone around. They checked the door behind the desk, which led to a small room equipped with a countertop fridge, a sink, and a kettle, a six-pack of Niddered Ale standing next to it with two bottles missing. The only other door had a large *Studio* sign on it, and a frayed, printed sheet of paper Blu-Tacked to it that read *On Air!!! Do not disturb!!!*

"So many exclamation marks," Adams said.

"Disturbing," Collins agreed. "Shall we ignore them?"

"No one else around," Adams said, and turned the handle, eased the door open just enough to peer inside. The volume of the music went up immediately, making her wince. A thin man wearing headphones over his sparse hair was seated at a rickety desk in front of a microphone, poking at a computer, and he looked up, startled. She held up her ID, inclining her head toward reception.

He nodded with surprising enthusiasm, tapped something on the computer, and hurried out to join them. He closed the door behind him, but whatever he'd done on the computer had evidently put the volume up out here. Dandy put his ears back, and Adams thought he was likely whining, but she couldn't hear him.

"Can you turn that down?" she asked, almost shouting.

The man pointed at his throat and shook his head violently.

"What?"

The man touched his mouth, then shook his head.

"You can't speak?" Adams asked. She supposed it wasn't *strictly* necessary to be a DJ, but it still seemed like an odd job choice. She could barely think with the music, though. About three different tunes were all trying to play at once, with some sort of marching band threaded over the top. Definitely not her sort of radio, but it took all sorts. "Can you turn the music down, sir?"

The man threw his hands up in the air, grabbed a notepad and a pen from the reception desk, and scribbled, *not music!!*

"Whatever it is, *turn it down.*"

The DJ shook his head violently, then wrote, *can't!!!*

"Something's broken?" Collins suggested.

The DJ rolled his eyes, took a deep breath through his nose, then opened his mouth very slightly, as if to let the tiniest breath out over his lip. A blare of noise – voices and guitars and drums and singing all tangled up together – swamped the room, the volume increasing to the point that Adams thought her eardrums might have permanent damage. She and Collins both ducked instinctively, as if the assault were physical, and Dandy fled as the DJ clamped his mouth shut again, the volume dropping to something almost bearable. They stared at him.

"That's *you?*" Adams asked, and he nodded. "*How?*"

He shrugged, both hands turned up the ceiling. Adams looked at Collins, and he coughed, then said, "Wouldn't happen to have started after you tried some of that Niddered Ale, would it?"

The DJ nodded violently, clutching his hands in front of his chest in supplication. He looked almost ready to cry, and the more upset he got, the more the volume went up, new instruments being added. There was a saxophone coming from somewhere now, and possibly some bongos.

Adams raised her voice. "Did anyone else have any?"

A shake of the head, and the roar of an accordion.

She handed him her card. "If anything changes, let me know. You can just message."

The DJ waved violently, and scrawled on his pad, *HELP ME!!!* It was accompanied by the screech of an electric guitar being played by someone with a grudge.

"We're working on a solution," Adams yelled. "We'll be in touch." She was already backing toward the door. They couldn't do anything, after all, and her ears were about to start bleeding.

The man threw his arms about, at once pleading and furious, and an entire orchestra fell into a pit full of cymbals.

Collins patted him on the shoulder. "Good luck, mate," he shouted. "I'm sure it'll be fine."

The DJ gave him a look that could have melted glass, and the inspectors fled.

# 7

# PEOPLING IS DIFFICULT

They could still hear the music all the way down the stairs, and it didn't fade away entirely until they'd reached their cars. Even then Adams thought she could still hear *something*, although it might've been the final echoes still dying away in her ears, caught there like the whisper in a seashell, only rather less appealing.

"So that was different," she said to Collins.

"No more so than small women throwing big men across gyms. Or DCIs punching journalists."

"That's not *so* unusual."

"It is, though. You can't get away with that sort of thing these days. Temper's lucky Ervin came to you instead of putting it straight in the paper."

"True," Adams admitted. "Weird he did, actually. He's not meant to remember anything about the … *other* stuff. That's what the cat said."

"When you're quoting a talking cat, I think you can use the word *magic*. You've already lost all credibility." Collins grinned as he said it, and she scowled at him.

"Why are you so relaxed about all this?"

"Because I am only involved tangentially," he said. "You're the magic detective with the invisible dog. I just tag along and arrest whoever pops up."

"Want to swap?"

"Not even slightly." He tucked his hands into his pockets, looking up at the sky. "I have a theory on how this beer's working, though."

"Do tell." She leaned against her own car, watching Dandy. He'd been waiting outside the door for them, and was now calmly eating dandelions.

"It's like Frankie said. Superpowers."

"*What?*"

"She said she works out and is stronger than she looks, but couldn't stop that trainer touching her. Suddenly she's super-strong. Poor old music-man up there's been talking music all his life, broadcasting it too, and now he's broadcasting constantly, all the music in the world."

Adams thought about it. "What about Temper? His superpower is punching annoying journalists?"

"It does fall down a bit there," Collins admitted. "But the brewer said they'd been working on refining the brew. Maybe he meant it. Maybe the results are a bit erratic. Or … people get into policing for all sorts of reasons. Maybe Temper's motivation has always been about the chance to get the boot in, rather than any moral drive. And his superpower is a complete disregard for consequences."

Adams frowned. She couldn't say he was wrong about the reasons people became police. But although she didn't much like Temper, she didn't think he was *that* bad, either. Unless he just hid the darker parts of himself well. Plenty of people did. "And Ervin with his car-jumping woman and violent editor?"

"No idea. More information needed," Collins said cheerfully. "The theory is a work in progress."

"I know what your superpower would be."

"Oh?"

"Being overly affable."

"Affable?"

"It's a word."

"I know it is. Your superpower might be having an excessive vocabulary, though." His grin widened. "Or something to do with over-caffeination."

"No such thing."

"Tell your doctor that."

She snorted and straightened up. "I'm going into Leeds. I want to see what's happening with Isha and Temper, and I'll see if James has got his hands on some beer."

Collins rocked on his heels. "I'll chase down some more samples here. Odd that Dixon gave us the list of places so easily. Kind of suggests there's nothing to be found in the beer. You know, even if your James gets a sample."

"I know. Run down every possibility, though, right? And maybe ..." She hesitated, then sighed. "Maybe the traces are simply going to be a bit more esoteric."

"*Esoteric.* Definitely vocabulary-based superpower."

She scowled at him. "I wish there was someone we could talk to about that side of it."

"Dragons?" he suggested.

"And end up with the sodding Toot Hansell Women's Institute in the middle of things? I can't see that making anything easier."

"Oh, bloody hell. Imagine the superpowers on that lot!"

Adams shuddered. "I'd rather not." They'd either be baked goods–based, or would have to do with the way ladies of a certain age just *did* things while no one could quite figure out how to stop them, and those particular ladies were far too skilled with both already.

"Thompson, then."

Adams sighed. "Really? The cat?"

"It's worth a try. He might know something, and if not maybe he can have a sniff of the bottles and figure it out."

"Good point. See if you can find him. He seems to like you."

"He likes my bacon butties."

"Well, get him a bacon butty, then." She swung into the car, and added, "Still going to try the beer?"

"Abso-bloody-lutely not."

THE ROAD from Harrogate to Leeds was already feeling deeply familiar, even though it hadn't been that long ago she was out here for the first time, chasing down the sorcerer's necklace. This time, at least, she didn't have to pull off the main road and go exploring tiny little back lanes where she was as likely to lose a wing mirror on a wall as she was to be run off the road by dangerous magic workers. Dandy kept his head out of the window all the way, dreadlocks flying, and she let him despite the coolness of the grey day's air channelling around the car. It stopped him drooling on her.

The midday traffic wasn't heavy, and she parked in the same car park as before, taking her backpack from the boot and slinging it over one shoulder. She could've used the station car park, of course, but she didn't feel like announcing her presence, particularly not if Temper was on some sort of super-powered, up-the-system rampage. She'd try and get in and out as quietly as she could.

She went via the coffeeshop to stock up first, then trotted up the steps to the main door of the station. The desk sergeant buzzed her in without comment, and she headed straight for Isha's office, figuring she should get that over with before she went in search of James. The computer tech's room was deep in the bowels of the building, the corridors echoing under Adams' boots and making her feel unaccountably nervous. Although that was likely to do with where she was heading, she had to admit.

Isha's door was closed and Adams knocked lightly, getting an exasperated *"What?"* from inside. She put the hand clutching a large iced coffee around the door first, then peered through the gap. "I come bearing gifts."

Isha looked from her to it and said, "Adams." Her tone was non-committal, and she didn't smile.

Adams couldn't really blame her. Things had been *nice,* in a way, dinners and drinks and so on, but then Adams had transferred to Skipton, and that had been that. Well, she'd made it that, she supposed. She put her other hand into the room, holding out a paper bag. "Chocolate brownie?"

"You owe me a bit more than that. I've never been bloody ghosted before."

"I didn't ghost you," Adams protested. "I *moved.*"

"To Skipton. It's hardly John o' Groats, is it?"

"Sorry. It's been busy."

Isha looked at her for a long moment, then said, "Come in, then. I'm not having this conversation with the door open to the world."

Adams came in obediently, although she had no intention of having any conversation that wasn't work-related. These sorts of things were always so messy and complicated, and people might say personal connections were necessary, but she'd never found them much more than straight-up *difficult.* Plus Isha had used her first name a few times, which was just not on.

She put the brownie and the coffee on the desk and settled herself into the spare chair. Isha had somehow acquired even more plants since Adams had been in here last. One entire wall was a mass of overgrown greenery, and she looked from it to the three monitors on the desk and said, "Is that safe with all your electronics and stuff in here?"

Isha shrugged. "As long as I don't start misting the computers as well as the plants, it should be fine."

Adams nodded, feeling that effort at small talk had not gone as hoped. "Fair enough."

Isha took her coffee, sipping it with her eyes on Adams. She was a tall woman with strong shoulders and long fingers, the gold stud in her nose collecting the light from the computer screen. "What can I do for you, then?" she asked. "Since I'm somehow doubting this is a personal call."

Adams took a sip of her own coffee, looking at the plants. "It really has been busy."

"I'm sure. How many sheep have you caught?"

"Last one was a bull. Very dangerous, bulls."

Isha snorted, then looked annoyed at herself. "I'm still not happy with you."

"Fair. I'm sorry. I'm not great at *this.*" Adams waved at the space between them, and Isha raised her eyebrows.

"Oh? And what was *this?*" She waved as well.

"I don't know. I told you, I'm not great at it."

"No kidding." Isha opened the paper bag to examine her brownie, leaving a sharp-edged silence in her wake.

Finally Adams said, "How have you been?"

Isha narrowed her eyes at her. "Why?"

"Just making conversation."

"You never just make conversation," Isha replied. "And you sure as hell wouldn't just be dropping in to see me on a whim, would you?"

"No," Adams admitted, the back of her neck too hot.

"So you want something. What is it?"

Adams sighed. "There's a beer going around that seems to be having some kind of strange side effects. I think some samples were dropped off here, and I wondered if you'd heard anything about it. Had any weird reports in."

Isha stiffened slightly. "Side effects?"

"People acting out of character, or inexplicable things happening."

"Inexplicable? Like your necklace case? The one you promised to explain to me and never did?" Isha was gripping her cup a little too tightly, indenting the sides.

"Erratic behaviour, is all."

"Like ghosting someone when they thought everything was going just fine?"

Adams opened her mouth to apologise again, then stopped. "I'm here for work, Isha. That's all."

They stared at each other for a moment, then Isha nodded. "Well, I'll be sure to let you know if anything comes in. If you read my messages, of course."

Adams got up. "Thanks." She hesitated, then added, "I really am sorry. I'm just … not great at personal stuff."

"There's being not great at it, and there's not trying."

Adams accepted that with a nod, wondering if it was worth bringing up the beer again. She had an idea she wasn't getting anything else out of Isha, though. She turned to the door just as it flew open, revealing a dishevelled man in civilian clothes. His T-shirt was torn at the collar and stained with tea, and he pointed at Isha. "*You*," he said.

She just stared back at him, both eyebrows raised, and took a sip of her coffee.

"You're messing with my program," he said, his voice wobbly with emotion.

"It's not your program," Isha replied. "It's the department's program."

"I'm the one that maintains it."

"And I'm merely showing you what would happen if someone hacked us."

Adams looked at her. "You hacked the department?"

Isha shrugged. "It was easy. This guy thinks he's some sort of security genius. I was through it in five minutes."

"You've got the passwords," he snapped. "You *stole* them."

"You shouldn't have had them anywhere I could steal them."

The man looked at Adams and said, "She's completely messed with everyone's salaries. Accounting are having a meltdown. And half the cases have vanished or been reassigned to other officers who are *completely* inappropriate for them, and somehow she's got herself a three-year bonus."

Adams looked at Isha.

"I was merely demonstrating the flaws in the system," she said. "If you did your job properly and maintained the security at a decent level—"

"I shouldn't have to protect it from the *inside!*"

"You should be able to protect it from *everyone.* I should have done this years ago. Useless bloody IT muppets."

They glared at each other for a long moment, then the man grabbed a plant off the nearest shelf, raising it threateningly.

"*No!*" Isha shouted, and he clutched the fern to his chest as he sprinted out the door.

She leaped from her chair and charged out of the room behind him, yelling for him to bring her plant back. Adams followed, leaning out into the hallway to watch the man crashing through the door to the stairs and vanishing. Isha plunged after him, still yelling.

Adams waited for a little while, standing in the doorway and drinking her coffee, but Isha didn't come back. Dandy leaned against her leg and she looked down at him. He licked his chops a little guiltily, and she glanced at the desk. Both the brownie and the iced coffee were gone.

"Well, that's not going to win me any points," she told

him. Dandy didn't quite shrug, but there was definitely a shrug in his look. Adams sighed. She couldn't fault him for his love of caffeinated beverages, or even for the brownies, but he wasn't exactly helping.

She went up the stairs, keeping a careful eye out for either Isha or the plant thief to come thundering back down, but apparently they'd taken their fight elsewhere. She let herself back into her old floor, looking around warily for Temper, but he didn't seem to be about. James was hunched over a computer, clicking away at the keys with a speed and accuracy she rather envied. She sat down in the chair opposite him, and he looked up, startled.

"Alright, James," she said.

"Alright, Adams," he replied. He looked even more tired than the previous day, his usually neatly groomed hair featuring some stray tufts, and a shadow of pale stubble on his jaw.

"Anything new?" she asked. "Did you get me a bottle?"

He looked around nervously, then took his backpack from under the desk and fished inside it, bringing out a tote bag. He slid it across the desk to her like contraband. "Just one," he whispered. "Temper almost bloody caught me, too. In his office!"

Adams winced. "How's he been?"

"Weird. Barely around. Still keeps muttering about how there's too many rules and regulations and there's better ways to sort things." James wiped his mouth. "Is this ... is it a *thing*? Like those muggers?"

"They were just some feral kids," she told him firmly, hating the slight shake in his voice. "And we have a theory this is some sort of fungal contaminant from using the wrong sort of vats."

"Really?"

"Really."

He leaned back in his seat, rubbing his hands over his face. "Bloody hell, that's good to hear. I was starting to think ... I don't know. I still dream about those muggers sometimes." He frowned. "The lab didn't find anything in the bottles, though."

"They'd've been looking for some sort of chemical additive, not fungus."

"I suppose," he said, still not looking entirely convinced.

"I spoke to Isha," she said, more to distract him than anything else.

"And you got out in one piece?"

Adams snorted. "Mostly because someone stole a fern, and she ran off after him."

"That'll be Troy. He's not happy with her."

"Kind of got that."

James clicked something on his computer and turned it around so it faced Adams. "This is the screensaver on everyone's computer," he said. "The system's still working, but if you leave it for two seconds this comes up." The screen started to cycle through a slideshow of various officers, all of them evidently taken from social media on nights out, wearing embarrassing costumes, in compromising positions, and, in one particularly unpleasant case, vomiting into someone else's welly.

"Oh, bollocks," she said.

"That's kind of what Temper said, only with better swearing."

"Why's she doing that?"

"No idea. All people she had a bit of a falling out with, though."

"Great," Adams said. "That's just great." She glanced around the room. "Temper's not about, is he?"

"Don't think so. He's pretty sneaky at the moment, though."

Adams frowned. You could normally hear Temper coming from two rooms away. "Right. Well, I'm on it. Keep me updated with anything new here."

"I can help," he offered, without much enthusiasm. "Look into things at this end."

Adams shook her head. "No, just keep your head down and let me know any new developments with Temper or Isha."

He gave her a look of unmistakable relief. "If you're sure."

"I am." She put the beer, still wrapped in its tote bag, into her backpack, then took a couple of Yorkie bars out. "Have these."

He frowned at her. "I don't really do sugar."

"Just this once," she said, placing them on the desk in front of him. "Call it medicinal. You look tired, and it's probably low sugar." She pointed at his flat belly. "It's not natural, that."

"Thanks?" he said, examining one of the bars.

"Eat them. You'll feel better." She got up and headed back downstairs, having to duck into an office as Isha went charging past, still in pursuit of Troy. He was plucking leaves off the fern and scattering them as he ran, which seemed unlikely to end well.

Back at the car, Adams took one of the bottles the brewery had given them from the boot, scratched the label to mark it, and put it in with the other in the tote bag inside her backpack. She turned to head for the street again and almost walked straight into Temper, who was looming over her, angular and glowering.

"Sodding *hell*," she said, clutching her chest. "Where did you come from?"

"What're you doing here, Adams? Thought you'd run off to chase sheep in the Dales."

She sighed. "Bulls, actually."

"Not too many of those here, either. What're you doing?"

"Shopping," she said, pointing at the market.

"I watched you come out of the station, Adams."

"Possible connection between a case of mine and some incidents here."

"And you just walked into the station without asking me?"

"I had a couple of questions for James, is all." She watched him warily, one hand straying to the baton tucked into the side pocket of her bag. His face seemed even redder than its usual ruddy hue, his eyes colder and paler, and he was clenching and unclenching his fists rhythmically. She thought suddenly that, for all his blustering, she'd never heard a single story of him actually laying a hand on anyone, until the whole thing with Ervin. And she wondered again what the hell sort of superpower this was meant to be, or if she and Collins were reading *way* too much into it, and it really was a fungus. One of those ones snails get that turn them into zombies.

"I'm just nipping across the road to get a coffee," she said, nodding in that direction.

"Shouldn't drink so much coffee, Adams," he replied, not moving.

"Probably not, sir," she agreed. "Maybe I'll get a decaf."

He scowled at her as if suspecting her of taking the mick, but when she took a step forward he reluctantly moved aside. Adams walked away at a measured pace, trying not to look back. She managed until she got to the entrance to the street, when she finally glanced over her shoulder, sure he'd be standing there staring after her. He was gone, though, or looked to be. The hair on the back of her neck was still crawling, as if some instinct suspected him of lurking in the shadows, waiting for her return.

She touched the baton again, then headed for the market.

# 8

# BROOMSTICKS DON'T FLY

THE MARKET WAS NEVER CROWDED, AND ADAMS WONDERED, AS she always did in these sorts of places, how any of the shops made a living – or even enough to pay the rent. There were some people about, of course, but half of them marched through with grim determination, using the market as nothing more than a thoroughfare, and the rest seemed a little lost and mildly panicked, giving the impression they'd strayed in from the street and didn't know how to find their way out again. All were intent on the nearest exit, careful not to look too closely at the enclosed spaces of the dusty stalls and their silent keepers, as if afraid the faded goods might suddenly come rushing after them, demanding to be bought.

The front entrance, the one closest to the town centre, was the part that was still most alive, as if the market were putting its best face forward to tempt the unwary. A florist's cart overflowed exuberantly just inside the gates, spilling lilies and roses and sunflowers onto the floor, as well as other flowers Adams couldn't identify but which were a riot of colours. They smelled of life in green spaces, fighting with the sugary scent of a cake shop just next to the cart, and here the painted walls seemed a little less faded, the windows a little less dusty.

But the deeper into the market one went, the more colours faded out, the way they do as water gets deeper, shadows creeping in to leech the brilliance. The stalls got stranger, too. Unattended sweet shops with unlabelled jars and softly petrifying displays of desiccated marshmallows and faded, misshapen coconut ice, and stalls so crammed with vast barrels of spices there was no room to pass between them. The slowly dwindling promise of unmade meals wafted from them, and jumbles of quietly browning fruit and unripe vegetables were stacked in big bins in some half-hearted attempt at attracting the trickle of passing trade.

At the far end of the market, for those who persisted past the ghostly stands at its heart, big doors opened into the walled, open-air portion. It featured the ubiquitous trailers selling phone cases and knock-off handbags, scratchy jumpers and fake leather boots, with handwritten signs and a jumble of stock. The fruit and veggie stalls with their shouting vendors were here too, all fighting to promise the best deal on tomatoes, the freshest potatoes, the tastiest pumpkin. It was always the busiest part of the market, and Adams liked those stalls. She doubted the produce was any better than at Tesco's, but there was something to having a human tot up your total rather than a machine, the sense she'd *been to market*, more satisfying than just *down the shops*. Never as convenient as doing everything in one place, though.

This was the way she came in today, still glancing over her shoulder now and then in case Temper was sneaking after her, darting from shadow to shadow like a kid pretending to be a ninja. There was no sign of him, though, and she passed the veggie stall, ignoring a man shouting at her to try his plums. She headed straight through the market doors instead, into her least favourite part of the whole place. It was always busy here too, or as busy as the market got. The meat market to one side, the fish market to the other, stall after stall of slabs of marbled meat and fat sausages and luminously marinated chicken, coils of eels and the glittering silver sides of sardines and the exposed, severed spines of salmon, exclamations in pink flesh. The whole place stank of scales and blood and bone that had been soaking into the ground for centuries, from long before the market had grown up around it. This had been a trading place for much longer than it had been a city, or even a town, and it wore its history with a certain insolent secrecy.

Adams didn't linger, breathing shallowly as she hurried past the stalls and into the shadows of the market, where the air was dustier but thankfully less *meaty*. She angled toward one of the inside walls, skirting shadowed alcoves which were half boarded up, waiting for new shops or for the market to slowly shutter around it. A few places were open – a barber's with a traditional red and white pillar outside, slowly turning, a man in the chair having his horns polished. A nail salon where a woman was massaging oil into the leathery wings of a creature that had its back to Adams. A tea shop that looked like it had never even heard of hygiene standards, with a table of five elderly ladies playing a fierce game of poker, cackling delightedly to each other. Adams went past that one as quickly as she could. Otherwise, this part of the market was even more quiet than the rest. An upper mezzanine ran along the walls above her, holding offices, but it was as empty as anywhere else.

Dandy loped up to her and offered her a bone. She pulled away from him, not wanting to get muck on her trousers. "I don't want your bone," she whispered.

He twitched his ears, and she wondered where he'd stolen it from. Not that she could do much about it. She had no idea how one was meant to discipline an invisible dog. Or get him to do heroic sidekick things, for that matter. He evidently had his own metric for when he was needed, and it seemed to err on the side of remaining uninvolved.

Having said that, he had proved himself exceptionally helpful in the middle of summer, during an altercation at a farmhouse deep in the Dales. They'd walked into the middle of a pitched battle between what appeared to be armed mercenaries and an army of women of a certain age, who were rather more effectively armed with dragons. It had threatened to descend into utter carnage, and probably would have, except for the fact that the dragons were better behaved than any of the humans, and Dandy had been irritated enough that he'd *expanded*, to the point that he was able to pick one of the hired thugs up like a chew toy and put an abrupt stop to things. Being that big evidently rendered him visible to everyone, and Adams didn't think Collins had quite recovered from the shock yet. She wasn't sure *she* had recovered from the shock, and she didn't really want a repeat, but wished she could at least sic him on people when she fancied it.

Dandy, currently in his more usual Labrador size, tried to give her the bone again.

"I don't *want* it," she hissed at him.

He gave her an insulted look and trotted off, head high. She followed, and they stopped outside a small shop set deep into the alcoves. *The Occult Onion* was painted in gold leaf on the glass panel in the door.

Adams peered through the front window. Purple curtains sealed the shop off from view beyond it, and the display had changed since she was here last, bringing in some rather belated summery motifs with gourds and ears of wheat. She pushed through the door, setting a bell jangling, and hesitated just over the threshold. The interior was scented with an accumulation of old books and the faintest trace of incense, less from burning sticks and more from the built-up layers of old artefacts collected over time, the quiet, deep energy of a place that welcomed in every second-hand item that came its way, honouring their past lives and promising them a new one.

The shop filled two of the alcoves, and Adams couldn't see anyone in this one, so she headed through to the second, discovering a skinny, dark-haired young woman in a tank top stacking small animal skeletons into a display case.

Adams squinted at them, trying to decide if they were plastic or not. "Early for Halloween, isn't it?"

Chloe looked up, giving her an appraising glance then a grin. "Never too early for Halloween," she said. "Some of us like it year-round."

"Rather not. Everyone goes a bit bonkers as soon as they put a costume on. Give someone a mask and they'll do anything."

"Don't we all wear masks? You wear your police mask. I wear my shopkeeper's mask."

Adams raised her eyebrows. "You wear a hedge witch mask, don't you?"

"We all wear lots of masks," Chloe said. "But that's one. Why?"

Adams unslung her backpack. "I need a bit of help."

"*Ooh*. Are you investigating magical things, DI Adams?"

"Much to my disappointment, yes. Or I think so. That's what I want you to tell me." She fished the tote bag out of her backpack and held it out. "The lab says it's just beer."

"But?"

"You tell me."

Chloe took the bag from her, peered into it and wrinkled her nose. "Phew."

"Can you smell something?"

"You've had a curry in this bag."

"Other than that?"

"Well—" Chloe broke off with a yelp, jumping back as Dandy shoved the bone into her leg. "What the hell was that?"

"Sorry. It's Dandy." Adams clicked her fingers at him, and he ignored her.

"Your familiar?"

"He's not a familiar. He's very unfamiliar, in fact."

Chloe patted the air around her knees warily. "What does he look like?"

"Doglike, sort of. He wants to give you a bone."

"What sort of bone?"

"I don't know. He probably stole it from the butcher's. He's very criminally inclined."

"Of course he is," Chloe said with a grin, and turned her hand palm up. Dandy deposited the bone in it, and she gave a little gasp. "It just appeared!"

"Yeah, anything he's holding onto seems to go invisible for most people."

"Very cool," Chloe breathed.

"Not so much. Do you know how much he thieves?"

"Well, nobody can see it."

"I'm a *police officer*. I can't have him thieving."

"It's him, not you."

"It happens *around* me, though."

Chloe chuckled, and patted the air until Dandy put his head obligingly under her hand. "You're a good dog, really, aren't you?"

Dandy wagged his tail and gave Adams a reproachful look. As much as she could tell through the thicket of hair, anyway.

"If you've finished bonding, can you take a look at those bottles?"

Chloe huffed. "Fine. Come on."

She headed behind the counter, the bag in one hand and the bone in the other, and Dandy trotted after her. Adams followed through another curtain, into a shadowed room with big Turkish carpets covering the concrete floor. A sagging, well-stuffed sofa stood in the middle of them, a coffee table in front of it, and a small table with two chairs stood against one wall, a deep purple tablecloth draped over it and something covered in a black cloth in the centre.

"Is that a crystal ball?" Adams asked.

Chloe glanced at it as she put the bone in a sink in the little kitchenette, which held a kettle and a toaster and not much else. "Yes. What do you think he wants me to do with the bone?"

"No idea. I think it means he likes you. Why do you have a crystal ball?"

"To tell fortunes. I'm glad he likes me."

"Of course you are." Adams leaned on the sofa, watching the younger woman set the two beer bottles on the kitchenette's tiny worktop. She raised them to the light, one then the other, turning them slowly, then checked the labels. She made a thoughtful noise and Adams said, "What?"

"Nothing, yet. Just gathering some first impressions."

Adams folded her arms, pressing her fingers into her opposite forearms, and tried to remind herself that hedge witches probably didn't really go in for urgency. There couldn't be much that was urgent in a hedge.

Chloe twisted the top off one bottle, sniffed it, then frowned slightly and found a glass to pour some into. She took another sniff and started to raise the glass to her lips, and Adams said, "I wouldn't."

Chloe looked at her. "Why?"

"Seems to be causing some unusual behaviour. That's what I'm trying to get to the bottom of."

"Okay," Chloe swirled the beer in the glass, sniffed it again, then repeated the whole process with the second bottle. She looked from one to the other and said, "Well, they're definitely different."

Adams joined her, peering down at the beer. "What's different?"

"Here." Chloe handed her the glasses.

Adams sniffed one, then the other, but all she could smell was the hoppy scent of a good ale. "They smell the same."

"Stop smelling. Start *sensing.*"

Adams frowned. "You realise smell *is* a sense."

"Yes, but it's not the sense you need to use right now."

Adams tried again, closing her eyes, trying to find something beyond the smell, a feeling or an image or just some sort of *reaction,* but there was nothing. She made a little noise of frustration and put the glasses down, looking at Chloe. "I've no idea. I don't know how to do this."

Chloe examined her and said, "You should keep trying."

"I don't have time for that. I need to get this sorted, so what can you tell me? What's the difference?"

Chloe leaned over the glasses, her hands set wide on the counter and a frown tugging at the corners of her mouth. "I'm not sure *exactly.* I need to do a little experimentation. One of them's definitely got something going on."

"Like?"

"Like it's been charmed, or it's had some pretty unusual ingredients added, or it's been stirred widdershins, or brewed in the moonlight."

"Stirred widdershins," Adams said flatly.

Chloe nodded solemnly, then grinned. "Okay, not really those last two. But you never know, right?"

Adams resisted the urge to press both hands to her forehead, and took a deep breath instead. "I don't know why I thought you could help."

Chloe clicked her tongue. *"Rude.* Of course I can help. And I *will* help, despite your attitude. But you brought these in here like two minutes ago. How long does your lab take to turn things around?"

"Twenty-four hours if they do a rush job," Adams admitted.

"So give me time to work." She pointed at the door with one imperious finger. "Off you go."

Adams frowned at her. "Really?"

"DI Adams, your lab might be able to find if it's been dosed with ketamine or whatever, but if you thought that was the issue you wouldn't've come here. Trust me. I'm no sorcerer, but I'm a bloody good hedge witch."

"What exactly is a hedge witch? Plants?"

"The hedge refers to the border between this world and the other. Liminal spaces," Chloe said. "But also, yes, plants."

"Neither of those sound—"

"Do you have another witch you're waiting to take these to?"

"No," Adams said.

"Then go away and let me work." Chloe lifted her chin, tapping her purple-painted nails on her hips.

Adams gave up. Chloe was right. She didn't have a lot of options. "You've still got my number?"

"Of course."

"Alright," Adams said, then added, "Thank you."

Chloe inclined her head slightly, looking at the beer labels, then said, "Knaresborough. Have you checked it out?"

"I had a word with the owner today."

"And you didn't notice anything odd?"

"Not particularly."

"You're *weirdly* insensitive."

"Thanks."

"I just mean in the magical sense. Are they doing brewery tours and tastings for the festival?"

"Not sure. I know they're part of the festival. That's why I need to get on this beer soon as we can."

Chloe pulled her phone from her jeans, tapping it briskly. She looked up at Adams. "There's a tasting tomorrow."

"And?"

"And we should go."

"There's no we," Adams said. "This is a police investigation."

"Is it, though?" Chloe said. "I mean, you said yourself, your lab's not coming up with anything. I can already tell something's up, and by tomorrow morning I'll have a better idea exactly what. Probably even have a potential counter-charm worked out. If we go to the brewery, I might be able to tell whether this charm was put on in the vats or whether someone did it after the bottles left the brewery. Get it at the source."

Chloe was grinning, and Adams swallowed a groan. Talking cats and hedge witches. These were her resources now. The police were as clueless about the Folk that moved around them as the general public were. For the most part anyway. After the necklace incident Temper had let slip that he had *some* knowledge of things, but given how he was acting she could hardly go to him. Not that she probably would've anyway, since he seemed as determined to ignore it as she'd once been. So it was hedge witches or nothing.

"Fine," she said aloud. "But all you do is tell me what you feel at the brewery. You don't get involved in *any* other way."

"Great! It starts at ten."

"Can you meet me there or do you need picking up?"

"I'll meet you there," Chloe replied. "I'll just whip over on my broomstick." Adams stared at her until Chloe burst out laughing. "I don't have a broomstick. Nobody rides broomsticks."

"*Could* they ride broomsticks?"

"Of course not. Broomsticks don't fly."

"Right. The invisible dog thing throws me off sometimes, and I start wondering."

Chloe nodded. "Yeah. I can see how that could happen."

Adams left the hedge witch to her experiments, wondering if the world would ever make sense again. She was starting to doubt it.

Worse, she was starting to get *used* to it.

# 9

# A SMALL DECEPTION

ADAMS DIDN'T SEE TEMPER ON THE WAY BACK TO THE CAR, BUT she still felt observed, as if he might be lurking in the shadows of the buildings somewhere, likely tapping his fingertips together and laughing in an improbable manner. She texted James once she was inside her Golf with the doors locked, feeling ridiculous – she was a police officer, after all, and he was a *DCI*, not a cartoon character – but also better.

*Any sign of Temper?*

He texted back almost immediately. *No. He's not been in all day.*

Adams wasn't as sure of that as James seemed to be, given Temper's unexpected ninja skills, but she just sent *Keep me updated. And eat your Yorkies.*

*Yes Mum* came back, and she huffed at the phone. She had no idea what the chocolate actually did, but just as the small brass duck that always lived on her keyring was simply *useful* in ways it shouldn't be, so it seemed chocolate helped people get through certain Folk-related things. Maybe it was just the comfort of a sugar rush, but she didn't think so. Maybe she should ask Chloe about it. At some stage she was going to have to learn all these things, but she had to admit to a certain resistance. Learning about it meant accepting she wasn't ever going back to being a regular detective with regular, common, sex-and-violence cases, and she wasn't sure she was ready for that yet. She didn't even know *how* to be ready.

She headed out of the city, happy she was going to be gone before the afternoon rush kicked in, rolling her shoulders as the buildings began to thin and the sky opened up. That lasted about five minutes, until she suddenly realised that she was actually *relaxing* at the sight of a drystone wall, as if to be caught up in the tangled entrails of the city was somehow a horrifying and stressful thing, rather than her natural environment.

"That's not good," she said to Dandy, who huffed at her. He apparently hadn't forgiven her yet for refusing his bone. "Am I going country?"

He looked back out the window, dismissing her, and she turned the radio up. The country was definitely infecting her. She'd be buying Hunter wellies and a Land Rover next.

COLLINS WAS BACK at his desk when she pushed through the door into their office at the Skipton station, a very late lunch in the form of an uninspired supermarket salad in one hand. It was astonishing how some places could actually make food that was *less* than the sum of its parts.

He looked up from his computer, peering at her over his reading glasses, and said, "Any observations to add for the bull case?"

"Absolutely not. I'm a sidekick on any case involving livestock."

"You're going to have to take the lead on them at some stage."

"Outside my skill set."

"You know we're into continuing education in this station."

Adams opened her mouth to say that she thought cow herding was unlikely to be on the professional development programme for the UK police when a voice behind her said, "More to the point, you're going to have to start doing *any* reports at some stage."

Adams jumped, almost dropping her salad, and moved away from the door as DCI Maud Taylor ambled into the room with her hands in her pockets. She was a small woman, even shorter than Adams, which sometimes made Adams wonder if she'd used booster shoes to make the old-school minimum height requirement for the job, or if she'd applied after it had been dropped. There was a startling solidity to her though, a sense of well-packed and well-used muscle that belied her gently greying blonde hair and Mrs Claus–style twinkling blue eyes.

"So … what are my two favourite detective inspectors doing hanging around inside on such a fine crime-solving day?" she asked them.

"*Only* detective inspectors," Collins pointed out.

"Yes, and I need to justify having two of you, so what are you doing to make yourselves useful?"

"Writing Adams' reports," Collins said.

"It was a shared case," Adams protested.

Maud looked at her. "Would it make a difference if it wasn't? I've forgotten what one of your reports even looks like, it's been so long."

"Sorry," Adams said. "I'll catch up."

"With more detail than *caught bad guy, booked him*, please. I thought you Londoners would have more of an elegant turn of phrase for such things." Maud smiled as she said it, and there was no bite in the words.

Adams nodded. "Can't compete with the land of the Brontës."

"Of course. All London has is Dickens and Shelley and Byron and—"

"I'll get to the reports," Adams promised.

"I bloody well hope so. What're you working on?"

"Something going on at a brewery in Knaresborough," Adams replied. "We're still trying to work out exactly what it is."

Maud nodded thoughtfully. "I know you're new here, but you realise that's not Craven?"

"Um, yes." Adams wondered if it'd help to mention she'd been called in by Leeds, but that was even further off her patch. "A contact brought it to my attention."

"*Hmm.* Anything to do with some posh sort who was looking for you earlier? I asked if he wanted to see Collins and he said no, he'd come back later to talk to you."

Collins chortled, which Adams didn't think she'd actually heard anyone do in real life before. "Maybe," she said. "I talked to the landowner where the brewery's renting its premises. Sounds like it could be him."

"What I found interesting," Collins said, still looking at his computer, "is that while he is undoubtedly posh, he used his first name. Just pointing that out, Adams."

She sighed. "You know I'm not posh. Adams is just my name."

"Like Cher," Collins said, poking away at his keyboard, and Maud chuckled.

"Alright. I will assume you have good reason to be off in Harrogate, and that it doesn't involve posh landowners with nice shoulders. Keep me updated. We've still got a spate of holiday home break-ins and a stolen car ring to deal with, so don't be poking around just because you want an invite to the beer festival."

"It's not that," Adams said. "We think there might've been some contaminants in the beer. Still trying to figure out what, exactly, and how it's working."

"Have you taken some samples to be analysed?" Maud asked.

"DC James Hamilton in Leeds did it."

Maud considered that. "We do have access to labs here, Adams. You don't have to run off to the city every time you want something done. We small town stations can still get the job done."

"Oh, no – he'd already done it. I didn't ask him to. I know I could've done it here. It was … he called my attention to the beer, and he'd already taken it to the lab."

Maud looked at Collins. "She's still touchy, isn't she?"

"Oh, you wouldn't believe it," Collins replied. "The face she made when she stepped in a cow pat."

Maud laughed and headed back out the door, calling as she went, "You're alright, Adams. We're not that precious."

Adams sighed and carried her salad to her desk, thinking she wasn't the one being touchy. Although she realised Maud was just winding her up. It was hard to tell sometimes, though. The north didn't welcome London cops all that easily. Not that she wasn't used to not being that welcome. Her skin and her gender had already done plenty of that for her, in plenty of spaces.

SHE'D JUST SHOVELLED a large forkful of limp salad in watery dressing into her mouth when Dandy pricked his ears and shot out the door. It was only slightly ajar, not really wide enough for a dog to go through, but it didn't even move in his wake, and Adams wondered again just what sort of pocket of physics Dandy occupied. It had nothing to do with the sort of physics she'd learned at school, that was for sure.

There was a timid knock at the door. "Yes?" Collins said.

"Is DI Adams there?" a hesitant voice asked.

"Come in," she called around a mouthful of lettuce.

PC McCleod eased the door open, looking at her as if he thought she might throw her salad at him. "You've got a visitor. Maud said you were expecting him, and to let him straight through."

Adams hurriedly swallowed her salad as Rory edged past the PC, who retreated rapidly.

"Detective Inspectors," Rory said, giving them both that easy grin, and glancing out the door before shutting it behind him. "Nervous sort, isn't he?"

"It's Adams," Collins said. "She has that effect on people."

Adams scowled at him, and said, "How can we help you, Mr Acklesfield?"

"Rory. Hope you don't mind me dropping in. I had a bit of business in Skipton, so thought it might be easier than calling."

"Sure," Adams said, although really texting, emailing, *or* calling would all have been easier than having some lanky great land baron in their office. She pointed at the chair opposite her desk. "What did you need?"

Rory sat down and leaned back in the chair as it creaked dangerously, crossing his legs at the ankle. He was wearing trainers and jeans, a long-sleeved shirt rolled up the elbows, and there was something annoyingly *effortless* about him. "Are you still looking into something at the brewery?" he asked.

"We are. Why?"

He ran a hand back through his hair. "This could be nothing. Probably I wouldn't have thought anything of it except for the fact that you were asking around."

Adams nodded, giving an expectant little *carry on* wave. "All information is welcome. We can figure out if it's relevant."

"Right, of course. It's just that I haven't seen Alistair – the owner – for a while. I thought he'd be around a lot with the festival coming up, and the new brew or whatever it is they're doing, but he's been gone for a couple of weeks at least."

Adams frowned. "We just saw him this morning."

"No, he wasn't there. I went in right after you, but there was only Marcus."

"Marcus?"

"The manager. And, to be honest, I thought it was a bit weird when he turned up. Alistair was there one day, then the next thing it was Marcus. Didn't seem to be any sort of transition."

"Are you sure?" Adams asked.

"No," Rory admitted. "It's not like I'm there every day. But I am always around, and I notice what happens on my land. It was a quick change, that I'm sure of."

"Did Alistair talk about getting a manager in?"

"No. It's not that big a place."

"*Would* he have talked to you about it?"

Rory made a thoughtful noise. "We did talk. He was one of my first tenants, and we'd have a drink after work here and there. But we're not *close*, so maybe he just didn't think to mention it."

"Have you tried phoning him?"

"Oddly enough, it did occur to me," Rory said. He grinned as he said it, and Collins snorted.

Adams shot Collins an irritated look, then turned back to Rory. "I'm taking it you couldn't get hold of him."

"Straight to voicemail. Nothing about when he was going to be back. It seems really odd, with the lead-up to the beer festival, that he wouldn't be here. That brewery was a *passion*."

"Interesting," Adams said. "Can you send me his number?" She took a card from a holder on the desk and held it out to him, but he waved it away.

"I've already got it." Rory fiddled with his phone, and a moment later, Adams' mobile dinged.

She checked it. "Thanks. We'll look into it."

"Great," he said, not moving. "I was thinking of going for a coffee. Would you like one?"

Adams resolutely didn't look at Collins, even though she could see him grinning out of the corner of her eye. "I'm working."

"Right. I would've thought that'd just preclude a beer. Are you not allowed to have caffeine when you work either?" He was grinning again.

"I've already had plenty today," she said, and Collins gave a strangled and very unconvincing cough. "Thanks anyway."

"Alright," Rory said, not sounding exactly devastated by her refusal. "Let me know if you track down Alistair? He's a good sort."

"Shall do."

He got up. "I'll be off then. Let me know if you need anything else." He nodded at Collins and headed out the door in a slouching, easy pace. He really did have very nice shoulders, which Adams wished Maud hadn't mentioned. She wondered where the collies were, and hoped Dandy racing out earlier hadn't been because he was off to harass them.

She looked at Collins, who was grinning broadly, and said, "Not a word."

"Who, me?"

Adams went back to her salad, trying Alistair's number as

she ate, but just as Rory had said, it went straight through to messages. She tapped disconnect and said to Collins, "No answer. It's probably off, but maybe we can get last location."

"Jules can do that. No need to go back to Leeds."

She huffed. "Hilarious. I'm going to take a couple of those beers for Lucas, too. I know James got them tested in Leeds, but …"

"You think the lab there might be compromised?"

"Maybe? Temper's acting really strange."

"You know that if it's Toot Hansell stuff, it's not going to show up in any sort of analysis, no matter where you do it."

"Sure. But seems a bit careless not to check."

"True," he agreed. "Off you go then. If you hurry, you should be able to catch Rory and get yourself that coffee."

"Too posh for my taste," she replied and stood up, tapping her fingers on the desk. "We need to talk to the brewery again. I'm assuming that was Marcus we spoke to."

"Yeah, and he didn't say he wasn't Alistair, which seems a bit odd."

"We didn't ask," Adams pointed out. "We said we were looking for Alistair, and that worker brought back Marcus. We just assumed it was Alistair."

"Bit sloppy of us," Collins said. "Were you distracted by the thought of gentry?"

Adams ignored him. "There's an open day at the brewery tomorrow."

"Oh? Want to check it out?"

"I'll do it," she said, and hesitated before continuing. "I'm meeting someone there."

"Who?"

"She's a bit of an expert in … Toot Hansell stuff."

"Oh, nice. So she can tell if there's magic being used?"

Adams wrinkled her nose. She *knew* she was asking a witch to chase down a charm, and had an invisible dog stealing her coffee, and dealt with dragons on far too regular a basis, and those weren't even the only things in her life best termed magical, but that didn't mean she had to use the word. Not that she'd found a better one yet. "I hope so," she said aloud.

"I'll leave you to it, then. I'll finish this report then get back to tracking down all the samples. That might give us a better picture of what's going on."

"Deal." She headed back to the car to collect a couple of the beer bottles, then went in search of Jules the computer tech, and Lucas, who was technically the crime scene tech but also did pretty much any other lab-related job the Skipton station could handle. It was hardly as large or well-equipped as Leeds, but neither was anyone kidnapping potted plants or hacking social media accounts. The whole place felt remarkably calm, in fact, and it made Adams uneasy, as if all the public disturbances and criminal activity and general mischief was on hold, just waiting for some mysterious catalyst to send it spiralling toward an unseen centre, intensifying like a tornado with the beer festival at its heart.

# 10

## NOT QUITE PEACEFUL

LUCAS WAS NOWHERE TO BE FOUND, AND JULES HAD SOMEHOW managed to reduce her communication to even fewer syllables, meaning she just took the phone number without making eye contact with Adams, and pointed at the door. Adams took the hint, retreating back to the office not long after she'd left it, and found Collins taking his jacket from the back of his chair, car keys in hand.

"Where are you off to, then?" she asked.

"I called a mate from Harrogate station. They weren't on the list of places that got samples, but I wanted to give them a heads up about it all, unofficial-like. Turns out he's currently attending a bit of a disturbance at the beer festival site."

"It's not open yet, though, is it?"

"No, just stallholders by the sounds. But he was properly wound up. Kept on about people needing putting on leashes, which isn't his usual style."

Adams frowned. "You think they might've had some beer?"

"No idea. Couldn't get anything out of him other than the fact that the general public are feral."

"Not entirely wrong."

"No. But I thought we should go and check it out, then maybe swing by Alistair Dixon's home address." He waved his phone at her. "Since we'll be in the area."

"Can't stand missing out, can you?"

"Nope," he said cheerfully.

She pulled her car keys out. "We don't need two cars this time. I'll drive."

"I could drive for once."

"You could, but I like driving."

"Well, I'd hate to deprive you," he replied, and shoved his keys back in his pocket.

They hurried out into the deepening grey of the after-noon, clouds rolling grimly across the sky, and Adams shivered, pulling her coat on as she went. She thought she'd been used to the hard edges of the wind in London, where it came off the Thames sharpened on salt and brown water, but the north was different. There was insis-tence to the chill here, even on warm days, as if the weather itself was determined to provide a constant reminder that it was within touching distance of frozen seas.

Despite the lack of sun, she left the windows wound down as they headed out of town, still half suspecting she could smell manure. Dandy was relegated to the back seat, but he kept his head jammed between the passenger's seat and the side window, his chin almost on Collins' shoulder. Collins kept flinching away, and eventually made a disgusted noise and touched the shoulder of his coat. His fingers came away damp and he showed them to Adams.

"Is that invisible dog slobber?"

Adams glanced at him. "I'd say so."

"Fantastic. He could've kept that to himself. Is his hair visible as well?"

"I haven't noticed," she admitted. "I always worry about the smell, though. Do I smell of dog?"

"I have not come close enough to sniff you, Adams, and I'd rather not. That'd be pushing the limits of our friendship a little too far."

"Partnership," she replied. "Work partnership."

He gave her an affronted look but didn't say anything, and she stared fixedly at the road. That hadn't come out quite right. Collins was a decent sort. But work was work. It had to be. One couldn't go about being friends with everyone. Next thing it'd be drinks after work and birthday cards and watering each other's plants if they went away, and she wasn't good with plants.

"So what other details have you got on the feral populace of Harrogate, then?" she asked.

"Well, it's not just a brawl. Myles wouldn't be so wound up about that."

"I hope it's not a brawl. These are the people meant to be *selling* the beer, not drinking it." She thought about it. "Unless the Dixon's lot are sabotaging the other brewers by giving them contaminated beer? Bit of a friendly *here try our stuff and we'll try yours* thing?"

"And then the competition get a bit unruly and get themselves arrested."

"*Huh.* Your mate mention anything about people leaping marquees in a single bound?"

"No, just that everyone's out of order, something about permits not being filled in right, and not even knowing what permit's needed for fire walking."

"*Fire walking?*"

"Yeah, you know. When people walk over coals."

"I do know, but why fire walking? Hardly Harrogate behaviour, is it? Thought it was all fur coats and G&Ts."

"I suppose we'll find out soon enough."

"And the permits are the bit he's worried about?"

"Seems so. Myles always was a bit by-the-book." Collins patted around until he found Dandy's head and tried to push him away from the window. Dandy didn't budge. "Could you please tell your invisible dog to stop slobbering on my shoulder?"

"He doesn't listen to me."

THE SUN FORCED its way through a break in the clouds as they arrived into the centre of Harrogate, setting the afternoon shadows long and rich across the Stray, hinting at the encroaching autumn. The marquees bloomed in the green grass, glaringly white and unexpected, like angular puffball mushrooms pushing out of the loam. Few of the passing joggers and dog walkers seemed to be paying them much attention, though. All through summer there was a steadily rotating series of shows at different venues or in different fields, vast ticketed things like the Great Yorkshire Show, or smaller, more local events such as flower shows or vintage car displays, inviting anyone to wander in. At some point they just became part of the scenery.

Adams pulled the car half onto the grass not far from where she'd parked the day before and got out, Dandy leaping past her and standing with his snout lifted to the cooling air, nose twitching.

"Anything?" she said to him in a low voice, and he looked at her then trotted off to investigate a lamppost. She took that to mean *nothing urgent*. Hopefully, anyway.

Collins had been on his phone as they arrived, and now a short, wiry man with a head of white-streaked dark hair came hurrying toward them from the direction of the marquees. Shouting drifted after him, and a snatch of what sounded like a sea shanty. Myles was in uniform, and looked like he was thoroughly looking forward to taking his baton to someone. Adams took hers from the car, tucking it into the pocket of her coat, and Collins said, "Adams, this is Sergeant Myles Hill. Myles, DI Adams."

Myles gave her a quick, sharp nod, holding his hand out. "Thanks for coming."

She shook it, feeling calluses on his grip. "So what's going on?"

"Absolute bloody carnage, is what. I've never seen anything like it. I've been doing the festivals for twenty years, and I've never seen it fall apart like this. Festival's not even started! It's the damn *stallholders!*"

Collins made a sympathetic noise, and Adams said, "Sounds pretty bad."

"It *is*. And, fine, you expect it on the last night, when everyone's had a few too many beers. Maybe even mid-festival, if you get someone who can't hold their drink. But *now?* Without even any *punters?*" He seemed to be taking it personally.

Adam nodded. "Right. So what's happened?"

"They're just …" He trailed off and waved furiously at the marquees, seemingly at a loss for words, then burst out, "They're just being *impossible!*"

Adams rubbed the nape of her neck and looked at Collins, who said, "You might have to be a tad more specific, Myles."

*"They're making a mess!"*

"A mess?" Adams said.

"And the paperwork … no one's got paperwork! It's … You'll see. Come on." He beckoned them to follow, and headed across the grass toward the circle of marquees, their fronts facing inward to the clear area in the centre, gaps left between them where food trucks would go. The flooring was complete in all of the marquees now, and through the clear plastic in the sides of one Adams could see barrels set up as tables, tall stools surrounding them. Another had folding tables set up along all the walls, waiting for displays to be brought in. A few of the others had blinds pulled down over the clear plastic panels, padlocks holding the door zips closed, and those she assumed were already set up for the next day. One largish marquee wasn't sealed up, but she still couldn't see into it, as it was utterly overgrown with greenery on the inside. Vines coiled out through the gaps at the door, and a branch had punched its way through the roof. She frowned at it.

A bonfire burned in a large barrel in the middle of the circle, surrounded by a dozen or so workers sitting on stools and bean bags and folding chairs pilfered from the marquees. A couple of big crates crowded with dark glass bottles sat among the chairs, and someone had supplied sausages. A few people had threaded them on sticks and were trying to cook them over the fire, with mixed results.

Myles pointed at the fire and yelled, *"I told you to put that out!* You don't have a permit for it!"

"Sod off, copper!" one of the sausage toasters shouted back, and the group laughed. It was a relaxed sound, though, and no one moved. They just stayed settled in their seats, drinking their beers, comfortable as holidaymakers at a beach bar.

Myles growled and looked at Adams and Collins. "You see? Nobody's even listening to me. No one's got any respect for us anymore!"

A few other coppers in uniform were standing around looking half-heartedly stern, hands tucked into their stab vests. None of them seemed as agitated as Myles, or at all inclined to interfere with the impromptu barbecue, and Adams could see why. There was simply no need. Maybe the bonfire wasn't strictly legal, and maybe the group weren't listening to Myles, but there was no aggression here. It felt more like end of summer can't-be-bothered-ness, the last event of the season leading to a long breath out. Adams was fairly sure she knew what the other officers were thinking – that there was no threat *now*, but it was easy enough for things to get unpleasant. And heavy-handed police coming down on people just having a couple of drinks was both unnecessary and unlikely to end well.

She glanced at Collins, inclining her head at Myles, and Collins nodded slightly. "Myles, mate, give me a walk around. Show me what's been going on."

"Right, well. I just wanted to check their permits, and—"

Adams tuned him out as she turned her attention to the fire, tucking her hands into her coat pockets, baton in one, duck in the other. She strolled over to the ring of chairs and said, "Nice set-up."

"Want a sausage?" a bald man asked her, winking.

"They vegetarian?"

"Best ones never are."

She smiled as the group laughed, and nodded at one of the crates. "What're you drinking?"

An older woman in a fleece that read *Totally Baked* reached for the nearest crate and handed a bottle to Adams. "Help yourself."

Adams took the bottle, already recognising the winking otter on the label. "Good, is it?"

"Free," a young man said. "Can't get better than that."

"Fair point." She looked around as a shout went up from the overgrown marquee. "What's going on there?"

"No idea," the woman said. "They've not come out all afternoon."

"It's the florists," the young man said. "One of them thinks the other killed his orchids, or something."

"They normally have florists at beer festivals?"

"Anyone who wants to pay for a tent," the woman said, and pointed at her fleece. "I do cakes."

Adams thought cakes made more sense than flowers, but what did she know? Maybe everyone did a little impulse plant shopping after an afternoon of beer tasting.

There was a thunderous crash from the florists' marquee, and the branch sticking through the roof shuddered in fright. Adams handed the beer back to the woman and jogged toward the tent.

"I wouldn't," the young man called after her.

She paused to look back at him. "Why not?"

"I went to ask if they wanted to join us – thought it might calm them down, like – and got a load of compost in my face for my troubles." He pointed at his cheek, and she could see remnants of muck still clinging to his collar.

"Thanks," she said, and approached the marquee a little more circumspectly.

She couldn't see much from outside, the canvas walls bulging with the weight of vegetation pushing against them, leaves hiding the interior from view completely. She tried the door, finding it opened outward, bringing a spill of coiling vines that looked a lot like overgrown ivy with it. The shouts were louder now, and she moved a wall of giant dahlias aside to discover a fragrant, humid clearing beyond. Flowers and green plants were entangled all across the walls and creeping along the ceiling, and a wash of grass and poppies turned the floor into a meadow. A middle-aged woman in a pretty blouse and a younger man in some sort of leather utility apron were in the centre of it, fencing with bamboo sticks while screaming obscenities at each other. The whole place was scattered with smashed pots and over-turned buckets, and the scent of lavender and crushed stems drifted around them. But neither the impromptu sword fight nor the inexplicable jungle were what made Adams blink in astonishment. No, that was because, as the two battled and fought, great swathes of vegetation tumbled to the floor, collapsed into rot, blighted and blackened. At the same time, new ones surged into being from their remnants, life and death on a massively sped up scale.

She watched for a moment, wondering how to interrupt without sharing the kid's experience with the compost. There was plenty of it lying around. Finally the man tripped over a broken pot and went sprawling, and the woman charged him with her stick waving in the air above her like she really thought she could impale him with it.

"Hold up," Adams called, still not venturing past the dahlias. "That's enough of that."

Both florists' heads snapped around, and they gave her matching glares. "*What?*" the woman demanded.

"Put the stick down," Adams said.

"It's *my* stick. I'll put it where I want to."

The man scrambled to his feet. "Yeah! What business is it of yours?"

"DI Adams, North—"

"Oh, *police,*" the woman said, putting both hands on her hips. "Come to spoil all our fun?"

"This is fun? You're trashing the place, and you've got to put it all back together by tomorrow."

The man huffed. "She underestimates us."

The woman clicked her fingers, and a sunflower unfurled from the floor, shooting up until it bumped into the canvas roof and started trekking across it. Adams watched, trying to remember she was meant to be keeping the peace, not being fascinated by enchanted flowers.

"Still think we can't put it together by tomorrow?" the woman asked.

"Alright, fine, but I doubt your mate here wants to be belted about the head by a bamboo stick."

"You have *no idea* what I want," the man said, and he and the woman exchanged fond glances.

"We're *competitors,*" the woman confided to Adams.

"Right?"

"Enemies to lovers? Heard of it?" the man asked, slinging an arm over the woman's shoulders. She jabbed an elbow into his belly, and he yelped.

Adams looked from one of them to the other, then nodded. "Fine. Ah – as you were?"

They didn't even acknowledge her, just turned to face each other again, sticks at the ready, and she clambered back through the undergrowth to a soundtrack of profanity-laden shouting behind her.

Takes all sorts.

❦

COLLINS AND MYLES were talking to an older woman wearing lavender leggings, a houndstooth suit jacket, and a rather elegant pair of boots, only slightly marred by the mud being smeared on them by three chihuahuas, all of which were trying to reach a bemused-looking Dandy, who was perched on top of Adams' car. She wished he wouldn't do that. She wasn't sure how heavy he was, but when he slept on her feet at night it seemed more than heavy enough to dent the roof.

"Those aren't regular cigarettes," the woman was saying, pointing toward the fire with a perfectly mani-cured hand.

"I *knew* it," Myles muttered.

"The situation is evolving, but it's under control," Collins said.

The woman raised her eyebrows. "Yes, the greenhouse in particular looks *very* controlled."

Adams joined them, and the woman gave her an appraising look.

"There's no threat to the public," Collins said. "We have officers on site."

The woman waved impatiently. "You misunderstand me."

"Not at all," Myles said. "You're quite right to be concerned about this *rabble—*"

"You." The woman pointed at Adams, her tone just a little too imperious.

"Detective inspector," Adams said, her own voice flat.

"Wonderful. You're the only one who appears to be doing anything useful."

"What?" Myles demanded.

The woman ignored him. "You were in the greenhouse, Inspector."

"There's no *greenhouse*," Myles said. "It's just two florists flinging mud at each other and making a right mess."

"You need to get your eyes checked, young man," the woman said, and turned back to Adams. "Are they growing anything ... *special* in there?"

"They're mostly working out some differences with the help of sticks," Adams said. She still didn't like the *you*, but she was getting the impression the woman talked to everyone the same way.

"Dammit," the woman said. "No one at the fire has any spare, and my supplier's on holiday in Malta. *Malta.* One would think they'd make arrangements for regular customers." Then she walked off, dragging the dogs after her.

The officers watched her go, and Myles said, "Completely dotty. A greenhouse?"

Collins looked at the tent, and Adams watched his gaze go to the sunflower, which had found a way out and was still climbing, apparently auditioning as a beanstalk. "*Huh*," he said, then looked at Myles. "What do you want to do?"

"Clear them all out. Run them out of bloody *town,* if we can."

"It's all pretty peaceful," Adams said. "I'd just keep an eye on things and let them get on."

"This your patch, is it?"

Collins clicked his tongue, rocking on his heels gently. "Your team there seem pretty calm about it all, Myles. They can keep an eye on things, don't you think?"

"They're *soft.* Everyone's gone soft these days! No one wants to do the hard stuff." Myles' hands were clenched at his sides, and he glared at the group by the fire, who were currently attempting an enthusiastic but inaccurate rendition of "Wellerman".

Collins looked at Adams, and she nodded, heading for the car and beeping it open. She sat in the driver's seat, one leg out in the cooling air, watching Collins and Myles. Collins seemed to be mostly listening, his face serious as he nodded, and slowly the tension drained out of Myles. He waved at the fire one more time, and Collins said something. The shorter man shook his head and laughed, then walked away at a more relaxed pace than Adams had seen from him so far. Collins stayed where he was for a little longer, waiting, then strolled back to the car and got in.

"Sorted?" Adams asked.

"I think so. He's not normally that …"

"Fanatical?" Adams suggested.

"I suppose."

"Any of that beer make it to the station?"

"I'm guessing it did, yeah." Collins peered at the tents again, where Myles was talking to the officers.

"Do you think he's going to be alright? Not going to bulldoze the place to the ground and arrest everyone in a five-mile radius?"

"I don't think so. But what does that mean? His super-power is over-policing?"

Adams made a doubtful noise. "I'm not sure it's *all* about the superpowers. It really seems to be upping the aggression levels too."

"Nice combo."

"Yeah."

They looked at each other, then Collins said, "Check on Alistair Dixon, or straight to the brewery?"

"We're too late for the brewery. Besides, I don't want to tip him off before we get to poke around tomorrow."

"Dixon it is, then."

"Looks like." She started the engine, and a moment later they were creeping through the clotted traffic in the centre of town. The sun had vanished, leaving the afternoon low and grey and whispering of cold days coming.

# 11

## DOGS GONE WILD

ALISTAIR DIXON LIVED IN ONE OF THE OLD TERRACED HOUSES that overlooked the Valley Gardens, a long green stretch of land driving straight to the centre of Harrogate. The Gardens began in an elegantly coiffed arrangement of ponds and playgrounds and pretty pockets of seating areas and plantings near the Turkish Baths, then became increasingly unruly as it expanded, running all the way out to join the bigger Harlow Carr Gardens and finally farmland. Many of the houses that faced the Gardens had been turned into apartments, and Dixon's was one, all bay windows and high ceilings.

There was no answer to the doorbell, and Adams tried the other apartments until a woman with a thin, posh voice answered. "Yes?"

"DIs Adams and Collins, North Yorkshire Police. We're looking for Alistair Dixon in apartment 3A," she said. "Any chance you can buzz us in?"

"I take it he's not answering, so no. I'm not letting any random stranger in," the woman replied.

"Not a random stranger, two detective inspectors."

"I can't tell that from here. You could just be saying it."

"Then come down and we'll show you our ID."

"And have you mug me on my own doorstep? I know how you scammers work!"

Adams scowled at the intercom, glad there was no video as she mouthed some things she wouldn't have said aloud.

Collins leaned past her. "We're very sorry to disturb your evening," he said, his voice warm and mellow. "We're just a little bit worried about Alistair. He hasn't been at work, and we want to make sure he hasn't hurt himself or taken ill or anything like that."

"Detectives don't do that sort of thing," the woman said, and Adams gave Collins a smug look.

"Not normally, no, but a friend's asked us to. It's a wellness check. It's so important to keep an eye on our friends, don't you think?"

"Why didn't you say that to start with?" the woman said, and the door buzzed open.

Collins gave Adams a rather better smug look.

"Sickening," she said.

"Only because you're no good at it."

"I don't *want* to be good at it."

"Catch more flies with honey and all that."

"I have no interest in catching flies. I use fly spray." She led the way into a white-painted hall with a deep green carpet that matched the runner on the stairs. Some faded oil landscapes hung on the walls, and a spindly-legged hall table had a small collection of post stacked on it. The whole place had a genteel shabbiness to it, as if modernisation wasn't something it was entirely convinced by, and it smelled of sunlight in still spaces and quiet dustiness.

Each floor held only two apartments, and the creaking stairs took them to the top floor, where 3A was marked on one of the old white doors. There was no response when

Adams knocked, not that she'd expected there to be one, and she tried Alistair's phone number again. It still went straight to messages, and she looked at Collins as she hung up. "It is a well-being check. He could be unconscious in there."

Collins frowned slightly. "He could also just be off on a week away."

"On the eve of the beer festival, when he's about to launch a new brew?"

"Family emergency."

"Marcus didn't even mention him," Adams pointed out.

"We didn't ask."

"The guy at the brewery said, *someone for Al.* You don't think Marcus might've thought to say anything?" Adams raised her eyebrows, and Collins sighed.

"No, right." He knocked, using the side of his fist against the door. "Mr Dixon," he called, "if you're in there, you need to let us know."

They both listened, but there was no movement.

"We have reason to believe he might need assistance," Adams said.

"Not really," Collins replied. "Your mate Rory said they weren't close. We don't *know* anything's wrong here."

Adams sighed, and looked at Dandy, who was panting next to her. "You could help," she said to him, and he huffed.

"Do I want to know how the invisible dog helps you break into apartments?"

Adams started to say something, then there was a crash from inside. Collins banged on the door again immediately, and Adams looked back at the floor. Dandy was gone.

"Good enough?" she said.

"Yeah, yeah. Reckon anyone's got a spare key around here, or should I go and get your crowbar?"

"No need." Adams took her lock-picking kit from her pocket and bent to inspect the lock. After a moment's fiddling there was a satisfying clunk, and she pushed the door open.

"You're uncomfortably good at that," Collins said. "You and your bloody dog both."

"He's a bad influence."

"Evidently."

The apartment smelt faintly of burnt coffee and laundry soap. It was small, just one bedroom, but the windows were tall, and the white walls and high ceilings made it bright and airy. The bed was made, and Adams couldn't see anything obviously missing from the wardrobe, shoes lined up below full hangers.

Collins emerged from the bathroom and said, "Toothbrush's still there."

"Phone charger's still by the bed," Adams said. He could travel with a different one, of course, but she had an idea he hadn't.

The living area was open plan, the walls smooth and featureless and the floors old, polished wood with a couple of big rugs thrown over them. A comfy sofa faced a large TV, and a breakfast bar with a couple of stools tucked in behind it separated off the kitchen area. The whole place barely looked lived in, let alone as if there had been a struggle of any sort. The only thing out of place was a metal fruit bowl that had spun to the floor off the coffee table, scattering a couple of remotes, some change, and a bunch of old receipts to the floor.

Collins looked at the bowl, which had managed to travel quite a distance across the rug to bang onto the wooden boards. "This just casually toppled halfway across the room, did it?"

"Maybe there was a small earthquake."

"Maybe someone helped it," he said, looking around suspiciously. "You've got to stop him messing with crime scenes, Adams. We can't have him eating the evidence again. That could've gone very badly last time."

"This isn't a crime scene," she said, checking the fridge. "Half a bottle of milk, just in date, and some old takeaway."

"You don't leave that in your fridge if you're going for a trip."

"Not usually, no." She closed the fridge door and looked around. "Well, there's nothing here. We need to find out if he's got a partner or something."

"Could head out to the brewery and see if Marcus wants to answer some questions."

Adams looked at her watch. "Definitely too late. And I really want Chloe to get a look at the beer before they get spooked and maybe start shifting stuff around."

Collins shrugged amiably. "Fair enough. What d'you reckon, then – take a walk through town, get a feel for things? See if anything else seems off?"

Adams nodded, still examining the flat and wondering if she were maybe a little more *sensitive*, if she might feel something here. She couldn't, though. It was a perfectly pleasant place, a little bland but harmless. "Good call," she said aloud. "I'm sticking with whisky, though."

"I could go for a nice white wine," Collins said, leading the way out of the flat. Adams followed, pulling the door shut behind her and checking it was locked. No point letting anyone else break in.

⁂

THEY LEFT the car parked where it was rather than trying to find a space closer to the town centre, and walked through the lower part of the gardens with its wide gravel paths and graceful trees, small duck pond and exuberant water plants, the flowerbeds still bursting with colour even as autumn drew in. On the other side of the main road, not far from the end of the gardens, was the conference centre, a banner advertising the beer festival hanging outside. It promised equipment stalls and educational displays for home brewers and industry ones alike, and Adams angled toward it.

Even as they crossed the road she could hear the heavy beat of music blasting wildly from inside. A young, slightly rotund man in a security guard's uniform was standing by the door looking uneasy, and he straightened up as they approached. Adams showed him her ID. "Is there something on inside?"

"Not meant to be," he said. "I reckon they've been sampling the wares."

Adams and Collins exchanged a glance, then pushed through the big doors into the convention centre, unleashing a rush of air-conditioned air, somehow both stale and full of an anxious, animal scent. She could feel the music in her joints, a hard, driving beat, and they followed it across the empty lobby and into the main hall, which had been transformed into an Ibiza-level rave.

Half the crowd seemed to have lost significant portions of their clothing, while the other half were still wearing suits and ties, or waistcoats and shirtsleeves, or tailored dresses, or skinny jeans, or some combination of the above. Lights flashed and rolled across the crowd as they bounced and cheered, swigging from bottles and pint glasses, crashing into each other and reeling away, full of hectic energy. It was painfully loud, and a brewing sense of barely-contained belligerence rose from the crowd, as if the spark that would light a riot was not just expected, but welcome. It was the sort of feeling Adams recognised from the end of football matches, or after Friday night pub-closing time. Everyone running on alcohol and adrenaline, all waiting for someone to put the first boot in, or fist.

But for now everyone seemed happy bopping to a remix of something that had the strains of a Crazy Frog song running through it, and there was nothing the two of them could do but potentially be the spark, and get themselves some hearing damage if they hung about for too long. They retreated, Adams rubbing her ear, and she stopped by the security guard. "You got anyone else on with you?"

"Just me," he said. "It's only meant to be people setting up, not this."

"Call your manager and give them a heads up," she said. "You might need some help."

He nodded, taking his phone out, and as they went back down the steps Collins said, "This doesn't bode well for tomorrow."

"No," Adams agreed. "But we should probably move on before your friend Myles starts accusing us of stepping on his toes again."

"That was you, not me," he said, but fell into step with her as they followed the curve of the road that led in a round-about way to the heart of town. There were scruffy edges here still, pawn shops and takeaways and second-hand places with dusty windows, but they rubbed shoulders with flashy delicatessens, organic food shops, and jewellers. Further on, altogether gentler music drifted from sleeker streets full of wine bars and restaurants, gas heaters roaring over outside tables filled with people sipping on cocktails and nibbling on tapas.

There was nothing obviously untoward at any of the bars, but Adams had a feeling that was *not yet*, rather than *at all*. The whole town was building toward something, and the beer was at the heart of it. She checked the tables as they walked past, spotting a bottle of Niddered Ale here and there, but there were more wine bottles and cocktail glasses than anything else. For now, anyway.

They didn't stop for a drink in the end, Collins evidently as unsettled as she was. Instead they looped around the city centre with unconsciously slow, measured strides, restlessly watching the drinkers and passersby. Adams was also trying to ignore Dandy helping himself to chicken wings and charcuterie boards at pretty much every place they went past. He seemed to be the most criminal element in evidence, the crowd otherwise mellow, although she still thought she could feel that lingering, charged energy lurking in the corners.

As they left the last of the restaurants behind on their route back to the car, she took her phone out and called Chloe. It rang enough times that she was about to hang up, then there was the click of connection and Chloe said, "Hello, Inspector. What can I do for you?"

"Any luck with those beers? I realise you haven't had your full twenty-four hours, but I thought you might make faster progress than police labs do."

"Oh, I do," Chloe said, a smile in her voice.

"Really? You know what it is?" Could it be that easy? She looked at Collins, who was watching her with an expectant expression that she thought probably matched her own.

"Not exactly. It's tricky, breaking down a charm when you don't know who's placed it or what the purpose of it is. It's a complicated process. But I'm almost certain it's in the beer itself, rather than on the bottle, and I think I know how to fix it. I'll be sure once we've checked out the brewery tomorrow."

"I don't know if you should go," Adams said. "If they're putting charms on it there, you going in could be risky. What if they realise what you're doing?"

Chloe clicked her tongue irritably. "Have your witchcraft skills elevated so much in the space of an afternoon that you can now not only sense a charm, which you couldn't do this morning, but you're going to be able to reverse it?"

"Well, no. But I have an invisible dog and a very large stick."

"See how well either of those do against a hefty charm."

Adams sighed, feeling Chloe was underestimating the value of an invisible dog and a very large stick somewhat. She'd done very well with both so far. "Fine. Ten o'clock at the brewery. Wait for me in the car park. Do *not* go in alone."

"Sure," Chloe said cheerfully, in the sort of tone that said she'd known exactly how this conversation was going to go, and also that she'd been going to do exactly what she wanted even if it hadn't gone her way. "See you tomorrow."

Adams hung up and took her keys out as they approached the car, beeping it open.

"That your witch, then?" Collins asked.

"Hedge witch, apparently. Any sign of Thompson yet?"

"Still waiting. I put some kibble out and it was gone this morning, so he might be around."

"Kibble's not going to work. Last time I had to deal with him in Leeds he demanded cod, then ate so much he went off it and wanted herring."

"He's a fussy little thing, isn't he?" Collins said.

A lazy voice replied, "Expertise doesn't come cheap." A tabby tomcat with a kink in his tail and ragged ears was crouched on the top of Adams' car, watching them with wide green eyes.

"Would everyone stop sitting on my car?"

"Lovely to see you too," Thompson said, and jumped to the ground, looking expectantly at the door. "Are we getting in? It's a bit chilly on the whiskers out here."

Cats were always such a pleasure to deal with. Adams took a moment to be grateful that Dandy was of the canine persuasion, then opened the door. Thompson jumped through to the back seat just as Dandy arrived in it, by methods Adams wasn't entirely certain of. Thompson hissed, and Dandy huffed.

"Don't hiss at him," Adams said to the cat. "This is his car."

"Hissing's the least I should be doing. I keep telling you, hanging around with a devil dandy dog is not going to do you any good whatsoever."

"Well, he's proved more useful than you have. On several occasions." She might be stretching the truth a bit, but Dandy *was* useful. When it suited him.

Thompson jumped through to the front passenger's seat. "I'm sorry, who do you always call when you're stuck? Not Red-eyed Rover here."

Adams swung into the car and said, "Never mind that. We seem to have a bit of a situation here."

"I can feel that," the cat said. "I thought this place was all fancy tearooms and bobbing about in baths, but it seems to have its party pants on."

"We think it's something to do with the beer," Adams said. "It's charmed, maybe."

"Interesting. What does it do?"

"Mixed results," Collins said, pushing Thompson over so he could get in. "We've seen super-strength and a few talents like that cropping up, but it seems to be shifting and making people behave erratically. Strange abilities and aggression."

"They're humans," the cat pointed out. "Are you sure they're not just drunk?"

"This is something else," Adams said. "Can you have a sniff around and see what you can find out? We think it's all based in one of the breweries. I'm going out there again tomorrow, and it'd be good if I had a better idea what I was dealing with."

Thompson shrugged. "Sure. I'll have a nose around. Not really my turf, though."

"Are you cats pretty territorial?" Collins asked.

"Cats, reasonably. Watch, more to the point, very much so." The Watch were a council that policed the divide between the human and Folk worlds, making sure that humans didn't stumble into knowing anything they shouldn't, and at the same time ensuring Folk didn't draw too much attention to themselves. The Watch were a desperately old and deeply entrenched organisation, regarded with reluctant respect and a good dose of fear in the Folk world, even if they were entirely unknown in the human one. They were also cats, and Adams had wondered more than once if their main method of control was simply annoying people into behaving themselves.

"Is that going to be a problem?" she asked aloud. "You asking questions here?"

"Shouldn't be, as long as we don't bring any dragons into it. I can be devastatingly subtle."

"I'm sure."

He arched his whiskers at her. "You, on the other hand, are not subtle."

"What?"

"The whole necklace thing was hardly going to go unnoticed, was it? And then there was that nest of Thrummy Caps in Leeds, and the bogeymen in Skipton."

"The *what?*" Collins asked.

Adams waved at him impatiently. "Do I need to worry about this?"

"Look, a magical detective and her demon dog are just going to draw attention. No helping it."

Dandy growled, and Thompson hissed at him.

"Stop that," Adams said. "He's not a demon dog. He might be a devil dandy dog like you keep saying, but he's not a demon. He's a very good boy." Dandy's tail thumped at that, and she reached back to scratch his ears.

"Part of the Wild Hunt, devil dandy dogs," Collins observed.

"Yes," Thompson said. "Which is *so* much better. You understand the wild bit doesn't mean he wears skimpy knickers and does body shots, right?"

Adams and Collins both stared at him.

"Why would he do that?" Collins asked.

"That's what humans do when they go wild, don't they? I saw it on TV."

Adams tried not to think about what sort of TV the cat was getting his information from, or who he'd been watching it with. Instead she said, "Will you ask some questions or not?"

"Sure," Thompson said. "But don't be surprised if some questions get asked back."

Then he was gone, sliding sideways into some gap between the dimensions, or maybe deep within them, leaving behind the whisper of his vanishing and a faint scent of fish. Adams didn't know how cats travelled, or how they were able to appear exactly where they intended whenever they fancied, and she wasn't sure she wanted to. It was enough to know it was bloody annoying.

Dandy whuffed and looked at Adams. She scratched him behind the ears again. "I know," she said. "Cats are the worst."

But on the other hand, they could also be rather useful.

# CONNECTION BREEDS
# COMPLICATIONS

THE NEXT DAY DAWNED BRIGHT AND SHARPLY POLISHED, THE clouds of the previous night chased away and the threat of rain dragged with them. Adams ran in the clear, still hour before the town had fully woken up, feet following their accustomed route to the castle and through the woods that bordered it. Her footfalls were quiet on the hard-packed earth, and the mingled scent of old growth and moss-edged streams stole the presence of the town. The woven willow sculptures of the Huntress and the Horse were rendered otherworldly in the low light, and she raised a hand in greeting as she passed. Just in case.

Dandy ran with her, one shadow among many, occasionally vanishing up a tree in pursuit of squirrels but always catching up again. She used to worry he might get stuck, since she'd never heard of tree-climbing as a canine skill, and she didn't fancy having to figure out a way to rescue a large invisible dog from the branches. She couldn't exactly call out fire and rescue for that. But Dandy navigated trees the same way he navigated walls and space – with scant regard for physics and without Adams ever quite seeing him do it. He never seemed to catch any squirrels, but he definitely enjoyed chasing them, and also terrorising any other dog they passed, although she had a feeling that was more accidental than anything else.

At least this early there weren't many people out, and other than setting a quartet of little white dogs in colour-coordinated jackets yapping and snarling hysterically, transforming them into enraged marshmallows, the run was uneventful. Although the toothed puffballs managed to get so tangled in their own leashes and around their equally irate owner that Adams almost stopped to help him sort it out. That'd only keep Dandy in the area longer, though, so she just waved apologetically and kept going, wondering why it was always the small dogs that felt they could take on a large, red-eyed, supernatural beast. It said something about their personalities, and she wasn't sure if it was admirable or not.

Even after she'd showered and dressed it was still too early to head for Knaresborough, so she filled a travel mug with coffee and drove to the station instead. Collins was climbing out of his car when she got there, and he raised a matching mug to her in greeting, although she knew his would be full of tea. She wasn't quite sure why he brought it from home when decent tea, at least, was the one thing that seemed to be available in every station. It was the coffee that was almost always an absolute disgrace, and they seemed to be having the same problem here as they'd had in Leeds, in that the machine was always empty. Although she had a sneaking suspicion she knew who the culprit was, and she gave Dandy a warning look as they headed inside.

"Any news from Myles?" she asked Collins by way of greeting.

"Morning to you too. Sleep well? Nice weather we're having." He grinned at her, taking a sip from his mug, then said, "Myles is still a bit miffed that we wouldn't help him bring the full might of the Yorkshire constabulary down on the party, I think. I haven't had any updates from him, but I called the station and they couldn't tell me anything. Usual night, few drunk and disorderlies but nothing out of the ordinary."

"Assuming it was reported." Adams was thinking of Myles all but vibrating with rage, and that late-Friday-night feel of the town, violence bubbling just below the surface.

"Not much else we can assume," Collins said, waving her ahead of him into the building. "I'm going to go and have a word with Jules. I sent a request for her to try tracking Alistair's cards last night, and to look into Marcus, but she didn't reply."

"Oh yeah – I asked her to try and find last location on Alistair's phone, too. Check on it for me?"

"Sure."

In the office, Adams opened the window to let out some of the night's stuffiness as she called Chloe. The young woman answered sounding almost unbearably bright. "Good morning, DI Adams. How may I direct your call?"

"You set for today?"

"I have my best witchy earrings on. For luck, you know."

"Good to hear. Ten o'clock, right?"

"I haven't forgotten since yesterday." Chloe sounded far too amused, and Adams wished there was a way to impress on her that this wasn't just some field trip into policing, that it was serious, that there could be consequences if they got this wrong, but she wasn't even sure she was convinced of that herself. After all, other than one journalist getting a black eye, what had really happened? Maybe she was too sensitive after the bridge and the necklace, seeing threat where there was nothing but coincidence. Seeing enchantment where there was just fungus.

Aloud, though, she said, "Right. Of course. See you then."

"Wouldn't miss it for the world."

Adams' phone rang again just as Collins ambled into the office, Isha's number coming up on the display. She grimaced, watching it ring.

"Dodging calls now, Adams?" Collins said.

"It's Isha."

"Wasn't she going to call you with anything unusual?"

"Yes, but ..." But she didn't fancy another uncomfortable conversation. She could only apologise so many times, after all, and it all came back to the fact that personal stuff was messy, and she should've just stuck to work. Work made sense. Most of the time, anyway. Personal always ended up like this. Complicated, and confusing, and everyone left with a bad taste in their mouths.

The phone was one ring away from going to messages when she hit answer, trying to make her voice breezy. "Isha, hi."

"Bloody hell. You answered!"

"Sorry. Yes. Bit busy."

"Those sheep'll keep you on your toes."

"Devious beasts." Adams took a sip of coffee, relaxing slightly. Isha sounded *normal*. Maybe the effects of the beer were wearing off.

"So I've got some files here," Isha said. "Interesting reading."

"Oh?"

"Take a look."

Adams' phone vibrated, and she took it away from her ear, putting it on speaker as she opened the message. More cases of weird behaviour? Something about the brewery?

Instead, a collection of links filled the screens, each with Isha's notes next to it.

*Cryptids Today: Detective Battles Bridge Monsters!*

*Secret London: Hero Detective Flees London! The Police Cover Up The TRUTH!!*

*Leeds Insider: Bridge Monster Cop in Leeds – Why Is She Here? What Are They Not Telling Us??*

Adams stared at them, not clicking on any, then, her voice flat, said, "What's this?"

"Well, you refuse to tell me anything, so I did some digging. Oh, hang on."

Adams' phone vibrated again, and again, and again, and she scrolled through a collection of text messages. They were between her old DCI in London and Temper, but not via any official messaging account. They were both personal ones, and she tried not to read them, but lines leaped out at her anyway.

*She's got a way with Yorkies.*

*I hate that sodding stuff.*

*So put her on it.*

*I'm not having some London copper having a breakdown up here. Not my department.*

*She'll be fine.*

*File says mental break.*

*Of course it does. She'll still be fine.*

She took the phone off speaker and put it to her ear again. "Where did you get these?" Her stomach was protesting the coffee, and her cheeks were too hot, her hands too cold, but her voice was hard-edged and steady. She was aware of Collins looking up at her from his computer, and Dandy rising to his feet on the far side of the desk.

"I'm good at what I do," Isha said. "I can find anything I want. And do with it what I want."

"And what do you want to do with this?"

"That depends on you."

"How, exactly?"

"Tell me what's going on, and how much truth's behind all this. Like you promised to after the necklace case."

Adams closed her eyes. "I never promised that."

"You implied it."

"Isha, I'm in the middle of a case. Can we talk about it after?"

"No. You can make the time to talk to me now, or I'll assume you're not going to, and the consequences will be on you."

Adams checked the time. "I'm not doing this on the phone, and I need to go and meet someone. I'll come by after."

There was a long pause, then Isha said, "Fine. Make sure you do."

The line went dead, and Adams stared at the forwarded texts, then set her phone carefully down.

"What's happening?" Collins asked.

"Isha's got hold of a bunch of stuff about me. London and … Toot Hansell stuff. I don't know what she's going to do with it, but she says if I don't go there and explain everything, she'll do *something*."

"Well, just to make your morning better, we've got another problem." He leaned back in his chair, nodding at the computer screen, and she got up to peer over his shoulder.

"A *disciplinary note?*"

"A warning. Maud sent it. Apparently DCI Ian Bell in Harrogate has heard I've been off my patch, and complained."

"The DCI complained?"

"I think Myles was not a fan of our approach."

Adams sighed and picked her phone up, swiping Isha's messages away hurriedly. Just the sight of them made her stomach go into revolt again. *Mental health break.* Yes, it had been an excuse – sort of – but it was also *private*. She opened her emails instead. "I've got the same— Wait. No. I've got *two*."

"What?"

"Temper's complained too."

"So you have to go to Leeds to see Isha, but also can't because he'll think you're sneaking about his patch."

"Bloody *hell*."

"Quite," someone's voice said, and they looked up at Maud, standing in the door. Dandy huffed at her. "You've been making a nuisance of yourselves, haven't you?"

"Not deliberately," Collins said. "Or no more so than usual, anyway."

"DC James Hamilton requested I assist him in Leeds," Adams said.

"And you didn't run that by Temper?"

"It was sort of … unofficial?" She pushed her coffee cup away, wondering what emails Maud had exchanged with Temper. What was being said about her behind closed doors, the strange detective with her *way with Yorkies*. Which was better than being talked about for being unstable, she supposed, but right now it felt like the same thing.

"Same in Harrogate," Collins said. "A mate of mine said there was a bit of a situation that we thought might be related to the brewery, and we went to check it out. He didn't quite get the help he thought he was going to get, so I think that might be why he's gone and complained about it."

"Which may also be related to the beer," Adams put in. "It's looking more and more likely it's affecting people's behaviour. We suspect Harrogate station may have been sent samples, the same as Leeds, which means they're not going to be thinking straight about it."

"And the effects may be worsening," Collins added.

Maud looked from one of them to the other. Her face was a little pink, and Adams couldn't tell if it was with annoyance or atmospherics. She hadn't figured out how to read Maud yet, and she had a sneaking suspicion it was never going to be an easy task.

"You're a right tag-team these days, aren't you?" the DCI said.

"Positively besties," Collins said, grinning.

Maud shifted her weight from foot to foot, an uneasy little movement, then said, "This beer. What was it called?"

"Niddered Ale from Dixon's Draughts," Adams said.

Maud sighed. "Well, bollocks. I knew I felt a little off this morning."

"You *had* some?" Adams said. "But we said yesterday that there were samples—" She broke off as Maud raised her eyebrows at her. "I mean … what happened, boss?"

"Hubby and I were having a drink in the garden last night. I like my beer in a glass. I'm not twenty. He brought me one, and it was very tasty, so I asked him what it was. He likes supporting all the local breweries by trying different brews, and I like drinking them."

"He bought Niddered Ale?" Adams asked.

"No. It was on the doorstep when he got home. He thought I'd ordered it online as a surprise for him."

"They delivered it to your *home?*" Collins asked.

"Yes." Maud crossed her arms, tapping her fingers restlessly on the opposite biceps. "I don't feel right, but I don't feel *bad.* And I've sent you your warning notes, so that's the last I want to hear about it. Stay away from Leeds and Harrogate."

"But—" Adams started.

Maud turned on her heel, already heading out of the door. "And I don't want to know anything about what you're doing in your spare time." She raised her voice as she walked away. "Plus it seems some beer was delivered here last night.

I'll be confiscating it, but there's only half a crate left. Just so you know."

Adams slumped back in her chair, rubbing her hands over her face. "*Bollocks.*"

"With bells on," Collins said. "What's the plan?"

Adams checked her watch. "I'm going to meet Chloe."

"In your unofficial capacity."

"Yeah. You?"

"See if I can track down Alistair Dixon, and do some digging on Marcus. If I find anything I'll send it through to you."

"Didn't you go to see Jules on that?"

"I did. But she's blacked out her office windows and has apparently disembowelled half the station's computers. She's sitting in there on the floor with a head torch, a screwdriver, and a bulk lot of energy drinks, and I swear she growled at me when I opened the door. I'd usually think she was just having a moment, but if some beer was delivered last night ..."

"Between her and bloody Isha they're going to take out the entire defence network."

"No, Isha's too busy torturing you," Collins said, then added with a grin, "Don't tell her about your landed gentry, whatever you do. She really will burn the world down."

"I don't have a landed gentry, and even if I did, that's nothing to do with why Isha's upset."

"Are you sure about that?"

Adams got up, ignoring the question. "Come on, Dandy. Some of us have proper policing to do."

SHE WAS on the outskirts of Harrogate when her phone rang,

and *Ervin Giles* popped up on the car's display. She sighed and hit reply. "Ervin."

"Adams. Where are you?"

She frowned. The journalist normally sounded like he was sporting a Cheshire Cat grin, but not today. "On the way to Knaresborough. Why?"

"Okay, good. Meet me?"

"I'm on a schedule."

"It'll only take a few minutes. It's important."

"Can't you just tell me?"

"No." His voice was flat, and she sighed. She *wanted* to be able to ignore him, but he'd brought the info on the beer samples. He could be useful.

"Where?"

"Knaresborough, under the bridge."

Bloody bridges. And that one was over a river, too, which was her least favourite combination. But it was the middle of the day and a long way from London, so she said, "Alright. This better be good." She hit disconnect before he could answer, and swore at the crawling traffic. She could probably still make it to the brewery by ten, though.

There was parking down by the river, where the long brick legs of the bridge grew up out of the water and the greenery to either side with the graceful disproportions of a giraffe. A few people were out in pedalos and rowing boats, and the ice cream shop was already doing good trade. Ervin was waiting for her on the path that curled along the river, watching the ducks paddling back and forth and keeping a wary eye on some swans. Adams marched up to him, Dandy bouncing ahead.

Ervin gave Dandy a good scratch around the ears, earning a wary glance from two women striding past with prams, and said, "Thanks for coming."

"You said it'd be quick," she replied, looking at her watch.

Ervin looked around like he was a spy about to sell state secrets, then took his phone from his pocket, scrolling through it. He talked as he did so, his voice low. "So, you know I told you my editor-in-chief had a bit of a go at me."

"Richly undeserved, I'm sure."

"It *was* richly undeserved. And even if it was deserved, it was assault. You should be against that sort of thing."

"I'm not sure when it comes to journalists."

Ervin shook his head. "The reason I got an award to the ribs was because I suggested running a story about the Yorkshire panther being seen stalking children on the Stray was maybe not responsible journalism at its finest. Today, the printer got fired for refusing to run this: *Aliens descend on Harrogate Festival.*"

"Sorry, what? What newspaper do you work for?"

"*Craven Chronicle.* And the editor's usually *fierce.* The fact-checking he makes us go through is ridiculous, but he says we're the last bastion against fake news. And now this."

"Some sort of prank?" Adams suggested.

"We've also got a sighting of the Loch Ness Monster in the River Nidd. And then in sports, a touring team of mini-golf players from outer Mongolia have just won the national snooker championships."

Adams stared at him. "But that makes no sense." And she didn't just mean the stories. If the editor was so fierce on good reporting, then how had his superpower become making up fake news?

"I know. But no one can stop him. He just says that he gets to make the news."

Now that made sense, in a warped sort of way, but then everything was a bit warped at the moment. "Okay," she said aloud. "Could've just told me this over the phone."

Ervin looked at the swans and said, "I didn't think it was a good idea."

"Why?" she asked.

He handed his phone to her silently, and Adams stared at the message on the display. It had been forwarded from an unknown number, but she recognised it. She'd read it just a couple of days ago. It was from her mum, asking if she'd been shopping, and if she'd tried the aubergine recipe her aunt had sent her. She looked at Ervin, and he shook his head. "I don't know who they're from. There's more, but I haven't opened them, I swear."

She went back into his messages and opened the next one. It was from Collins, asking her if she wanted to try a coffee-flavoured goat's cheese, and included her response that he should arrest the cheese-maker. There were more too, going back at least for the last month, but she didn't open any. She just looked up at the slender span of the bridge, scowling, and wondered if ducks worked on computer techs.

"I'll delete them, obviously," Ervin said. "I didn't know if you might want to see if you can trace them or something."

"I know where they came from," she replied, handing the phone back.

"That's something, then. But see why I didn't want to talk about it over the phone? You've likely been hacked."

Adams gave a grunt of acknowledgement, pulled her phone from her pocket, and powered it down. Isha had been far too good at tracking her in the past, and though it had been helpful then, it felt like a threat now. "Have you got Collins' number?" she asked him.

"Sure," Ervin said. "But it's possible they've got my phone too. I took it offline as soon as I talked to you."

"Fair point." She looked at her watch, turning to walk away, then paused and said, "Thank you."

"Told you I could be useful. But quid pro quo, right?"

"Civic duty, right?" Adams jogged back to the car. She was

going to be late for Chloe, but she had to make a stop before she headed to the brewery. She reached for her phone, intending to search the nearest phone shop, then swore and started the car instead. She'd have to do this the old-fashioned way.

Fifteen minutes later, after asking at the nearest garage and being directed to a small, rather scruffy shop down a side street that had stock she suspected of being of dubious origins, she was walking out with a new SIM card and a pay-as-you-go mobile that was as far removed from a smartphone as it was possible to get these days. That was both for practical reasons and budgetary ones. She'd had them put the SIM in at the shop so she wasn't faffing around with it, and now, as she hurried back to the car, she plugged Chloe's number into the new mobile. There was no answer. She threw the phone into the passenger seat and pulled out of her parking space fast, swinging the car into a U-turn to head toward the brewery. Not answering didn't mean anything. Maybe the signal was a bit patchy, or Chloe was driving and witches didn't use hands-free, or she simply hadn't heard it. There were all sorts of possibilities.

She had to stop jumping to the worst conclusions. It was getting to be a bad habit.

Not an unfounded one, though.

## CAUTION, LOITERING WARTS

THE BREWERY DOORS WERE STANDING OPEN, THE SPACE directly outside set up with big tables and a scattering of stools, and a couple of open-sided gazebos had been erected to give some shelter from the sun. The tables had thyme and rosemary plants set in the centres, looking as if someone had suddenly thought a nod should be given to decoration and had grabbed them from the supermarket on the way into work. A few early starters were already talking to workers in otter-festooned Niddered Ale T-shirts, and there were small tumblers of beer being handed out freely from a keg set up just inside the doors. Beyond them, Adams glimpsed more tables waiting for guests. Evidently Marcus was expecting a good turnout.

She parked in the same place as yesterday. The BMW she'd noted before was there, along with a couple of white delivery vans, but nothing that shouted *witch's car*. Not that she knew what that would look like anyway. Not a broom-stick, evidently. She tried Chloe's phone again, but there was still no response. Maybe she'd already gone in.

"Ready?" she asked Dandy, and he whined at her from the passenger's seat. "You don't much like the smell, do you?"

He wagged his tail at her gently, and she sighed.

"Is it the beer smell, or is it the charms?"

He tipped his head.

"One bark for beer, two for charms?"

Dandy just whined, so Adams got out of the car and looked at the brewery, the old stone bright in the sunlight. "Heel?" she suggested to Dandy as he slipped out behind her, having shrunk down to spaniel size. He turned around and vanished into the trees. "Right. As you were."

She went straight past the assembled drinkers, nodding at the young man she'd spoken to the previous day, and stepped into the rich scents of the brewery. It was dimmer in here, even the strong lights no competition for the sun. But she spotted Marcus heading toward her quickly enough, his slightly too-long hair curling to meet the collar of a matching T-shirt to the other workers. The otter's winking face was far too knowing, and she frowned.

"DI Adams," he said, smiling. "Lovely to have you back again."

"I'm looking—"

"For your friend, yes. She said to give you a message."

"Sorry?" Adams said.

"Chloe. She said you were meeting her here, but she couldn't wait." Marcus was smiling genially, his hands in the pockets of his jeans.

"She left?"

"Yes. Her phone had died, so she asked me to let you know when you arrived."

Adams didn't return his smile, just examined him thoughtfully. He gave nothing away, just met her gaze with a sort of affable interest, and finally she said, "That was all she said?"

"I'm afraid so, yes. Can I interest you in a tour at all?"

"I'm more interested in why you pretended to be Alistair yesterday."

"I never said I was him."

"You never said you weren't."

"You never asked." He grinned, then immediately looked contrite, holding a hand out to her. "Marcus Gallagher, brewery manager."

Adams regarded him steadily. "Why not say that yesterday? Especially when your mate there specifically said we were looking for Alistair?" She nodded at the young man, who was currently flirting shamelessly with a much older woman. She looked as delighted as her companion did bemused.

"He knows anything for Al comes to me."

"Why?"

Marcus's smile finally faded. "Al's gone on a little break."

"You're going to have to be a bit more detailed here, Marcus. I can't reach him on the phone, have concerns for his welfare, and you're hanging about being at least cagey, at worst obstructive in the legal sense."

"Easy," he said, and she raised her eyebrows. "I just mean I didn't realise it was that serious."

"It is."

"Okay, come on." He turned and headed for the door. Adams took another look around, seeing a few people already being led through the vats, still clutching their samples as T-shirt-clad workers pointed at pipes and valves and well-polished taps.

"Hang about," she said. "I'd like a look around."

"I'm not talking about Al here. It's private."

She looked from him to the cavernous brewery, debating, then nodded. "Alright, tell me. Then you can give me a tour."

"With pleasure, Inspector."

MARCUS LED her toward the parked cars, leaning against the
flashy BMW with his arms folded across his chest, biceps
smooth and tanned in the sun. Adams leaned against her
own car, taking a surreptitious look for Dandy, but evidently
he was off on his own adventures.

"So?" she said.

"So Alistair's taken a mental health break."

She frowned. "By choice, or do you mean he was hospi-
talised?"

"No, by choice."

"He just walked out and left you in charge right before the
launch of a new brew? That hardly seems like it's going to
help his stress levels."

"It was a bit more than stress. He broke up with a long-
term partner last year, and he's been struggling. Bloody
genius with the beer, but not with much else. He couldn't
cope with the lead-up to the festival, so he brought me in.
He's taken himself off to some sort of retreat, no contact
with the outside world, milk some sheep and pet some cows,
all that sort of thing."

Adams didn't answer straight away. Out here in the
sunlight, she found herself second-guessing the thought that
Marcus's edges were too sharp, that there was something
other than human to him. Maybe she hadn't seen it at all. Or
maybe he was better at hiding it here than he was in the
shadows.

"Do you have any details for this retreat?"

"No. He didn't want anyone to know. He just said he was
going, and to expect him when we saw him."

"Puts you in a difficult situation as manager."

"No. Lets me get on with my job, is all."

She nodded, still watching him. He was smiling again, just slightly, and she could see the tips of his canines. They irritated her for some reason, and she had the sudden urge to ask if he needed a chew toy. Last thing she needed was for him to file a complaint against her, though.

"Did you want that tour?" he asked.

"Did Chloe go inside at all?"

"She had a look. She seemed a bit impatient to get off, though. Don't think you'll be popular."

"Sounds about right," she muttered, mostly to herself, then straightened up. "Alright. Give me the quick version, then."

"You can't rush good beer, Inspector."

"I'm not making the bloody beer, am I?"

He laughed, a gruff, delighted sound, and led the way back toward the brewery. "No mention of Al in here, though, right? Everyone thinks it was a family emergency. No need for the whole team to know."

"Fair enough."

There were more people arriving all the time, walking up the lane from wherever the official car park was. There weren't hordes of them, but there were enough that none of the half-dozen workers were standing idle, kept busy either drawing beer from the keg or talking to the tasters, or leading them inside in couples and little groups. She caught snippets of conversation as she and Marcus passed.

"—Harrogate water has excellent clarity—"

"—as much as possible local grains—"

"—brewing temperature is carefully maintained—"

"—then the bloody stoat only up and bit his—"

She blinked at the last one, but by that stage they were already in among the looming vats, the air heavy with hops. Marcus was talking about the viewing ports that allowed them to keep an eye on the brewing process, pointing to barriers set up around some of the vats as he explained they were for …

"Loitering warts?" Adams said, startled.

"W-o-r-t."

"Oh."

"And l-a-u-t-e-r-ing is the process by which—"

Adams had been more intrigued by the concept of loitering warts, and now she mostly tuned Marcus out again, nodding and *mmm-hmm*-ing in what she hoped were suitable places. The majority of her attention was on the building itself, scanning for doors that might lead to back rooms, anywhere someone might be kept out of the way and unheard. Although, the unheard part could always be arranged.

"Do you have a toilet I can use?" she asked, interrupting Marcus mid-spiel about whirlpools, which really seemed as if it should have nothing to do with beer.

"Of course." He pointed to a door at the back of the brewery, *Beer Out* burned into a wooden plaque on it. A second, unmarked door stood next to it.

"Thanks." Adams headed over to them, and tried the unmarked one first.

"Other one," Marcus called.

"Right, sorry," she said, but she'd already turned the handle on the unmarked door, finding it unlocked, so she just added, "Oops," and pushed it open. Inside was a small staffroom, equipped with a table and a few chairs, some beers with wonky labels collected on a little worktop and a fridge groaning away in the corner. There was no Chloe trussed up on the floor, and no signs of struggle. She went back to the toilet door and let herself in, finding a single loo behind a second door, plus a cupboard of cleaning supplies. Everything was spotlessly clean and smelt of soap, and there was nowhere a hedge witch could've been stashed.

Marcus was leaning against the wall outside the toilet when she came out, and he grinned at her. "Can't find your friend?"

"Why would you think I was looking for her?"

"Coppers have suspicious minds."

"It tends to come with the job."

He straightened up, still grinning. "Come on, then. On with the tour."

"I think I've learned as much as I want to about brewing."

"Sure. But you haven't checked behind this door." He led her to one at the back of the brewery, which was marked with a *Private* sign, a combination keypad set above the handle. He tapped a code in without bothering to hide it from her. *9-8-5-2-9*. She filed the number without thinking about it, and he pushed the door open. "There you go. Then you can let us get on with work, DI Adams."

She walked into a big storeroom, crates of beer stacked high on one side, metal kegs on the other. There was a clear path to an oversized door at the other end of the room, likely where they backed the vans up for loading, and straps and heavy-duty gloves were hanging from hooks on the wall. Marcus waited at the door, and for one moment she was seized by the certainty that he'd slam it shut, sealing her in here with the almost certainly charmed beer. She wondered if she could breathe the spell in, and what would happen if she did.

Instead, Marcus said, "Do you want to see the room with our safety gear and decontamination shower, too?"

"Sure," she said. "Since I'm here."

He gave a startled huff of laughter. "I honestly thought you'd say no."

"Never leave a job half-done and all that."

"As you say." He pulled the door of the storeroom shut after her, then led the way to the wall near the office, where another door lurked behind a vat. It was adorned with a large yellow, white and black sticker that read *Safety Equipment Do Not Obstruct,* and it wasn't locked. He rolled a hand toward it, giving a mocking little half bow, and she opened the door to reveal an overgrown wardrobe. Overalls and hard hats, safety goggles and more heavy gloves were all hanging in carefully designated spaces, and there was a big first aid kit fixed to one wall. There was also a cheap plastic shower taking up most of the end of the room, with an eye-washing station next to it.

"A lot of kit."

"Brewing's not for the fainthearted."

"Evidently." They smiled at each other, and in the shadows behind the vat, both of them leaning into the safety room doorway, shoulders almost touching, she thought she could smell him. Heat and hunger and something fiercely contained.

But she couldn't *sense* anything, no more than she had with the beers, when Chloe had said she could sense the charms on it. Maybe Adams could see that sharpness in people, and right now she could smell something *other* on Marcus, something that cut through the hops and yeast and alcohol, but she couldn't *sense* it, nor could she *make* sense of it. She gripped the rubber duck keyring in her pocket like it could clarify things, lend her some of its essential un-ducki-ness, or whatever it was that made it not just a keyring and not just a duck.

Nothing changed, though, and she shut the door again.

"Happy?" Marcus asked.

"How much beer are you shipping out for this festival?"

"We've got our own stand, which we're getting set up for tonight. Plus quite a lot of pubs in town do stock our brews, so we're going to rotate staff around them throughout the different nights so that we can offer tastings at as many of them as possible. We're also doing tastings here every day. So ... as to how much? As much as we can. It's the general business model when you're selling things."

Adams couldn't even hazard a guess as to how much that would be, but there was plenty of beer in that back room. If the festival ground last night had been an example of what one crate could do, she hated to think what all of those bottles and kegs were capable of. "What would happen if you had a bad batch and had to recall it?"

"It'd be a bit of a nightmare," he said, gesturing for her to lead the way to the doors. "We do all we can to avoid anything like that happening. Obviously we have to adhere to Food and Hygiene standards, but we consider them a minimum. We test every batch at various stages throughout the brewing process, and we've got systems in place to minimise any risk of contamination. So, with all that, the odds of a bad batch are pretty slim."

"Do you have a method for recalling it if it did happen?"

"Sure. We have to. It's not foolproof, of course, because we can only go as far as distributors. It's not like we have a database of every punter who picks up a bottle at the bar."

They'd stopped just outside the brewery's big double doors, and Adams watched a polished, highly tanned couple in athletic gear lugging two six-packs each down the lane, both of them looking a little pink and delighted. Of course it was impossible to track everyone down. But the effects didn't seem to be easing, if Isha was anything to go by. They seemed to be intensifying.

She looked at Marcus. "Thanks for the tour."

"My pleasure. I hope you can get hold of your friend." He strolled over to one of the tables and took half a dozen bottles from a crate, fitting them into a cardboard holder. "Here you go," he said, holding them out to Adams.

"No thanks."

"Non-alcoholic. And still cold. Just the thing for a hot day."

"I can't take gifts."

He grinned. "Give us a fiver, then. I'm telling you, these are *excellent.*"

"I'm sure," Adams said, and wondered about taking them to test, but just as he was unlikely to be showing her incriminating doors, he wasn't likely to be giving her charmed beers if he thought she knew what she was looking for. Not that she did. "Good luck with your open day," she said, and headed for her car, leaving him holding the bottles.

She could hardly shut the brewery down. Not only did she have no evidence to wave in front of anyone, she wasn't even meant to be here. If Myles was anything to go by, she'd have zero support from Harrogate, and with Maud on the beers now too she had a feeling it was only so long before the directive to go ahead unofficially was revoked. There was nothing she could do except keep poking around and seeing what came loose. And it would come loose. It *had* to.

Not least because Chloe was simply *gone.* And that was on Adams. She should've been here on time.

She swung back into the car and started the engine, jumping as Dandy raised his head cautiously from the back seat. He was smaller than he had been when she left, terrier-sized, and they looked at each other warily.

"I don't like it either," she told him, and he whuffed softly. She looked back at the brewery. Marcus was talking to someone outside, sunlight shining on his thick hair. He moved with an easy, sloping sort of grace, and she wished again that she could figure out what he was, because he definitely wasn't entirely human. He made her think of the bodyguards at the house earlier in the summer, the ones that she'd kept thinking of as *good boys* for some unknown reason, even though they'd been as human-shaped as Marcus. No horns or wings or hooves or extra appendages. But he was unsettling, just as the good boys had been, some instinct recognising him for what he was, even if her mind didn't.

She sighed and put the car into reverse. She wasn't getting anywhere here. But she knew somewhere she might.

# 14

## BAIT AND WITCH

Instead of following the lane back toward the main road, Adams turned deeper into the estate, following the drive as it uncoiled between green fields, graceful trees, and a number of *Private Property No Entry* signs. The final one was very large and attached to a gate that advised visitors to both *Keep Out* and *Please Shut The Gate*, which she felt was sending somewhat mixed messages. The final stretch of drive beyond it was distinctly less well gravelled, and seemed determined to assault the suspension of her car, but before long she was pulling up in front of what she assumed was Featherstone Manor, or House, or Hall – whatever had given its name to Featherstone Estate.

Rory hadn't actually been being self-deprecating. It really wasn't a particularly stately home. It rose to two storeys over the main door, but the wings were only one storey each, as if the builder had run out of enthusiasm or funds to make them match up. The one to the right was slowly crumbling into oblivion, plywood sealing the windows and patches in the roof covered with hasty repairs. The section to the left looked a little healthier, although the windows seemed to be original, single-paned sash ones, and Adams shivered at the thought of how cold it'd be in the winter. Despite the disrepair, the house still had a crumbling beauty to it, ivy clambering over the walls and a wilderness of flowers scrambling about in the neglected beds. The stone had weathered elegantly, and, unlike most of the country houses Adams had seen, it looked as though it had been lived in and loved, not just used as a status symbol.

She parked to the side of the main door and climbed the curved steps to ring the bell. Dandy padded after her, back to his Labrador size and looking around curiously.

"You're happier," she said to him while they waited, and he twitched his ears at her, then pointed his nose around the house to the left. She followed his gaze, and when no one answered the door she started back down the steps. Dandy immediately trotted off, heading for a low stone building that looked like it used to be stables or something similar, wooden double doors lying open to the day. There was a quad bike sitting outside it, and as she got closer she could hear the clash of metal, accompanied by some inventive and colourful swearing. Adams paused on the threshold, waiting for her eyes to adjust and expanding her vocabulary quite impressively. Then a dog gave a short, warning bark, and the swearer yelped as they dropped something with a clatter.

"Dammit, Midge!"

"Mr Acklesfield?" she said, as the two border collies emerged from the shadows with their heads down, eyes fixed on Dandy. They stopped just inside the doorway, teeth showing. Dandy wagged his tail at them cheerily.

"Hello?"

Her eyes had adjusted now, but the interior of the shed was still somewhat mysterious. There were vats and barrels and pipes and valves, just like in the brewery, but on a smaller scale, and a curious mix of alcohol and botanicals invaded the space, strong enough to make her wrinkle her nose. The floor was hard-packed dirt, and the equipment had been erected on a patch of somewhat rudimentary wooden flooring plonked in the centre of the space. The only light came from the doors, and there were a couple of chickens picking around the place.

"It's DI Adams," she said, wondering what Marcus's Food and Hygiene would have to say about the chickens. And the dogs. And probably the dirt floor. Nothing good, she imagined.

Rory emerged from around the vats, his hair dishevelled and mucky handprints on his jeans where he'd wiped them. He gave her a wary look. "How much of that did you hear?"

"Enough to think that public school really does widen your vocabulary."

He laughed. "All that money's got to buy you something, right?"

"Apparently. Everything alright in there?"

He examined the knuckles on one hand, where the skin was torn. "I just got a new still, and the bloody connectors are all the wrong size. I've managed to get imperial instead of metric, and now I've messed up the threads, can't get it back off, and won't be able to return it even if I do, because I might have hit it a couple of times with a hammer to try and make it fit."

"Can't imagine why that didn't work," Adams said. "Do you have a moment?"

"Sure. I need a break, anyway. Do you want a cuppa or something?"

"This won't take long—"

"Come and tell me while I put the kettle on, then," he said, and somehow she found herself falling into step with him as he headed toward the corner of the house, circling around the wing to the back.

"Trying to break into the beer market too?" she asked as they walked.

"Not quite. My current goal is a decent non-alcoholic gin."

"Really?"

"Really. Huge market in non-alcoholic spirits now, and I thought *Featherstone's Featherweights* might make for a good label."

"Did you?" Adams said, trying to channel Collins' approachable tone. Apparently she hadn't nailed it, as he gave her a sideways look, his grin widening.

"No. It's a terrible name. But I was trying to distil whisky and I am very bad at it. As in, terrible. I exploded a still, and it's a good thing that old shed's got solid walls."

"And that no one was in there."

"Well, I did lose a chicken." He pressed a hand to his chest and bowed his head, and Adams surprised herself by laughing. "Anyway, I decided gin might be safer, but my first couple of goes were about 500 proof. So then when I was trying to get rid of some of the alcohol I discovered I could get rid of almost all of it. I'm just working on how to get it down the final bit to within the limits of what it can be to sell it as non-alcoholic. I'm almost there."

"Seems like dangerous business," Adams said, looking at his hand pointedly.

He examined his knuckles. "For me and the chickens," he agreed, leading the way across an unevenly paved patio and through a sweep of bifold doors into a big kitchen. Evidently the renovations had started here, as while it still had a stone-flagged floor and a deep double butler sink, the cabinets were too uniform to be anything but new, and the worktops were smooth, polished wood. A big gas cooking range was tucked into an alcove that would probably have once been for a hearth, and a long, scrubbed wood kitchen table stood in the middle of the room. A clutter of papers, charging cables, and mysterious pipes and attachments filled one end of the table, along with a discarded pizza box.

Rory kicked his wellies off at the door, waving at Adams to keep her boots on, then filled the kettle at the sink, not without some difficulty. It was full of discarded mugs already. He rinsed a couple off and said, "I'd say it's the staff's day off, but that sounds unbearably posh, doesn't it?"

"Unlike the country house," she pointed out.

"Well, you've seen it now," he said.

"I do see why opening it to tourists wasn't an option."

He grinned, drying the mugs. "Yeah, it wouldn't really be up to that standard even if bits didn't keep falling off." He looked around. "I do actually have someone come in and clean once a week, but I think she's going to fire me. Coffee or tea?"

"Ah – neither. I spotted a camera down by the brewery. Any chance I could take a look at the footage?"

"Sure. Is this to do with Alistair being missing?"

"Among other things. Had you heard he was struggling at all?"

Rory frowned, dabbing at his knuckles with a cloth. "Struggling how? He always made his rent, if that's what you mean."

"Personally. As in, would it seem likely he'd need to step back for a break due to stress?"

"Not that I know of. But you know how it is. Some of the stigma's gone, but if you're suggesting it was a mental health issue, I don't know that he'd have felt comfortable enough to talk to me. I'm still his landlord." He shrugged. "Also, guys, you know?"

Adams nodded. She hadn't really expected anything else. She was still hovering on the threshold, and she glanced outside as Rory abandoned the mugs and unearthed a laptop from under a drift of invoices. Dandy was sprawled on the roof of a dilapidated greenhouse, having a staring contest with the border collies, and she couldn't tell if it was friendly or not.

"What date do you want?" Rory asked, as the laptop powered up.

"Start with this morning, just before ten," she said, coming to stand next to him as he logged into the cameras and started scrolling through files.

"What happened this morning?"

"Maybe nothing."

"I can see why you want to look at it." He clicked through the files, pulling up the right ones. "Here it is." They were looking at the front of the brewery, the angle suggesting it had been taken from the camera Collins had spotted in the trees. It showed both the lane and the brewery's front doors, and as Rory skipped the frames forward people emerged and vanished, all in the Niddered Ale T-shirts. Then, just as the clock ran a few minutes past ten, a slim figure appeared on the lane.

"Stop," Adams said. "Play from there."

Chloe stopped in the lane, hands cradled in front of her as if she were holding something, watching the brewery with a curious tilt to her head. She didn't move for a while, just stood there until one of the workers waved at her. She waved back immediately, smiling, one hand still staying in that cradled position, and Adams said, "Can you zoom in on her hands?"

"Not a lot," Rory said. He tried, pausing the recording, and it pixellated before they could see what she was carrying. There was only a vague suggestion of something that seemed to be brown-ish. "Phone?" Rory suggested.

"Maybe," Adams said. "Keep playing."

Chloe walked toward the brewery, putting whatever she

was holding into her jacket pocket as Marcus emerged from inside. He offered her a cup, which she took but didn't drink from, and they stood talking for a while, Chloe glancing back down the lane every now and then.

Marcus pointed into the brewery. Chloe shook her head, waving a couple of people ahead of her. She took a seat at a table, taking her phone out and checking it.

"I don't think she was holding her phone before," Rory said. "She just took that from her back pocket."

"Could be," Adams said.

The second time that Marcus pointed at the brewery, Chloe had a look at her phone, then nodded. They vanished inside.

"Okay, fast forward till she comes back out," Adams said.

Rory skipped the frames forward, both of them peering at the screen as they watched more beer tasters begin to arrive, and the workers scuttling in and out finishing setting up and welcoming people in. But Chloe didn't come back out, even as the recording ran all the way to the point where Adams' Golf pulled up and she got out.

"Alright, stop there," she said. "Where's everyone parking?"

"Down the lane," he said. "You'd have driven past it on the way in. It's just a field, not an official car park. I opened it up for the tastings so it'd keep the punters out of the way of the other businesses."

"I don't suppose you've got a camera there?" she asked.

He shook his head. "No, it's not really been used before. I just have cameras covering the drive and fronts of the buildings in case of break-ins or anything. I can take a look at those, too, if you want?"

"Do they show any other ways out of the brewery?"

"There isn't one. I mean, there's the loading doors, which the cameras don't cover, but she'd still need to come back down the main drive to leave." He clicked into another screen anyway, humming softly to himself.

Adams took both mobiles from her pocket, started to tap Collins' number into her new one, then stopped. She had no idea how Isha had got into her phone, and while she imagined simply calling Collins wasn't going to pose any risk, certain aspects of technology were more mysterious than charms to her. She looked at Rory, who was flicking through the other cameras to trace Chloe's walk from the car to the brewery. "Can I use your phone?"

He looked at the two mobiles in her hands. "You've broken both of them?"

"Small issue with hacking. I bought a burner, but I don't really want to use it too much, in case that one gets picked up too."

"Of course," he said, handing her a glossy black mobile. "Get mine hacked instead. Absolutely no problems."

"You don't have a landline?"

"No. And it's fine. Sure you don't want that cuppa?"

"I'm not really a tea person."

"I've got coffee." He pointed to the corner, where a large, stainless steel espresso machine stood, gleaming quietly in the shadows.

"Well, in that case, yes. Thanks."

Rory busied himself with the machine while she tapped Collins' number into the phone, stepping out onto the patio with it.

It had barely rung twice before Collins answered. "DI Collins."

"It's Adams."

"Ay-up, Adams," he said, the relief evident in his voice. "I've been trying to call you. Thought you'd maybe fallen in a barrel."

She ignored that. "Listen, I'm using someone else's phone.

Call me back from the office landline." She hung up before he could say anything else, and a moment later Rory's mobile rang.

"What the hell's going on?" Collins demanded.

"My phone's been hacked. Odds are it's Isha, and she's probably just targeting me, but ..."

"But Niddered Ale."

"Exactly. I have no idea how this stuff works, but if she got in through the network at the station, your phone could be compromised too."

"You really need to get better at break-ups, Adams."

"It wasn't a break-up."

"Ghosting is no better, as you're evidently discovering. So what's up?"

"Chloe McGill's the owner of The Occult Onion in Leeds. I don't know her home address, but I need you to see if you can find what car she drives and get me the number plate."

"Should be able to do that."

She could hear him scribbling something on the other end of the line. "Grab yourself a pay-as-you-go phone and message me on this number." She spieled the number off the SIM card pack that was still in her pocket. "Don't connect it to the wi-fi."

"Got it. What's happened to Chloe?"

"I was late arriving after the whole hacking thing came up, and she went into the brewery. She doesn't seem to have come out."

"That doesn't sound good."

"No. What's happening there? Why were you trying to reach me?"

"Maud went out for coffee and came back having threatened to arrest three people for jaywalking, one for using his phone on speaker in a public place, and one for wearing those barefoot shoes in town."

"The ones with the toes?"

"Those are them."

"I kind of see her point."

"Maybe, but she's currently sitting in her office trying not to look at anything. She told me she has this feeling that she can fix *everything* if she just enforces the rules enough."

"And Jules?"

"She may have succeeded in scaring PC McCleod even more than you do."

Adams snorted. "I suppose that's something, but it's not looking good, is it?"

"No. I've been trying to round up everyone who had the beer, see how they're doing."

"And?"

"And we have one sixty-year-old sergeant shouting *hi-ya* and kicking everything like they've been watching Karate Kid, a constable who's turned the meeting room into what looks like a serial killer's lair, and has so far traced every crime in the last ten years back to one five-year-old girl, three others I'm seriously worried are going to start a riot, plus a sergeant and another constable who've simply vanished."

"Great." She rubbed a hand over her face. "Anything from Thompson?"

"Not so far. Where are you?"

She started to say *the brewery* just as Rory leaned out of the kitchen and called, "Milk or sugar?"

"Neither," she said.

"Who's that?" Collins asked, and she could hear the grin in his voice. "Are you having coffee with your fellow posh person?"

"I'm not posh, and I'm just having a coffee while I wait for you to get that number. So the sooner you get back to me with it, the sooner I can leave." She hung up and looked at

Rory as he emerged from the kitchen with a mug in each hand. She could smell it from here, dark and rich and full of the promise of, if not energy, at least some form of motivation.

"Grab a seat," Rory said, nodding at the outside table. "This is a great spot. If I face the fields I can't see what part of the house is going to fall off next."

Adams took her coffee and sat down, wishing she could deal with the bits falling off this case just as effectively.

# 15

## WOLFY AT TIMES

By the time Adams had finished her coffee, Collins had texted the details of Chloe's car to her. She left Rory to continue swearing at his non-alcoholic still, managing not to mention the fact that it smelled like a stray match could result in more dead chickens.

"I'll keep you a bottle," he said as he walked her to her car.

"I think I'll let you test it on someone else first," she said, and he shook his head.

"Admit to one small explosion and no one trusts you anymore."

Adams drove back down to the collection of outbuildings, paying attention to the little printed *parking this way* signs now. They were stuck to gardening stakes and jammed into the verges, and she'd been so intent on getting to the brewery to meet Chloe she hadn't paid much attention to them on the way in. In fact, she'd driven right past the designated field. There were only half a dozen cars in it, all huddled under a strip of shade cast by a large tree. No one seemed to be monitoring it or directing anything, so she simply drove in and pulled up behind the cars, leaning over the wheel as she examined them. No old green Vauxhall Astra. She double-checked the plate number on her phone anyway, in case witches had ways of disguising their cars, but there wasn't even a remote match.

Adams sat there for a moment longer, fingers tapping on the wheel, then got out and circled the field. She wasn't sure what she was looking for, exactly. The ground was dry after a surprisingly hot summer, and even if she'd been able to find tyre tracks, she had nothing to match them to. But sometimes just walking settled things into place, the mind clearing and connections rising to the surface as the clutter settled. She supposed it was *possible* Chloe could, for some reason, have crept out of the brewery via the loading doors then ducked into the woods, so avoiding all the cameras. She could've then circled the buildings, got back to her car, and driven off. And Adams had been calling her from the pay-as-you-go, so maybe she didn't answer unknown numbers for personal, witchy reasons.

All of that was unlikely, but not impossible. And what was the other option? Marcus had realised what Chloe was up to, jumped her in front of however many punters were already at the tasting, then bundled her into a van pulled up to the storeroom? Or he had some other, hidden room Adams had yet to find? Maybe, but how to find out? She looked around for Dandy, but he'd vanished while she was having her coffee, leaving Rory's dogs whining, and hadn't reappeared since she'd left.

A message beeped onto her phone. *It's Collins. New number.*

*Got it,* she texted back. *Can you check any vans registered to NA, or used by them? Thinking they may have moved something.* Which was both vague enough to be confusing to Collins, and probably not vague enough to throw off anyone snooping. She sighed. Not being able to use her phone properly was really very limiting.

*Imagine me sending a thumbs up*, came back.

She'd circled back to the cars, and now she rubbed the back of her neck, feeling the tension in it as she wondered what to do next. Movement in the next field caught her eyes, the long grass parting, and Dandy bounded toward her, setting wildflowers shivering over his head. He jumped the wooden fence enclosing the field easily and loped over to join her, looking up at her with his dreadlocks falling away from his red eyes.

Adams checked no one was around, then gave his head a good scratch. "Alright, you. I wondered where you'd got to."

"He got to me," a new voice said, and she looked up to see a dishevelled Thompson following Dandy over the fence, his ears back. His fur was damp in places, standing out in strange directions, and there were bits of grass stuck to it.

"What happened to you?"

"Your *mutt* happened to me," Thompson spat.

Adams took another quick glance down the lane, making sure no one was about to wander over and see her talking to either an invisible dog or a cat. "What d'you mean?"

"I was just minding my own business, doing a little surveillance on some imps, and the next thing that stinking animal dragged me off by the scruff of my neck. The *scruff!* I am *not* a kitten."

Adams looked at Dandy, who was chewing on some grass, presumably to take the taste of cat out of his mouth. "Sorry. I think he was just trying to help."

"It did not help me. Fright of it just about lost me another life, you want to know the truth. I don't know how he travels, but it's not the same as how a cat travels, and I do *not* want to experience that again."

Adams frowned. "But you do the whole teleportation thing."

"Again, it's not science fiction. Cats don't *teleport*. It's magic. Cats step out of the world and back in again somewhere else. Simple as that."

"Right. And this was different how?"

Thompson shuddered. "I don't even want to think about it. The Inbetween's bad enough, but what he just dragged me through …" He looked down at himself. "I feel like my atoms have all come apart and gone back together again, and I might have bits of dog in me."

"That's teleportation, then," Adams said, and the cat huffed.

"What do you *want?*"

"Did you find out anything about the beer or the brewery?"

"Not yet. Humans acting up aren't a huge concern for the Watch, as long as they're not stumbling across Folk. No one's been interested enough to see what's going on."

"Handy."

Thompson narrowed his eyes at her. "The Watch is responsible for keeping the Folk and human worlds separate, not for babysitting booze-addled humans. Is that all you set your mutt on me for?"

Adams felt the problem was more likely that cats were astonishingly selective regarding what they deemed to be their responsibility, and, going by the one cat she was acquainted with, it tended to be whatever they felt like on the day. Aloud, though, she just said, "I need some help with something else."

"Astonishing. You mean your utter refusal to learn about the Folk world hasn't paid off?"

She scowled at him. "I've learned plenty."

"Mostly by falling into it," the cat pointed out, and she

crossed her arms. She couldn't actually argue, though. She'd watched *Game of Thrones* in the name of research, only to be roundly told off about how it was a grotesque misrepresentation of dragons. She'd kind of given up after that.

"Will you help, or do I need to get Dandy to throw you back?" she asked.

The cat gave a long-suffering sigh. "Tell me what the problem is."

"We're missing someone. She went into the brewery and doesn't seem to have come back out. And she must've driven here, but there's no car that matches hers."

"She borrowed a car?"

"Still doesn't explain how we've got her on camera going into the brewery but not coming out."

"*Hmm.* Alright. What do you expect me to do, though? I'm not a tracking dog. Get Loathsome Lassie on it."

Adams looked at Dandy, who was chasing a butterfly across the field. He went through the fence and vanished into the long grass, without jumping or otherwise navigating it. He was just on one side, then on the other, with no in between. "He doesn't take direction well," she said.

"Neither do cats," Thompson replied, grooming himself. He made a gagging sound. "*Gross.* I've got hellhound slobber on me."

"It doesn't matter if you can't track her. I want you to see if she's still in the brewery, and also tell me about the workers there. I don't think they're entirely human."

"Plenty of people aren't entirely human," he said around a mouthful of fur. "Humans are just very human-centric in their assumptions, and get a bit funny when things aren't just as they think they should be."

"I'm not being funny. I'm worried about Chloe, and it might be relevant to know who's running the brewery."

"And how do you think knowing that's going to help you?" Thompson asked.

"I'm not sure," she admitted. "But I also thought you might do better than me at having a nose around. I tried, but I couldn't spot anywhere she could be being held, and I can't get in there unnoticed. You're better at all that."

"Flattery doesn't get you as far as some decent trout," the cat said, twitching his ears.

She sighed. "Trout can be arranged. But this is in your interests too, you know. If part of your deal is keeping humans and Folk separate, then making sure these brewers aren't some sort of Folk trapping witches and using them to fire their stills comes under your jurisdiction."

Thompson examined her. "Whatever TV shows you're watching, you should do less of it."

"I don't need to watch TV shows. I'm police. I can think of much worse things that could've happened to her, and it's my fault she was here at all. So please – will you help?"

Thompson gave a little huff then stood and shook himself off. "Fine. But it better be organic, hand-caught trout. And you can come too. Be a distraction if anyone spots me."

They left the car where it was and walked back toward the brewery, Adams retracing the steps she imagined Chloe had taken. She looked for more cameras as she walked, spotting them tucked up high on the buildings' eaves, or strapped to trees like the one by the brewery. There weren't a huge amount of them, and given the poor quality of the picture Rory had shown her, she had a feeling his security budget was as stretched as his one for house repairs evidently was.

Thompson kept to the fields, appearing on fenceposts and vanishing again, until they reached the trees near the brewery, where he faded away. Dandy had walked up the lane with Adams, dwindling in size all the way, and by the time he darted off into the trees after the cat he wasn't much bigger than Thompson was. Adams leaned against the nearest fence, watching the little crowd in front of the brewery. The place was hardly doing a roaring trade, but it wasn't lunchtime yet, and it was midweek. She had an idea that by Friday the whole area would be heaving, and the Harrogate police would be well above quota on their traffic stops.

Marcus emerged from the shadows, glanced over at her and smiled immediately, giving that big, white-toothed grin. He took two beers from a crate and popped the tops off, then walked over to join her.

"Non-alcoholic for the inspector," he said, offering it to her. The label read *Dixon's Wonkybrau*, and had a grinning donkey on it.

"No thanks."

"Suit yourself." He swigged from the other bottle, and they both surveyed the brewery. "Have you found your friend yet?"

"Not yet."

"You still think she's here somewhere? Think we've stuffed her in a vat or something?"

Adams regarded him, trying to get the *feel* of him. It was ridiculously frustrating, like a splinter evading tweezers. If she could just put a name to what he was, then it felt as if everything might fall into place. "Have you?" she asked, and he laughed, taking another mouthful of beer.

"That would definitely get Food and Hygiene's knickers in a twist."

Adams nodded. She couldn't see Thompson or Dandy, but they seemed to share a similar disdain for the laws of the universe as she understood them, so she had to assume they were inside. Or hope they were, anyway.

She tipped her face up to the sun and waited.

Marcus kept trying to talk to her, and she put up with it as long as she could, then finally told him to call her if Chloe turned up. She still hadn't seen the cat or the dandy, so she walked back to the car alone. Unless they'd ended up in a vat, they'd meet her there.

As it turned out, they'd beaten her to it. Dandy was sprawled under a tree in the shade, belly turned up, and Thompson was a couple of metres away, where the tree's shadow thinned and turned dappled with sunlight. Both of them seemed to be asleep, and she slapped her hand against the side of her car. Dandy rolled straight to his feet with a strangled bark of alarm, and Thompson opened one eye.

"How long have you been here?" she demanded.

"Oh, we came straight back."

"You didn't even go in?"

Thompson closed his eyes again. "Didn't even cross the boundary charms, which are *everywhere*, by the way."

"Super helpful, both of you. I was stuck there talking to Marcus for ages." Talking to him, and wasting time when she could've been looking for Chloe.

"I didn't need to get any closer. I knew what they were from halfway down the lane, but I had to make myself scarce. Didn't want them catching a whiff of me."

"And you couldn't have checked inside for Chloe?"

Thompson opened his eyes properly. "The whole place is shift-locked, meaning I'd have to walk in. And I wouldn't have survived two minutes if any of them had caught my scent. Someone would have had my head off before you could say *organically brewed*."

"What?"

The cat looked at Dandy. "Your mutt there's got the right idea as well. He wasn't going anywhere near the place and risk them sniffing him out."

"You think they can see him?"

"Not as they are now. Not even most Folk can see dandies. It's only those who are meant to, and the really old ones like dragons. Sometimes sorcerers, but not even always them. As they get older, their senses get more attuned, so sometimes they can."

"You can see him."

"Of course. Cats see the world as it is, not as we want it to be, and that includes seeing invisible demon mutts. Most animals are like that."

Dandy huffed.

Adams pinched the bridge of her nose. "So we're no further forward with Chloe. Can you tell me *anything* helpful?"

"Sure," Thompson said, yawning. "It's run by weres."

Adams stared at him. "Wheres?"

"Yeah, you know, human some of the time, wolfy other times."

"*Werewolves?* Humans that change into wolves at the full moon?"

"No, the full moon thing's a myth. Bit of handy misdirection. They can change whenever they want. They have a bit more of a struggle staying human at full moon because the moon gets in your blood, but that's the same for all kinds. Everyone goes a bit bonkers at the full moon."

Adams looked back up the lane as if she might see wolves sprinting down it, but it was empty. She looked back at Thompson. "So, would these be like the werewolves at the farm the other month?"

Thompson bared his teeth at her. "Look, there were charms on the house, slaughtered livestock – of course I thought they were weres."

"They were dogs, though," she pointed out.

"Weres are basically dogs, except for the fact that they're smart, mercenary, and know what cats really are, so there's no way I'm setting foot in that place. Weres and the Watch do not get on."

"Just because they're a bit like dogs?"

"No, we've got history."

Adams raised her eyebrows, and he sighed. "I'm not your personal tutor, you know? Read some books."

"Not a lot of time between now and trying to get Chloe back from werewolves."

"Weres. Put it this way – the Watch has been pretty extreme over the years. There are certain factions that think we still should be, and some of those think weres are an abomination. They're well known as being for hire when people don't want to get their own hands dirty, which means there have been *incidents*, and now the weres stay well away from the Watch, and we stay well away from them."

"Incidents?" Adam said.

"Weres have, at times, been sent against the Watch's interests by their employers." Thompson hesitated, then added, "And, like I say, a lot of the old school just don't like canines. Whole packs have been wiped out simply for being weres."

"That's horrific."

"Yeah, the weres think so too. I don't disagree, but I also don't feel like having the sins of my ancestors taken out on me. And that *will* happen if they find me on their territory. Not even sure your Dandy would do too well against a whole pack of weres."

Adams reached out to Dandy, and he leaned against her legs. No wonder he'd stayed hidden. "Good dog," she said quietly.

"Doubly so, although I hate to say it. Your pretty were at the brewery is as confused by you as you are by him. Your scent is strange. It's human but not, and he won't have smelled anything like it before. But if Dandy had showed himself, he'd know *exactly* what you are."

"I'm just police," she muttered, and the cat looked at the sky.

"Sure you are. But fine. Go in all police-like."

"I've got no grounds for a warrant."

"That doesn't stop you going in," Thompson pointed out.

"I went in. I had a tour, even, but I can't exactly ask them to show me their secret dungeon, can I?"

"Who said anything about asking?" the cat said.

Adams shook her head. "I can't just go in and search somewhere without a warrant."

"You need to stop thinking in purely human terms. You're working against people who don't think of *you* in that way – or won't for long, anyway – and if you keep putting limits on yourself your little chocolate tricks aren't going to help you." His eyes were glittering in the bright sun, and Adams rubbed her forehead.

"Do I want to know how you know about the chocolate?"

"I told you. You're attracting attention, Adams. That's happening whether you want to admit to being not just police or not, so I'd get comfortable with admitting it fast."

She hated that. She couldn't even explain how much she hated that. It was worse than the word *magic*, the idea that, when police was what she'd always been, that she was suddenly *not just police*, with everything that entailed.

But arguing with a talking cat was hardly reassuring either.

# 16

# RUNNING DOWN THE OPTIONS

ADAMS WASN'T TOO SURE WHERE TO GO FROM THERE. COLLINS was tracking vans, but Chloe still being inside the brewery somewhere remained the most likely option. If there was another room, something behind the office, or hidden among the vats, they needed to find it, and since Thompson couldn't get in and sniff around, it was down to her.

But practically, she couldn't do anything until the brewery had closed for the day, and officially she couldn't do it at all. Which meant keeping Collins away from the place so if anything went wrong she didn't drag him down on her hunch, and also not going back to Skipton where Maud could suddenly decide to flex her by-the-book superpowers.

She joined Thompson and Dandy in the shade and called Collins.

"Anything your end?" she asked when he answered.

"The brewery has one van registered to it."

"I've seen at least two," she said, frowning.

"The others may be rentals."

"How about Marcus Gallagher? What did you get on him?"

"Very little. Or rather, a small assortment of Marcus Gallaghers, none of whom raise any flags. More details would be needed to see if he is who he says he is."

Adams sighed, then thought of the red BMW. "Try his car. Number plate …." She hesitated, trying to remember, then looked at the cat. "Pop back and get the number of that red BMW?"

Thompson blinked at her lazily. "Cats can't see red."

"The BMW, then."

"Not much up on car makes, either."

"It has a little round logo thingy on the boot and bonnet that's divided into blue and white quarters. How's that?"

He huffed. "Fine." He got up, stretched, took one step forward and simply ceased to be, the grass not even bent where his paws had been.

"Is that Thompson?" Collins asked.

"Yeah, for all the help he is."

"He couldn't tell you anything?"

"Apparently there's no one on his side worried about the brewery. I asked him to take a look himself, but he wouldn't go in."

"Not into beer?"

"Not into werewolves." She listened to the silence on the other end of the line.

Finally Collins said, "Actual ones?"

"Apparently."

He was silent for a little longer, then said, "And you think Chloe might've been kidnapped by werewolves."

"I don't know. But if Thompson can't go in, I need to. I did a tour, but of course I didn't see anything useful."

Collins sighed. "You know no one's going to give us a warrant."

"I know. But on the cameras I can see she went in, then didn't come out again. *Something* happened."

"We need more than that. Especially with Harrogate and Leeds complaining about us already, and Maud ... Well, Maud just suspended PC McCleod for using a blue pen instead of black. I thought the poor lad was going to cry."

"We can't *get* any more without getting in there. And whatever we get ... it's not police stuff, Collins. We're not going to find any bloody fungus in the beer. Not even warts."

"W-o-r-t-s?"

"Whatever. But you know we can't prove anything, and we need to fix this. Or I do, anyway."

"You're still police, Adams."

She wished she believed him. That part of her world seemed to be drifting, not quite within reach anymore, less real than talking cats and artisan werewolves. "I can't just leave Chloe," she said. "The only reason she's involved is because I asked for her help."

"Sure," Collins said. "I get that. But don't listen to that bloody cat too much, alright? I think he's a bad influence."

"Excuse *me*," Thompson said, appearing so close to Dandy that he *whuff*ed and jumped backward. "I'm only braving were-infested forests for you."

"It's a country estate," Adams pointed out.

"Even so. D'you want that number plate?"

"Yes. Tell him." She put the phone on speaker and bent down, holding it out to Thompson as he reeled off the letters and numbers. It sounded close enough to what Adams remembered that she thought he'd found the right car. Whether he'd got the number right was another question, but she didn't feel that going back to the brewery a third time herself was sensible. Not if Marcus, for the moment, still thought she was only police and therefore wouldn't be looking for anything more than a human answer to the beer issue. It gave her a tiny advantage for now, but the more she was around the more likely he was to literally sniff out the truth of her.

"Got it," Collins said. "I'll run that. What're you up to now?"

"Getting trout," Thompson said.

"I want to check in with James," Adams said. "See if there's been anything new happening there."

"Fine. Just keep your head down, alright? We seem to have every DCI in the area getting scratchy."

"Yeah, coincidental that, isn't it?"

"Meow," Thompson said, and she stared at him.

"What—"

"Ay-up. That place does a right good brew, doesn't it?" a cheery voice called.

Adams straightened up hurriedly, taking the phone off speaker. "Um, yes," she said to the two men heading for a glossy Skoda in the middle of the parked cars. They were both clutching crates to their substantial bellies, and with their red noses and close-shaved heads they looked oddly similar, like beer-loving versions of Tweedledum and Tweedledee.

"Not sure you should be driving, though, love," one of them said. "Not if you're making phone calls for a cat." They both laughed, and Thompson half closed his eyes.

"It's … a joke. With my friend."

"Whatever you say," the second man said, and they both laughed again, loading the car up and climbing in. Adams watched them go, wondering if she should intervene, but they both seemed steady enough.

"Adams?" Collins asked.

"Yeah, sorry. Small interruption."

"It's fine. I've got the registered address for the car. Want it?"

"Definitely," she said, and scribbled it in her notebook as he reeled it off. "Thanks."

She hung up before he could tell her not to go out there on her own. It wasn't like she was going to go in, after all. Just see if it looked like any brewers or witches were being held prisoner. Although he'd have had to be quick off the mark to sneak Chloe away and get back again.

It was something to do, though, while she waited for the brewery to close for the day. And it should keep her out of the way of any other police. She hoped.

THE ADDRESS the car was registered to was, her GPS informed her, in a village on the outskirts of York. She supposed that worked quite well, as she had yet to upset anyone from the York station that she knew of. This way she could make a hat trick of it.

It wasn't a long drive, and it was A-road all the way, smooth and mostly straight, with none of the bottlenecks and squeezes – and tractors – of the B-roads. The village itself was called Nether Poppleton, which sounded like it belonged on either a children's programme or one of those somewhat suggestive 1970s BBC comedies. It was all detached and semi-detached houses with smooth green lawns and old trees and substantial garages. In other words, the glossy red BMW made sense.

The address itself was on the edge of the village, where farmland rolled up to the back garden, and was a fairly plain red brick detached house, two storeys with white window frames and a garden that needed a little more TLC than it was currently getting. It was neither scruffy enough to attract comment nor flash enough to, and there was nothing about it that screamed *werewolf den*. Not that she was even sure what would. Piles of bones and some chew toys, perhaps?

Adams parked across the road, leaving the engine on, and examined the front of the house. Thompson was still with her, and he put his paws on the door to peer out the side window. Dandy had been relegated to the back seat, where he was currently sulking.

"Anything?" Adams asked the cat.

He gave her a narrow look. "I'm across the street in a car with the windows up. D'you think I have x-ray vision?"

She shrugged. "I don't know how you sense charms."

"Oh, there'll be plenty of those. Don't need to sense them."

She looked at the house for a moment longer, then turned the engine off and opened the door.

"What're you doing?" Thompson demanded.

"Going to look in the window."

"Great. Then when wolfman gets back he can sniff you out instantly."

Adams hesitated. He had a point. But she wound the cat's window down then got out anyway, going to the boot.

"I'm not coming in," Thompson called. "You're on your own."

Adams opened the bin bags and pulled out her wellies, which she hadn't used since they'd had to deal with a pig farmer whose competitor had vanished. There had been a certain amount of poking around in unsavoury things, since pigs really could be as violently ravenous in reality as half a dozen thrillers had made them out to be. They hadn't found the competitor, who, it turned out, was in a bit of a financial sinkhole and had staged the whole thing. She'd borrowed some protective coveralls for the poking around, and they were still tightly bundled up inside multiple bin bags with her wellies. She should've got rid of them earlier.

"Gods, what's that *stink?*" Thompson called.

"Shouldn't you be keeping your mouth shut?" Adams asked him, rather more quietly, as she reluctantly pulled the coveralls on, trying not to gag. Dandy whined from the back seat.

"Can you see anyone around here?"

She didn't answer. She was trying not to breathe too much as she zipped the coveralls up and pulled her wellies on. She hadn't thought it'd be possible for pig muck to smell any worse dry than it did fresh, but she now had evidence it really could.

Still breathing as shallowly as possible, and trying not to let her hands come in contact with the coveralls any more than they had to, she crossed the road to Marcus's house, letting herself in the gate. She assumed the cat was right about the charms, but she felt nothing more here than she had at the brewery, and she just hoped they didn't work as an alarm system (she supposed, if they were the same as the brewery ones, that they didn't, given the amount of people traipsing in and out there), or that she had enough time to get out if they did. She knocked on the front door, a quick, breezy rap, and when there was no answer she went around the side of the house, into the back garden. It was in the same state of gentle neglect as the front, the lawn festooned with nodding dandelions and the flowerbeds a wilderness of weeds and blowsy blossoms gone to seed. A garden shed with a broken window stood near the back fence, and over it fields rolled toward the River Ouse where it bordered the village. She supposed it would be quite a good place if one spent part of the time as a wolf. Lots of room to run.

She knocked on the back door, but there was still no answer, and she stepped back to examine the house. She wasn't sure what she'd been hoping for. A sign saying *captives this way*? Someone yelling from inside? One of Chloe's witchy earrings on the path? There was nothing, and she couldn't break in. She had even less reason to believe anyone was being held here than she did at the brewery, and she wasn't ready to go fully rogue yet. Besides, the stink of pig muck would be a bit of a giveaway that someone had been here.

She checked the shed, but it was empty except for the abandoned debris that collects in every garden shed. Empty plastic plant pots and cobwebbed rakes and crumpled gardening gloves like sloughed animal skins. She banged on the back door, listening carefully for anything from inside, but it was silent, and she circled back to the front on the other side of the house.

"Are you alright there?" someone called, and she looked around to see an older man with a neatly buttoned cardigan watching her over the fence, a frown on his face.

"Yes, thanks," she said. "Just seeing if anyone's home."

"It's usually pretty quiet in the day," he said. "Astonishing, really."

"Why's that?"

He looked around, and put both hands on top of the fence so he could hiss, "It's *overrun* at nights. I think he's running an illegal boarding house. All sorts in there!"

"Oh? How do you mean?"

"Well, they can't all be his family. I mean, he's … some of them are quite *foreign*."

"Oh?" she said again, reminding herself that she might get something useful out of him if she could manage not to be rude for a moment.

"Yes. I think they're probably illegal." He hesitated, looking her up and down, his frown deepening. "You *sound* English. You're not—"

"How many would you say is a lot, sir?" she asked, but he was still inspecting her.

"What did you say you were doing again? And what's that *smell?*"

Adams pulled her phone from her pocket, finding the photo of Alistair she'd saved off the brewery website. She turned the phone so the man could see it. "Have you seen this man?"

"No. Is he illegal? He looks like he could be foreign."

Adams found Chloe's contact card and showed him that photo. "And her?"

"No. She looks a bit rough. Who are you again?"

"Just looking for some people," she replied, putting her phone back. "Thanks for your help."

"Are you from immigration? I heard they were doing sweeps." He was clutching the top of the fence still, fingers tight with anticipation, and suddenly the stink of the coveralls was too much to stand.

"Thanks," she said again, and headed back to the car.

"Are you undercover?" he called after her. "I won't tell anyone!"

She felt a sudden sympathy for the werewolves. Persecuted by cats and dealing with neighbours like that. No wonder they got a bit bitey.

THOMPSON COMPLAINED SO MUCH about the stench that she ended up driving back to Harrogate with the windows down. Admittedly, she could still smell pig muck on herself, too, and she stopped at a lay-by to stuff the coveralls into a bin and slather her arms with hand sanitiser before bundling her wellies in an extra two bin bags, just to be on the safe side. Then she leaned on the car and punched James's number into her new phone.

"DC James Hamilton," he answered, his voice strained.

"It's Adams," she said. "You alright?"

"*Adams,*" he said, her name coming out in a sigh of relief. "I've been trying to get hold of you."

"Yeah, small issue with my phone."

"Did Isha hack it?"

"Um. Yes. I think so, anyway."

"She's gone *completely* rogue," he said, his voice low. "Although, half the station has, to be fair. Temper's never in his office, just appears now and then, lurking in a corner, then vanishes again."

"Weird," Adams said, although she felt she could probably use that word a bit more sparingly now. Hunting werewolves in a pig muck disguise was currently winning in her stakes of weirdness.

"It gets better. Check the socials for *masked vigilante Leeds.*"

"What?"

"Just take a look."

"I can't. No smartphone."

"Oh. Well, someone's been going around in a cloak and a mask, stopping muggers and busting car thieves over the head with a cricket bat. I'm pretty sure it's Temper. He turned up with a black eye this morning, and he keeps muttering about *cleaning this town up.*"

Adams pinched the bridge of her nose. "Great."

"I know. So have you made any progress? It was the beer, wasn't it? Some sort of contaminant?"

"I think so, and I'm working on it." She took a breath. "You said Isha's gone fully rogue. How bad?"

"Bad. Troy just had all his bank accounts frozen. And she's been putting everyone's Tinder messages on the station forum."

"Ouch."

"Exactly. And I have no idea what to do." There was tremor in his voice, and Adams sighed.

"I promise I'm working on it. You just keep your head down and try to keep out of everyone's way."

"Isn't there anything I can do to help things along? We need to get back to normal soon, or the whole bloody place is going to fall apart."

She thought about it, trying to decide what would keep him relatively out of harm's way. "Just try to make sure no one's doing anything that's going to get out. Last thing we need is a huge public mess."

"I can try."

"Good man," she said. "And eat more Yorkies."

She hung up and looked at the cat, who'd jumped to the roof of the car while she'd been talking. Dandy was standing on the bonnet, looking put out, and she scratched his ears.

"So?" Thompson said.

She didn't answer at once. She hadn't found anything else out. Chloe was still missing. The beer was still affecting everyone. She'd exhausted all the possibilities. All the *official* possibilities, anyway. She checked her watch. The afternoon was wearing on, but it wasn't late enough yet.

"I'm going to have a look at the festival," she said. "See what the brewery tent looks like and all that."

"And then?"

"And then we'll see," she said, getting back into the car. Although she already knew.

Then it'd be time to try the unofficial route.

# TECHNICALLY ILLEGAL ACTIVITY

Back in Harrogate, the already trickling traffic had all but congealed. Adams figured there was a good reason most festivals were held on the outskirts of town and not on the Stray. The old streets simply didn't have the capacity to cope with the festival-goers as well as the residents, and she gave up before she even caught a glimpse of the marquees, leaving her car in a pub car park at the far end of the Stray. A large A-frame blackboard promised free tasters of Niddered Ale the following day, and she frowned at it, then turned toward the festival grounds. There was nothing she could do about that yet.

The Stray was a long, roughly rectangular green, bordered with roads and sliced crossways by them in a couple of places. Adams walked its length, passing a football game that was being cheered wildly by a small group of supporters, the traffic still grumbling away next to her. Joggers crossed the grass, and someone was trying to fly a kite without much success. There was enough wind, but Adams had an idea they'd put something together backward. A couple of passersby had a near miss as it plunged to the earth. Thompson walked next to her, hissing at dogs, and Dandy sprinted across the green with his dreadlocks flying, in pursuit of pigeons.

The marquees had multiplied, spreading like a fairy circle, and Adams had the same sense of unreality when she looked at them, as if she'd stumbled into something that wasn't meant for her. The bonfire of the night before didn't seem to have done any damage, the barrels tidied away and the space in the centre of the marquees cleared. Picnic tables and benches ringed it, and a small stage had been set up at one end. Music was already drifting from its speakers, something innocuous and quiet, and people hurried between vans and the stalls with trolleys, carting kegs and clinking crates and boxes of paper plates and napkins. The barriers were still in place, signs at regular intervals reading, *Open 5 p.m.!*, but Adams simply walked through a gap without being challenged. No one was monitoring it.

She stopped in the shelter of one of the marquees to watch the workers setting up. There was nothing she could put her finger on, no one scuttling about in wizard's robes yelling curses, or hunched figures lurking in hooded cloaks, dropping the contents of mysterious vials into glasses, but there was more here than the usual sense of last-minute tension ahead of an event. The atmosphere was *charged*, as if the pressure was dropping ahead of a storm, and she could almost taste that barely suppressed edge of Friday-night violence once more. Thompson bounced sideways in the swirling gusts of wind that tugged at the canvas of the marquees, making them sag and bellow like the lungs of great beasts.

"Don't like it," the cat hissed.

Adams crouched down to pet him and said quietly, "Anyone here to be worried about?"

"All of them. Particularly the humans. They're always the ones you've got to watch for."

"Unhelpful." She straightened up, tucking her hands into her pockets and deciding she'd just have to do things her way, which meant having a quiet walk around and simply observing, letting the place tell its own story. Places, like people, tended to do that when they were given a chance.

She wound her way through the marquees and food trucks, staying out of the way of the hurrying vendors and workers, noting that they were almost all human. She was surprised by how strange that felt to her. She'd become used to seeing Folk everywhere, but particularly in places like this, in the sort of jobs that gave a certain freedom. But it also made sense. If Marcus and his team – or pack, she supposed – had something planned, she was fairly sure Folk would be staying well clear.

The florists' tent was still violently overgrown, and was now sporting an entire tree spreading its canopy over the roof. It looked rainforest-y, Adams thought, but beyond that she couldn't identify it. Beneath it, though, some sort of order had been established, as jasmine grew in a fragrant, delicate bower around the entrance, and further in she could see the sort of gentle wilderness that made her think of botanical gardens and enchanted forests. In a food truck next door, a butcher specialising in wild game had a hot plate set up to one side of her stall, prices for venison sausages in a bun, boar burgers and rabbit bites on the board behind her. The butcher herself was currently elbow-deep in a vast vat of marinade, massaging what Adams assumed were bits of rabbit with the sort of pleasure that made her feel she was intruding.

She walked on, spotting a skinny man with a long ponytail arguing with a large man who had a plaited beard and a shaved scalp. She went close enough to them to eavesdrop, but the discussion seemed to relate to whether they needed more passionfruit champagne or strawberry spritz on the stall. Marquees were given over to woodworkers and metal-workers, soap makers and clothing designers, all of them restlessly changing around displays and checking stocks, full of the usual anxiety that came with the start of any event. The biggest marquees were allocated to the brewers, though, logos emblazoned on banners and flags, stools and upturned barrels lined up in front of each stall, the brewers shouting good-natured abuse at each other as they stacked cups and checked kegs. There were half a dozen smaller brewers in each of two big marquees, as well as in a couple of vans set up as bars. She couldn't see a stand for Niddered Ale or Dixon's Draughts, but everywhere she looked there were banners and signs for the ale, including hanging over the stage, the movement caused by the wind making the otter's wink lewd and unsettling.

"Bit of a crock, isn't it?" someone said, and she turned to find a slight, older woman with thick white hair pulled back in a ponytail staring up at the banner as well.

"What's that?"

"Everyone else gets one little stand, and they get their logo splashed everywhere? Here *and* in town?"

"How does that work, then?" Adams asked. "They're not that big a brewery, are they?"

"No, but someone's got deep pockets. Town's just about drowning in bloody otter bollocks. Heard they've already been handing out freebies, so I doubt tonight'll be any different. Don't know how the rest of us are going to sell anything with that going on."

"They're sponsoring the show, then?"

"Not officially."

"You think they paid off the organisers?"

The woman shrugged. "I think the rest of us have wasted

our money." She walked off, her back rigid with irritation, and Adams hoped she wouldn't take any free samples from the competition. She didn't like to think how that might end.

Adams kept up her circuit of the field without discovering much more, other than a stressed faun who was rapidly shuttering a coffee truck.

"Any chance of a coffee?" she asked him.

"Closed," he said, not looking at her. He was securing syrups so quickly he was in danger of smashing the bottles, and a cake stand was on its side on the counter, a coffee cake collapsing inside the cover.

"It hasn't even started yet."

"And I'll be out of here before it does," he said, finally looking at her. His eyes narrowed for a moment, and she wondered if he was aware of Dandy with both paws on the counter, his nose twitching toward the machine. Apparently not, though, as the faun turned back to what he was doing, dismissing her.

She left him to it, wandering out through the barriers and looking back at the bustle of activity as if a little distance could give her the perspective she needed to understand what was going on. What was the beer intended *for*? What was the end goal? Was it just to create chaos? There had to be a reason behind it. No one hijacks a brewery, mixes up a load of enchanted ale, rigs a beer festival, and kidnaps a witch just because it seems like fun at the time. She supposed it could all be a money-making thing, creating an addiction to the beer so it was the only thing anyone wanted to drink. But it didn't explain the side effects, and it also simply didn't seem like reason enough. Marcus could've accomplished that without taking over a fairly minor brewery.

She stood there for a while longer, arms crossed over her chest, Dandy sitting to one side of her with his snout raised to the wind, and Thompson on the other, paws pressed together, all three of them watching the slow build of pressure in not just the festival grounds, but the town. She still hadn't seen anyone from Dixon's Draughts, but they wouldn't be much longer. The afternoon was running out, and her patience with it.

EVEN WITH SEPTEMBER starting to make its presence felt, the sunset was in no hurry in the Dales. There was still plenty of light when Adams turned back into Featherstone Estates, passing the informal car park without slowing. It was already empty, the last of the tourists gone, and she drove on a little further before turning down a rough lane she'd spotted while she'd been looking for Chloe's car. A wooden gate with a *No Entry* sign blocked the route, but it wasn't locked, and she was soon bumping gently toward a crumbling stone shepherd's hut that had sprouted a few saplings. She coaxed the car around it, where it'd be hidden from the lane, grateful that it hadn't rained much recently. She didn't fancy getting bogged down in werewolf territory.

"Coming?" she asked Thompson, as she got out and took her pack from the boot, checking she had her torch and baton. She considered her very large stick, but the baton was more subtle.

"I'd rather not. But I will, because I see a dozen ways this is going to go wrong."

Adams clicked her fingers to Dandy, who was investigating the ruins, and for once he left what he was doing and ran to join her immediately. Without any snotty remarks, either. She was more and more sure she was a dog person at heart. She headed across the field with Thompson trailing her and Dandy trotting on ahead. Walking up the drive risked running into someone from the brewery, plus if she kept to the trees and fields she'd be off the cameras. Between potential werewolves and not exactly being on police business, it seemed best to keep as low a profile as she could.

"These boundary charms," she said to the cat as they walked. "Are they like an alarm system? Will they know if we cross them?"

"Unlikely," the cat said. "They're probably basic boundary charms – marking their territory to let other Folk know to stay clear. Trigger charms are high-level magic work."

"You don't think any of them could do it?"

He wrinkled his snout. "They're weres, not magic workers."

"Couldn't they be both?"

The cat stopped and stared up at her, so startled that she looked over her shoulder, in case he'd seen one of the creatures in question creeping up on them. Then he said, "I suppose it's *possible*. But they're basically dogs. They've only so many brain cells to rub together."

Dandy huffed over Thompson's ears, making him jump sideways, spitting as he went.

"You deserved that," Adams said. "So you think we can just walk into the brewery?"

"We *can*," the cat said. "But we better be bloody sure about what we're doing, because they'll know we've been in the moment they get back. They'll have our scent."

Adams suddenly wished she hadn't dumped the pig-fouled coveralls. They sounded better than a werewolf having her scent.

They followed the tree line all the way around the buildings, keeping out of sight of the brewery. The other businesses were already closed, windows dark and parking spaces empty. Adams saw no one until they were peering out from the cover of a hedgerow at the back of the old barn, out of view of Rory's cameras. A van was pulled up to the big double doors that led to the storeroom she'd seen earlier, the interior floor raised a decent distance above the ground outside. A tall woman with broad shoulders was taking crates from a slightly pot-bellied older man as he hefted them down to her. She stacked them effortlessly into the van, muscles moving under her T-shirt. She'd rolled her sleeves up, and her skin was warm brown in the long shadows of the evening.

Adams settled in to watch from the shelter of an oak tree. They didn't have to wait long.

"We're full," the woman said, and the man grunted.

"That'll have to do, then." He looked back inside. "Bloody hell, we've a lot to shift still."

"It's going fast enough once it's out," Marcus said, appearing from the shadows of the storeroom to lean against the doorframe next to the pot-bellied man. "Samir and Ines are dry already."

"You getting them to do another run?" the woman asked.

"Not tonight. Got to leave the punters wanting a bit more," he said, and grinned.

The woman nodded, slamming the van's back doors closed. "We'll head off, then. Get this lot to the grounds."

"Won't be far behind you," Marcus said, and clapped the other man on the back as he jumped to the ground from the storeroom's raised floor.

It was a simple movement, that jump, economical and without flourish, but there was a *flow* to it, an unexpectedly un-human naturalness, that made the breath catch in Adams' throat. She found herself crouching lower behind the tree, making herself smaller and smaller while one hand squeezed the duck keyring so painfully she could feel her tendons creaking.

"There it is," Thompson said, his voice barely more than a breath below the wind rifling through the branches.

"There what is?" Adams managed, surprised to find her own voice still worked.

"Instinct," the cat said. "There's hope for you yet."

By the time the van had vanished around the building and down the lane, Adams thought she could probably trust herself to stand up again. She didn't, though, because Marcus was still loitering at the storeroom's double doors, arms crossed over his chest and legs wide as he looked out into the mellow light of the evening, his head raised just slightly more than was usual. More than was *human*. Adams wondered if he could smell as well in human form as he could in wolf. She was wondering a lot of things, actually, and reluctantly concluding that Thompson was right, and she was going to have to try a bit harder to find some reading material that hadn't been made into a TV show.

Marcus tipped his head one way, then the other, and Thompson whispered, so softly she could barely hear him, "We need to go."

Adams didn't answer. That awful sense of instinctive fright, that need to make herself invisible, unnoticeable, was back in her belly, and she wondered about the boundary charms the cat had said were *everywhere*. Wondered if they *were* alarmed somehow, and they'd blithely gone tripping through them, or if Marcus – if the *werewolf* – was simply scenting them out. She should've considered wind direction, she thought vaguely.

Marcus jumped lightly down from the double doors and put his hands in the pockets of his jeans, strolling forward with a rolling, easy gait. The low, warm light turned the ends of his thick hair to ruddy gold and painted the muscles of his arms with flattering shadows, and when he smiled his canines showed, white and sharp and just that touch too long.

"DI Adams," he said, looking almost directly at her tree. "You may as well come out. I know you're here."

Adams closed her eyes, and considered giving her forehead a good bang against the tree for thinking she could sneak up on a *werewolf*. Instead she whispered to Thompson, "Get out of here."

The cat didn't argue, simply faded into the undergrowth, and Adams held a hand out to Dandy in a *stay* gesture. He licked it.

"Inspector? It's no use hiding. I assume you have no warrant and no right to be lurking about my brewery, so why don't we just have a nice little chat?" His voice was as smooth and muscular as his arms, and Adams took a breath, slipped her baton out of the pocket of her pack, and walked out to meet the wolf.

# BREWING UP TROUBLE

ADAMS CROSSED THE LONGISH GRASS BEYOND THE TREES, stopping at the edge of the gravel drive. Marcus smiled at her, hands still in his pockets, and she kept the baton tucked behind her leg as she said, "Where's Chloe McGill?"

He tipped his head slightly. "Who's that? Your little friend?"

"That's the one." Adams weighed her options, then added, "You might know her as a hedge witch." She imagined the werewolf had sniffed out what Chloe was immediately, so there didn't seem to be much point dancing around, pretending she knew nothing of such things.

"Is that some sort of horticulturist?" he asked, his grin widening. Adams was starting to understand the meaning of the term *wolfish*.

"I don't think so."

They looked at each other, neither speaking, and Marcus's smile slowly faded. "There's nothing that concerns you here, Inspector."

"There's plenty. Let's start with how the beer's affecting people."

"Getting them drunk, you mean?"

"It's more than that. And Chloe knew it as well. So what did you do to her?"

He kept his gaze fixed on hers, a warm brown that paled to hazel toward the pupil, and she wondered distractedly if they stayed the same colour when he was in wolf form. "I suggest you stop asking questions," he said.

"My job description is asking questions. Especially when it comes to beer that's sending half the county bonkers. What're you planning with it?"

"To sell it, obviously."

"Why?"

"It's what breweries do."

"You know that's not what I mean. Why *this* brew? Why the charms?" She was almost vibrating with impatience. "What's your end goal here?"

He tilted his head, the grin resurfacing. "I could tell you, but then I'd have to kill you."

"I hope you're not threatening a police officer. I could arrest you for that."

"You could try, see how it ends up. How did your DCI like her beer?"

She held his gaze, feeling her own lips drawing back in a grimace that was almost a smile. "It makes people controllable? Is that it? They drink the beer, and now you've got half the police in the place in your pocket?"

Marcus took a few slow, stalking steps toward her, and she shifted her weight, still keeping the baton hidden. She was aware of the size of him, a good head taller than her at least, and broad as well, his body sleek under the T-shirt and his movement full of an economy of power. He stopped a couple of metres away, looking down at her, and she stared back steadily, smelling something musky and feral rising from his skin.

"You need to drop this," he said, his voice warm and almost gentle. "I did some digging this afternoon, and I heard about the necklace in Leeds. But this isn't some little scam run by a moonlighting copper. This is far more than you can handle. And if I can give you some advice: go back to regular policing. If your only sidekick is some hedge witch, you're just asking to end up on someone's lunch menu."

Adams didn't look away from him, her chest tight and her face hot. He hadn't mentioned invisible dogs, so presumably that part of her reputation had yet to get around. "If I need career advice I'll ask for it, and it won't be from a brewer who's disturbing the peace and inciting riots, has imprisoned at least one person against their will and likely kidnapped another, plus is endangering the public through distribution of contaminated goods."

"And you think you can prove that?"

"At least that. I'll think of some other things when I get a chance."

He grinned, and this time she was sure he was deliberately showing his teeth. They might even have been a little longer than they had a moment ago. "I heard you were persistent. No one said you were funny."

He took another step toward her, and she adjusted her stance, still keeping the baton hidden. She was going to need every scrap of advantage she could get, given the size of him. Movement caught her eye, and she saw Dandy stalking around the side of the building, his head low and his eyes gleaming red through his dreadlocks, brighter and more intense than usual, as if reflecting the day's dying light. She lifted her free hand just slightly, in a *stop* gesture, and he paused, his gaze never shifting from Marcus.

Marcus looked around, his nose high. "What's that? What've you got here?"

"Tell me what you're planning with the beer."

"You're in no position to make demands," he replied, glancing back at her.

"Chloe, then. Where is she?"

He looked around again. Dandy had crept closer, his mouth hanging open to expose sharp white teeth, far more than Adams thought a regular dog should have – or even than he normally had. He'd bulked up to the size of a Newfoundland, and even though she knew he was on her side, a shiver still trekked up her spine and curled around the base of her neck.

"What *is* that?" Marcus asked. There was a growl in his voice, and Dandy gave voice to an answering one. Marcus cocked his head, moving in small sharp movements as he cast about for a scent.

"Where's Chloe?" Adams demanded.

"Why can't I see it?" Marcus's voice had grown rough edges, and his stance changed, shoulders hunching forward and hands sliding down to rest on his thighs as he turned away from Adams.

"*Hey.* I'm talking to you." She brought the baton out from behind her leg, snapping it to its full length. Marcus's head whipped toward her at the sound, his lips drawn back from his teeth. Nothing about his appearance had changed, but in that moment she could see the wolf anyway. "*Where's Chloe?*" she said again, holding her free hand out to Dandy. He paused, but his stance was all coiled springs.

Marcus's gaze went to the baton then back to her. He didn't straighten up, and a growl laced his words as he said, "Have I been a naughty boy? Are you going to *punish* me?" He was grinning, canines biting into his lips.

"Arrest you, more like. Where is she?"

He straightened up slowly, and said, "She's safe. And if you pull your neck in, she'll stay that way. Once we're done we'll release her."

"Done with what?" Adams caught the sound of an engine somewhere, and she hoped it wasn't the other werewolves coming back. One was *more* than enough.

"Our work," Marcus said impatiently.

"Controlling people through the beer? But for *what?* And why the superpowers?"

"Superpowers?" he said, sounding suddenly fully human again, and somewhat confused. "What superpowers?"

"People jumping cars and climbing up buildings, and skinny women throwing big men across gyms. DJs playing music through their mouths."

"*Huh.*" He looked at the sky for a moment, considering. "Interesting. Well, there were always going to be some side effects before we got the mix right."

"Right for what?" Adams demanded.

"Back down, Inspector. Or it won't be Chloe you need to be worrying about. Just get on with your murderers and car thieves and all that normal, human stuff. It's not like there isn't enough of it to keep you busy."

"Fine. Marcus Gallagher, I'm arresting you for—"

Marcus lunged for her, the movement all power and laced with that unnatural grace, and Dandy gave a sharp, warning bark, leaping forward as Adams jumped back, already swinging the baton. It connected with Marcus's side, but it was a glancing blow, because he'd spun to meet Dandy, hearing him on some wolfish level. He couldn't seem to see him, though, and Dandy crashed into the werewolf, carrying him to the ground.

"Dandy! *No!*" Adams snapped, as Marcus's snarl rose, barely a trace of anything human in it.

Dandy let himself get thrown back and took up position between her and the werewolf as Marcus came to his feet in one fluid, furious movement.

"What the hell was *that?*" he demanded. There were

scrapes on his forearms from Dandy's claws, and he looked at them, then at her, his eyes narrowed. "What do you have, Inspector? What's your pet beast?"

"Never mind. Now tell me where Chloe is, or I *will* arrest you."

Marcus grinned at that, and now she was sure his teeth were longer and sharper than they had any right to be, his face more angular. "Two can play at these games," he said softly.

Dandy snarled, a visceral, ugly sound, and Marcus returned it, teeth bared and face tightening as he stared around, and Adams was quite certain she was about to discover just what a werewolf looked like when it changed. She shifted her grip on her baton, chest tight with fright, and just at that moment, while Marcus was still clearly human yet somehow very much not, Rory walked around the side of the building and called, "DI Adams? Everything alright?"

Marcus froze, and she could actually see the effort it took for him to stop the transformation. He growled, his eyes on Adams, bright and hungry, and she stared back at him.

"Marcus?" Rory said, his tone a little sharper. "What's going on here?"

Marcus took a breath, closing his eyes, and pulled his shoulders back. His face still had all the wrong lines, and without looking around he said, "We're fine, Rory."

Rory looked at Adams and said, "I spotted you on the cameras and came down to make sure everything was okay."

Marcus kept his eyes on Adams, his mouth dropping open to show his teeth, and she nodded just slightly. "Yes, fine, Rory. Marcus was just helping me with some enquiries."

"Always happy to assist the police," Marcus said. There was still a snarl under his words, and he kept his back to Rory.

Adams put one hand on Dandy's head, quieting his

growls, and she and the werewolf stared at each other. "Where *is* she?" she hissed.

Marcus inclined his head just slightly, indicating Rory. "I'll tear his throat out, then yours. *Leave.*"

"If you've *touched* Chloe," Adams started, and Marcus growled.

"I told you, she's safe. *Go.*"

And what was she going to do? She couldn't arrest him. Couldn't risk Rory seeing what he was, and certainly couldn't risk one or both of them getting mauled. Or turned into a werewolf themselves, if that was how it really worked. Another thing she needed to ask the cat. So Adams went, Dandy keeping himself between her and the werewolf.

She crossed the gravel to join Rory and said, "It's all good here. Let's go."

He examined her for a moment, then his gaze slid to Marcus, who still hadn't turned around.

"This way." Adams waved Rory around the building, where the day was being swallowed by the long shadows of the evening, full of the scents of sun on long grass and trees slipping toward autumn slumbers. She took a long, shaky breath as they left the werewolf behind, trying to escape the stink of her own adrenaline, and shook herself like a dog coming out of the water. Every muscle in her body felt like it had been on the verge of cramp.

Rory pointed at his quad bike, sitting outside the uphol-stery shop. "Can I give you a lift?" Then he blinked. "That cat's on my seat." He raised his palms at the two border collies, who were on either side of the bike, watching Thompson with their ears back and their teeth showing. They didn't seem keen to get too close. "You two are useless. Won't go near the brewery, don't know what to do with a cat – I'm going to trade you in."

They trotted toward him, tails waving happily, and

Adams said, "A lift'd be great." She glanced back at the building. Marcus wasn't visible, but Dandy was standing at the corner looking back toward the loading doors, his ears back. She followed Rory to the quad bike, where he clapped his hands at Thompson.

"Go on, get out of it."

Thompson gave him a flat look, then jumped to the ground. Rory swung onto the bike and fired it up, then looked at Adams.

"Hop on."

She did, and Thompson promptly jumped up behind her, pressing against her back. She could feel him trembling slightly, and she reached around, pulling him into the space between her and Rory. The cat didn't resist, and Rory put the bike in gear, turning in a wide circle as he whistled to the dogs. They galloped after the bike, and Dandy abandoned the brewery, falling into loping step with them. The border collies seemed less bothered by him than they had by the cat.

Rory accelerated down the lane, and Adams leaned forward to point at the junction, calling, "My car's parked down there, by a bit of a ruin."

"We're not going there," Rory said, barely audible above the engine.

"What?" She touched the baton, back in her bag. *Saw me on the cameras.* Only no cameras covered the back of the brewery.

"I've got something to show you." He opened up the throttle, roaring past both the turn to go to the house and the one to leave the estate. Adams gripped the back of the seat with both hands as the lane got rougher, and before long Rory stopped at the entrance to a field. Adams got off to open the gate, and close it again after the bike and the dogs were through. Trees marched off ahead of them, foliage reflecting the green glimmer of grass below.

"Where're we going?" she asked, before she got back on.

Rory looked back along the track, his easy smile gone, leaving tight lines behind it. "Get on," he said. "I don't want to risk Marcus seeing us."

Adams climbed back on, raising her eyebrows at Thompson. He arched his whiskers back, which told her precisely nothing. Dandy had decided to match the size of the border collies, though, which made her feel better.

"I saw tyre tracks coming up here." Rory raised his voice as they headed off again, following the faint ruts of old tractor routes. "I thought maybe someone was joyriding in the field, or sneaking out to the tarn for a picnic, so I went and took a look."

"Right," she said. "And?"

"It's not far." He fell silent, and they growled into a stand of mature trees as the trail rose in a steady slope ahead, their shadows running with the dogs alongside them and colours rendered rich and golden as the sunset started. They cleared the trees as they reached the crest of the hill, a rich wilderness of grass washing toward a distant wall, and Adams spotted the tarn immediately. It was a little reed-skirted thing lit on fire with the reflected sky, but that wasn't what caught her breath. No, the thing that did that was mired in the tarn, about ten metres out from shore. It was a faded green Vauxhall Astra, the water lapping around it quietly.

"Oh, *bollocks*," Adams said, and Thompson leaned around Rory to see what she was talking about.

Rory brought the bike to a halt a couple of metres from the water, where chunky rocks littered the grass shoreline. "Is that anything to do with your missing woman?"

"I think so."

"I was afraid of that." He rubbed a hand back over his hair as Adams swung off the bike. "I think they were probably hoping it would sink, but it's not really a tarn. It's more of a pond. It dries out if it's a really hot summer."

Adams walked to the edge of the water and scowled at the car, then pulled her boots off and rolled her trousers up to her knees. Dandy joined her, nose twitching.

Rory watched her, then said, "I've checked. There's no one in it."

"Did you touch anything?" Adams asked.

"I opened the door so I could pop the boot, but I used my sleeve."

She gave him a questioning look, and a shadow of a grin passed over his face.

"I watch crime shows."

"I'll be sure to pass that onto the crime tech. He'll be very happy."

His grin widened. "Do you want me to come with you? In case you need help?"

"No, stay here."

"Good. The water was too deep for my wellies, and the bottom's squishy." He gave an almost theatrical shiver.

Adams braced herself for the squishiness and walked into the tarn, finding the bottom distinctly rocky and uncomfortable for the first couple of steps. Dandy bounded past her in great, splashing leaps, and Rory exclaimed, "Bloody hell! Are there *pike* in there? Mind they don't get you."

She hit the squishiness on her next step, mud oozing between her toes while grass and water plants did their best to get tangled around them. She waded on stolidly, the water slowly rising to her knees as she reached the car. She unslung her backpack and found a set of disposable gloves, pulling them on before she tried the driver's door. It was open, and inside she could see the floor mats floating gently. Whoever had driven out here had likely just kept going until the engine stopped.

There was nothing of interest in the glovebox or behind the mirrors, just a bundle of herbs trussed with twine dangling from the rearview mirror. It gave her an odd stab of homesickness. It looked just like the ones her mum always made, handing them off to her children as if the simple act of belief could ward off life's disasters. The back seat was empty too, and Adams went to the driver's side to find the button for the boot. She popped it open and waded around the car to peer into the interior, thinking that at least she knew there was no body to be found. But that still raised the question of where Chloe was now.

The boot held a jumble of reusable shopping bags, a couple of twisted pieces of wood, and an entire bag of pinecones. None of which were very useful, but inside the shopping bags Adams found a soft tote bag with The Occult Onion's logo on the outside, containing what looked like an old, stained recipe book, a newer notebook, a few unlabelled envelopes full of herbs, and some ibuprofen. That last didn't seem particularly witchy, but what did she know? Maybe that was what all the modern witches were using. She took a couple of photos of everything in place, then tucked the tote bag into her backpack and settled it securely into place.

She straightened up and stood looking around the tarn. The colours of the sunset were intensifying, light shattering on the edges of the ripples her movements were creating. She rubbed the back of her neck. They were still missing Chloe and Alistair, she and Collins had both been told to step away, things were escalating in Harrogate, and she'd almost been noshed on by a werewolf. A werewolf who had told her that all these events were *side effects* while they tried to get the mix right. But right for what? What was it all leading to? If Marcus had some sort of control over the police, she could understand that being handy for some scheme – a bank robbery, if you wanted to go classic, or a drug ring. But a whole *town?* What could he possibly need that for?

She jumped as Thompson appeared on top of the car, lost his footing, and slid down the windscreen. She grabbed him before he could tumble off the bonnet into the water, and he hissed at her.

"You're welcome," she said, letting him go.

"Sorry. Instinct."

"Smell anything?" she asked, shifting from one foot to the other. She had a feeling small fish were nibbling on her.

Thompson padded across the bonnet and peered in the open driver's window. "Werewolves," he said.

"Huge surprise." She turned and headed back to shore, where Rory was leaning against the quad bike, playing with his phone, while somewhere in the distance Harrogate's peace slowly crumbled to chaos.

# 19

# DANCING WITH WOLVES

ADAMS CONSIDERED CALLING CHLOE'S CAR IN, BUT GIVEN HER current, compromised situation, she decided the Vauxhall might have to languish where it was for a little longer. Instead, she called Collins while she wiped her feet in the cool grass, trying to get the worst of the mud off, and let them dry out a little before she put her socks back on.

The signal was awful, whether due to the astonishing lack of features on her phone, or the vagaries of the Yorkshire countryside, but eventually she managed to connect.

"Ay-up, Adams," Collins said when he answered.

"Any news?" she asked.

"I have made myself scarce from the station. Maud's having conniptions over grammar errors."

"You should be fine, then."

"My ego won't take it if I'm not, though. I'm on my way to Harrogate."

Adams shook a sock out and pulled it on, phone cradled between her shoulder and her ear. "Anything new on Marcus?"

"No records, nothing of note at all. No social media. My

limited skills ran out there, and Jules is still growling at anyone who goes past the door, so I'm not asking her."

"Understandable," she said, moving onto her other foot. "We found Chloe's car."

"We?"

She grimaced. "Well, Rory found it and showed me."

"Ah, *that* we."

"Sure. Anyway, it's in a tarn. She's not in it, at least."

"That's something." The amusement had gone from his voice. "Any chance we can wrangle a way into the brewery?"

"Probably not now."

"Ah. You had a go?"

"I did, and didn't have time to find anything before I had a small run-in with Marcus. He's a werewolf. An actual one."

There was a long silence while Collins didn't answer, then he said, "I really shouldn't be surprised, because the cat did say, but still. *Werewolf.*"

"Yeah. He didn't exactly change, but I saw enough." She pulled her boots on over her damp socks and stood up. "I found Chloe's notebook in the car. With any luck she's written down what she figured out about the beer."

"Are we still sure—"

"Yes. Marcus basically told me he's got the police in his pocket through the ale, and they've got some final version of the brew going out tomorrow night, for the main festival event. The superpowers and so on are *side effects*, apparently."

"That sounds great. What're you up to now?"

"Heading for the festival. There were some pretty miffed brewers there. Not happy about Dixon's Draughts flooding the market with free samples. I'm thinking I might be able to get them to make some sort of official protest against it, stop the beers being distributed."

"If he's got the police they'll just move them on by whatever means necessary."

"Not if we've got some media attention."

Collins made a surprised noise. "Are you going to call in your favourite journalist?"

"No, you are. The signal here's terrible."

"Fair enough. I'll call him now and see you in town."

"Meet you there."

Adams headed back to the quad bike, grimacing at the dampness between her toes.

Rory put his phone away and said, "Did you find something?"

"Some evidence, hopefully," she replied. "Can I get a lift back to my car?"

"Of course," he said, swinging onto the bike and starting it up.

Adams was just climbing on behind him when she heard ... something. She paused, looking for Dandy. He was standing with his paws still in the tarn, his head raised and pointing in the direction they'd arrived from. "Did you hear something?" she asked Rory.

"Um ... maybe?"

Neither of them moved for a moment, then she caught the noise again. It still wasn't clear over the sound of the engine, and Rory turned it off. They waited. Adams' stomach was rolling slowly over, her chest tight.

This time, with only the softness of the wind and the pound of her own heart in her ears to compete with, the noise was clear and almost musical, the soundtrack of a hundred horror movies. The border collies, who'd been nosing around the tarn, sprinted for the quad bike, tails tucked.

"That's not what I think it is, is it?" Rory asked.

"I don't know," Adams said.

"I mean, it sounds like a wolf. But we don't have wolves in Yorkshire."

"I suppose not," she said.

The howl went up again, haunting and unmistakable. Dandy loped out of the tarn, swelling to his Newfoundland size again, or even a little bigger, and she found herself willing him to grow more, to become the giant beast that had picked a man up by the arm earlier in the summer. Although she supposed what he gained in size he lost in agility, and now there were two howls, or maybe three, intertwining and shivering against each other, coming from below the brow of the hill, still out of sight.

"I *know* there's no wolves in Yorkshire," Rory said. "But, on the other hand, I've never heard a dog sound like that."

Adams opened her mouth to say something, and Thompson leaped straight into the gap between her and Rory, yowling, "*Go!*"

And Rory, rather than questioning why Adams suddenly sounded like she smoked a pack a day yet still presented a BBC culture show, opened the throttles so fast she had to clutch his shoulders to stop herself falling off the back.

"Sorry!" he yelled.

She didn't bother replying. They were heading back across the field a lot faster than they'd arrived, the bike jolting on the uneven ground. The border collies sprinted behind them, and as they surged off the bald top of the hill and dived into the trees she had a moment's hope that the howls had been further away than they seemed. Then, as the trees closed over them, movement among the trunks caught her eye. She turned her head to watch, almost reluctantly, as if to look made it real. But facing things was the only way to fight them, and she let go of Rory with one hand to retrieve her baton from the side pocket of her pack, snapping it out without taking her eyes off the wolf.

And it was a wolf. There was no denying that once she saw it, big and barrel-chested, running in long, hard lopes as it arrowed out of the trees to meet them, movement graceful and effortless. Rory swore and jerked the handlebars over as the creature plunged into their path, narrowly avoiding both it and the nearest tree. He swung them back onto the track, accelerating again as Dandy shot past, dreadlocks flying. He launched himself at the wolf as it lunged for the bike, and the creature swerved with a snarl, barely avoiding colliding with him. Dandy followed it, driving it back with snapping teeth, and Adams twisted to watch as they fell behind. The wolf was big, but Dandy was at least half again its size, and the wolf backed up, not quite fleeing, but drawing Dandy away from the bike.

Rory braked hard, sending Adams lurching forward. Thompson gave an outraged squawk as he was squished between them, but she ignored him, peering over Rory's shoulder. Two more wolves had emerged onto the track, heads down and front paws wide, blocking the way.

"Keep going!" Thompson yelled, and Adams clamped one hand over his snout. He shook her off and vanished.

"What?" Rory asked.

Adams looked over her shoulder. The first wolf was darting from one side to the other, trying to get past Dandy, and suddenly it shot into the trees. Dandy hesitated, then whirled and sprinted toward the bike. He didn't slow as he came, and the two wolves surged to meet him. They crashed together with the dull thud of heavy bodies meeting and teeth snapping, and the border collies, who'd been making themselves scarce, came pounding out of the shadows, fleet and silent, piling into the fight.

"Midge! Pinto!" Rory yelled. "What the hell – did those two wolves just start fighting *each other*?"

"Go back the other way," Adams said.

*"Midge! Pinto!"*

The fight was surging back and forth, the wolves struggling with both Dandy and two collies to deal with. One broke free and shot away through the trees, and Rory whistled, sharp and hard. The dogs hesitated, and Dandy slammed into the remaining wolf, sending it flying.

"*Go!*" Adams shouted.

Rory reversed the bike, getting it turned in the tight confines of trees and track, and the next moment they were charging back the way they'd come. He opened the throttle up still further, and Adams clung to him with one arm, the other hand still clutching the baton as she half-turned, watching the trees behind them.

All three wolves came out of the trunks like ghosts in the failing light, greys and browns and softly luxuriant whites. They evaded the border collies, running hard, aiming for Dandy. The dogs plunged after them, still not barking, and with the bike's engine drowning any snarls there was a surreal quality to the pursuit. Dandy turned to face the wolves and Thompson flashed out of nothing, sprinting across their path. He took one graceful leap to slap a wolf across the snout, landing in a sprint and vanishing into the trees. The wolf tripped as it tried to change direction and follow without stopping, and almost face-planted into the ground. It recovered and plunged after the cat, while the other two wolves slammed into Dandy, teeth flashing in the dim light. He went down under the combined assault, rolling over twice, then came up again, hair flying and eyes gleaming.

"*Stop,*" Adams yelled at Rory.

"*Why?*" he asked, but he'd already jammed the brakes on. She threw herself off the bike, sprinting back toward the wolves, yelling as she went, the baton raised over her shoulder. The bike revved behind her, and she hoped Rory was smart enough to get out of here and call for help from somewhere safe. But even as one of the wolves broke free of

Dandy, charging toward her, the bike tore past, driving hard at the wolf. The creature swerved away, and Adams spun to slam the baton across the hindquarters of the second wolf where it rolled across the ground, still locked in battle with Dandy. It yelped and scuttled away, but only far enough to join its packmate. Dandy stood between them and Adams as Rory whistled to his dogs. They retreated toward him, and the third wolf emerged from the trees. It was licking its chops, and Adams hoped that was due to Thompson's slap.

There was a moment's stillness as they faced each other off, they three wolves eyeing Adams and Dandy distrustfully. They could certainly see Dandy now. Maybe they were close enough to animal in this form to see things as clearly as the cat did.

Rory had turned the bike again, back toward the tarn, and now he said, "Get back on the bike."

Adams took a step toward it, and the wolves matched it with a few steps of their own. She stopped again. Dandy was panting, his head low and his shoulders high

"Forget the bloody cat," Rory said. "I can't believe you got me to stop for a *cat.*"

Thompson stalked out of the trees as if on cue, his ears back, and Adams said, "Well. Couldn't see him get eaten."

"Absolutely bonkers," Rory said, but with a certain amount of admiration.

The wolves took a few more steps forward, paws unnaturally big in the thick grass, and Thompson took another run past them. One snapped at him, but otherwise they kept their eyes on Adams. Dandy stepped in front of her again, and she grabbed a handful of his hair, pulling him back next to her, not even caring if Rory saw. Three wolves were too much for even a dandy. She readied herself, the baton half-raised.

"*Adams,*" Rory said. "I don't want my dogs to get eaten, so can you get on the bloody bike?"

She couldn't explain to him that her invisible dog was at risk of getting torn limb from limb by the bloody wolves, but she couldn't let his dogs get hurt, either. She hesitated, and Dandy shot a look at her, growling slightly. Thompson appeared by her feet, ears back. "*Go*," he hissed. "He's only fighting because you are. And I'd rather no more wolf slobber on my coat."

She hesitated, looking from him to Dandy, and the wolves crept closer. Then she turned and ran the couple of steps to the bike, throwing herself on as Rory opened the throttle up once more, sending them slaloming back along the track. He whistled again for the collies, and this time they ran ahead of the bike, sprinting off into the coming night.

Adams twisted in the seat to look back. The wolves had broken after them, trying to avoid Dandy rather than confront him, and on the rough track they were easily as fast as the bike was. Thompson was flashing in and out of sight, a tabby shadow in the dusk, laying a scratch here and a bite there, but barely getting a shrug from the wolves as they pelted into pursuit. Dandy crashed into one, sending it tumbling into the trees, and the fastest surged up to the bike. Adams whipped the baton across its snout, sending it stumbling away with a piteous yelp.

They crested the hill, back into open ground, Rory pushing the bike as fast as it would go. Adams kept one hand twisted into the back of his shirt to help keep her balance, lashing out with the baton with the other. She caught another wolf a glancing blow across the snout and it snarled, shaking its head violently as it peeled away from the bike.

"Hold on," Rory yelled, and they went tearing through a ditch so fast Adams almost tumbled off. She grabbed for Rory with both hands, losing hold of the baton and swearing.

"Sorry," he yelled.

"I've lost my baton," she yelled back.

"It's alright. We're going to be out of here in just a sec."

She peered over his shoulder and saw a gate coming up fast. "We've still got to get over that," she said. "And don't you think they can jump?"

"Not going that way." He swerved to run along the wall, still going fast, the quad bike rocking under the momentum. She spotted a stone hut looming up in front of them, looking in distinctly better condition than the one she'd left her car at. One side of the doors stood open, and Rory didn't slow down. He tore toward the gap at full speed, and Adams found herself trying to breathe in, as if that would somehow make the bike skinnier. A wolf surged up next to them and she planted a boot into its jaw. It fell back, snarling, then lunged for her leg and she jerked it away. Dandy shouldered the wolf aside, forcing himself between it and the bike, then they were through the door, the border collies still racing ahead of them and the opening so tight Adams was sure she grazed both knees on the way through.

She was off the bike before it even stopped, running back to the doors, Rory a stride behind her. He grabbed the sagging door, half-lifting it to force it over the uneven ground, and Adams snatched up a rock that had crumbled from the wall, hurling it at the nearest wolf with an accuracy that drew an exclamation from Rory. It smacked the wolf directly between the eyes, and it wobbled off to the side. She already had another rock in her hand, but Rory swung out from behind the recalcitrant door to put a boot in the next wolf's face. It staggered, and Adams threw her weight behind the door too, trying to get it moving. The third wolf shot for the unguarded gap, already gathering itself to leap at Rory. Adams grabbed him, pulling him clear of the wolf's path, and Dandy plunged out of the shadows of the shed, catching the wolf by the throat and carrying it back out into the deepening dusk.

"What the hell happened there?" Rory asked, trying to see where the wolf had gone.

Adams ignored him, heaving the door closed and putting her back to it. "Is there a way to secure this?"

"Sure. One moment." Rory ran back to the quad bike, put it in reverse, and backed up until it bumped into the door. "Locked," he said, and grinned at her. The grin faded rapidly, though. "Did we just get attacked by wolves?"

"I think that's a safe assumption."

"But we don't have wolves in Yorkshire. We don't have wolves in *England*. The UK, even!"

She pointed at the door. "Tell them that."

They looked at each other, barely visible in the fragments of low light creeping in around the door and from little apertures in the stone.

Rory ran a hand back through his hair and said, "This is about when I should start carrying a flask of whisky with me."

"Wouldn't say no myself." She took her phone out and inspected it.

"No signal?"

She sighed. "No. You?"

"No." Rory sat down with his back against the door, knees up and forearms resting on them. Midge and Pinto flopped down next to him, and after a moment Adams joined them. They sat in silence, listening to the dogs panting and the occasional sound of paws on soft ground outside, while the last of the light faded and left them in darkness.

# 20

# DRAGONS AS A GATEWAY DRUG

A WHISPER OF MOVEMENT DEEP IN THE BARN STARTLED ADAMS, and she looked up sharply. Dandy separated himself from the shadows, sloping toward her, and she wanted nothing more than to throw her arms around him and fuss over him. But she couldn't exactly do that with Rory right there, so as the dandy slumped to the ground next to her she petted him as surreptitiously as she could, trying to feel if there was any blood in his fur. He didn't respond to her prodding, just wagged his tail gently, so she supposed he was okay.

A skittering noise and a thud came from deeper in the building, and Adams picked up the torch she'd taken from her bag. She flicked it on, shining it over the rubbly floor and old stone, and Thompson appeared in its beam, stalking toward them with his ears back and his tail lashing. He narrowed his eyes at the light and the border collies surged to their feet.

Rory grabbed their collars. "That looks like the same cat."

"I suppose it does," Adams said.

"Is it yours?"

"No. Why would it be?"

Rory didn't answer immediately, then he said, "It appeared out of nowhere when I was heading back to the house, and the dogs took off after it. I went after them, and it took us straight to the brewery. Dogs never go anywhere near the building, but I followed the cat, thinking I could catch it, and there you were, having a bit of a to-do with Marcus, by the looks."

"*Huh,*" Adams said, looking at Thompson, who raised his chin in a way that she was fairly sure meant *I want duck liver and caviar.*

"Don't know how it's found us here, though," Rory said. "Maybe there's a whole colony of them. I'll have to get some traps from the RSPCA."

"Sure. After we deal with the wolves."

"Yeah, those." He got up, still holding the dogs, and tried to peer through the gap around the door. "I can't see them. D'you think they're still out there?"

Adams stayed where she was, looking at Thompson. "Probably. It's a pity I can't call Collins, what with having no signal."

The cat bared his teeth, tail whipping even harder, and hissed something that sounded very much like *trout* before trotting back off into the shadows of the barn. Better than caviar, she supposed.

"Seems a bit feral, that one," Rory said. "Not looking forward to trying to catch him."

"Yeah, I think he'll probably be quite tricky," Adams said, and settled herself back against the door, flicking the torch off.

Rory let the dogs go and they rushed off to investigate the rest of the building. He leaned on the bike. "So we just wait?"

"For a while, anyway. I don't fancy a repeat."

"No," he agreed. "What's your first name, then?"

"Adams is fine."

Rory laughed. "I thought near-death experiences were meant to bring people closer."

"It'd have to get nearer than that."

COLLINS HAD EVIDENTLY BEEN WELL on the road to Harrogate when they'd spoken, because it wasn't much longer before they heard the rumble of a car engine in the quiet beyond the doors.

Rory looked at Adams, raising his eyebrows slightly. "For you?"

"I imagine so," she said, getting up as headlights leaked around the door and a car horn gave a polite little double beep.

"I thought you had no signal."

"I told Collins where I was when we were at the tarn. Must've followed the tyre tracks from there."

"Right," Rory said, without much conviction. He started the quad bike and moved it far enough forward that Adams could drag the door open a crack and peer out.

Collins had parked a few metres away, headlights washing the front of the shed, and as she watched he got out, looking around warily. Dimly, beyond the lights, she could see Thompson inside the car with his paws up on the dashboard.

Adams nodded at Rory. "Looks okay." He pulled the bike further forward, then came back to help her heft the door open again.

"Bloody glad I never got around to fixing this," he said. "We'd never had made it in if it had been shut."

"I'm just glad it didn't fall off its hinges," she said, as the wood groaned warningly.

"Ay-up, then," Collins said. "What've you two been up to?"

"Wolves," Rory said. "Actual wolves."

"Wolves, huh?"

"Four paws, big teeth," Adams said, checking the field. Dandy had emerged to stand next to her, and the border collies were padding around, snuffling at the ground. None of them seemed concerned, so she supposed they were safe enough. It was full dark now; stars swept across the sky above them while the loom of lights from the town in the distance washed the horizon to pale grey.

Collins followed her gaze, hands tucked into his pockets, and said, "Didn't see any on the way up."

"That's something."

Rory backed the quad bike out of the barn and turned it to face back toward the tarn. He looked from Collins to Adams and said, "Thanks for the excitement. I'll be off home, then."

"We'll go with you," Adams said. "Don't want the wolves sneaking up on you."

He grimaced. "True. I'd appreciate that."

They set off in convoy, Rory leading the way on the bike and Collins' car jouncing along behind it. He looked at Adams. "Werewolves, then. Thompson said it was a bit of a sneak attack."

"It was. Rory brought me up here to show me the car, and we were just leaving when they jumped us. Three of them."

"Mutts," Thompson said, with some feeling. He was balancing on Adams' knee, flatly refusing to be in the back with Dandy, who had his head out Collins' window. Collins kept flinching as Dandy panted on his neck. The headlights lit the tarn as they approached it, turning it into a flat, darkly reflective sheet, the Astra forlorn and motionless in the centre. Adams thought it looked like an art installation.

"How did your man there cope?" Collins asked, nodding at the quad bike's taillights.

"Remarkably calmly. Thought they were just wolves, though, obviously."

"In Yorkshire?"

"True, but I think at the time we were more worried about not getting eaten than the specifics."

"You can thank me for the not getting eaten bit," Thompson said. "I do an excellent line in distraction."

"We can thank Dandy and the dogs, too," Adams said, reaching into the back to rub Dandy's ears. She still hadn't been able to inspect him properly, but he was moving normally, so if he was injured it couldn't be bad. She was evidently going to need to learn some DIY vet skills if this sort of thing kept up, though.

Thompson gave a grudging huff. "They weren't completely useless, I suppose."

"High praise," Collins said. "What now?"

Adams nudged her backpack, which was lying in the footwell. "I managed to keep hold of Chloe's notebook. I'm hoping she's got some sort of counter-charm in there."

"What, you're going to try reversing the charm yourself?"

"It may be our best option. *Only* option. If we can figure it out fast enough, we make the counter-charm and take it to the festival with us. We fire up the other brewery owners, get Ervin covering everything, and bring everything to a stop at once. Then we worry about finding Chloe."

"Do we have time to mess around with the counter-charm?"

"I think we have to. If we try stopping them without it, and Marcus *can* actually control everyone who's drunk the beer, we've no chance."

"She speaks sense," Thompson observed.

"That's almost a compliment," Adams said. "Watch yourself. You'll be saying Dandy's pretty decent next."

Collins was silent for a moment as they followed the

track down through the trees, then he said, "I think I'm starting to understand how you feel, Adams."

"Oh?"

"I used to have proper cases, too."

She waved. "Sheep cases. This is a step up." She grinned when Collins snorted, but her chest had a different sort of tightness to it now. This was her fault. She'd dragged him into this chaotic, illogical facet of the world without so much as a by-your-leave, and now he couldn't get out again. He'd *never* be able to get out again, far too immersed for the cat to do his mind-wiping thing, and if she was attracting attention, he would be too. And he didn't even have a Dandy to protect him. She'd been so careful to try and keep James out of everything, but she'd just let Collins fall straight in, by way of dragons. Dragons as a gateway drug. She put an elbow on the door, rubbing her forehead with her fingers.

They followed Rory all the way up to the house, Adams getting out to do the gates with Dandy shadowing her silently, the night feeling vast and exposed, their headlights the only anchor to the land. Rory pulled the bike into an open shed next to the one that held his still, then walked back to them, shoving his hands in his pockets. He leaned down to peer in Adams' window. "You want a cuppa? Or something stronger? I'm personally going with a full-alcohol whisky."

"No, we're still working," Adams said. "Stay inside for tonight at least. We'll report this to the RSPCA and see what we can figure out."

"RSPCA? They have a wolf capture division?"

"They usually work with a zoo," Collins said. "You know, for unusual escapes."

"Fair enough," Rory said. He didn't straighten up, looking from one of them to the other, then at Thompson, who'd half-concealed himself behind Adams' backpack. "That *is* the same cat."

Adams looked at the cat, and Collins said, "I picked him up on the way in. We'll give him to the RSPCA too."

Thompson bared his teeth.

"None of this is making an awful lot of sense," Rory said.

"No," Adams agreed. "But we'll sort it."

He still didn't straighten up, watching her thoughtfully. "Do I need to be worried about what's happening on my farm?"

Neither Collins nor Adams replied for a moment. Finally Adams said, "It's an ongoing investigation, but you're not a suspect in anything."

"Good to know, but I was actually thinking that there's bloody *wolves* running around, and I've got farmers who rent my land to graze their sheep. I need to tell them if this is going to be a problem."

"I don't think it will be," Adams said.

"No? Those wolves looked pretty hungry to me."

She didn't know how to explain that she doubted the werewolves would jeopardise their operation by munching livestock in their own backyards, so she just said, "We'll get the RSPCA out here straightaway."

Rory didn't say anything for a long moment, his face unaccustomedly serious, then he straightened up. "I think, considering this is all happening on my property, you could be a little bit more forthcoming with what you know."

"We don't really know anything yet," Adams said.

"Absolute bollocks." He turned and walked away, heading around the house toward the kitchen.

Collins looked at Adams. "I think you might be blowing your chances there."

"Shut up and take me to my car. We've got a spell to cast."

HER CAR WAS STILL where she'd left it, tucked in behind the ruins of the shepherd's hut, and she climbed out of Collins' car warily, checking the shadows. Collins got out too and said, "Let's have a look at this book, then."

"Not yet. Last thing we want is another run-in with bloody wolves." She looked at Thompson, "Can you check if anyone's at the brewery?"

"I'm not a *dog*. You can't just order me around."

"I'll buy you some prawns."

"Back in two. Don't do anything till I get back." He vanished, and Adams and Collins looked at each other.

"You've got him sussed, then," Collins said.

"A bit. Did you get hold of Ervin?"

"Yeah, he's at the festival already, talking to people. I've told him not to agitate things too much, not until we can get in place, and to stay clear of any other coppers."

Adams took Chloe's old, battered, recipe-style book from her bag. "Think he can manage that?"

"Soon find out."

Thompson reappeared in almost the same spot he'd vanished from, looking around with a certain air of self-satisfaction. "No cars, and no lights on. No telling if anyone's inside, though."

"Thanks," Adams said, and opened the book. Collins clicked his torch on, shining it on the pages.

"*Whoa*," Thompson said. "Slow your ponies."

"What?"

"That's a full-on spell book."

Adams stared at it. She couldn't feel anything from it, no heat or distasteful hunger as she had with the previous magical book she'd handled. There was nothing at all. "This isn't like the sorcerer's book."

"No. But there's more than one type of magical book."

"Bloody fantastic."

Thompson put his paws on Adams' leg, trying to get a closer look. She started to bend down, but he jumped straight to her shoulder, balancing easily.

She clicked her tongue in irritation. "Do you have to do that? You'll get hair all over my jacket."

"It's a hell of a lot harder to talk to you from down there, and I can't see the book properly. Let me have a sniff." She raised it up so that he could snuffle the pages, his ears twitching. "Okay, it's pretty mellow. No innate power. But it's old school. Look at it properly."

Adams examined the book, Collins leaning over her other shoulder. It actually did look a lot like her mum's recipe book, all handwritten in dozens of different inks, extra sheets and scraps of paper stuck within the pages, a pressed flower here and there. The remains of spices and blurred outlines of spilled liquids stained the pages, tears and loose leaves here and there. Even the smell was almost the same, a whiff of spices and warm kitchens. It was definitely older than Chloe.

Adams checked the front and back covers, looking for a name. There was nothing, but the handwriting changed as she moved through it, from fancy, curving script to spidery capitals and everything in between.

"Family heirloom," Collins suggested. "Aunty Miriam's got one just like it. It was Gran's."

"My mum's got one too." She thought about it. "Pretty sure she's going to give it to one of my brothers, though. Don't think I'm getting it."

"You astonish me," Collins said, and grinned at her when she scowled.

"Okay," she said to the cat. "So it's basically a recipe book. What's the problem?"

"Probably nothing with the book itself—"

"Well, thanks for that."

"*But* you need to check. You can't just jump into things. Plus, stuff doesn't have to be intrinsically magic in order to create magic. Humans always think there has to be some sort of power source, like it's all external. Even the power in a sorcerer's book comes from the sorcerer themself initially. Magic's about what you *do*, not about what's in your little bits of para-what-have-ya."

"Paraphernalia," Collins said after a confused moment.

"That."

"Okay, understood, but if it's not magic itself, then there's no problem, right?" Adams asked.

Thompson huffed in her ear. "Magic has a scent, and a feel. I don't *think* there's any weres in the brewery, but I can't search the whole bloody farm. Last thing you want is to be halfway through a charm, and you get munched on by a were. Nobody needs half-finished charms floating about the place."

"The getting munched on sounds unpleasant, too," Collins observed.

Adams sighed, closed the book and stuffed it back into her bag. "Fair point. We need somewhere quiet to do this, then." No one answered her, so she said, "Back to Skipton?"

"That's going to waste a lot of time," Collins replied. "What about your man?"

"I don't have a man."

"Rory, then. You know he'd let you use a shed or something."

She pinched the bridge of her nose. "We don't want him any more involved than he is. He's already at least a bit suspicious after the whole wolves and Thompson thing."

"I'm not suspicious," the cat said. "And I agree with Big

Man here. I can always give the toff a bit of a mind wipe. We're wasting time."

Adams rubbed her face. She wanted very much to argue, but they were both right. They *were* wasting time, and they needed to get this counter-charm sorted before the whole festival exploded, or Marcus decided to accelerate his plans and roll out the new, improved brew tonight, if he hadn't already. She took her keys from her bag and beeped the car open.

"*Fine.* But can we try to make sure he doesn't need his mind wiping? I'm sure that shouldn't be our first line of defence."

Thompson yawned. "You humans don't use that much of your brain, anyway. It's fine."

"That's actually a myth," Collins said, heading for his own car.

"It's not," the cat said. "Have you seen yourselves?"

# 21

# WRONG SKILL SET

RORY GREETED THEM AT THE KITCHEN DOOR WITH A GLASS OF whisky in one hand, the dogs peering around him. "That didn't take long."

"Sorry," Adams said. "Any chance we could use a room for some … research?"

"Maybe the kitchen," Collins put in, and Adams looked at him. "We could need a pot. And a stove."

"A pot and a stove," Rory said.

Adams gave him a slightly helpless smile. "It's difficult to explain, but it's all part of the investigation."

He scratched his jaw with the hand holding the glass, the liquid tipping dangerously. "See, if I hadn't just been chased by wolves – which absolutely categorically do not exist in Yorkshire, I asked Google – I'd probably have more questions about why two detective inspectors are at my door in the dark, wanting a pot and a stove, while accompanied by a cat that keeps popping up in improbably distant locations, and which I saw attacking the impossible wolves. But right now I'm just going to have another whisky and you can help yourselves to my kitchen." He stepped back to let them in, and they filed past him obediently, Dandy and Thompson trailing the inspectors. Rory clicked his fingers at his dogs. "Leave it," he said, then added, "Hi, cat." Thompson twitched his ears and the border collies whined, but seemed more interested in Dandy.

"Thanks," Adams said to him.

"Sure. Want that cuppa?"

"A coffee would be great, actually."

"Tea for me, please," Collins said, and Rory busied himself with mugs and water while Adams put Chloe's tote bag on the big table and pulled the book out. Collins set the beers from Adams' boot next to it.

"How do we figure out which spell to use?" she asked, her voice low as she paged through it.

Collins poked into the tote bag, coming up with the envelopes of herbs and the much newer notebook, which had a glittering cover that said, *A little fairy dust, a little don't touch me.* He picked it up, fanning through the pages, then turned it around so Adams could see.

"I reckon the one with the yellow Post-it saying *beer.*"

She took the notebook from him. Chloe's handwriting was rounded and bubbly-looking, and the page he'd shown her was a mess of crossed-out lines, arrows, exclamation marks, and finally a large circle swirled around a note that said, *Reversal 23, 1979, use beer not grass, widdershins three times and right way five, pure water for distilling. DO NOT SNEEZE.*

She frowned, and turned the page. It was blank, so she flipped back in the other direction, finding shopping lists and stock orders, to-do lists and fragments of things that might've been spells or song lyrics. She went back to the Post-it page. "Why in here instead of in the book?"

"It looks like she was experimenting, so I imagine she didn't want to write it up in there until she knew it was going to work."

"Great. So we don't even know if she got it right."

"It's the best we've got."

Adams paged slowly through the older book, finding every recipe – she was still having trouble thinking of it as a *spell book*, and *recipe book* sat so much better – was dated. The seventies were around the middle, and she found Reversal 23 without too much trouble. They both leaned over the page, squinting at the ingredients.

"Do we have all of this?" Collins asked, finding his reading glasses and popping them on before running his finger down the page.

"Better hope so. Can't exactly nip out to *Spells-R-Us.*" She riffled through the envelopes. "Nothing's labelled."

Thompson prowled down the table and sat next to them, head tilted to read the book, as Collins picked up one of the envelopes and sniffed it. "Star anise?"

"That's not even in the recipe," she said, tapping the page.

Rory set their mugs on the table and sat down across from them, chair turned sideways and long legs stretched out, crossed at the ankles. They both looked at him. "Don't mind me," he said. "As you were."

"It's police business," Adams said.

"It looks like you're making a stew," he said, leaning across to pick up the envelope Collins had put down. He sniffed it. "Allspice."

"Still not in the recipe," Adams said.

"Also known as pimento berry, or sometimes just pimento."

She looked back at the page. "Oh. Yes, that's it."

"I think you need some help, and since this is my kitchen, I'm going to have to insist."

Adams sighed, and scanned the recipe. "Alright. D'you have that pot?"

"What size?" Rory asked, getting up.

"Let's go with a big one." She had no idea what was going to happen when they mixed this up. Maybe nothing. Maybe everything.

Rory came back with a large, heavy-bottomed pot that he placed on the table, and Adams spread the envelopes out, inspecting each one and checking it against the recipe. Collins went through them with her, finding thyme and baking soda (neither she nor Collins wanted to touch any unidentified white powder, but Rory licked his little finger and stuck it in the envelope before making his announcement), pine needles and grey salt from distant plains, fish scales and turmeric and Bisto gravy granules. There was more than enough of each to make the recipe ten times over, and eventually they had them all laid out in the same order they appeared in the book. Thompson prowled along the line of envelopes, sniffing each and twitching his ears expectantly.

"Are they alright?" Adams asked, and the cat just looked at her.

"They're all there, at least," Collins said.

She looked at him. "Are you sure you don't want to do this?"

He shook his head. "You do it. It's more your skill set."

Rory sucked air over his teeth. "I hope you're not suggesting she's more suited to cooking. That seems dangerous."

"Not that skill set," Collins said. "Specialist knowledge."

"Definitely not cooking," Adams muttered, reading the recipe for about the tenth time. "We need something to decant it into. Do you have any clean bottles?"

"Plenty in the shed," Rory replied. "Back in a mo." He ambled out of the kitchen door, looking surprisingly relaxed about the current turn of events.

Thompson watched him go, then said, "Let's just get him in on it."

"I've already said, no mind wiping. Or only minimal," Adams replied.

"Yeah, but I guarantee you're going to need my help, so I'll have to talk at some stage, and we don't want him freaking out in the middle of the charm and wrecking everything."

"I just have to follow the recipe," Adams replied. "I think I can manage that."

"Do you?"

She scowled at him. "Can you at least keep your mouth shut until absolutely necessary?"

Thompson huffed, but he didn't say anything as Rory came in and set a crate of empty bottles on the table, then went back to his seat and picked his glass up again.

Adams lit one of the burners and shifted the pot on top of it, then checked the recipe again. "Do you think we need to add oil?" she asked Collins.

"Doesn't say oil," he replied, and they looked at each other doubtfully.

"No oil," Adams decided, and started working through the recipe. A pinch of this, a pinch of that, turn the pot three times anti-clockwise, add the scales, stir twice with the left hand, add the turmeric, half a turn clockwise … She tuned out the kitchen, unaware of the cat watching with narrowed eyes, or Rory leaning forward, both elbows on the table. She barely even noticed Collins standing next to her, handing her the sachets of ingredients. Then she paused. "What does that say?" she asked, pointing at the book.

Collins, Rory, and Thompson all crowded around, and even Dandy got up to put his chin on the table. "Shake it?" Collins suggested.

"Smoke it?" Rory offered.

Adams turned hurriedly back to the pan, where the scent of heating spices was rapidly turning to burning. "I'm going with shake," she said, grabbing the pan's metal handles with both hands, then letting them go with a yelp, employing a couple of the more colourful phrases she'd learned from Rory earlier. An acrid smell was rising from the pot as she snatched up a couple of cloths and used them to hold the handles, shaking the thing vigorously. It wasn't just the simple scent of burning spices, but something astringent and sharp that plucked at the back of her throat and made her eyes water. Rory hurried to open the back door while she snuffled helplessly, sneezing and wiping her eyes with one hand. Thompson had his ears back and his snout wrinkled, and Dandy vanished out the open door.

"Beer," Adams managed, waving at Collins.

He cracked the top off one and she took it, looking at him and Thompson. "Here we go." She added a splash to the smoking pan, jumping back as she did so.

The result was instantaneous. A percussive *bang* tore through the kitchen, rattling the dishes in the sink and toppling a broom from where it leaned against the wall. Adams dropped to the floor, both hands over her head. Thompson fled, Rory dived off his chair, and Collins hit the floor next to the table. The acrid stench intensified, thick billows of choking smoke boiling out of the pan, far too much of it for the meagre amount of ingredients Adams had used. It swamped the whole room, until Adams could barely see the table, and a smoke alarm started going off, beeping wildly.

"Out!" she wheezed, and Collins grabbed Rory, pulling him outside as Adams jumped up, grabbing the dish towel and waving it wildly, trying to calm the smoke alarm.

"Adams!" Collins shouted from the door. "Move yourself!"

She took a couple more swings at the smoke detector then gave up. It was a bit more than some burnt toast in here.

She staggered out onto the patio and stopped in the thankfully cool night air, both hands on her knees as she coughed and gasped. The stink of something that was a combination of burning hair and melting plastic washed out of the kitchen along with the smoke, and she stepped back a little further, wiping her face with her forearm.

"Sorry," she said to Rory. "That was unexpected."

He nodded, his eyes still streaming. "I'm so glad I let you mess around in the only liveable part of my house."

She grimaced. "I did say this wasn't really my skill set. I'm better with big sticks and handcuffs."

Rory snorted with laughter. "Why does that not surprise me?" he asked, then added, "And I mean that as a compliment."

"Well, it's going to need to get *in* your skill set," Collins said. "We need to do something about this bloody festival."

"You've already done plenty," someone else said, and they turned to look at three newcomers who had just walked around the corner of the house. Dandy was standing a little distance away, his head down and his teeth showing, and Adams clicked her fingers, then held her hand out to him, careful not to make the movement too big.

"DCI Temple," she said. "What're you doing here?"

"Looking for you," he said.

"Why?"

"Because I'm arresting you for harassment, soliciting bribes, and threatening behaviour."

"*What?*" she demanded.

"That's ridiculous," Collins started, and Temper held a hand up, silencing him.

"You too, DI Collins."

"You've no grounds," Adams said.

"The complainant, Marcus Gallagher, would disagree.

Apparently you trespassed on his property not once, but *twice* today. At his home *and* workplace."

Adams swore, and looked at Collins. He had a grim expression on his face, arms folded over his broad chest. There were two unfamiliar officers with Temper, and she had an idea they'd be from Harrogate. "Marcus Gallagher is a suspect in kidnapping, distribution of a controlled substance—"

"I hardly think beer is a controlled substance, Adams."

"This one should be," she said. "Why are *you* here? This isn't West Yorkshire Police territory."

"A small favour for the DCI here. He thought I might be able to talk you down a bit easier than a stranger."

"Talk me *down?*"

"You're endangering others and behaving recklessly. I'm arresting your colleague here more to keep him out of trouble than anything else. I'm sure it'll turn out you're the one who engineered the unrest in Harrogate. We've already taken in a journalist who's a known associate of yours, and I'm sure he was acting on your instructions, stirring up some sort of protest among the stallholders at the festival."

Adams looked at Rory, but he seemed utterly bewildered. She doubted he'd been the one to call the police on them. She winced inwardly at the thought. She *was* police. This shouldn't be happening.

"Come on," Temper said, waving them forward. "Let's do this with some dignity."

"Hang about," Collins started, and Adams shook her head.

"Leave it," she said. "We'll call Maud as soon as we're in."

"That's not going to change anything," Temper said. "Your behaviour can't be allowed to continue, and I'm certain she'll be in complete agreement. The festival *must* go ahead without interference."

"Why?" Adams asked, and saw a sudden shadow of uncertainty on Temper's face, as if the question hadn't occurred to him, then it was gone.

"Because it's good for the local economy. Now are you moving yourselves, or do I have to put cuffs on you?"

"No." She walked forward, not even reacting when one of the younger officers pushed her past him, making her stumble on the grass. They left the circle of patio light behind, the house looming high above them as they followed its walls around to the front. An old but sleek black Volvo was parked in front of a police van, and she and Collins were escorted to the back of the van, where one of the officers opened the door to the rear, caged section.

"Oh, come *on*," Collins started.

"In," Temper ordered. "We're not taking any risks."

"We're hardly going to kick off," Collins snapped.

"Do you want us to push you in?" the DCI asked, and Adams looked at the two officers. They were both young men, and there was a tense, nervous energy about them that suggested they very much wanted the opportunity to do some more pushing.

"It's fine," she said, climbing in and sitting down cross-legged on the floor. It smelled faintly of vomit, which wasn't as bad as it could've been.

Collins scowled at Temper. "I'm filing a complaint," he said, but got in and sat down opposite Adams, folding his legs somewhat awkwardly. He looked too big for the space.

The doors slammed shut, Collins hissing as it banged into his knee, and Adams looked around with a sigh. She'd never imagined she'd end up on this side of the divide.

The two officers climbed into the front of the van and started the engine, and a moment later they were rumbling down the drive.

"What the hell do we do now?" Collins asked, his voice

low, even though they weren't likely to be heard. There was a row of seats between them and the front.

"I don't know," Adams admitted. She didn't even have her duck keyring with her. It was in her bag, back in Rory's smoky kitchen. No duck, no baton, no chocolate, and no plan.

She wasn't quite sure how this could've gone worse. Other than burning down the whole house, of course. At least she'd avoided that.

# 22

# A BREAKOUT

THE RIDE TO THE STATION WAS SILENT AND UNEVENTFUL, neither of them with much to say. The van slowed as they drove through Harrogate, and Adams heard pounding music, shouting and cheering outside. It sounded like the celebrations after a major football win, spilling all through town, full of excitement and delight and just needing that one extra drink to tip into something darker. Collins stood and peered through the grill, trying to see something through the windows in the front of the van.

"Anything?" Adams asked him.

"Can't see much," he said. "Town's not burning yet, anyway."

*Yet.* That was the key. It was only a matter of time, with the beer flooding the place and no way of stopping it. She crossed her forearms over her knees, her thoughts wheeling in circles. They hadn't found Chloe. They hadn't made the counter-charm. They hadn't stopped the beer being distributed. They hadn't even succeeded in turning the public against Dixon's Draughts, because Ervin had been arrested too. She rested her forehead on her arms. There was a way out of this. There was always a way out. She just couldn't think of what it was.

They pulled into a covered car park, and the van stopped. Adams found herself tensing as the officers got out, as if she expected to be dragged out and beaten, or thrown to wolves, or to be delivered to the ravenous crowds at the festival, offered as sacrifices. Instead, the younger of the two officers, the one who had pushed her, opened the doors. "Out," he said, standing back with one hand on his baton.

They got out obediently, Collins stretching and shaking his limbs out. "Bloody outrageous," he muttered.

"I'll take them from here," Temper said, strolling around the van.

"Really?" The young officer looked disappointed, and Adams had an idea she wasn't the only one who'd been thinking about beatings. She pressed her lips together to stop the distaste showing on her face.

"Yes." Temper nodded at the van. "Get back to the grounds. Make sure there's no one else trying to film or stir things up, like that bloody journalist."

"Boss," the older officer said, nodding, and headed for the front of the van. The younger one followed, still looking put out.

Adams looked at Temper, and some small hope that maybe he'd turn to them and whisper that he was on their side *really* faded as he pointed them toward a door not far from the van. "Off we go," he said, sounding far more jovial than usual.

The hallway beyond the door delivered them to the custody suite, a long brightly-lit corridor with white-painted walls and floor, doors lining it. A uniformed officer with a thick plait of dark hair was frowning at her computer in a pocket-sized, enclosed office, hefty plexiglass dividing her from the room. She looked up as Temper walked Collins and Adams in, and her frown deepened.

"Who're you?"

"DCI Temple," he said, showing her his warrant card.

She squinted at it. "Leeds?"

"Yes. But you can check with DCI Bell. He knows I'm bringing these two in."

She looked from Adams to Collins. "ID?"

"Not on me," Adams said, then added reluctantly, "DI Jeanette Adams, North Yorkshire Police."

"DI Colin Collins, same," Collins said.

The woman paused, fingers poised above her keyboard. Her name tag read *Sgt. J. Pahal.* "You're both DIs?"

"Yes," Adams said.

"I'm holding them pending an internal investigation," Temper said, his voice sharp. A flush was rising on his scalp. "Flight risk."

"I need to check this with DCI Bell," Pahal said, picking up the phone.

"Sure, if you want to interrupt him. He's a bit bloody busy with all the chaos in town at the moment, which these two are responsible for."

"That's ridiculous," Collins snapped. "How could we *possibly* be responsible for that?"

"I'll prove it," Temper said, and looked at Pahal. "You must have a free cell."

"Sure. Weirdly, to be honest. I thought it was going to be bloody busy, what with the beer festival on. But I can't just bang up two DIs without—"

"I'm a DCI and you'll do as you're bloody told," Temper said, punching one forefinger into the desk on his side of the divider.

Pahal gave him an unimpressed look. "You're not *my*

DCI." She hit dial and tucked the phone between her shoulder and ear.

They waited, Temper muttering under his breath, and after a moment Pahal hung up. "Not answering his mobile."

"I told you—"

"Just trying his office." She hit dial again, and Adams shot a look at Collins. He was grinning slightly. "Hello?" Pahal said. "Is he in? No? Any idea where he is? Huh. Uh-huh. Okay." She hung up again, and looked at Temper.

"Now will you lock them up?" he demanded.

"I'm not processing them until I know what's going on, but I'll put them in an interview room," she said.

"That's not secure," Temper protested.

"It's a good sight better than chucking a couple of coppers in a cell, particularly if we get as busy as I think we will." She got up, picking up the phone handset. "Thank you, DCI Temple." She let herself out of the office, pulling the door closed behind her, and looked up at him. "You can go now."

Temper opened and shut his mouth a couple of times, then turned and stomped toward the door, tugging on it enthusiastically until Pahal said, "Oh, hang on." She went back behind the desk and buzzed him through. He didn't say anything, just threw them a furious look and headed off. Pahal waited until the door closed behind him, then said, "Interview room okay? No loo or bench to stretch out on in there, but it'll smell a bit better at least."

"No chance of just letting us go?" Adams asked.

"No," Pahal said comfortably, leading them down the long alley of doors. Holding cells were off to their right, the doors blank metal with numbers on the outside, and to the left were doors labelled as a processing room, a medical suite, a consulting room, and finally the interview rooms. She opened the first one. "In you go. Anything to drink?"

"Water would be good," Collins said.

"Can do." She turned to leave.

"Hang on," Adams said. "Have you had an Ervin Giles brought in? Journalist?"

"He's in a cell."

"Can I talk to him?"

"No," she said, and closed the door.

Adams sighed, and took one of the chairs at the interview table, resting her forearms on the scarred surface. "Bollocks."

"Pretty much," Collins said.

THE INTERVIEW ROOM was all but soundproof, and they spent what felt like five days, but which Adams' watch informed her was less than two hours, shifting positions in the moderately uncomfortable chairs, counting cracks in the ceiling, and trying to figure a way out of this. They were arguing about whether an interview room constituted a cage, and that was the reason Thompson hadn't turned up (Collins' theory), or if he'd been distracted by salmon (Adams'), when the locks in the door rolled. They both looked up as Pahal opened the door and said, "You can come out now."

Adams jumped up and hurried to the door as if she thought Pahal might change her mind if she lingered. "What happened?" she asked.

"I called your boss," Pahal said, and Adams looked past her, stomach suddenly tight. Maud was standing in the middle of the floor, arms crossed, one foot tapping impatiently, and behind her hovered DC James Hamilton, towering over the DCI and looking as if he wished he could shrink.

"No *paperwork*," Maud spat.

"That's why I didn't book them," Pahal said, strolling back across the room. "They're all yours."

"That Temper," Maud started, shaking a finger at James, who raised his hands.

"I'm here to help, remember?" he said.

Maud took a deep breath, then turned back to the DIs. "Come on, come on. I shouldn't be bailing my detectives out, you know. I *should not.*"

"Thanks, though," Adams said, then added carefully, "Can you bail one more person out?"

Maud flung her arms wide, looking at the ceiling as if in supplication, and Adams was sure she was about to get a bollocking. Instead, Maud yelled, "*Yes!* Dammit. I am ..." She pressed a hand to her chest and took a couple of deep breaths, then managed a little more calmly, "Yes. I assume they're needed to sort this ... *this utter balls-up*"—she bellowed the last few words, then calmed herself again—"situation out?"

"It's the journalist," Adams said. "And yes, I think we need him. It's going to give us some insurance."

"*Fine.*" Maud strode after Pahal, yelling for her to get her keys, and Adams looked at James.

"What're you doing here?"

"She called me when she heard you were in here. Knew I'd been working with you on this and said she didn't quite trust herself to get you out, as she's ... not quite herself." James looked a little wide-eyed, and Adams wondered how bad the drive over had been.

"Good man," Collins said, heading toward Maud and Pahal. Maud had both hands clenched in fists, and was trying so hard not to shout that her face was almost comically red.

"Thanks," Adams said to James. "I think she was right."

He nodded. "What the hell's going on? Looks like bloody New Year's Eve out there, and Maud is *not* good."

"It's the beer."

"That's all you can say?"

She hesitated. "It's all I *want* to say. The rest is kind of … small muggers and that sort of thing."

James rubbed the back of his head. "Do I need to know the details to help?"

"I don't think so. We need to distribute an … an antidote to the beer. And people are going to try to stop us, probably violently. That pretty much sums it up."

He examined her, then nodded. "That'll do, then."

They joined Collins and Maud, who was scribbling furiously on release forms, muttering under her breath. Collins took the form away as she started correcting some of the printing, and handed it to Pahal.

"*Careless,*" Maud hissed, and scribbled out the apostrophe on a printed sign that said *Please present ID's*.

Pahal checked the form, then went to one of the cells and opened it. Ervin slouched out, looking even more dishevelled than usual, his dimples missing. They reappeared as soon as he saw the little group by the desk, though.

"Adams! Colin! I knew you'd come through."

Pahal looked at Adams as she pushed a form toward Ervin for him to sign. "You hang about with journalists?"

"Not by choice," she responded.

"Hurtful," Ervin said, and took his satchel and a sealed bag containing his shoelaces and the contents of his pockets from Pahal. "But I know you don't mean it."

"Behave yourself or we'll put you back in," Adams said.

"And brush your hair," Maud snapped. "You look like an urchin."

"Salty and delicious?"

"Unwashed and on the streets."

Ervin nodded, as if that made sense.

"Let's move," Collins said, clapping his hands together. "We need to find our cars."

"Now my detectives are losing their cars," Maud muttered, striding toward the door. "*Unbelievable.*"

THEY DIDN'T WASTE time in the car park, Adams, Collins, and Ervin all squeezing into the back of James's Nissan Leaf, Ervin in the middle with his knees uncomfortably high.

"Sorry," James said, looking back at them. "I didn't think we'd have only one car, but Maud said she couldn't drive because she'd want to ticket everyone."

"I should ticket *you*," Maud said, buckling her seatbelt. "You were speeding at least three times, and you didn't stop fully at a junction." She leaned her head against the seat, closing her eyes, and said almost plaintively, "Is this going to stop soon?"

"We're working on it," Collins said, and patted her shoulder.

"Where to?" James asked, driving the laden car out onto the street.

"Head for Knaresborough," Adams said.

James hadn't been wrong about it looking like New Year's Eve, although Adams also thought *Mad Max* would've been a fair description. It was almost midnight, and every bar was packed, revellers spilling out onto the streets, James having to use the horn to clear them. Banners for Niddered Ale were tacked to awnings, and flyers were plastered to lamp posts, and there were stands set up outside the bars, dispensing plastic glasses of beer to anyone who passed. Adams spotted a brewery van too, driving slowly along the main road, the muscular woman she'd seen earlier leaning out of the back and handing more glasses to the crowd that crushed around it. It might not be the entire town who'd drunk the beer, but it was enough that anyone who hadn't would be staying well away.

"Outside licensing hours," Maud said, pawing at the door like a dog spotting a rabbit. "Drunk and disorderly. *Littering.*"

"Get a move on, James," Adams said, and he accelerated as much as he dared.

Once they were past the centre of town and the packs of singing, dancing, almost-but-not-quite brawling drinkers surging toward the festival, the roads were clear. James ignored the speed limit and pushed the little car as fast as it could manage, while Collins grabbed Maud's arms from behind the seat to stop her hitting the detective constable around the ears. Ervin put his shoelaces back in his trainers, watching with some fascination, and finally said to Adams, "You owe me this story."

"I got you out of a cell."

"Helping you put me in it."

She couldn't argue with that, so she ignored him and called directions to James over Maud's enraged shouts. Before long they were charging back up the lane to the crumbling country house, skidding a little in the gravel at the corners. James stopped next to Adams' car and pressed his hands against the steering wheel.

"Dangerous driving," Maud told him. "You're a *disgrace.*"

"But we're here," he said, his tone somewhat clipped, and climbed out, shaking his head.

Adams released Maud and said, "Don't arrest him. It was on request."

"*I know,*" she said, shoving her door open. "This is a bloody *nightmare.*"

No one had come to meet them, and Adams couldn't see any lights on in the house. She turned to lead the way around the long arm of the house's wing, then saw light spilling from the shed where she'd found Rory the day before. She hesitated, frowning, and headed toward it. She could hear voices before she reached it, and the clinking of bottles, and the sound of something bubbling wildly. A strange scent drifted out into the night air, salty and spicy all at once, something that tingled the tip of her nose and made her lips curl up at the corners.

The door was ajar, and she held a hand up to stop the others, then stepped up to the gap warily.

The inside of the shed was full of warm, golden light from dangling overhead bulbs, and the still Rory had been working on was humming and vibrating, steaming from a couple of joints and bubbling at a brewing port. She could see one valve that was cranked up into the red zone, and Dandy was staring up at it dubiously, his ears back. The border collies lay next to him, one of them nosing a rubber ball toward him and the other offering a bone. Rory was leaning over a crate of bottles, filling them from a hose that was attached to the still, his T-shirt sporting dark patches of sweat, wearing heavy-duty gloves and safety goggles. Next to him, Thompson had his ears back and his tail whipping furiously.

"I'm *telling* you," the cat yowled. "You can't just keep *making* it! We don't even know if it works. What if it makes them *worse?*"

"Look, it didn't blow up this time," Rory snapped back.

"You didn't even follow the recipe properly! I doubt there were sodding *salmon scales* in the original!"

"Didn't stop you bloody well eating the salmon, though, did it?"

"Couldn't waste it."

Rory stopped filling the bottles to glare at the cat. "Do you ever do anything useful, or just sit around criticising people?"

Adams pushed the door open before anyone got bitten,

and they both turned to look at her. Dandy jumped up and rushed toward her, tail wagging cheerily. "We've got a tester here," she said, and beckoned Maud to join her.

"Great," Rory said. "I was about to dose the cat just to see what happened."

Thompson hissed, and Maud stared at the still. "This is a health and safety *nightmare.* Do you have a licence? What's your emergency procedure? Where's your spill kit? Are you wearing *slippers?*"

Rory looked at the hose in his hand, then at Maud, and aimed the nozzle at her.

# 23

# A CANDY FLOSS PLAN

Adams jumped out of the way as the spray splattered straight into Maud's face. Rory had his thumb over the end of the hose, forcing the liquid through a small gap so it had a bit more pressure. Even so, it barely reached the DCI, and she gasped, flinching back. Rory crimped the hose, and they all stared at Maud. She wiped her face with one hand, flicking droplets away, and glared at Rory.

"A *little* warning would be nice," she said, sounding just as irate as she had a moment earlier.

"Would you term that assault?" Adams suggested, and Rory gave her a reproachful look.

"No, I—" Maud stopped, and grinned suddenly. "No, I would *not!*"

Adams took a deep breath, letting it out in a rush as she sagged against the door, one hand finding Dandy's head. "It worked."

"Really?" Rory and Thompson both said.

"Really," Maud said, staring at her hands and turning them one way then the other. "I feel a bit ... tingly."

"Faint?" Collins suggested from the door. Adams could

hear the journalist somewhere behind him, arguing with James that he should be allowed to see what was going on, and James's sharp answers.

"Not exactly," Maud said, and giggled, then clapped a hand over her mouth, looking at Adams with wide eyes.

"Oh, good. She's *drunk*," Thompson said, and Maud turned her gaze to him, her eyes getting even wider. She dropped her hand.

"Did that cat—"

"No," Adams said firmly. "Side effects. You don't feel like arresting Rory for having a dangerous workplace, then?"

Maud shook her head, and slung an arm around Adams' shoulders, making her jump. "Nope. And I'm not drunk. But *you*, you are *the best*. Did I ever tell you how much I like having you on the team? You're just …" She trailed off, thinking about it. "So cool," she finished, and hugged Adams.

"Thanks," Adams said, trying to disentangle herself. "But are you sure you're not drunk?"

"I'm not." Maud looked at Collins. "And you! My other favourite detective. You're both so *clever*." She released Adams and went to hug Collins. He backed outside with her following him, and Adams looked at Rory.

He grimaced. "I did follow the recipe."

"Sort of," the cat said.

"You probably shed in it," Rory said.

"Stop *talking*," Adams hissed at Thompson, and he huffed. She looked at the still. "You've made a lot."

"We've got a lot of people to dose," Rory said. "I figured I'd be better to have it done by the time you got back."

Adams thought that showed a certain, previously unsubstantiated level of faith in them being *able* to come back.

"But it doesn't *work*," Thompson said, and bared his teeth at Adams when she scowled at him. "There's no one here."

"It does work. She no longer wants to arrest anyone."

"No, just hug them all."

"It's an improvement?" Adams could hear the doubt in her own voice.

"Maybe it was too high a dose," Rory said, looking at the hose. "I cranked the heat up to get it through the distillation fast, and maybe it concentrated it too much. Reversed it too far, or however these things work."

Collins put his head in the door. "I don't think she's drunk. I've got her standing on one leg reciting tongue twisters and she's fine. Just really happy."

"But is she going to stay like that?" Adams asked. "She *hugged* me."

"The horror," Collins said. "We can wait and find out before we do anything else, I suppose."

Adams thought of town, the surging crowds and breathless anticipation of violence. "I don't think we can," she said, and looked back at Rory. "How much have you made?"

"Shedloads, to use the technical term." He turned the hose off at the still and pointed to the crates of bottles stacked by the door.

"How do we distribute it?" Collins asked. "It's a lot, but nowhere near enough to give it out to everyone."

"I'm pretty sure you don't want anyone drinking a full bottle anyway," Rory said. "I've got a couple of cordless pressure washers with tanks from when I was doing up the buildings, and a bunch of spare batteries. They've been charging since you left. We fill the tanks from the bottles and spray it over the crowds. It'll go a lot further and be a lot easier to distribute." He nodded at the door, and Maud beyond it. "It doesn't seem to take much, after all."

"Great, then we'll just have a whole town of giddy drunks to deal with," Thompson pointed out.

"Better than murderous ones," Rory said.

Collins looked at Adams. "Your call."

She rubbed the back of her neck, looking at Dandy as if he held the answers. He just stared up at her, tail waving softly, and offered her something. She leaned down, holding her hand out, and he dropped her duck keyring into it, slick with slobber and reassuringly hard in her palm as she closed her hand over it. Her car key was attached to it too, but it was the duck that mattered.

"What the hell was that?" Rory asked.

"Never mind," Thompson said. "You'll forget it all soon enough."

Rory scowled at him. "You're very threatening for something I could pick up by the scruff of the neck."

"Try it, posh boy. I dare you."

"Are there any bottles of beer left?" Adams asked Rory, ignoring Thompson.

"Sure." Rory took one from a cluttered workbench, holding it out to her.

She put it in front of the cat. "What does it smell like?"

Thompson snuffled the bottle, his tail twitching. "Boots and sacks and broken bones."

"That's the charm?"

"Yeah."

She looked at Rory. "Dose the bottle."

He did, squirting a tiny amount of the solution over it. Adams pulled her sleeve down, wiped the bottle off, then set it back in front of Thompson. He sniffed again, shook his head so hard his ears snapped, then head-butted the bottle. It toppled over and he collapsed on top of it, rolling it under him and purring so loudly that Collins said, "Bloody hell."

Adams nodded. "Good enough. Collins, you and I start at the brewery, dose the whole place so they can't come out behind us with more. James can load up as much as he can, then take Maud and Ervin back to the festival and keep us updated." She looked at Rory. "How much more can you make?"

"I'm pretty much done," he said. "This is the last batch."

"Alright. It'll have to do – bottle it all up and we'll grab it once we're done at the brewery."

"I'll get James and Maud off," Collins said, ducking outside.

Rory was watching Thompson, who was still rubbing his face against the bottle, and now he looked at Adams. "I'm not going to ask too many questions," he said.

"I'm not going to ask why you seem quite comfortable with the talking cat. And wolves."

He smiled slightly. "I'm not sure comfortable is the word. But you've got to accept what's in front of you, don't you?"

Adams inclined her head in some sort of acknowledgement, then nodded at the still. "How did you get this to work?"

"It's just a recipe. You follow it, it works. It's not magic."

"Not usually," Adams agreed.

"I've brought the laptop down with me," Rory said, screwing the caps onto the bottles. "No one's come back to the brewery yet."

She examined him for a moment longer, but he just calmly kept on with what he was doing, so she nodded. "I'll get my car and we can load up."

"Ready when you are," Rory said, already heading across the shed to where the pressure washers were leaning against the wall. "I've got your bag, too."

Adams went back out into the night, filled with a sudden, rickety hope. Their plan was precarious, and had so many weak spots it'd collapse like candy floss if she looked at it too closely, but it could work. It *could*.

And right now, that was enough.

JAMES COULDN'T GET many crates into the boot of his car, but they wedged what they could into the back seat with Ervin as well, and he drove cautiously off with the bottles clattering and Maud singing "I Predict a Riot" in the passenger seat. Adams had to admit that she didn't seem impaired, as such, but she was alarmingly jolly.

They'd lost too much time sitting in Harrogate station, and it was still passing far too fast. Adams could almost feel the growing frenzy of the festival, the marquees and grounds bloated with alcohol and threat, building to an explosion. So rather than load her car up fully, she and Collins simply stacked a couple of crates in the back to refill the pressure washer tanks at the brewery. The sooner that was taken care of, the better. They'd have to come back for the rest, and Rory was still bottling the last of it anyway.

"How much more have you got?" Adams asked.

Rory checked the still. "Only another couple of crates' worth, then I'm out of turmeric."

"That shouldn't bother you," the cat said. He seemed to have recovered from his sudden affection for the bottle. "You were using pine sawdust instead of pine needles in the last batch."

"They were pine *shavings*, you philistine, from a pine dresser that'll never be the same. And it's at least in the same family. I don't think I can exactly use Thai curry paste instead of turmeric. Who knows what the fish sauce would do."

"Still. Gods know what effect *pine shavings* are going to have."

"As long as it stops anything getting worse, I don't think I care," Adams said.

The cameras were still clear, so they left Rory finishing

up and headed for the brewery, Dandy in the back seat and
Thompson balancing on Collins' lap. Despite the fact that
they knew there wasn't – or shouldn't be – anyone around,
Adams found her hands so tight on the wheel that she had to
will herself to ease her grip. In the back of her mind she
could still hear the howls of the wolves in the trees.

She didn't bother being subtle about their arrival, just
pulled straight up in front of the brewery, and they sat there
looking at it, as if waiting for it to reveal itself.

Finally Collins said, "Are we doing it?"

"Might as well get it over with." Adams looked at Dandy.
He'd already left the car by his own mysterious means, and
stood on the gravel outside, his head raised and his nose
twitching. She opened her door and looked at him. "All
clear?"

He glanced at her, tail wagging, then padded up to the
brewery. She looked at Thompson, who hadn't moved from
Collins' lap.

"I'm going in after you do," he said. "Let them nip you
first."

"Dandy thinks it's fine," she said to Collins.

"We'll go with that, then," he said, opening his door and
dislodging Thompson. "This one might be hungover."

"I'm *sensible*," the cat said.

The pressure washers consisted of a longish metal pipe
with the nozzle at one end, while the battery nestled into the
handle at the other. The tanks were on wheels, and had an
extendible handle on top, looking much like a carry-on case.
The DIs set them on the ground and looked at each other.

"I feel like a geriatric Ghostbuster with a granny trolley,"
Collins said, rolling his back and forth experimentally.

Adams handed him a reusable shopping bag with half a
dozen spare bottles of solution in it, and shouldered her pack
with the same. "Not such a bad thing," she said. "The grannies

we know would probably have the werewolves doing party tricks by now."

"True."

They went in through the office, using a set of keys Rory had given them, flicking the lights on as they went. There was no use hiding their presence. If the werewolves turned up, they'd sniff them out in an instant anyway. Adams led the way into the brewery itself, and Collins looked around as the lights flooded the space, gleaming softly on the expanse of mellow copper and bright stainless. Things ticked and groaned and bubbled, as if the brewery was a living thing in restless sleep, and the yeasty scent was so heavy the air felt syrupy with it.

"I forgot how big this place was. Are we going to have enough?"

"I hope so. We just do what we can, and Thompson can have a sniff after and see if it's worked."

"I'm not a bloody lab rat," the cat called from the door to the car park.

"No, they're more helpful," Adams said, and pointed at the door to the storeroom. "We'll start on the bottled stuff. They can't exactly wheel the vats out to town."

They hurried through the forest of pipes and pots and hoppers, the hulking forms of the vats crouching high above them like prehistoric beetles. Adams half expected one of them to gather itself up with a screech of metal and lurch into their path, but nothing moved, and they stopped at the storeroom door,. Adams closed her eyes for a moment as she pictured Marcus punching in the code. *9-8-9-2-5*. No, *9-8-5-2-9*. She opened her eyes and entered the numbers, then tried the handle. It opened easily, and she pushed through, examining the crates and kegs to each side. There were a lot in here still, maybe even more than there had been when she'd been there earlier. She looked at Thompson, who'd trailed them in with his ears back.

"Are these charmed?" she asked him, and he reluctantly joined her, sniffing around a couple of the crates, then gagging.

"*Yes.* Ugh. Worse than that bottle at the house."

Adams looked at Collins. "Marcus said they were refining the brew."

"Best get on it, then," he said.

Adams nodded, and towed her tank with her to the end of the storeroom, by the external door. She started on the right-hand side with the crates, Collins taking the other with the kegs

They worked quickly, methodically, spritzing the crates and kegs then dragging them out of place so they could reach those lined up behind. Thompson followed, snuffling the dosed items warily and purring. The stacks of crates were five or six high, and three or four deep in most places, and Adams' back was soon aching with the bending and lugging. She kept going stubbornly though, and was halfway down the length of the wall when she stood to stretch her spine out, and found herself staring at the corner of a heavy metal door set into the stone wall. It had been concealed behind the stacks, but now she was looking she could see the scuff marks that showed where the crates had been moved aside regularly.

She dropped the pressure washer and grabbed the stack of crates in front of the door, almost falling over when she pulled it. The bottles were empty, and the stack moved so fast she had to put her shoulder to it to stop it toppling.

"Collins," she called, and he looked around. "I've got something." She banged on the door with the side of her fist as he abandoned his pressure washer and came to join her. "Chloe?" she called. "Are you in there?"

There was silence, and she banged again, putting her ear to the door and wondering if it was soundproof. "Chloe?"

"Adams?" The reply was faint, but unmistakable. "Is that you?"

Adams closed her eyes for a moment, sagging against the door. Chloe was alright. Or alive, anyway. "We'll get you out," she called. "Hang on."

"Well, I'm not exactly going anywhere, am I?" came back faintly.

"I'll check the office for a key," Collins said, already hurrying away

Adams dug through her pack for her lock-picking tools, then crouched down to peer at the door. The lock wasn't as heavy-duty as it could've been, but it was still substantial. It was going to take some work. She started, Thompson sitting beside her and looking on with interest, still purring steadily.

A few minutes later Collins wasn't back yet, and she was cursing both the lock and her cramping hands when her mobile rang. She pulled it out of her pocket and set it on the floor, hitting speaker, then went back to the lock.

"Yeah?"

"You've got company," Rory said, his voice sharp and clipped.

"How many?" she asked, jabbing at the lock frantically.

"A van and a car. Coming down the lane, fast."

She looked at the cat. "I thought you said those boundary charms weren't alarmed."

"I said *probably*. Or maybe the door's alarmed," he said with a shrug, and she swore. There were no interior cameras – she'd checked for that – but she hadn't thought of the possibility of the door having some sort of silent alarm.

"*Collins!*" she shouted, just as she heard running footsteps.

He appeared at the storeroom door. "Someone's here."

"Rory's just said." She attacked the lock with renewed ferocity, and Collins hurried to the back door, unlocking it.

"Adams, come on. We can come back once they're gone."

"It'll be too late." She was so *close*. She could feel the lock almost ready to give.

"*Adams.*"

"*No,*" she replied, and the lock popped. She wrenched the door open, and Chloe shoved her way out, looking like she wanted to punch someone.

"Where's that hairy bloody—"

Collins opened the exterior door a crack and swore, slamming it closed again. "There's a van. Try the other way."

"Wait here," Adams said to Chloe. She grabbed the long metal nozzle of the pressure washer and unclipped the hose from the end, then ran for the door to the brewery, opening it enough to peer out and check the main floor. There was no one in sight yet, and she stepped onto the brewery floor just as Dandy plunged out of the office and ran to join her, bulking up as he came, until he was back to Newfoundland size. He spun around before he reached her, turning to face the office door, and she gripped the metal pipe in both hands as the wolves boiled into the brewery, lean and muscled and full of fury, one, two, *four* of them.

"Incoming," she called to Collins, and braced herself for the attack, the world gone sharp and cold at the edges.

## TICKLING PHYSICS

The werewolves didn't waste time with posturing. There was a brutal efficiency to them as they flowed into the brewery, muscles moving smoothly under their heavy pelts. There were four of them, and they went straight for Dandy. He crouched as they approached, then launched himself forward, hitting the first one chest to chest and bowling it backward. One dived to join the fight, and the remaining two arrowed toward Adams.

She stepped forward to meet them, twisting to slam the pipe into the snout of a slim grey wolf and setting it into a yelping retreat. The second one, bigger and more solid, leaped to meet her, and she dodged sideways as a beer bottle flew out of the storeroom, smacking it between the eyes. The wolf spluttered, shaking its head wildly, and Adams landed a blow on its haunches, sending it skittering away.

She risked a glance at Collins, standing in the storeroom doorway with a crate at his feet. "We have to dose the rest of the beer," she shouted.

"Chloe's on it." He hurled another bottle, and Adams backed up until she had the wall behind her, watching

Dandy. He'd thrown off the two wolves, but they were circling him with their teeth bared and ears back, snarling steadily.

The skinny grey wolf darted out of the cover of a vat to Adams' right, and she barely had time to bring the pipe up to meet it. She couldn't swing properly, the bloody creature was on her too fast, so instead she just grabbed the pipe with both hands, holding it crossways as she jammed it against the wolf's throat. It was so close she could smell the heat and meatiness of its breath, and she pushed herself off the wall, throwing the wolf backward. It dropped onto its haunches without losing ground and lunged for her again immediately, and she met its snout with her boot, the impact jarring up her leg and wrenching a yelp from the wolf.

"Adams, get in here!" Collins shouted, hurling another bottle at the bigger wolf. It dodged, ready for the attack this time, weaving its way forward past his missiles. The skinny one darted at Adams again, and she whipped the pipe at it. It stopped its charge before she could make contact, snarling.

"*Dandy!*" Adams yelled, taking a step back. "*Move!*"

The wolves surged forward, and she ducked behind Collins into the storeroom as he hefted the entire crate and its two remaining bottles at the beasts. He jumped inside and Adams slammed the door, but not quick enough. The bigger wolf already had its head and shoulder through the gap, and it snarled and twisted, trying to force its way in, snapping at Adams as she threw her weight against the door. She jerked away from its teeth and the door jolted open a little further. The wolf snarled in triumph and surged against the gap, and Chloe ran forward, smashing a bottle straight onto the wolf's snout. It yelped, pulling back, and Adams put her shoulder to the door as the skinny wolf took the first one's place. Collins pushed Chloe away and raised his foot, meaning to boot the wolf back, but it snarled and ducked away, and the door slammed shut. Adams kept her back to it, bracing her feet on the floor. She didn't know how quickly wolves could turn back into human shape.

"How many out the back?" she asked Collins.

"I just saw the van," he said, grabbing up her abandoned pressure washer. "No idea how many in it." He looked at Chloe. "How much of the beer did you get done?"

"It doesn't matter," Adams said. "We need to get out of here."

"All of it," Chloe said, somewhat smugly.

"What?"

She pointed to a smashed bottle of the solution lying in the middle of the floor. "Magic is kind of like tickling physics. I just expanded it into mist."

"Worked, too," Thompson observed. "But not much help to us if we're going to get eaten."

Collins hurried to the back door, opened it a crack, then jammed it closed again at a snarl from outside. "Two at least."

"We split up," Adams said, abandoning the door and grabbing her backpack. "I'll make a commotion in the brewery, hopefully get those two to come around. Once it's clear, you go out the back. Take the pressure washers and get to the car."

"No—"

"Thompson, help them. Run interference if the wolves are still out there. You're no use in here anyway."

"I'm a very supportive presence," the cat said.

"We're not splitting up," Collins said. "That's a terrible idea."

"I've got a dandy," Adams pointed out. "Chloe, can you do that physics-tickling thing on a large scale?"

"Like in the festival?" she asked. Her face was paler than ever, but her eyes were bright. "I should be able to."

"Perfect." Adams looked at Collins. "You need to get her

there. Give me some cover while I get into the brewery, then you go, alright?"

Collins rubbed a hand over his short-cropped hair, looking at Chloe, then nodded, his face grim. "Chloe, you grab the pressure washers," he said. "I'll deal with the wolves." He looked at Adams. "You're sure?"

"Only option," she replied, handing Chloe the pressure washer nozzle and putting her hand on the brewery door. "Ready?"

"Ready," he said, stepping up next to her. She nodded, then went through the door fast. Two of the wolves were skulking not far away, and one let out a howl. The second rushed her, and Collins hurled a bottle at it. It caught the wolf a glancing blow on the shoulder, and Adams whistled, loud as she could, breaking into a sprint across the floor. She heard the crash of another bottle behind her, and another, Collins yelling as he threw them, and she risked a glance back. The wolves had already abandoned him, coming after her with their eyes bright and intent in the sharp light. She reached one of the big tables in the centre of the room and vaulted onto it, racing down the centre with her boots squeaking on the smooth surface.

She whistled again, but there was still no Dandy, and she tried not to think about him battling the two wolves when she'd run into the storeroom. She didn't have time to look for him. The wolves were pacing her easily on either side, and she was about to run out of table.

Adams didn't slow as she reached the end. There was no time to think about it, no time to judge distances or second guess. She threw herself into a leap, body arching and legs pulling up as she imagined the wolves underneath her.

She almost didn't make it. She crashed into the ladder that ran up one of the double-stacked vats, her boots slipping on the rungs and her chin smacking the metal painfully. She grabbed on with both hands, eyes watering, and scrabbled for purchase with her feet, barely finding it in time to scramble out of reach of the wolves. One of them snagged her ankle, her boot resisting its teeth but the pressure painful nevertheless. She kicked back, hard, and it let go with a yelp. She clambered out of reach and hooked an arm through the ladder to hold herself in place, breathing hard.

From this vantage point she could see Collins at the door to the storeroom, still watching.

"Okay?" he shouted.

"Fine," she yelled back, searching for the other wolves. They needed to be in here, it was no good if Collins tried to go out the back and— *"Move!"* she bellowed, and he threw himself back into the storeroom, barely making it before the wolf she'd seen sidling through the shadows launched itself at the door. She could see him fighting to close it, then it slammed and the wolf stepped back, growling. She let her breath out slowly, looking around the storeroom. She still couldn't see Dandy, and now she was stuck on a vat, treed by the wolves. They weren't wasting time jumping and snapping, just stood watching her with those strange, not-quite-animal eyes. The third wolf joined them, and they looked at each other, some communication passing between them.

Adams shifted her position, settling herself more securely, and said, "Which one of you's Marcus, then?"

The wolves looked at her, then at each other, huffing. She couldn't tell if that meant they were amused or insulted.

"Well, I don't know," she said. "I never saw you in wolf form." She eased her bag off one shoulder, checking the contents. Still the six bottles of solution, which were a bit bloody heavy to be carting around, if she were honest. Good missiles, though. Her duck keyring, which she squeezed a couple of times for comfort, then put in her trouser pocket, as it didn't seem to be offering any solutions right now.

Torch. Lock picks. No baton. No phone, as it was probably still on the floor of the storeroom. Half a dozen Yorkie bars.

She waved one at the wolves. "Want one? Is it poisonous for you? Or do you still have kind of a human stomach?"

The wolves didn't answer, and she put the chocolate bar back, zipping her bag up again and settling it on her shoulders. Three in here. That meant Collins was still dealing with three on his side, if the fourth had gone out, and it probably had. She was suddenly grateful Dandy wasn't here. Maybe he was helping them. She *hoped* he was helping them, as she didn't like the thought of any other options for why he wasn't here.

There was a tap at the bottom of the top vat, near her foot, and she knocked it with her boot absently. The two bigger wolves had circled back to the storeroom, sniffing the door, leaving the skinny one below, and it growled. Adams looked at it, feeling the heat rising from the tank. She couldn't remember what these ones had been for. Was this the one with the warts? The loitering? She should've paid more attention, but on the other hand, she didn't need to know the technical details. It was hot, and the wolves had bare paws, which told her as much as she needed. She kicked the tap again, with a little more feeling, and this time the wolf snarled.

Adams grinned. "Oh, don't much like that, do you?"

She booted the tap a third time, and this time it burst open, releasing a trickle of brownish-yellow, steaming liquid, smelling of alcohol and rotting wheat. The wolf sneezed, backing up a couple of steps, and gave an imperious yap. The other two turned away from the storeroom, ears up. Adams kicked the tap again, and the trickle turned into a flood, splashing across the floor, hot and stinking, making the skinny wolf dance back. Adams scrambled down the ladder, leaning precariously across to wrench the tap of the next vat on, the liquid gushing enthusiastically across the hard floor. The wolf dashed toward her, paws slipping in the treacherous flood, then yelped and reversed again, shaking its paws out with a whine. It was hot enough to be uncomfortable, but that wouldn't last long.

The other two wolves broke into a run, rushing around the tables, and Adams jumped to the floor, running for the next vat to open its tap, then to the next, working her way toward the double doors in the midst of a splashing, steaming overflow that made her head swim with fumes. The wolves spun to follow her, sliding in the muck, and she tried to go faster, but her footing was treacherous, even more so than theirs, and she wasn't going to make it. She couldn't get to the door and get it open before they reached her, and one of them gave a little snarl of triumph, so near she had to bite down on something that was too close to a scream for comfort, her heart pounding.

The two wolves converged on her, and she grabbed for a ladder, meaning to scramble out of reach again. As she did, the storeroom door burst open and Collins came charging out with a crate of beer clutched under one arm and a bottle already in another, yelling a wordless, wild battle cry. Chloe raced out behind him, a bottle in each hand, and the wolves hesitated, torn between going after Adams or them.

"What're you *doing?*" Adams yelled. "Go back!" One wolf darted at her, and she booted its snout, hard as she could, sending it skidding back.

Collins and Chloe were still coming, and Chloe hurled one bottle then the other in quick succession. One caught the larger wolf on the hindquarters, and as it spun to face the attack the second exploded at its feet, sending it scuttling back.

"Office," Adams shouted, and started working her way in that direction. Chloe and Collins were still hurling bottles, rapidly depleting their supply, but it was keeping the wolves at bay for now. Then the biggest one gave a soft little half-snarl, and all three melted back into the vats.

"What's going on?" Collins asked, and Chloe froze, a bottle half-raised to her shoulder.

Adams turned, trying to keep track of the wolves, and at that moment the entire place was plunged into darkness. She swore, and shouted, "Climb! Find something and *climb!*"

She heard a crash as Collins abandoned the crate, the clang and yelp of someone running into a pipe, a clatter that she hoped was feet on a ladder. She shoved a hand into her pocket, closing it around the duck. It had tiny little LED eyes, and while she knew logically she'd be better finding her torch, she also knew, entirely illogically, that she wouldn't. She spun as she heard the heavy splash of running paws behind her, dropped into a crouch, and clicked the duck's wings down. Light blazed into the space, casting shadows hard-edged as glass, and the wolf leaping toward her howled in pain, throwing itself sideways. Adams clamped her eyes shut against the assault of the light, and let the wings go. Darkness again. She could hear panting, but wasn't sure if it was her or something else. She stayed where she was, waiting, eyes still closed, and when she heard an intake of breath behind her she swivelled in her crouch, clicking the wings down again. The wolf swerved, skidding past her, and she had a glimpse of Collins and Chloe, clinging to ladders like a couple of kids mid-game, then she let the duck go dark. It was impossible, that massive searchlight beam, and she knew it. But it was real anyway.

Movement, and she almost used the duck again, but she recognised the scent, or the feel, or *something*, and then Dandy's breath was on her face, the gleam of his red eyes just visible through his dreadlocks. She put one hand on his back, straightening up, and cocked her head. An engine. More wolves? She held the duck up, aimed at the oncoming engine, thinking for one absurd moment, *Stop or I'll use my duck!*

The engine was *very* loud now, revving hard, and she almost missed the movement behind her, but Dandy twisted under her hand, lunging away, and she heard the impact of hard, muscular bodies, and claws scrabbling on hard flooring, the splash of creatures slipping through the mire of hops. She spun around, already clamping down on the duck, and the double doors to the brewery exploded open behind her. She whirled back, one arm raised to protect her eyes from a flood of light. The vehicle's brakes screamed, and it carried the tables ahead of it as it juddered to a halt just short of the nearest vats. Two shadowy forms flashed around it, and she thought for a moment it was more wolves, then she saw the piebald markings of the border collies rushing past her.

"*Get in!*" Rory bellowed, leaning out of the Land Rover's window, and Adams ran to meet Collins and Chloe as they jumped down from the vats. Dandy and the border collies were charging and darting through the shadows, wolves scattering in confusion.

"Pressure washers," Collins shouted, angling toward the storeroom, and Adams shoved Chloe toward the Land Rover then sprinted after him. He'd left the door propped open with one of the pressure washers in the gap, and they had hold of them in a moment, turning to run back.

"Move it!" Rory yelled, then swung himself out of the Land Rover, wielding a golf club with an unnerving fury as he swung at a wolf chasing Pinto. "*No! Bad wolf!*"

Chloe hadn't got in, and was crouching down, one hand in the wash of released hops, muttering to herself. Adams broke into a jagged sprint, lugging one of the pressure washers, and as she did she saw the spilled liquid leap upward, transformed into an instant mist that filled the brewery and concealed everything. She ran into a table with a yelp, bounced off it and crashed into Collins. They both staggered but kept their feet, and aimed for the cones of the headlights glittering on the suspended droplets.

Dandy loomed out of the murk, the border collies racing next to him with their eyes rolling in fright, then the Land Rover was right in front of them.

"*In,*" Rory snapped. Chloe was already scrambling into the back, and Collins threw his pressure washer into the cage on top of the vehicle, snatched Adams' from her and did the same, then dived in after Chloe. Adams swung into the front seat and Rory jammed the Land Rover into reverse, backing through the ruins of the doors.

Adams couldn't see anything, not behind or in front, couldn't tell where Dandy and the dogs had gone, couldn't see where the wolves were. Then they were outside, and it was like walking through a curtain, the mist cut off on a knife's edge. Rory kept backing up fast, then threw the car into a leaning turn, gravel spitting from the tyres. The wolves appeared, four surging out of the murky brewery and four more racing around the building to join them. Adams didn't even know where the extra two had come from, but it explained where Dandy had been.

Rory jammed the brakes on. "Dogs!" he yelled, and Collins threw his door open. Rory whistled, and Midge and Pinto launched themselves into the car, scrambling over Collins. Thompson appeared from nowhere, leaping for the Land Rover as Rory floored the accelerator. The cat almost missed, claws screeching on the back door frame, and Collins grabbed him, bundling him in. They roared away down the lane, the wolves racing to keep up. Rory barely slowed as he took the turn onto the main drive, bottles clattering wildly in the back, then they were racing for the road, engine screaming.

Adams peered out the window, spotting Dandy flashing alongside the car, dreadlocks flying. The wolves were still pounding after them, but they'd fallen behind.

"Stop," she said, her voice sharp. Rory slammed the brakes on without questioning it, Adams bracing herself on the dashboard. Chloe, Collins, and the dogs all yelped, while Thompson screeched in disgust as he got tangled up with the border collies. Adams flung her door open and Dandy leaped in, landing on top of her and almost crushing her. She slammed the door, the wolves gaining fast.

"Go," she yelled at Rory, but he was already tearing off again, tyres skidding in the gravel. He didn't pause as they reached the main road, just hauled the wheel over to turn into it. They slid across both lanes, leaning precariously on the edge of the Land Rover's balance, and barely avoided a van coming from the opposite direction. Then they were back on their own side of the road, the whole car bouncing and the van's horn blaring furiously after them.

Thompson was wailing complaints from under the pile-up in the back seats, and Dandy huffed in Adams' face. She grimaced, both at the weight and the smell. "Please shrink," she said.

Rory glanced at her. "What?"

"Not talking to you."

He nodded. "I'm assuming it's whatever we just stopped for?"

"An invisible dog. He's crushing me."

"Right. Not my biggest surprise of the day, oddly enough."

She supposed it had been that kind of evening.

# 25

# TO THE HEART OF IT

PINTO AND MIDGE WERE WEDGED BETWEEN – AND LARGELY ON – Collins and Chloe, panting and whining occasionally while Thompson kept up a steady litany of canine-based complaints. Dandy had shrunk to a more manageable size, and Adams pushed him off her lap into the footwell. He put his head on her knee.

Rory looked at Adams and said, "Where to?"

"Festival," she said, and leaned into the back to look at Chloe. "Are you alright?"

"Well, being kidnapped by werewolves is a first," she said, inspecting her arms. "I'm not bitten, though."

"I didn't even think of that," Collins said, clutching his chest as if to check he was in one piece. "How about you, Adams?"

"No, all good." She ran her hands over Dandy, looking for tender spots.

Rory watched her with fascination. "Is it there?"

"Yes, he's there," Thompson spat. "The *stink* of him. Although, at least he didn't land on top of me like these two bloody mutts. No respect. *No respect at all.*"

One of the mutts in question licked Thompson's head, and he yowled in horror.

"They landed on top of us, too," Collins pointed out. "You're very overdramatic."

"I always thought cats would be a lot more chill," Rory observed, and Thompson spat at him.

Dandy's thick hair seemed to have fended off injury for the most part, although Adams found a couple of spots on his hindquarters that made him whine when she touched them. She parted the fur as well as she could, looking for blood, although she had to admit she didn't even know what dandy blood would look like. Hopefully it wasn't going to be bright blue or something. For some reason, that seemed like it would be even more alarming than the red eyes.

She couldn't find anything, though, and he didn't seem desperately worried. She wondered what would happen if he had been bitten. Would he become a were-human? She didn't imagine that he could become any more dog than he already was.

Collins leaned forward to look at Rory. "Question has to be asked, mate. You're very calm about all this."

Rory shrugged. "I have a very large, very extended family that are much more eccentric than our diminished finances justify. Honestly, this is nothing compared to some of our family reunions."

"Right," Adams said. "Have to fend off a lot of wolves at family reunions, do you?"

"Worse. Cousins thieving the family silver and aunts trying to snaffle all the vintage champagne. Plus an uncle trying to use the dinner service as clay pigeons."

Collins looked at Adams. "How the other half live."

"I lost my phone," she said. "Can you call James?"

"I don't have his number."

"Maud?"

Collins leaned back, digging his phone out.

"So what's the plan when we get to the festival, then?" Rory asked. He was driving fast, the roads nighttime quiet as they left Mother Shipton's Cave behind them and headed for Harrogate.

"Douse the place with the counter-charm and hope we don't get bitten," Adams said.

"Concise."

"Who did the counter-charm?" Chloe asked, leaning forward. "It's got an unusual … *flair*, shall we say."

"That's the pine air freshener," Thompson said.

"Rory," Adams said, nodding at him. "I tried, but I just about blew up his kitchen."

"To be fair, I busted two more pots before I thought to try the still."

"You sneezed," Chloe said to Adams. "That's what it did when I sneezed, too. My upstairs neighbour came down to complain about *young folk today*."

Adams thought about it. "I suppose I did."

"It was really hard not to," Rory said. "I think that's why the still worked. Contained all the fumes."

"Clever," Chloe said.

"It's James," Collins said, holding the phone out to Adams.

She took it, putting it on speaker. A burst of noise blared out, making her wince. It was probably meant to be music, as she could make out an electric guitar screaming, and possibly someone singing, but at the sort of volume that sounded like it was going to bring down some buildings.

"James? What's happening?"

"Adams? Can you hear me?" he yelled.

"Just. Are you alright?"

"It's carnage."

"How's Maud?"

"She keeps hugging everyone and telling them how

wonderful they are, and people aren't taking it well. Some woman who makes cakes with punny names just punched her."

"Ah."

"Yes. And someone keeps yelling *cannonball* and throwing pineapples through the marquee walls, there's a brawl breaking out over the sausages, the butcher appears to be trying to strangle the fishmonger with a string of said sausages, and—"

"Okay, okay. We've got more antidote and we're on the way."

"Can we start with what we've got?"

"Not unless you've got a good way to distribute it. Do you still have the journalist?

"He's here."

"Good. This is contamination in the beer, got it? He needs to document it, and get his ferrety little nose into the other brewers' business and tell them about it. We need them to help us stop any more beer being handed out, and Ervin needs to film it so that no one gets too rough."

"I think it's a bit late for that. Temper and some lawyer are having a throw-down brawl, there's about half a dozen other fights going on, and no one's *doing* anything. Half the coppers are *in* the brawls, and the other half are cheering them on, and that beer's everywhere, and how—"

His voice was rising and rising, and Adams snapped, "Detective Constable Hamilton, *stop*." He stopped immediately, the noise around him rushing in to fill the space. "Take a breath. Just get Ervin working, try to stop anyone from killing each other, and we will be there as soon as we possibly can. Got it?"

"Got it," he said, sounding a little calmer. "Sorry."

"See you soon." She hung up, and handed the phone back to Collins.

"I see your technique," he said. "Scare people into behaving."

"Works for me," Rory said, grinning at the road.

"Not to ruin the moment," Chloe said, "but is that car coming a bit fast?" She was peering out the back.

Collins and Adams both twisted in their seats. A set of headlights was bearing down on them, going even faster than they were, and Rory was already ignoring the speed limit.

"Floor it, mate," Collins said, and the Land Rover growled as Rory did just that. But it wasn't a young car, and it had never been built for speed. It was slow to pick up, and the other vehicle roared up behind them, not slowing. It bumped into the back of the Land Rover, setting the dogs barking. They were going fast enough that it wasn't a huge bump, but it still bounced them forward. Rory swore, leaning over the wheel as if he could will more speed out of the old car, and their pursuers flicked their headlights onto high beam as they fell back slightly.

"Left," Collins yelled at Rory, and he didn't hesitate, just spun the car into a side road that yawned up next to them, working through the gears and accelerating hard as the other car overshot, brakes squealing. They thundered down the narrow street, bouncing over speed bumps as headlights swung in behind them, their pursuers quick to recover. Collins hung between the front seats, shouting directions, leading them in a zigzagging route back to the main road again.

"Isn't there another way?" Adams asked, bracing herself against the dashboard.

"No, there's train tracks," Rory said. "There aren't many crossings."

They screeched back onto the main road and turned toward Harrogate again, only a few car lengths in front of the van. The train tracks loomed ahead, the safety barriers on their way down, lights flashing, and Rory said something that drew an impressed sound from Thompson.

"Do it," Collins said, his voice flat.

"I don't know—" Rory started.

"They're just going to push us onto it anyway."

"He's right," Adams said.

Chloe said something even more inventive than Rory had, and he dropped a gear and jammed the accelerator down as hard as he could. The Land Rover's engine screamed in protest. There was one car waiting on this side of the tracks, and he swerved around it, punching straight through the barrier on the wrong side of the road, setting them bouncing and skidding across the tracks.

The dogs were barking, Dandy setting up a yelp of sympathy, and Thompson, who had put his paws on the side window to peer out, screeched at the top of his feline lungs. Adams looked in the same direction, and saw the train bearing down on them. Its brakes screamed as they clamped down on the rails, and its headlight flooded the car, almost blinding her, so close she couldn't even seem to form a coherent thought. The only thing that occurred to her, disjointed and almost entirely irrelevant, was that she'd imagined such moments to happen in slow motion, but everything was so *desperately* fast.

There was one teetering moment where it seemed there was no way they'd make it across in time, then they were crashing off the tracks and back onto the road on the other side, the passage of the train buffeting them and Collins swearing almost as roundly as Rory was.

The other car had come to a violent halt on the far side of the tracks behind them, but Rory kept the accelerator down, swerving back onto the right side of the road and tearing toward the heart of Harrogate.

"That was a bit close," he said, his tones jagged for the first time.

"Just a bit," Adams replied, and looked at Collins.

He managed an unsteady smile. "You normally have more time than that when the barriers have just come down."

Thompson dropped down from the window and looked at him. "I know I have multiple lives, but I do have no desire to waste any of them dying in a car crash with *dogs*."

"Better than being torn apart by wolves," Collins pointed out. "Besides which, you can shift whenever you want. Why're you still here?"

"I was too traumatised by that stunt to even think about it in time," the cat said.

Rory looked in the rearview mirror at Collins and the cat and said, "I have a *lot* of questions."

"Me too," Chloe said. "And I'm a witch."

"Some witch," Thompson said. "Where's your familiar?"

Chloe reached into the pocket of her coat and brought out a small, sleekly brown snake, which coiled gently around her hand, flicking its tongue curiously. The dogs started barking hysterically, Rory bellowed at them to shut up, Collins pressed himself against the door, trying to get at far as possible from Chloe, and Thompson hissed wildly, his back arching and his tail pouffing out.

Adams sighed and leaned back in her seat, closing her eyes as she petted Dandy. They had half a moment to take a breath, and she intended to take full advantage of it.

THE ROUTE GREW MORE and more snarled the closer they got to the Stray. It wasn't traffic that was the problem, but the packs of people who surged and moved across the green and the pavements, spilling onto the road and blocking their path. The unruly crowd didn't consist of just the usual suspects, packs of excited, agitated lads or groups of men sporting T-shirts and aggression, although there were plenty of them, too. But there were also women in sensible shoes and cardigans, their hair wild, wielding golf clubs and tyre irons as they smashed car windows and climbed fences, yelling for the pure joy of being heard, while older people with canes and walkers thrashed through flowerbeds and took off in slow-motion escape with pilfered plants from doorsteps. Edging past the Stray, they passed a small pack of dishevelled men in respectable suits rocking a coffee truck until it overturned, all of them cheering.

"Hell of a mess," Collins muttered.

"Do you think we've got enough antidote?" Rory asked Adams.

"Soon find out." She was wondering how many of the crowd had drunk the beer, and how many were just taking advantage of the chaos it had sown. She supposed it didn't much matter. The end result was the same.

"We could have a little practice," Collins said, pointing through the windscreen. A van was trundling slowly down the street ahead of them, a tall man hanging out the back and tossing bottles to the crowd.

Good call," Adams said, unfastening her seatbelt and winding down the window. "Close as you can," she said to Rory, and lifted herself out to sit on the edge, one arm hooked inside the car to hold her in place as she grabbed one of the pressure washer nozzles out of the roof cage. Collins did the same in the back, and Chloe leaned out her own window, shaking her hands out as Rory rolled toward the van, the crowd parting reluctantly in front of them. Adams started spritzing the drinkers, the scent of the antidote rising toward her, soothing as lavender in the night, and Chloe caught some on her hands, muttering softly to herself.

The tall man's head snapped toward them, his mouth dropping open just slightly. Even from here Adams could see the slightly too-long canines, and she fired a spray of liquid toward him, aiming into the van. He moved fast, jumping into the crowd to lunge for her with fluid, muscular grace, knocking people out of the way as he surged forward. "Faster!" she called to Rory.

The Land Rover nudged forward, Rory laying on the horn as he carved a path through the crowd. The werewolf reached them, grabbing for Adams, and she smacked him with the spray nozzle, whipping it across his face and sending him stumbling back with a snarl. She went back to spraying as much of the crowd as she could. Chloe was still muttering, and the solution began to rise in a delicate, fragrant mist in the crowd, not as thick and choking as in the brewery, but something gentle and soft instead. Adams still wasn't sure how well it was going to work – or if it would at all – but they couldn't exactly hang around to check, not with a second van load of wolves likely not far behind them.

They were past the knot of people around the wolves' van now, and Adams lowered herself back into the car. Rory picked up more speed, and Chloe turned back into the car and said, "I think that worked."

"Really?" Adams asked, and Rory gave her an offended look.

Chloe pointed. "Those two guys were hitting each other with traffic cones, and now they're hugging. Wait – wow. Should *not* be doing that in public." She looked at her hands. "I hope I'm not doing that."

"No, it was making people a bit huggy already," Adams said.

"That's a bit more than hugging."

"She's right on both counts," Collins said, squeezing

himself back through the window. "Look, the crowd's already breaking up."

Adams leaned out of her window to look back. The cluster of drinkers was drifting away from the brewery van, losing interest as the charm crumbled. There was certainly a lot of excessive affection going on, but she supposed that was better than the alternative. "How do you do the mist thing?" she asked Chloe, and the young woman wiggled her fingers.

"*Magic.*" She laughed. "Told you. Tickle physics. Water wants to evaporate. I'm not breaking any rules, just helping things along."

"Can you help cars along?" Rory asked, looking in the rearview mirror. "The beer van's after us."

"Move it," Adams said, and he accelerated as much as was possible on the crowded streets.

It wasn't far to the festival grounds, and Rory didn't bother looking for a spot to park. He just came to a stop at the closest point to the marquees, half-blocking the road, and Adams and Collins swung out, Dandy following them. The van pulled in straight behind them, and the tall man threw himself out of the passenger seat.

"*Hey,*" he shouted. "What the hell was *that?*"

Adams raised her ID, yelling back, "DI Adams, North Yorkshire Police. Get back in that van or I'll arrest you right this moment."

"You can't arrest me," the man said, starting forward. "I haven't done anything wrong."

"We can start with disturbing the peace and go from there," Adams snapped. The driver had climbed out too, a big man with broad shoulders and a sloping belly, and he looked at Collins as he took the pressure washers from the roof of the Land Rover.

"What the hell d'you think that's going to do?" the driver demanded.

"Police work," Adams said. "Now, are you going to be a problem, or are you going to get back in the van and go quietly?"

The tall man growled, and she crossed her arms over her chest, legs planted wide, wishing she still had her baton. The crowd was thick here, swelling out of the festival, and Adams didn't think these two would risk changing into wolves. But when the other van turned up, they were going to be outnumbered, and then it wouldn't matter what shape the werewolves were in. They couldn't stop them by force.

"Collins, take Chloe and find James. Get him to help her with whatever she needs," Adams said. "Then grab Maud and we can regroup."

"You're alright here?"

"Sure," she said. "Nice civil discussion."

"Come on," Collins said, and Chloe grabbed the second pressure washer. They jogged off, vanishing into the crowds. Rory stayed with Adams. He'd let the border collies out and they flanked him, both of them growling, ears back and teeth bared. Dandy stood still and silent next to Adams.

"What do you think you're going to do with those mutts?" the big man asked Rory.

"Whatever I need to."

Adams took a step forward. "If you're not going to take advantage of my generous offer to ignore you, we may as well get on. I'm arresting you both for disturbing the peace."

The tall man stepped back. "Seriously? In the middle of *this?*" He gestured at the surging, chaotic crowd, music thumping wildly, voices raised in shouts and shrieks, and fireworks fizzing out of the green to explode above them, washing the night in ghastly colour.

"Got to start somewhere," Adams replied.

The big man retreated to the van, looking at his packmate. "Get in," he said. "We're out of here."

"But Marcus—" the other started, and the big man shook his head sharply.

"Just bloody well get in."

They climbed back into the van and Adams let them go. She wasn't going to be able to arrest all of them, but if she could just get Marcus and distribute the antidote, she could stop this whole thing in its tracks. She was sure of it.

Rory looked at her as the van pulled away. "What do you want me to do?"

"Look for Marcus. Don't engage with him – or anyone – just come and find me if you see him." She grabbed her pack from the Land Rover and turned to leave.

"Wait," Rory said, and handed her a plain spray bottle, like might be used for misting plants. He held up a matching one. "Got to help, right?"

She looked at it, then raised it in mock salute. "Can't hurt." She turned away, Dandy padding next to her, and pushed her way into the crowd, straining to see through the throng. It had become one organism, moving and surging, full of the sort of raging energy that made it hard to tell if people were laughing or screaming, fighting or dancing. This place should have been shut down hours ago, and it was all she could do not to start shouting, *Police, clear the area*. But that wasn't going to make any difference, and the last thing she needed was to draw attention to herself.

She put her head down, stuck her elbows out, and fought her way toward the tightest knot of the crowd, wondering where Collins was, and thinking that maybe they shouldn't have split up. But then again, what were two of them going to do against this, together or not?

What *could* they do?

# 26

# WOLVES FOR HIRE

THE MASS OF PEOPLE PACKED BETWEEN THE FOOD TRUCKS AND marquees was difficult to navigate but not impenetrable, and Adams hadn't been a London copper for nothing. She employed elbows and boots ruthlessly, not enough to harm, but enough that she steadily cleared a path through the throng toward the centre of the festival. She wasn't sure what she expected to find there – everyone wedged together in one furious snarl of adrenaline and enchantment perhaps, waiting for the spark that would ignite them into whatever final act of fury Marcus had planned, or some sort of mosh pit for the truly catastrophic music blaring from the stage. Not picnic tables and seating areas anymore, certainly.

But when she reached the edge of the marquees and pushed her way between a tall woman in leather trousers and a large lad in a kilt, who were yelling at each other about the cost of living, apparently in furious agreement, she stumbled abruptly into relatively clear space. The picnic tables had been pulled to the edges of the circle of tents, as had the big barrels set on end to use as tables, and people were sitting and standing on them, shouting and cheering. Adams had a clear view to the stage to her left, toward one end of the oval, where about four people were pounding on the drum kit with whatever they had to hand – bottles and fists and what looked like a sausage roll – while half a dozen others played different tunes on electric guitars, most of which she suspected weren't tunes at all. A few singers were giving it their best Axl Rose impression, and a wedge of festival-goers in front of the stage were headbanging wildly.

But other than that, the oval was clear, because it had become a gladiators' arena, complete with the bloodthirsty crowd baying for blood, but without the sandals and lions. Hand-to-hand combat raged across the torn grass, the fighters slipping on dropped burgers and tripping on discarded shoes. Women in twinsets and pearls brawled with tattooed youths in hoodies and trainers. Bespectacled banker types with black eyes and bleeding noses exchanged punches with farmers in wellies and torn shirts. A cheesemonger in a filthy apron pelted two barefoot, long-haired men with chunks of blue cheese, and she spotted the florists chasing a big-bellied man, wielding their bamboo sticks ruthlessly while he shouted threats involving weedkiller.

And those were just the fights that looked *normal*, heated and irrational, if a bit overwrought. There were others which Adams couldn't quite get the logical part of her brain to accept, although the very practical part of her simply pointed out that it was just more fighting, and she had a duty to stop it. She wasn't entirely sure how, though, as the combatants were hurling each other the length of the arena, throwing themselves into flips and somersaults, tearing their shirts and body-slamming each other like they were in a wrestling ring. Others sprinted from one side of the oval to the other, like kids playing tag, but with the addition of screamed invectives and a generous assortment of missiles they'd evidently swiped from the stalls. A lot of the runners were far too fast, and seemed to like throwing giant, ballet-style leaps into the middle of things, which was particularly impressive when quite a few of them looked like they should probably be using walkers.

Adams dismissed the fighting. None of it looked life-threatening, and she couldn't go in and arrest them all. She'd just end up shoved in a barrel with the offcuts from the butcher's stall, like the very distressed uniformed officer she could see by one of the benches, a large man casually pressing him back into place every time he tried to climb out. If Chloe could do her physics-tickling thing, the fights would be over in moments. What she needed to do was put a stop to more beer being handed out first, otherwise it'd all be for nothing.

Because the flow of Niddered Ale hadn't slowed. All through the crowd moved more werewolves in their brewer's shirts, handing out bottles and plastic glasses and jugs. That had to be her priority. *That* was what she had to put a stop to.

Someone shoved her, or bumped into her, and she stumbled forward into the ring, almost colliding with one of the fighters. He turned to her with a snarl, and she recognised Temper, his shirt torn at the collar and dotted with blood from a split lip.

"*Adams.* Just can't keep your nose out, can you?"

"We have a situation," she started, trying to appeal to the part of him that was still Temper, because it had to be there, didn't it? Maud had gone back to usual, after all. Or she had gone giggly, at least.

He shoved her, one hand to her shoulder. "Fight me."

"No."

"*Fight me.*" He shoved her again, harder this time.

Adams sighed, looked at the spray bottle in her hand, and blasted him in the face with it, as if he were a cat on the kitchen worktop. Temper yelped, covering his face with both hands, and staggered backward.

"You *cow!* You nasty little—"

"Adams!" Maud rushed across the litter-strewn grass to throw her arms around the DI, almost lifting her off her feet. "*There* you are!"

"Maud, stop." Adams struggled to twist out of the DCI's grip, spotting Collins jogging around the oval toward them. Someone had splattered him with tomatoes, and he looked seriously put out.

Temper staggered back toward her. "You," he started again, pointing at her, then looked at his finger as he wasn't sure what he was doing with it. "You," he tried again. "Um."

"Temper!" Maud sang, and let go of Adams to hug him instead. "Isn't this fun? All of us together?"

"Get off," he said, pushing at her ineffectually.

"No, we need this. Good hugs make for good policing."

"They *don't*. All this *empathy* and *hugs* and paperwork and new initiatives and community outreach—" He sounded almost like himself, building up to a rage. "I've had enough! We need to get back to *proper* policing!"

Maud hugged him harder. "You just need more hugs."

Temper sniffled. "I *don't*." His voice was slightly wobbly.

"You *do.*"

Adams looked at Collins as he reached her. He didn't have the pressure washer anymore, but he had his baton ready in one hand. "Chloe?" she asked.

"She's on it. Wants to use the stage to distribute the antidote. There's a couple of big fans up there and she thinks that'll disperse it pretty well."

"Great. James?"

"Helping her and muttering that he's going to need more than a Yorkie bar."

Adams grimaced. "Alright. And Ervin?"

"Inciting a riot, I think," Collins said, and pointed across the oval. Adams clambered to the top of the nearest picnic table, avoiding an irate soap-maker who tried to squirt bubble bath in her face, and stared across the crowds.

Ervin had a pack of people gathered around him, whom Adams assumed were the other brewers, and he was ... "Oh, bollocks," she said aloud. "He was just meant to stop it being handed out."

"Another one who doesn't take direction well," Collins said, and grinned up at her.

The brewers were attacking anyone wearing a Niddered Ale shirt, or even just carrying one of the beers, snatching the bottles and running off into the crowd, knocking plastic glasses out of people's hands, wrestling for ownership of crates and kegs. A couple of men wearing Niddered Ale T-shirts had been trussed up with packing straps and were being dragged into a marquee by half a dozen dishevelled men and women in competitors' shirts, which gave her hope that either Marcus's crew weren't all werewolves, or weren't going to change without warning.

The brewers seemed a little too enthused though, and as she watched, three of them tackled a man who was towing a Niddered Ale keg around on a small handcart. As they tussled, two drinkers took advantage of the distraction to grab the handcart and take off through the crowd, the brewers abandoning the fight to chase them. The man climbed slowly to his feet, head low and teeth bared. His eyes locked with Adams, and he raised his head slightly. It was the young man she'd met the first day, and his mouth dropped further open, revealing still more teeth. He turned, and she knew he'd be going straight to Marcus.

She jumped back to the ground and looked at Maud and Temper, who were still locked in an embrace, Temper bent over so he could rest his head on Maud's shoulder, while she petted his hair and made soothing noises.

"It's *hard*," he wailed. "You have to be *nice* to people. Since when is policing about being *nice?*"

"You don't have to be nice to *everyone*," she said encouragingly.

"But I don't *like* it! Why can't I shout?"

Collins tilted his head at the DCIs. "Were you counting on them?"

"We need to find the brewery tent," she said, ignoring the question. "Stop any more beer going out."

"Ervin'll know where it is," Collins said.

She handed him her spray bottle. "Get back to Chloe. James doesn't know what's going on, and I don't think we're getting any help out of these two." She nodded at Maud and Temper, who were now waltzing around the oval.

"You can't just run off on your own," Collins started, and she looked around. Dandy was a few metres away, scoffing sausages off a dropped tray. She pointed at him.

"I've got him. Chloe's key to cleaning this up. Worry about her." She didn't give him time to answer, just headed around the oval, watching warily for werewolves to lunge out of the crowd.

She made it around the oval unscathed, but not before she saw DCI Bell striding across the grass with a box of tomatoes under one arm (which likely explained where Collins had acquired his stained shirt from) toward Maud and Temper. He was bellowing for them to get off his patch, but all the other two DCIs did was crush him into a group hug, while he struggled and swore, trying to fight free.

Adams was just about to start forcing her way back into the crowd when a shout stopped her. She turned to see Collins jogging toward her with Thompson running next to him. As they went past the DCIs, Collins gave Bell a blast from the spray bottle, eliciting a howl of outrage, then delivered the same treatment to a couple of the other fighters before he and the cat reached her.

"What?" She needed to be moving to the heart of what was going on, not standing here poking at its edges. Dandy whined up at her.

"Rory's found Marcus," he said.

"Where?"

"In the bloody spa, where d'you think?" Thompson asked. His coat was damp in patches, and his pupils swallowed the green of his eyes. He leaped to Collins' shoulder, making the big man wince. "Straight ahead, go on."

THE TWO DIs forced their way through the crowd, following the directions of the cat, Dandy sliding through the forest of legs in his own unknown way. Adams could feel eyes on them, and she was tensed for someone to grab her, to try and drag her off like a deer snatched from its herd. She'd taken a couple of the bottles of antidote from her pack, gripping them tightly by the necks, and she wished she'd had a chance to get her very big stick from her car, or even that she still had her baton. But she had the duck at least, and the bottles, and Dandy looking back at her with red eyes.

They made it out of the thickest press of the crowd and into slightly freer ground, which Adams found rather less reassuring than she thought she would. There was less cover here, and as she looked around warily Thompson said, "There. Coffee truck."

Dandy gave a little whuff of excitement and ran to the shuttered truck, putting his paws up on the back door and looking at Adams hopefully. She felt about the same, but there was no time for stocking up on caffeine.

"Marcus is in there?" she asked doubtfully.

"Of course not," Thompson said. "But Lord Land Rover is."

Collins tried the door, finding it latched from the outside, but not locked. He opened it onto Rory on the floor with his back pressed to the counter, the spray bottle and a handle off the coffee machine both pointed at them. Midge and Pinto were sitting next to him, as far from the door as they could get.

"Alright?" Collins asked, and Rory lowered his weapons, sagging.

"Yeah. We kind of got trapped by a couple of the … of Marcus's guys."

Adams looked at Thompson. "You didn't mention that bit."

"Well, they're not here now, are they? And Duke of Dogs did find the beer tent."

"I did," Rory agreed, getting up and clambering out to join them. He pointed across the field with his coffee handle. "Come on."

"Do we have a plan?" Collins asked Adams.

"Arrest Marcus and seize the beer."

"How d'you see that going?"

"Probably not smoothly."

They hurried after Rory, the dogs trailing behind him, as he led them still further from the centre, the crowds thinning more and more until Adams felt uncomfortably exposed. Finally he skirted a flower-bedecked juice truck that seemed to have escaped mostly unscathed, although no one was in it. It was open, oranges still stacked in big bowls on the counter and pineapples resting next to them.

"There," Rory said, nodding around the corner of the truck to a marquee.

Adams leaned around him to see. There was no banner to mark it, and the clear plastic windows had blinds rolled down over them, giving her no clue as to what waited inside. No one was guarding the closed doors, but as she watched a small, muscled woman pushed through them, glancing around before pulling a trolley laden with Niddered Ale out with her.

Adams looked at Collins and Rory with their spray bottles, then handed them the spares she was holding, Rory dropping his coffee handle to grab his. "There's more in here still," she said, taking her bag off and giving it to Collins. "Once we get in, can you two douse everything?"

"Sure," Rory said.

"Why not," Collins said, looking at his spray bottle. "It's everything I thought policing would be."

"Thompson—" Adams started.

"No, I'm not scouting it out for you. There's shift locks around the whole festival, so I'm doing every bloody thing on foot, and those mutts are *fast.*"

"Fine," she said. "Go and tell Chloe we've found the beer, and she can get started on whatever she's doing to spread the antidote."

"Shouldn't we make sure we can actually get in there first?" Collins asked.

"We can," Adams said.

"How?"

She hoisted herself onto the counter of the fruit trailer, peering into the shadows, and found what she was looking for stuck to a magnetic strip under the counter. She dropped back down, handing each man a knife. Rory hooked his spray bottle onto his jeans, taking the knife and staring at it with a frown on his face.

"You two circle around the back," she said. "Give me a minute, then once you hear a bit of a commotion, come in. If there's no other doors, just stab a hole in the bloody tent and spray everything you can reach."

"Where're you going?" Collins asked.

"Straight in the front door." She turned back to the truck and pulled herself up until she could lie on her belly over the counter, grabbed a mop that was leaning in the corner, and slid back out again. "Come on." She marched toward the marquee with Dandy trotting beside her and the mop swinging in one hand. Collins and Rory scrambled after her, both of them running for opposite corners of the tent.

Adams didn't give herself time to wonder if this was smart, or even possible, just shoved the marquee door open and strode in, her head up and the mop loose in her hand. She stepped to the side as she came through, in case anyone was right behind her, and found herself facing four were-wolves, their edges so clear-cut as to be painful, more so than she'd ever seen before. Two were stacking crates of beer onto trolleys, another tapping a keg to fill a stack of plastic glasses, and Marcus was sitting on the edge of a folding table, frowning at his phone. He looked up as she came in, and a broad grin spread across his face.

"See, Andi?" he said to the woman tapping the keg. It was the same muscular werewolf Adams had seen at the brewery earlier. "I told you she'd come to us."

"Shouldn't be so bloody relaxed about it," Andi replied, sniffing the air. "She'll have that bloody monster in here somewhere."

"Can you see him when you're in human shape?" Adams asked, genuinely curious.

"No," one of the men stacking crates said. He was young, with a man-bun and a poorly trimmed beard. "Can still smell him, though." He peered around warily. Dandy stayed by Adams, panting softly.

"Interesting." She looked around the marquee. Kegs and

crates were everywhere, forming rough, chest-high walls, and a heavy reek rose off them that she knew she was feeling as much as smelling, redolent of fists and teeth, bottled violence waiting to be spread, the reek intensified in this small, hot space. Maybe she hadn't been able to sense it before, but she certainly could now, her pulse spiked with adrenaline. She looked at Marcus. "I want a word."

Marcus got up, pocketing his phone. "I know you're just doing your job here, but we don't want any trouble."

Adams raised her eyebrows slightly, spreading one hand out toward the door to indicate the carnage outside.

He laughed. "Okay, we want a certain *type* of trouble. But we don't want trouble with you. Your colleagues are having a good time. You could be too."

"They're not having a good time. They're beating the hell out of each other."

"Sure, but they're enjoying it."

"They won't when it wears off and they realise what's happened," she pointed out.

He leaned back against the table, hands on its edge. "Well, for some of them, sure. But if we got that last batch right, it's not going to."

"Sorry?"

"These things are always a bit experimental. The first batch was very short-lived and mostly made Frank here cry in the corner."

The third werewolf, a big man with hefty arms, scowled. "I wasn't crying. I was whining."

"So much better," Marcus said.

Adams tapped the mop against her leg. "So what's the big plan here?"

Marcus shrugged. "This is my job done, really. Roll out the new batch, make sure your witchy little friend doesn't get up to any mischief, and that's it."

"But why? What's your reason for it?" Movement behind Marcus caught her eye, the canvas wall of the marquee bulging just slightly.

"It's just a job."

Adams frowned. "A job?"

"Sure. Someone gives us money, we do some things? Just like you."

"That's all it is?" Thompson had said werewolves were mercenary, and it did make a frustrating sort of sense. She hadn't been able to figure out Marcus's why because there *wasn't* one. The why was someone else's.

"Sure. Plenty of people don't like getting their hands dirty, but we're not fussed, are we, lads?"

Andi growled, and Marcus glanced at her. "I'm not a lad," she said.

"Outdated language there," Adams agreed. The back wall of the tent was moving, rippling and shifting, and she said to Andi, "You could do him for that."

"I should," she said, giving Marcus a level look that suggested he wasn't an undisputed leader.

He raised his hands. "Mutts, then. How's that?"

"Steady on, Marcus," Frank said, and Marcus waved irritably.

"Who hired you?" Adams asked.

Marcus pushed himself off the table. "Client confidentiality, I'm afraid. I can't help you with that."

"Fine. What's the end goal? You must know that."

He shrugged. "They pay the bills, I do the job. Less questions asked, the better. And we're wasting time." He looked at the other three werewolves. "Let's get this bloody well done."

"I don't think so," Adams said. "Marcus Gallagher, I'm arresting you—"

The wolves turned toward her, Andi dropping to all fours in the same movement, the other two following in rapid succession until only Marcus remained standing, and a hideous crackling sound filled the marquee, visceral and stomach-churning. The werewolves collapsed down on themselves, bending and folding and twisting, and some part of Adams calmly observed that the noise was probably made by tearing flesh and ripping muscle, by the bones shattering and reforming. She took an involuntary step back as the more sensible part of her screamed hysterically that she needed to put as much distance between herself and this horror show as she could, but she couldn't quite look away. Instead she watched in horrified fascination as the human forms congealed into some unformed mass of organic matter, then re-knitted again in a different shape, the wolves rising out their shed clothes, heads low and teeth shining, beauty born from grotesquery.

She tore her gaze off them and looked at Marcus just as Collins burst through the back wall, spray bottle at the ready. Marcus didn't even look around.

"Run, Inspector," he said, his voice a growl. "I've got your scent."

He collapsed to the ground, and Adams grabbed the nearest stack of crates, toppling them into wolf-Andi as she lunged forward. Dandy surged toward Frank, Collins grabbed the folding table and swung it into the third wolf, and Marcus rose from the floor as a heavy, perfectly muscled beast, already launching himself toward her.

## SEEING SPARKS

Marcus leaped for Adams, sleek and deadly, and she had one moment to think he was a truly beautiful animal. That same balance of leanness and bulkiness he had as a human, legs long and shoulders muscled. His fur was a tawny mix of golds and browns, his eyes green-tinted and luminous, and ... And then she was mostly focused on the teeth, which were long and bared. She swung the mop to meet him, and he twisted mid-leap, so she only caught him a glancing blow on the shoulder. Dandy abandoned Andi and shot toward Adams, and the front door to the marquee tore open as more of the werewolves rushed in, collapsing as they came with that terrible sound of traumatised flesh.

"*Here!*" Rory yelled, leaning around a stack of crates, and Adams walloped Marcus across the jaw as he swung back to her, then sprinted for the back of the tent, yelling for Collins as she went. He joined her, barely a pace ahead of the wolves, Dandy snarling behind them. Adams toppled another stack of crates as she went past, spilling beer and shattering glass across the marquee's hard floor and into the path of the wolves.

She tumbled through the torn canvas into the night, Collins right on her heels, and shouted, "Get to Chloe, *go!*"

He wheeled left without arguing, grabbing Rory and hauling him along, vanishing into the crowds. Adams turned right, out into the night and the darkened green, put her head down, and ran. She was the one Marcus was after, and if she could draw him away, the others would hopefully either follow or lose interest.

She couldn't outrun wolves, of course, but she darted and weaved her way through the dregs of the crowd as she headed for open ground, pushing hard, using the straggling festival-goers as obstacles. Then they were gone, and the Stray was wide and bare before her, and a growl went up at her heels. She pivoted hard, using her momentum as she brought the mop around and slammed it into Marcus's shoulder, sending him tumbling sideways. He recovered fast, coming back to his feet as three more wolves joined him, pausing their charge as they looked to him for a cue.

Adams pointed the head of the mop at them all. "Are you sure you want to do this? For a bit of *cash?* I'll arrest the whole bloody lot—"

Before she could finish, Marcus lunged forward. Dandy leaped to meet him, and they crashed into each other chest to chest, tumbling to the ground, snapping and snarling. More wolves were arriving, spreading out to surround her, and she stole a look around. She needed something to put her back to.

There was a van parked in the middle of the green, side door open. A handful of kids were ferreting around inside, a fire burning next to it, and as Adams looked back at the wolves she heard the sudden *whoomph* of a firework going off. She feinted forward, taking a half-hearted swing at a wolf she thought was likely Andi, then turned and sprinted for the van, yelling for Dandy as she went. The wolves pounded after her, Dandy darting back and forth in her trail, unable to drive them back but keeping them at bay.

She reached one of the kids just as he lit the fuse on a rocket. She dropped her mop and shoved him out of the way, grabbing the firework out of the ground and hurling it back toward the wolves. It exploded right in the middle of the pack, sending them scattering as it shot off across the ground. One of the wolves went howling sideways, yipping in pain, while another turned and sprinted halfway back toward the marquees before it recovered itself. The others came to a skidding stop and waited, watching Adams. Only Marcus kept coming, his charge slowed to a prowl, his head low and hungry.

*"Run!"* Adams shouted at the kids, snatching a rocket and a lighter off the one she'd pushed over. She lit the firework and hurled it straight at Marcus. He side-stepped it and broke into a run, ignoring it fizzling in the grass behind him. She grabbed another and lit it hurriedly, flinging it at him even though she knew it wouldn't be fast enough. The previous rocket caught light and zoomed off across the field, making Marcus flinch sideways, checking over his shoulder, and Adams ran for the fire. The other rocket exploded behind her, and she skidded to a stop at the edge of the flames, grabbing a splintery section of pallet from the embers. She whirled around to face Marcus, putting her back to the fire as she brandished the burning wood at him.

"You do not want to do this," she said. "Stand down, now."

Marcus stopped, huffing something that might have been laughter, and glanced around. One of the wolves had vanished entirely, but Andi and the other, who she decided must be Frank, were still lurking behind him. She risked a look over her shoulder, seeing the kids huddled by the van. The oldest looked about fourteen, if he was lucky.

"Get out of here," she snapped. They looked at each other

then sprinted off across the green, and she took a deep breath, planting her legs as wide as she could. She couldn't arrest wolves, couldn't cast some sort of magic stun spell at them, and she didn't have her very big stick, but she had a large piece of flaming wood, and she was just going to have to make the best of it. "Come on then," she said to Marcus, her chin lifted. "Come and have a go, you *mutt*."

Marcus sank back onto his hindquarters then surged forward, and rather than meeting him she spun in place, jumping the fire from a standing start. The flames weren't *that* big, but she still felt the heat of them as she hurdled it. The wolves split, Andi coming from one side and Frank from the other, and as she landed she swung the piece of pallet hard, smacking Andi on the nose, then twisted back to wallop Frank. Dandy was holding Marcus at bay, their teeth clashing loudly, and for one moment she thought she could do this, that they'd be able to battle it out, then Marcus backed rapidly away from Dandy, raised his muzzle and *howled*.

The howl was answered from six furry throats, ten, a dozen – she didn't know, but she saw sleek, muscular bodies pouring across the Stray, pounding toward them, and her chest tightened with fright, the pallet suddenly impossibly heavy. They couldn't do it, not just her and Dandy. She needed some sort of magical damn dog catcher for this, but all she had was some burning wood and a box of fireworks.

Fireworks. Dogs and fireworks.

She lunged for the box, kicking it to the edge of the fire as she took a swing at Andi, waiting for the pack to get closer. Marcus was still trying to get past Dandy, and as the other wolves bore down on them she booted the box into the middle of the flames, smacked Frank over the head, parried another rush from Andi, then yelled for Dandy.

*"Heel!"*

He spun toward her, for once unquestioning, and she sprinted for the van. The side door was still open, and she threw herself in, Dandy bounding after her. She kicked Marcus as he lunged after them, and slammed the door to. The whole van rocked as the wolves leaped at it, the impacts shaking it on its suspension, snarls echoing in the night, and then there was a single, long moment of silence.

The first firework caught with an understated *pop*, nothing spectacular, and one of the wolves gave a questioning yip. The next was louder, a whistle that made Adams wince, then the rest of the box caught in a cacophony of explosions and screaming rockets, all but drowning out an answering chorus of yelps and howls, many of them rapidly retreating. Adams cracked the door open as the chorus of devastation continued, spotting wolves scattering in every direction, and she bit the inside of her cheek. It had worked, but it hardly felt like a victory. It felt like cruelty.

Piteous howling caught her attention, and she spotted Andi twisting wildly, dancing across the grass as she tried to reach a smouldering patch on her hindquarters. Adams threw the door wide, jumped from the van and ran to the wolf, tackling her and forcing her flank into the ground, smothering the burning fur in the damp grass.

"Sorry, sorry. I'm sorry." She rolled the wolf over, checking there were no smoking edges to the burn, and Andi looked at her with wide eyes, then scrambled up and shot off into the darkness. Adams sank onto her heels and ran a hand over her face, reminding herself it had been this or be turned into wolf fodder. Not that it made her feel any better.

The other wolves had made themselves scarce, and she was still on her knees when Marcus stalked slowly out of the depths of the dark green, his head low and his eyes fixed on her, shoulders rolling under his heavy pelt. There were scorch marks on his flanks and one on his nose, blood on his muzzle as he bared his teeth at her. Adams stood, backing toward the fire and grabbing another section of pallet from its edge without taking her eyes off him.

"Enough," she said, and nodded behind him. "You're on your own."

He glanced around, then turned those luminous eyes back on her and shrugged.

Adams scowled. "Go human again. I can't talk to you like this."

He growled.

"Well, I can't arrest a wolf," she said, shifting her grip on the wood. "But I can bloody well put you in the pound."

He snarled at that, all rage and frustration, and rushed her. She didn't want to do it, she *hated* to do it, but she swung the burning pallet as hard as she could. He tried to avoid it, but she already knew which way he was going to go, because there were only two possibilities, and right was into the fire. She stepped right at the same time as she swung, catching him solidly on the side of the head and shoulder, sending him tumbling into the darkness. He came to his feet instantly, and this time as he charged back toward her Dandy came out of the green like a freight train, a vast, dreadlocked beast cut of night and shadows. He bowled Marcus off his feet, and the wolf slid across the grass on his side, his teeth flashing in fury.

"Stay down," Adams started, but he was already coming up again, the fire in between them now. He launched himself over it, and she swept the piece of pallet up to meet him, her jaw clenched. He crashed into it, and she staggered back under the impact, but the collision sent him tumbling into the flames, scattering wood and embers and the remnants of the fireworks. He howled, scrabbling out of the fire with luminous embers and rocket casings stuck to his fur, and Adams dropped her pallet. She ran to him, grabbing the back of his neck with both hands, twisting away from his teeth as he tried to snap at her, and threw her weight against his body, forcing him to the grass and smothering the burning fur just as she had with Andi.

Marcus snarled, writhing in her grip despite the pain of the burns, still trying to get his teeth into her. Then Dandy was there, one massive paw pressing down on the wolf's side, with his own, much bigger teeth parting the hair over Marcus's throat.

"Are we done?" Adams asked breathlessly, and Marcus growled, straining to look past the fire, searching for support. "There's no one there. Back to human form before he puts his teeth in you."

Marcus glared at her, those not-quite-animal eyes narrowed and furious, then his body surged under her hands. She rocked back on her heels as he collapsed in on himself, and this time she had a close-up view of his furry body melting down into a rawness of flesh and bare tendons and chips of bone, something organic and horrifying and beautiful, reforming just as quickly into pale flesh and long limbs. A moment later he was lying in front of her, panting and leanly muscled, the burns on his shoulder and side standing as stark and brutal on bare skin as they had against the fur.

"Call him off," he said, glaring at Dandy.

Adams pulled Dandy back, and she and Marcus stared at each other.

"What *are* you?" he asked.

"Police."

"You're not," he said. "Or not only that."

Adams sighed. "Maybe. But I'm police enough to take you in. Want to make things easier and tell me what the end game was for this?"

"Told you. It was a job."

"For whom?"

"Someone who was willing to pay."

"Pay for *what*? A bit of chaos? Getting the police in your pockets?"

"*Their* pockets, and not just police." He glanced back at the marquees. "The superpowers would've been a nice bonus, too. Client would've liked that."

"But *why?*"

He looked back at her, grinning, and his teeth shone in the light of the fire. "You say you're police. Figure it out."

She frowned, then rolled him unceremoniously over before he could resist, twisting his arms behind his back. "Marcus Gallagher, I'm placing you under arrest for disturbing the peace and whatever else comes up."

"No, wait, you can't," he started, and she hooked her handcuffs out of the pocket of her coat and clicked them neatly closed on his wrists, feeling a sudden surge of satisfaction.

"Just did," she replied. "Come on. Let's find you a blanket." She pulled him to his feet while he tried to resist, shouting for his wolves. Adams turned him toward the road. "I don't think they're coming back," she said. "Didn't seem that into the fireworks."

"That was cruel," he snapped, and a horrified twist of guilt swallowed her satisfaction.

"Sure," she said, managing to keep her voice calm. "But so was dosing a whole town with enchanted beer."

"That wasn't cruel. They were all having a great time."

"That wasn't the point, though, was it?" she asked, steering him naked and pale toward a patrol car she could see at the side of the road. "It's going to go easier for you if you tell me why this happened."

"Loose lips lose pay slips," he replied, and the grin was

back in his voice. "Keep up like this and I'm sure you'll get closer to the answers than you want, though."

"What's that supposed to mean?"

He didn't answer, neither that nor anything else she asked as they crossed the Stray.

"You'll keep," she said, as they approached the patrol car. "A bit of time stewing might get some answers out of you."

"Won't come to that," Marcus said, and bared his toothy grin at the nervous-looking PC standing in front of the car, one hand hovering over her baton.

"DI Adams," Adams called to her. "You alright here?"

"Um, yes? Is everything okay? I was told to watch the perimeter, and I know it got really loud in there, but—"

But howling wolves and explosions would be enough to keep anyone out. "It's under control." Adams pushed Marcus toward her. "Get him in, would you?"

The PC grabbed the werewolf and manoeuvred him into the back of the car, ignoring his complaints as she told him to watch his head. She shut the door firmly, then looked at Adams and said, "Is he a flasher?"

"Something like that," Adams replied. "Probably have some more for you soon. See if you can call in some backup."

"Got it." The PC clicked the radio on her lapel, calling the station, and Adams turned back into the festival ground, Dandy back to Labrador size and strolling at her side with his head and tail high. She rested a hand on his head as they walked, finding the duck with her free hand.

Turned out she *could* arrest wolves. And she had every intention of arresting as many of them as possible.

## A SLIPPERY TRUTH

CHLOE OBVIOUSLY HADN'T WASTED ANY TIME, AS ADAMS could already feel the edge going out of things, that Friday-night ferocity sliding into a Sunday morning awkwardness. People were drifting away into the streets and toward town, clutching pilfered pork pies and inspecting their torn clothes with a bewildered air, and as she got closer to the tents she encountered a low mist whispering across the green, the sort of thing that rises on an early summer morning as the earth wakes. A scent of salt and spices came with it, and Adams smiled slightly. This sort of magic she could get behind.

She skirted the centre of the marquees, where a certain amount of pushing and shoving seemed to be persisting in a half-hearted manner, and went back to the Niddered Ale tent instead. She peered in the door warily, and found James standing in the middle of the floor, his arms crossed over his chest.

"No," he started, his voice sharp, then recognised her. His shoulders slumped in relief. "Adams, what the *hell* just happened?"

"Fungus in the beer. What're you doing in here?"

"Collins said to make sure no one touched anything until you gave the all clear."

Adams sniffed the air, but she couldn't smell anything except a faint whiff of beer and spent adrenaline. Whatever sense had kicked in before was gone now, and she had no idea how to reach it again. That was evidently just not how she worked. Aloud, she said, "I'll get someone to check it in a mo. Are you alright in here?"

"I think I prefer it to out there."

"Fair enough." She left him to his guard duty, and headed reluctantly toward the central oval, moving against the flow of the dispersing crowds. There was a lot of hugging going on, and a fair amount of crying, and an astonishing number of people singing "Jerusalem" for reasons she couldn't quite fathom. But no one was leaping tents or trying to set up an impromptu Fight Club, so that seemed like an improvement.

She found Chloe sitting on the edge of the stage, dabbling her fingers in a cup of what Adams assumed was the antidote, whispering gently and flicking droplets off her fingers. The pressure washers were abandoned behind her, among the ruins of the musical instruments, and the crates of spare bottles they'd brought with them were scattered empty across the stage.

"Are we okay?" Adams asked.

Chloe looked at her with bright eyes and grinned, breaking off her chant. "Hell, yeah. We *rocked* that counter-charm. The pressure washers were genius to get things going, and everyone's carrying the mist out with them. It might take a day or so, but it'll get all through town. Total win."

Adams wrinkled her nose. "I don't think anyone's going to be feeling too good tomorrow."

"It'll be fine," Chloe said. "Nobody ever believes it when this sort of stuff happens."

"Seen it happen a lot, have you?"

"Eh. Enough to know. All we have to do is offer a decent alternative truth for them."

"I know someone who can do that," Adams said, and left Chloe to it.

Adams picked her way through the debris-strewn grounds as they slowly emptied, finding Collins and Rory handing out the last of the spare bottles. They'd told the confused police officers and stall holders that it was a natural antidote to the psychedelic drug contained in the Niddered Ale, and there was a certain shame-faced eagerness to help in all of them. Police were heading back into town armed with a baton in one hand and some antidote in the other, with instructions to decant it into a spray bottle, since, Collins said quietly to Adams, he wasn't sure how much confidence he had in a self-sustaining mist. Adams felt that was reasonable, and reminded him to make sure James got some for Leeds, and that they had a bit to take back to Skipton. Collins gave her a thumbs up, and she went in search of the cat.

She was still hunting for Thompson when she came face to face with Temper, Maud, and the Harrogate DCI, who gave her an irritable look and said, "You're not meant to be arresting people on my patch."

"Well, technically I didn't," she said. "I handed him off to one of your PCs."

He squinted at her, then grunted and looked at Maud. "She seems alright. I heard she was a bit London."

"She is," Temper said, and Adams sighed.

"She is, yes," Maud said. "But she wasn't the one brawling in public." Both men looked anywhere except at Adams, Temper clearing his throat uncomfortably, and Maud patted

Adams' shoulder. "Good work," she said. "I'm glad one of us kept her head."

"Yes. Well done," Temper said, still not looking at her. "I'll buy you a beer later."

Adams stared at him until he met her gaze, and the corner of his mouth crooked up in a very un-Temper-like grin.

"Thanks?" she said.

Maud shook her head, crossing her arms over her chest, and said to Adams, "What do we do now?"

"Sorry?" Adams had thought Maud seemed to be back to normal, but the DCI was asking *her* what to do?

"You seem to have a better handle on what's going on than anyone else. What's next?"

"Ah …" She looked at Temper and Bell, but they just looked back at her expectantly. "Well, the head brewer's in custody, so we just need to tidy up here. And find out who paid him to, um, contaminate the beer. It was a contract, sounds like."

"That's for later," Maud said. "For now, does the rest of the beer need to be destroyed?"

"Probably be safest."

"Fair enough." Maud folded her arms over her chest and tapped her fingers gently, a short solid woman with dishevelled curls and drying tomatoes on her collar. She looked at the other two DCIs. "Best get on it, then."

She walked away, the other two falling into step with her, and Adams and Dandy looked at each other. He huffed softly, and Adams scratched his ears, then resumed her search for Thompson.

She found the cat sitting on the counter of a fish'n'chip van, chewing on a piece of raw cod as long as he was.

"You're not going to eat all that," Adams said.

"Can if I want," Thompson said indistinctly.

"My point is you won't, and nobody else can now you've been slobbering all over it."

"Well, someone has yet to provide the trout *or* the prawns I was promised."

"I've been a bit busy. What do we do about this?" she asked, waving vaguely at the emptying grounds.

"Too many for me to deal with."

"But we need to tell them *something*."

"So tell them something. What d'you expect me to do? I'm a cat, remember? Meow and all that." He put a paw on the fish to hold it in place as he ripped a strip of flesh off, ignoring her.

Adams scowled at him, but he simply continued eating, and after a moment's thought she decided that she probably did owe the journalist a story. She'd never said anything about it being a *true* story, after all. She left the cat to his trophy and headed off, moving quietly through the fading scent of enchantments as the night deepened into midnight beauty, watching for wolves and smelling distant shores on the mist.

❧

It was a week later when Adams bumped up the drive toward the ramble of Featherstone Estate. The brewery sign was gone from outside the warehouse, and a *For Rent* one had appeared instead. Alistair had been found in a remote village in the Outer Hebrides, where he had gone for his "nerves", like a Victorian maiden retreating to the seaside, and he steadfastly refused to return. Adams didn't blame him. While he hadn't mentioned any specifics, she felt that seeing a grown man collapsing into a pile of goo and then reforming himself into a wolf would take a toll on anyone's nerves.

It had certainly made its mark on her, and she kept

having nightmares about it. For some reason, in those dreams, when Marcus reformed it wasn't into a wolf. Instead he turned into an oversized cat who swore at her in a very colourful manner, then demanded apple crumble with custard. That much she blamed on Thompson, who seemed to feel that he had been pivotal in the whole werewolf situation, and had taken to haunting her house insisting he needed organic trout. Adams wasn't at all sure she agreed he'd been *that* helpful, but having found herself arguing with a cat one too many times, she'd just added trout to her shopping list and accepted that anyone she met in the supermarket would figure the stray cats around her house were the best fed in the country.

She pulled up in front of the dilapidated country house and got out, Dandy leaping lightly to the gravel and raising his snout to the wind. The air was cold, thin with the deepening autumn, and from the higher ground here she could see patches of light and shadow chasing each other across the mottled patchwork of fields and trees, pulling sheets of rain with them.

A yap of greeting rang out from the shed, and the dogs ran across the potholed gravel, ignoring Adams to collapse to the ground in front of Dandy.

"Hello to you, too," she said to them.

"Is your invisible dog stealing all the attention?" Rory called, and she looked up to see him emerging from the shed, an old jumper with a hole in the side hanging baggy over his jeans.

"He's evidently much more interesting than me," she said.

"As long as he's fixed. No one needs invisible puppies. Visible ones are more than enough trouble."

Adams gave Dandy a startled look. That thought had never occurred to her. "Your dogs—"

"Oh, *mine* are fixed, seeing as I'm a responsible dog-owner." He stopped in front of her, smiling. "I was hoping you'd come back at some stage."

"I owe you some thanks," she said. "And also a couple of questions."

"Does that mean I get to ask you questions?"

"I'd prefer the other way around, but I suppose I can answer a couple."

"Excellent. Come on." He led the way around the house and into the quiet warmth of the kitchen, where he put the coffee machine on without asking. The table was back to being piled with papers, spare parts, and a startling collection of mugs.

Adams looked at the scorch mark on the ceiling and said, "Sorry about the explosion again."

Rory followed her gaze and shrugged. "Ah, it's fine. It's more in keeping with the rest of the house now."

She snorted. "How did you really end up with this place? You don't seem ..." She couldn't think how to say it without being rude. *Toff* seemed a little harsh, given his helpfulness.

"The last owner was my great-uncle," he said. "None of his kids or grandkids wanted to take the house on because there was so much work to do, and selling it wasn't even going to pay off the debts. He had about three mortgages. I was ..." He hesitated. "Between jobs, let's say. So my cousins and I worked something out, the idea being I get it making enough money to pay off the debts, then we split the profit after. It has not gone entirely to plan so far, but I have to admit that plan did not include werewolves."

"Most don't," she said, wondering what sort of jobs he was *between*. "They didn't seem to bother you as much as they should have, though. Even given the eccentric family."

He set a mug on the table in front of her, then set another on the machine, leaning back against the worktop and crossing his arms over his chest. "I could say the same for you."

She took a sip of coffee, not answering immediately. Finally she said, "I've encountered a few things before. Not werewolves, but other stuff."

"That went without saying." He rubbed his chin, stubble scratching against his hand, then took his mug and sat down opposite her, clearing a path in the debris on the table. They looked at each other, his lips quirking up at the corners, and she frowned.

"Well?" she said, when he didn't offer anything else.

"Well what?"

"What have *you* encountered?"

He shrugged, and poked around in the papers until he uncovered a packet of Garibaldi biscuits. He pushed them toward her, and she gave the pack a horrified look. "Sorry. I need to go shopping." He opened it and took one anyway. "Not that much," he said. "Or not up close like that. I just … see stuff. My mum did too. She was also pretty good with herbal remedies and so on."

"That's why you were good with the, ah, recipe?"

"Maybe." He dipped a biscuit in his coffee and took a bite, then grimaced. "That's dire."

"Could've told you that. So your mum was a …" She could almost hear the volume her own mum would hit if she described anyone else's mother as a witch, so she tried, "Magic-worker?"

Rory gave her an odd, half-amused glance. "She was unwell, and over-prescribed. I think because everyone told her what she saw wasn't real, and she tried to believe that but couldn't. So she was caught in between, mixing up herbal recipes that weren't spells, but really were, and seeing things that didn't exist, but did, until it was all too much."

Adams was silent for a long time, then she took a biscuit and nibbled on it. "I'm sorry."

"Sure. But that's why it's interesting to meet someone who does handle it well."

She grimaced. "Maybe. But you obviously manage it just fine."

"I've been fired from every job I ever had, and now don't quite own a disaster of a country estate, which I'm trying not to blow up with a homemade still. *Manage it* is questionable."

Adams sighed. "So you don't have either a mystical mentor or a massive occult library passed down from generation to generation, where I'll find the answers to all my questions?"

He laughed. "No. But I do have a small, somewhat eclectic book collection that might help."

"Really?"

"Sure. Entrance fee is dinner."

She narrowed her eyes at him. "Dinner?"

"Unless you're seeing someone."

"I think I've gone off seeing anyone."

"The phone hacking?"

She grimaced. "Personal stuff just complicates things."

"Life complicates things," he said, and took another bite of his biscuit. "Did you ever get out of Marcus what he was up to? The big plan?"

Adams took a sip of coffee to wash away the taste of the Garibaldi, and handed the rest of the biscuit to Dandy. "No."

"Raisins aren't good for dogs," Rory said. "He wouldn't talk?"

"I'm not even sure he's technically a dog. And no. He was somehow released with no charges and no questions asked. He's vanished." She'd been by the house in Nether Poppleton, but it was empty and forlorn, and Marcus's unpleasant neighbour said (with deep disapproval) that they must've got wind of her upcoming raid, as they'd packed up and gone in the middle of the night.

"That's unfortunate," Rory said.

"It's more than that."

"People make mistakes." He regarded her for a moment then added, "But you don't think that's what happened."

She shook her head. She wasn't going to elaborate to him, but she had that itch in her fingertips again, the tingle that spoke of pieces of a puzzle that weren't quite coming together. Lindsay, with enough knowledge of the Folk world to use her position within the police to trade on it, trying to get hold of the sorcerer's necklace and take out half the magic workers in Leeds at the same time. And now Marcus, spirited away from under Pahal's undoubtedly conscientious nose, and the sergeant didn't even remember him being there. There was no paperwork left behind, nothing. Not even the PC Adams had handed him over to remembered the large, naked man with the pretty eyes. It was if he'd never even existed.

"Are you worried?" Rory asked.

"Well, I'm not particularly pleased there's someone out there who tried to turn a whole town into some sort of supernatural cage fight, for reasons unknown."

"No, are *you* worried? Personally, I mean. Do you think he might come after you?"

She considered it. "Maybe. But that's always a risk in the job. Anything can happen."

He finished his biscuit and made a face. "I should've given mine to your not-dog, too. So what d'you do now?"

"Keep looking, I suppose. The festival thing's already blown over, so just see what happens next, and try to keep a lid on it all." Even saying it made her feel tired. Was this what she did now? Had she somehow become Thompson's human counterpart, papering over the gaps between the worlds before anyone could fall in?

"You seem to have done a good job on that already," Rory said. "I saw the story in the papers, about the fungus in the yeast causing hallucinations and extreme inebriation. Good cover, that."

"Yeah, I had a journalist who was keen to have the exclusive, and my hacker was able to spread things online pretty easily. She kind of owed me a favour, considering she'd been sending my personal files to said journalist." Not that either of them had been entirely convinced by Adams' story, particularly Ervin, but that was a problem for another time. She'd mentioned it to Thompson, so hopefully he could tackle it.

Rory grinned. "That must've been a seriously bad break-up with your hacker."

"It wasn't a break-up." She considered it. "Or maybe it was. I don't know. These things are complicated."

"Evidently." He stretched. "You'll be pleased to know I have zero hacking skills."

Adams tried to find an answer to that, and came up with nothing except, "Um."

SHE LEFT NOT LONG AFTER, Dandy loping ahead of her with the dogs in pursuit, and Rory walked her back to her car, leaning down to look at her as she got in. "The library, such as it is, is there whenever you want a look," he said. "Dinner's optional, but the invitation stands."

"Thanks," she said. "I'll take you up on that."

"Which?" he asked, grin broadening.

"Books," she said, and closed the door firmly. He was still grinning when she pulled away, jouncing her car down the rutted drive, leaving him presiding over his crumbling house and rambling estate as the sharp, cold autumn rain washed across the hills to feed the fields and fill the tarn, now bereft of its Vauxhall. Darker days were coming, ones full of cold edges and wild winds, and the world was beginning to hunker down in front of them, small creatures padding their nests and birds turning their beaks south. The feel of change in the air was as clear-cut as the frosty dawns, and she wasn't sure what it meant.

More than just the blurring edges of the seasons, she was certain. But life was change, for all that one might desire it wasn't, and fighting it brought nothing. One could only navigate the wild currents and savage squalls as they came, be they werewolves or invisible dogs or sons of witches.

Adams looked at Dandy, sitting in the front passenger seat and panting at her, and rubbed his head. Change had its positives, too, she supposed.

She thought about it, then went through her contacts on the hands-free, hesitating on Isha's name before moving on and hitting *call*.

The phone rang a couple of times, then a familiar voice said, "Ay-up, Adams."

"Collins." She took a breath. "You going to the pub tonight?"

"Are you not running a marathon or drinking green smoothies?"

"Green smoothies are almost as much of an abomination as your coffee-flavoured cheese."

Collins laughed. "I'm meeting Lucas for a pint in a bit. Come and join us."

"Sure," she said, and hit disconnect, then settled into her seat as she swung onto the road back to Skipton, suddenly impatient to shake off Harrogate's crowded streets and spa-town elegance, already looking for the harsher, higher angles of the fells, looming under the press of grey sky and scattered with bright splashes of autumn colour as the trees changed. Dandy put a paw on her arm as she drove, and she scratched his head absently, accelerating into wilder land as town fell away behind her, thinking of dragons and cats and drifting puzzle pieces, and the far more complex and confusing puzzles that were people, and personal connection, and how one made any of it work.

But a pint with friends seemed like it should be a decent start.

As long as it wasn't artisan.

# THANK YOU

Lovely people, thank you so much for joining me on this latest venture into the surprisingly wild (in many senses of the word) hills of Yorkshire. I hope very much that you enjoyed it, and I shall take this opportunity to say that your local craft brewer is probably *not* trying to give you questionable superpowers, and that you can likely sip a nice ale with no risk of any but the usual side effects.

I make no claims as to whether your brewers are werewolves or not, though, as it's hard to be sure on such things. Probably don't offer them a belly rub, just in case they take it the wrong way. I mean, unless you already know them pretty well.

The next DI Adams will be on the way in the first half of 2025, full of teeth and snark and unhelpful canines, but until then I have a small request ...

If you did enjoy this book, I'd very much appreciate you taking the time to pop a review up at your favourite retailer or on Goodreads (or both, if you're feeling particularly generous).

Reviews are more intoxicating than enchanted beer to

authors, and they may even endow us with superpowers (or at least the belief we have superpowers for five minutes or so, until the realisation that we need to get back to work sinks in, along with the usual crushing self-doubt).

Plus reviews tickle the retailers' algorithms, and encourage them to show our books to more readers. Which hopefully means more sales, which means writers can buy more baked goods to fuel more writing, and send more strange tales out into the world in a delightful little cycle of story happiness.

But mostly it's the superpowers that we're interested in ;)

Thank you again so much for reading, lovely people. If you'd like to send me a copy of your review, suspicions regarding the human-ness of your local brewer, or anything else, drop me a message at kim@kmwatt.com. I'd love to hear from you!

Until next time,

Read on!

Kim

# THE HUNT IS ON

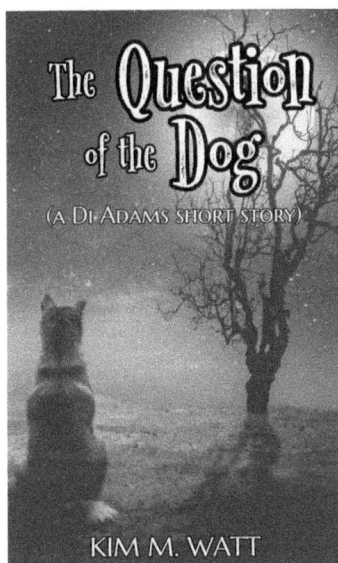

*If it even is a dog ...*

Thompson's not a young cat anymore. Toot Hansell's meant to be a cushy patch after some hard lives.

Except for the bloody dragons, the truly terrible influence of the Women's Institute, and now something that looks like a dog, sort of smells like a dog, but which is most certainly not actually a dog.

And is also most certainly going to be a problem …

*Thompson has some explaining to do (and threats to make) in this free short story download! Grab yours by scanning the QR code below, or heading to https://readerlinks.com/l/4362945/rm*

# MEET GOBBELINO LONDON, PI

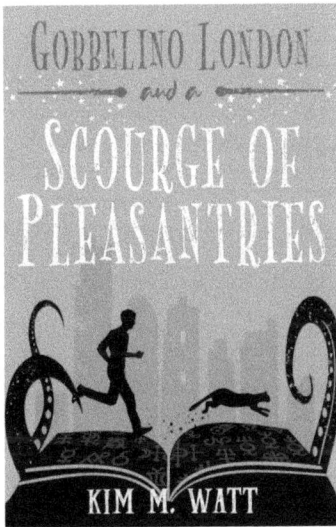

*"What've we got?"*

*"Tigers. Snakes. Alligators. Tears in the skin of the universe."* Susan shrugged. *"I think I saw a kraken in the sink, too."*

We were only hired to find a book. No one said anything about void-monsters, sink-krakens, or saving the world from a plague of niceness.

And there was *definitely* no mention of dentists …

Scan above or head to the link to discover Yorkshire's premier magical PIs today! https://readerlinks.com/l/3088744/g1b2r

# ABOUT THE AUTHOR

Hello lovely person. I'm Kim, and in addition to the DI Adams tales I also write other funny, magical books that offer a little escape from the serious stuff in the world and hopefully leave you a wee bit happier than you were when you started. Because happiness, like friendship, matters.

I write about baking-obsessed reapers setting up baby ghoul petting cafes, and ladies of a certain age joining the Apocalypse on their Vespas. I write about friendship, and loyalty, and lifting each other up, and the importance of tea and cake.

But mostly I write about how wonderful people (of all species) can really be.

If you'd like to find out the latest on new books, learn about giveaways, discover extra reading, and more, jump on over to www.kmwatt.com and check everything out there, or join me at ko-fi.com/kimmwatt for monthly short stories and weekly updates.

Read on!

amazon.com/Kim-M-Watt/e/B07JMHRBMC
goodreads.com/kimmwatt
bookbub.com/authors/kim-m-watt
facebook.com/KimMWatt
instagram.com/kimmwatt
youtube.com/@KimMWatt-yd1qb

# ACKNOWLEDGMENTS

As always, it's impossible to thank everyone, and doing this page always leaves me with the niggling worry I've left someone vital out. If I have, *it's not deliberate.* I love you all. But specifically, right now, thank you to:

My amazing beta readers, who point out the plot holes and shifting names and magically reappearing batons, and soothe my ragged writer nerves.

The delightful population of The Toot Hansell Auxiliary, as well as my newsletter readers and Ko-fi supporters (many of whom are one and the same), who not only laugh at my terrible jokes, but jumped in to create beer names *and* the book title, and who are truly the best people. I couldn't ask for better support.

My truly fantastic friends, online and off, who got me through a slightly (okay, very) hectic summer, and told me to eat and sleep and take days off and act like a human, and didn't even point out that I can be very bad at that last one.

My wonderful friend and editor Lynda, who accommodates my erratic schedule, patiently corrects all the *s's* I've scattered carelessly throughout the manuscript, banishes the persistent batons (seriously, I was starting to think it was a boomerang), and still takes the time to point out the bits that make her laugh. As always, all good grammar praise goes to Lynda, while all mistakes are mine. Head to her website at www.easyreaderediting.com for fantastic blogs on editing, grammar, and other writer-y stuff.

The fabulously supportive community of The Ripping

Scribblers, who are a ridiculously talented group of very funny writers, and particularly the lovely Bjørn Larssen. It turns out Bjørn is an absolute genius with cover design, and stepped in to create this book's cover when I was in a flat panic. Writer friends are *amazing*. (Also, go and read his book *Why Odin Drinks*. You will not regret it.)

And last but so very far from least, thank *you*, lovely reader. These books start with me but end with you. They are very much a joint effort, and it means the world to me that you're here with me for one more tale. I can't wait to share the next one with you.

Until next time!

Kim x

# ALSO BY KIM M. WATT

### The Gobbelino London, PI series

"This series is a wonderful combination of humor and suspense that won't let you stop until you've finished the book. Fair warning, don't plan on doing anything else until you're done ..."

– Goodreads reviewer

🐾

### The Beaufort Scales Series (cozy mysteries with dragons)

"The addition of covert dragons to a cozy mystery is perfect ... and the dragons are as quirky and entertaining as the rest of the slightly eccentric residents of Toot Hansell."

– Goodreads reviewer

🐾

### Short Story Collections

### Oddly Enough: Tales of the Unordinary, Volume One

"The stories are quirky, charming, hilarious, and some are all of the above without a dud amongst the bunch ..."

– Goodreads reviewer

### The Cat Did It

Of course the cat did it. Sneaky, snarky, and up to no good – that's the cats in this feline collection, which you can grab free by signing up to the newsletter. Just remember – if the cat winks, always wink back ...

**The Tales of Beaufort Scales**

Modern dragons are a little different these days. There's the barbecue fixation, for starters … You'll get these tales free once you've signed up for the newsletter!

**Need more stories?**

Join the Ko-fi membership site for monthly, member-exclusive short stories, behind-the scenes content, early access to ebooks, and more!

9 781067 011659